THE
LEAGUE
OF
ELDER

SYGILLIS OF
METATRON

The League of Elder

OF
Elder

SYGILLIS OF
METATRON

REN GARCIA

iUniverse, Inc.
New York   Bloomington

Cover art by Carol Phillips

iUniverse books may be ordered through booksellers or by contacting:

iUniverse
1663 Liberty Drive
Bloomington, IN 47403
www.iuniverse.com
1-800-Authors (1-800-288-4677)

Because of the dynamic nature of the Internet, any Web addresses or links contained in this book may have changed since publication and may no longer be valid. The views expressed in this work are solely those of the author and do not necessarily reflect the views of the publisher, and the publisher hereby disclaims any responsibility for them.

ISBN: 978-1-4401-2131-9 (sc)
ISBN: 978-1-4401-2129-6 (dj)
ISBN: 978-1-4401-2130-2 (ebook)

Library of Congress Control Number: 2009921063

Printed in the United States of America

iUniverse rev. date: 10/29/09

Contents

Part 3—The Fanatics of Nalls

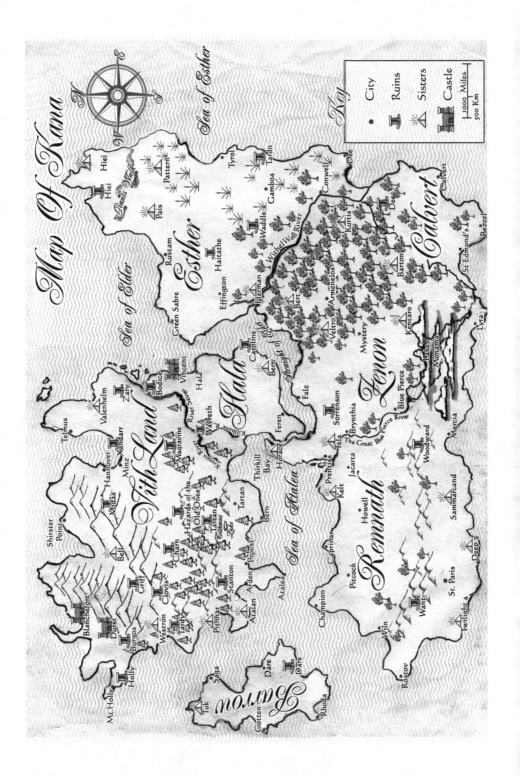

THE LEAGUE OF ELDER: SYGILLIS OF METATRON

PROLOGUE

The thing in the dark waited to dream again. It sat in the dizzying heights at the pinnacle of an artificial mountain within the hollow innards of an even larger artificial mountain all around. Vaguely, it heard the din of noise drifting up from the floor far below; a chorus of moans and anguished cries mixed together with the occasional mewling and grunting of some unseen animal lurking in the dark—an off-tune symphony of suffering. If a prisoner had been brought to it, as sometimes happened, it heard the person cry out in fear, sometimes offering bribes, sometimes shouting threats. In any case, when it felt ready, it would slowly drift down the steep stairway to the floor, awash in dreams, and deal with the newcomer, sometimes taking days in the killing.

It gripped the arms of the chair, digging in with its clenched hands. During these brief moments of hated lucidity, if it felt particularly angry and there were no prisoners about, it often seized one of the servants from below, filthy and naked, and lifted its terrified body up to the heights and killed it, sometimes in unthinkable and inventive ways.

And then, sitting back, calming, it dreamed the same old dream.

It dreamed of a flat expanse, the drenched ground clogged with mud and topped with a layer of rain-soaked fog that stubbornly clung there like a huge, ghostly hand. No mountains could be seen in its dream, yet it had the impression that there should be mountains, or rather hills, seven of them. Seven hills. It always wondered why there were no hills; where did they go? The landscape of its dream was dark—but it was a normal sort of dark, like a nighttime countryside sprinkled with little snatches of light here and there—a night that promised the eventual coming of dawn. This dark wasn't like the impenetrable and hopeless murk it and the miserable servants below lived in day after day. Certainly, such a bleak landscape might serve as the stuff of nightmares for most anybody else, but for it, living in an endless waking nightmare, the wet, fog-bound landscape awaiting the coming of dawn was an inviting paradise.

Then, in the rain-matted distance, it saw the Light.

It was a golden Light, panning, far away, inviting, warming the night, promising rescue ... promising salvation.

Slowly, the Light approached, bobbing slightly, like a hand-held torch. The Light called out to it, though no voice was heard. As the Light got nearer, it could see that it was actually two points of light, side by side, like a pair of eyes.

Standing there in the distance was a man, tall and looming, his eyes shining in the dark like a pair of searchlights. He stood with arm outstretched, hand open. And all it had to do was take his hand, and the dawn would come.

I've been looking for you, though I knew it not myself. Take my hand and let us away. I've come to take you home ...

Take his hand and the dream might end, and something new could begin. It wanted to go toward the man and the Light; to speak to him—to touch him maybe—but it could not move. It was rooted in stone, locked in place. The old wall of darkness held it firm, giving it no place to go.

The man and his Light were the loveliest things it had ever seen. His Light offered change, offered hope. With the Light, it could be more than what it currently was.

"It" was a she, a demon in female form. And she, sitting in her chair high above the floor in the moaning darkness, rife with suffering, could finally become something denied to her throughout her long, savage life ... she could become a woman.

*   *   *   *   *

It happened often, perhaps more often than it should.

Captain Davage of the League Main Fleet Vessel *Seeker*, the esteemed Lord of Blanchefort of the current line, would be in his spacious quarters, or occasionally in his small, comely office, and he would receive a message from the Com officer on the bridge. The Com, in the usual businesslike voice, announced that he had a pending message: from Fleet Command, from the League Office, from his ancient Vith home in the far north of Kana, or sometimes—painfully—from the House of Durst. He would then stop what he was doing, clear his throat, and accept the message.

Certainly nothing was unusual about a busy Elder like Captain Davage getting a message, but …

If the Captain had a visitor in his office or if his first officer, Lt. Kilos of the Stellar Marines, was there, then the message opened for a moment and then failed, the connection lost. A colorful League banner usually popped up stating that "technical difficulties" had been encountered, and that was that.

But if Davage was alone, then, every so often, the message was not as advertised—it would not be from the Fleet or the League Office or his home or from House Durst either.

It was sometimes from *her*, Captain Davage's mortal enemy: Princess Marilith of Xandarr, a Xaphan princess, Davage's eternal sworn enemy and near-constant antagonist.

* * * * *

The animosity between these two had been the talk of both League and Xaphan societies for decades. When they confronted each other in public—Davage in his powerful League vessel *Seeker* and Marilith mounting a various assortment of warships always called *Bloodsimple*—their spectacular, twisting, turning, soliloquy-laced, weapons-blazing confrontations were legendary and eagerly anticipated, almost akin to a popular sporting event. The stage, played out many times over the years, was usually the same: the lesser Xaphan ships parting as if in supplication to a greater power, an excited hush falling on the *Seeker*'s bridge, and there on the view screen would be Princess Marilith, the Arch-Xaphan herself—what a sight!

She was tall and fit, with a long head of straight hair with short bangs. Her hair was blue—bright blue, like a blueberry dream, a mark of royalty and a sure sign of arrogance and pending trouble. She always dressed in the Xandarr style, a colorful assortment of veils and light garments, like a dancer that, often-times, failed to account for the demands of modesty. Indeed, Lt. Kilos, always nined-up in her red Marine uniform, often said the princess dressed like a courtesan ready for bed. Her face was beautiful and somewhat feline in appearance, and was rather triangular in shape with a small, pointy chin and a fairly domelike forehead. Her long somewhat sleepy eyes, like her hair, were profoundly blue.

And there was the makeup—the fierce war paint she wore to distort her features and make her appear monstrous, demonic even.

Princess Marilith—no matter the time or place or the state of her dress (or un-dress) always commanded instant respect.

Captain Davage, on the other hand, was the model of a dashing Fleet senior officer and Lord of the League. Tall and lean, he wore the Stellar Fleet uniform of a captain: a woven dark blue coat with long tails embroidered generously with gold ivy and stars denoting his rank, striped black pants tucked into a rather oversized pair of tall black boots, a frilly white shirt, and a black command sash. Strapped to his waist was his gun belt, a finely decorated and enameled MiMs pistol holstered on his left and the CARG saddled in place to his right. The CARG was a large, coppery, beautiful weapon that looked something like a sword but was definitely not a sword. In standard Fleet tradition, the captain and the first officer were armed at all times. Topping it off was a large, dark blue triangle hat. The whole ensemble was modeled from military dress worn eons ago in another time and place—before they were Elder, before the Elders came and made them into what they were. The Stellar Fleet, though sporting the latest in fancy star-faring war machines, had a very old, very romantic soul. That was why Davage loved the Fleet so much.

Like Marilith, the stately old Vith trait of blue hair ran in his family as well. His hair and eyes were much darker blue than Marilith's, a deep azure that could often be mistaken for black. His hair was wavy and held bound in a tail, a usual standard for fashionable northern gentlemen in League Society.

And even though Davage was an Elder and Marilith was a Xaphan, they were both the still the same people—the Xaphans merely being Elders who had betrayed the League and became their enemy long ago. They both enjoyed the benefits of the ancient Gifts: lifelong youth, freedom from disease, and a series of powerful mental skills given to the tribe of Vith long ago. Davage and Marilith were both well over a hundred years old, yet they appeared young and healthy in the flower of their young adulthood. They were forever awash in the Gifts of the body and the mind—at least until one of them managed to kill the other.

Captain Davage also had that handsome Blanchefort face, those fine northern Vith features that so captivated ladies of standing all over the League. He was a bachelor, and his reluctance to take a bride, to make that lucky someone his countess, had been both a scandal and a source of endless gossip in League society for decades: Great House Lords certainly did not remain unmarried. They married, if not for love, then for politics, for the needs of the House for an heir were clear. Who was it to be, the ladies whispered? Who would finally be the one to capture his heart? Davage had no brothers, only two sisters, and the proud Blanchefort line hung, quite literally, in the balance, heirless—one well-placed shot from Marilith's guns could bring down the old Vith House for all time.

Who would win Davage's heart? He had remained frustratingly non-committal and sullen on the matter since the spectacular debacle of eighty years prior that was still the talk of the League, when he had in fact publically and proudly given his heart to that lucky someone after all ... to Princess Marilith of Xandarr.

Facing off, the two of them hurled insults and threats at each other and eventually, they fought. Marilith blasted away at Davage with her cassagrain energy weapons, a Xaphan staple. Davage's mighty ship was unshielded save for thick armor plating, and her guns could melt it to slag with only a few well-placed hits. Marilith held nothing back; she fought to kill. Davage though, being an old master helmsman, was extremely hard to hit, the *Seeker* rolling, diving, and jinking in a confounding manner, while Marilith, stuck in whatever old Xaphan tub she could get her hands on, gnashed her teeth in rage and watched as her shots found nothing but empty space.

Captain Davage, a master of his craft, always ended up sinking Marilith in the end no matter what sort of foul trap she sprang. A canister and shot-riddled heap, the *Bloodsimple* spun out of control, decompressing, caving-in violently in a mass of twisted, blasted metal as battered lifeboats, and assorted fleeing craft blossomed into a flailing cloud around the doomed vessel.

Princess Marilith, a master of her craft, always eluded his grasp, always escaped the burning wreckage of her destroyed ship, and was always just out of his reach, escaping back to the shadows, ever ready to try and kill him again.

That was in public—that was the fiery, hate-filled, guns-smoking image they maintained.

In private, though, things could not have been more different.

With Marilith's vast family fortune affording her access to elaborate technology that could fool League Com channels, she often contacted him and there, all alone, they stared at each other over their respective screens, Marilith's face free of her fierce makeup and Davage with his hat off. They spoke kindly to each other—almost tenderly, each silently lamenting what might have once been.

How they once were nearly married in a grand ceremony, the event of the year—of the decade. It was a wedding that was meant to end the League-Xaphan conflict forever and bring the two sides together as one.

In the usual tradition common to both societies, the wedding baton had to pass from the end of the procession to the front, and when the bride and groom touched it simultaneously, they were wed. There were thousands of esteemed guests present for this wedding, this seminal event, and thousands of hands accepted the lovely jeweled baton, held it for a cheering moment, and then passed it to the next person. It had taken a while—it had gone literally miles—and was nearly to the front.

Then, the gasps, the manicured, jeweled hands coming to shocked open mouths as the baton stopped, was held fast in a shaking grip and then thrown to the floor where it hit with a musical, somewhat anti-climatic "*ding.*"

The baton was stopped; it went no further. There would be no wedding.

Then there was confusion and outrage as Davage was dragged from the chapel ... by his sister, she who refused to see him wed to a Xaphan monster.

And their respective fates were sealed.

✳   ✳   ✳   ✳   ✳

So, now, here was Marilith, beautiful and alone, on his screen once again.

"Princess Marilith," Davage said, putting down a report in his office. The Com had said he had a message from Fleet, marked green.

"How are you, Dav?" she asked quietly, her beautiful face close to the flickering screen, a tiny, genuine smile on her lips. "It's good to see you." She backed away from the screen a little—a single veil wrapped around her otherwise nude body.

"Good to see you, too. I am fine—that was a particularly insidious trap you sprang at Hoban. You are an endlessly crafty person. Where did you get all those old ships from time and time again?"

Marilith smiled and looked at him hard. "Would you expect anything less of me? You know I can offer you no quarter ... though I know that you will come through alive. I know there isn't a trap I can think up that you can't escape from ... and I am happy for it."

They made small talk for a bit, chatting casually as if they were simply two close friends catching up—as if the last eighty years hadn't happened, as if the baton hitting the floor hadn't happened.

Then, after a bit, she closed her eyes and looked sad. She appeared to have something on her mind.

"I can see something is troubling you, Marilith. Out with it. You can tell me."

She took a deep breath. "I can divine the future. You know that, correct?"

"I did not. Is that a Xandarr Gift?"

"My family can do it sometimes. Sometimes I can interpret the future. I saw the future before our wedding ... but I did not understand it."

"What did you see?"

"I saw a cloud ... a thundercloud. I did not understand. Perhaps if I had I could have taken preventative steps. I could have ... done something. I ... so wanted to marry you."

Marilith paused and caught her breath, her eyes momentarily anguished.

She continued. "Something is searching for you, Dav," she said as matter-of-factly as she could. "I can feel it, and I am afraid for you. I fear you are in danger, and I wanted to warn you of that."

"Danger? What did you see?"

"In a dream I saw a figure, a terrible, lonely figure, sitting atop a tall mountain. There were impaled bodies struggling for life all around it. It gazed down from the heights, looking for you, Dav. I don't know what it is, but I saw it sure enough in the darkness. I pray you heed my warning and look to yourself. The figure was terrifying. It wants you. It waits for you."

"I see. You still dream of me, Marilith, even now?"

"I do, every night; I'm not afraid to admit that. Promise me you'll look to yourself."

"Look to myself, so that you can kill me later?"

"Yes ... yes. Promise me you will be careful, please. Will you do that for me?"

"I will, Marilith, and thank you for thinking of me."

She put her hands on her screen, her blue eyes growing misty. "When next we meet, Dav, I pray you fight well ... for I shall show you no mercy. I cannot ... I cannot."

She wept.

Davage felt a pang cross his heart. He touched his screen where her hands were.

And the two wept, the mortal enemies ... who loved each other still.

Part 1

THE PRISONER REQUESTS ...

They say a Black Hat's heart does not beat.
They say it sits in her chest and rots.
Maybe all it took to change all that,
Was one brave man, and a woman who had a second thought.

1

THE LORD OF BLANCHEFORT

All of his life, Captain Davage, the Lord of Blanchefort, had been a pursued man. He was hunted and given no peace.

He ran, his tall Fleet boots rising and falling on ancient stone, through the splendid corridors and vast halls of the sturdy old castle. The Vith castle, located high in the mountains of the Kanan north, was huge. Here, within the cold hallways of his ancestral home, he had space to run and run. He could run all he wanted. He could run to exhaustion and still not reach the end.

As a boy, he'd run from his father—Sadric, Lord of Blanchefort. Sadric, well thought of and influential, was the consummate man about town, a diplomat, well-placed in League Society, and Sadric, the Society man, wanted his only son to learn the stern and exacting ways of League Society as well. Sadric chased his son through the hallways of the castle with a set of dress clothes and a fancy pair of stylish shoes, determined that he put them on. Davage ran from him, as if Death itself pursued.

Davage, for better or worse, was born into the House of Blanchefort. House Blanchefort was an ancient House, founded long ago in the time of the Elders from the fabled blue-haired Vith heroes of old. It was Lennybus, the Vith and original Blanchefort, who built the massive expanse of Castle Blanchefort, the place of endless halls and towering spires in the spiny mountains of the north. It was said he made it complex and confusing to keep the Demon of Magravine, his arch-enemy, from being able to locate him and exact vengeance. Lennybus also planted the Telmus Grove behind the castle, a huge orchard of mystical trees and Vith courtyards fed by ancient streams to keep out the giants. He was also said to be the first Blanchefort to be laid to rest atop Dead Hill—a mushroom-shaped hill in the Telmus Grove where all future Blancheforts, except those lost in distant battles, were entombed—though his particular vault had never been located.

The House of Blanchefort, like most modern Great Houses, maintained a Lord and a Countess. They designed their own regal clothing in a distinctive style, forged their own weapons, minted their own coins, and were generally expected to be trendsetters in Blue League social circles. The firearms they once designed were the prize of the League—the Blanchefort PtVa was a legendary pistol, the famous old "Poltava" being a template for many modern firearms, including the prolific Grenville 40, though no Grenville ever admitted that. Sadric, however, frowned upon the practice of producing firearms and eventually abolished it, turning the old weapons factories the villagers worked in into textile mills for creating fine Blanchefort fabrics.

The Lords of Blanchefort, accordingly, were expected to throw lavish parties, attend other Houses' parties, and generally be Blue—Blue being of Vith, Remnath, or Zenon heritage, the Viths being the "Bluest" of the lot.

And so there was Davage, a Blue Lord who really wanted nothing to do with parties and social circles and setting trends. He'd much rather go to ground in common clothes, see the world, travel the by-ways of Kana, and visit the stars.

Davage was a reluctant Lord who withered in the dainty shoes and the fine clothes he was expected to wear. He hated all of the Lords and Ladies who came to gawk at him, to poke and prod and see the next Lord of Blanchefort. The worst of all was Countess Hortensia of Monama, a mountain of a woman in a black gown who was said to have visions, the Monamas being a strange, black-eyed lot. "Oh," she gasped every time upon seeing him, which was frequent, for she was his father's personal seeress. "Something evil dreams of you even now, my boy. I am afraid for your soul."

What a horrid woman.

At first, to find refuge, Davage ran into the arms of his mother, Countess Hermilane, formerly of House Hanover. Davage had inherited much from his mother. He'd inherited her tall, lanky frame. He'd inherited her stately blue hair. He'd also inherited her restlessness, her spirit. His mother was once known for her quick temper and her able sword-hand. She was a lady of standing who was notorious for her knack of getting into and winning duels. How a powdered fop like Sadric survived to court a savage Black Widow like her was a real mystery. In later years, his mother taught Davage how to sword fight, a skill that eventually served him well.

But for now, his mother simply handed her son over to his lurking father, throwing him back into the stately fire that had been set for him.

And the endless drilling and sessions began, the fine clothes and fancy shoes confining and galling. He was forced to learn how to stand, how to walk, how to bow, how to hold a fork—forced to study the traits, habits, and identifying characteristics of the Great Houses, forced to endure all the things he rather not have learned.

Sadric put him through his paces, then, armed with this useless knowledge, Davage was loosed upon the battlefield—the luncheons, the stuffy morning get-togethers, and the high-brow cotillions. It was a hoity-toity battlefield that was every bit as dangerous and fraught with peril as a real one.

There were the rules—the unbending rules.

Do not be early.
Do not be late.
Do not speak out of turn.
Do not speak like a commoner.
DO NOT USE … PROFANITY!
Do not eat until the proper moment.
Do not eat your foods out of order.
Do not eat your foods with the improper utensil.

Do not miss a step when dancing.
And on and on ...

Breaking the rules had repercussions. There were the footmen who stood behind every chair at the dinners and luncheons. Any breach in the rules of etiquette and decorum, any at all, and the footmen seized one's plate and took it away. A seemingly harmless punishment ... yet Davage often went meal after meal and managed to not eat a bite, his plate ruthlessly removed after he'd violated some rule early on. He always managed to mess something up. Lady Hathaline of Durst, a House from a nearby castle, was good friends with Davage, and she often tried to help him, to correct him under her breath. She'd somehow remove her complicated Durst shoe and kick him in the shin when he was going wrong, and many times her efforts were detected by the footmen and she lost her plate right along with Davage, the pair of them going hungry. He once went a whole week without eating a thing. Pacing the castle, he was ravenous. There was not a crumb of unsecured food to be found, and near collapse, he ate the wax bindings out of a stained glass window one day. It was a tasteless, unnourishing meal but something he could get his teeth on.

He told his father how hungry he was, and his father, not realizing how bad the situation was, told him he may eat when he accepted the rules of society and followed them to a mark. His father had no idea his son was literally starving to death; a feast of food and not a bite to eat.

And Davage ran from him, determined to find food, determined to put something, anything, into his belly. Sadric, chasing, caught him and punished him. A seemingly frail and dainty man, Sadric could nevertheless exact a terrible punishment on his unseemly son.

He put Davage to a Hard Stare—the Gift of the soul, putting him into wrenching pain before his gaze. When he was a younger boy, Davage shuddered and cried under the Stare, and Sadric, not a heartless or cruel man, held him and said it was for his own good, that he simply wished for him to become a fine lord. As Davage grew older, he simply stood there and took it ... enduring the Stare, feeling the pain but ignoring it, putting his mind elsewhere.

Those painful Stare sessions were what first gave rise to his thoughts of going to the stars, to put Castle Blanchefort behind him. As he stood under the Stare, feeling his guts turning inside out, he looked skyward and Sighted through the room, through the walls of the castle, through the empty northern skies, to the starships floating high on the horizon, the Fleet starships soaring so graceful, so carefree, so unchained ... In his frequent Stare sessions, he came to know the ships by heart. There were the *Venture* and *Midnight*, the *Great Expectations* and the *Fictner*, to mention a few. Able to see through the ship's hulls, he came to recognize their crews and their captains as well. He watched them eating and drinking in the mess halls; all that food, all that drink and good fellowship—oh, how he craved it. He watched the ships launch from their berths, going to wherever it was they were going. He watched them return to port weeks later, sometimes with battle damage. Sometimes, they didn't come back at all, their berthing docks empty, and he, missing their presence, mourning the lost crews, wept. His father, not a hard-hearted man, stopped the punishment, thinking he was hurting his son too much.

Those ships had been destroyed in space by the Xaphans. The enemy. The betrayers. The Xaphans weren't so bad his father, ever the diplomat, said. The Xaphans should be welcomed back into the League. Remembering the lost ships, the dead and wounded crews that he had befriended from afar, he stood and told his father to be quiet ... to shut up in front of a shocked luncheon. The Xaphans were evil.

More Stare ... the hardest yet, the longest, the most angry.

Another indignity Sadric subjected him to was letter-writing—endless correspondence to this Great Lord and that Great Countess, all people he neither knew or cared to know. A fashionable trend in the League was to forgo the usual methods of communicating—no holos, no tele-vids, or insta-types. No, Great Lords were expected to write letters longhand using ink and fine paper, the way the ancients before the time of the Elders did it. Three hours a day of letter-writing was Davage's bane. He swore his hand was going to fall off, his fingers hurt so badly. Another hour a day was spent reading the letters coming back to him—letters from peers and ladies of standing from other

Houses who might be agreeable to court one day. The letters he got back from Countess Hortensia of Monama were characteristically dark and depressing, full of the usual warnings regarding a terrifying evil presence that searched for him across the stars. In one letter, Countess Monama drew a picture of a strange pyramidal shape that she had seen in her frequent visions. Within the pyramid was a smaller one with a crudely drawn stick figure sitting at the top. At the base of the pyramid were many prone and weeping stick figures. "Here, the evil searches. Here the evil commands," she wrote. "Beware this place."

Good Creation, why couldn't the evil force be done with him already and give him peace?

✳   ✳   ✳   ✳   ✳

Much later, no longer a boy, as a handsome young man Davage again ran through the castle. By this point, his father was mad, locked in his tower, and his mother had passed away, resting in her tomb on Dead Hill.

He ran, this time from his sister, Pardock, the new Countess of Vincent.

How could his sister have done this to him?

Davage had two sisters, Pardock, again, the newly married Countess of Vincent, and Lady Poe, several years her younger. Both sisters were decades older than Davage, their faces unchanged with time, ever young. Pardock, like their mother, was tall and statuesque. She was blue-haired and beautiful. Additionally, like her mother and her grandfather Maserfeld, she was rowdy, and she could be downright mean too. She often stood firm against Sadric, arguing with him in public, defying him at home, spurning his efforts to make a proper lady of standing out of her. Sadric couldn't punish her with the Stare like he did with Davage because Pardock had the Stare too. Two Starers couldn't Hard Stare each other, so that was that. So, there was yelling— lots and lots of yelling—and slammed doors.

Pardock, rough and tumble with outsiders and an obstinate rock with her father, always loved her brother, always looked out for him. Seeing him suffering, starving in his room, going meal after meal without getting a bite to eat, she often smuggled him food, just a bit of cheese and some fruit wrapped in a cloth, but Davage, grateful, devoured it. She had a habit of sneaking out of the castle and going to the village by the sea. When Davage was old enough, she took him with her. They dressed up as peasants, and using the tunnels running under the castle, they snuck into the pubs and wharf-side bars. Davage was astounded. He loved talking like a commoner, walking among them, not being judged at every turn. And the food—to simply order what you wanted and be able to eat it at your leisure … truly remarkable. And fights; Dav and Par often got into fights in the bars, bouncing their fists off of commoners' faces and then mug-hoisting with them afterwards, no hard feelings, no harm done.

Davage's incognito forays into the village with Pardock were some of the most wonderful adventures he'd ever had. How he cherished his sister.

And then there was Poe, his other sister. Poe was often away from the castle for long periods of time—where she was or why she was gone for so long, Davage didn't know. When she was there, she was strange, silent, gazing at something that only she could see—not even Davage with his Sight.

It was unheard of to be sick in the League. Sickness, other than embarrassing and seldom spoken of fungal infections, was a scandal, a sure sign of weakness and bad breeding. And Poe was sick, badly sick in her brain. She was mentally ill.

She was crazy, to use the vernacular. One could smell the sickness on her … a strange, metallic, basic smell.

Were House Blanchefort not so highly placed, were Sadric not such a skilled gentleman at spinning a topic in League circles, her illness could have brought the House down in a scandal-ridden heap. Sadric, though, was very protective of Poe. If he was strict and harsh with Davage, if he was angry and argumentative with Pardock, he was patient and doting on Poe. Somebody had to be, for she was so sad, so lonely in her haze-clouded little world. Everything about her seemed to be flawed … imperfect. She was attractive but not beautiful like Pardock. She was tall like her brother but frail, bent, teetering. She had blue hair like her brother and sister, but only in strange wispy patches—she was mostly blonde-headed. Platinum blonde—a commoner's hair color.

Sadric often tasked Davage and Pardock to watch Poe after their mother's passing during the days when he was away at a function. They sat there with her for long periods of time, two sisters and a brother—one tall and fierce, one tall and restless, one sad and sick.

It was hard not to love Poe, though—that innocent face, that silly head of blonde-blue hair, her shy, slightly comical bearing. Davage and Pardock passed the time by trying to entertain Poe, they took her into the huge, mysterious Telmus Grove behind the castle and showed her the wondrous plants and animals there, and she laughed and clapped, her blue eyes full of wonder.

Then, before long, her eyes always grew blank, and she fell into a spell. Such was her life. Pardock once knocked the teeth out of a lady who had made a crass public comment about "Crazy Poe," and said that she "smelled" funny—Dav and Par eventually became as protective of her as their father. She was their sister, sick or not, and they loved her.

* * * * *

Davage ran through the castle … pursued this time by his sister Pardock.

As they ran, they both wept, Davage heartsick and in grief, Pardock out of fear and love for her brother.

Gasping for air, his heart fluttering, Davage stopped and slumped to the floor, weeping in wracking spasms. Pardock caught up to him, she in her blue House Vincent gown, Davage in his best, his wedding attire.

The wedding the Pardock had just prevented from happening. The baton rolling on the floor of the chapel, his Xaphan bride who was, even now, shooting her way back Xaphan space ahead of an angry mob.

Pardock put her arms around him. He tried to pull away.

"Dav!" she cried. "Dav, look at me!"

"What have you done to me? Do you hate me so?" he sobbed.

Pardock, in a panic, put her hands on his face. "Dav … you don't know … you don't know what I saw … you don't know what she is—what she would do to you!"

Dav reared his head back. "Marilith!" he cried.

Pardock, weeping, held her brother to her. "I'm sorry, Dav. I did it for you! I threw down the baton for you! You can hate me if you want.

You can hate me as much as you need to. As long as I know your soul is safe, that's all I care about."

And Davage stood, composed himself, and walked away from his sister. He looked around at the walls of stone and felt them closing in on him.

He ran.

Unable to stay in the castle any longer, seeing little bits of Marilith, Princess of Xandarr, everywhere, he left. Wearing common clothes, he went to the city of Minz and joined the Stellar Fleet ... to go to the stars, to get away from the woman he loved but couldn't have, to get away from the sister who had prevented his marriage—for his sake, she had said.

The common clothing was a quaint touch, the Lords at the Fleet office thought, but everybody knew the Lord of Blanchefort—the Unable Groom, the man who couldn't be married to that randy, half-naked Xaphan iconoclast. His public shame made him a celebrity of sorts. His family connections undeniable, he was accepted as is without the usual Letter of Recommendation and was oathed at once. He became a junior helmsman aboard the *Faith,* a rickety old *Webber*-class starship. Nobody expected much out of him—a spoiled Blue Lord who was going to probably quit on his own or get drummed out in shame. It happened all the time.

But what a helmsman he was. Before long, he was flying the *Faith,* that old tub, like she was a Main Fleet vessel ready for war. Those regal hands of his—hands that could properly hold a fork after years of drill, hands that could flatten a roughneck in the bars, hands that could write out a letter in flowing, exquisite script—could turn a mean wheel, could fly a wicked starship. He was magical; he could make a ship dance. It was said he could fly a starship through a thunderstorm and not get the ship wet. He quickly became a master helmsman, a man of great renown, and Fleet captains fought over his services. He recalled the first time he helmed a starship into battle with a new Xaphan enemy, an angry rising star in the evil Xaphan ranks—Princess Marilith of Xandarr, his once love and future antagonist.

He had just been promoted to full lieutenant, ten years to the day after joining the Fleet, when he took some time ashore and went to see his sister Pardock at Castle Vincent on Nether Day—a warm, solemn holiday, a holiday for families, for togetherness. Pardock, usually regal and proper, upon seeing Davage in his blue Fleet uniform and hat, put her children down and ran to him. She ran down the tree-lined lane as fast as her confining House Vincent gown allowed her, and Davage ran to her as well. They embraced when they met, ten years of pain and hurt erased in one moment.

He had forgiven her. Perhaps she had been right. Perhaps Marilith was a monster after all and Pardock's courage had saved his soul, though the pain he'd endured at her loss was unimaginable. As he sat down to eat the Nether Day feast with his sister and her family, his heart entered a long period of dormancy, of numbness. Marilith, his Zen-La, was gone, now an enemy at arms though he loved her still. In the years ahead he had his occasional romantic encounter, the momentary distraction for his broken heart, but they never lasted or provided any real comfort. He looked to his to his duty, and eventually to his command to provide relief, for seventy years—ever the Elder, his face not aging, his body remaining strong and fit, but his heart laboring in a battered cage of hidden sadness. He was an old, wounded soul in a young, healthy body.

He could not have known, could not have expected, that seventy years later, an emergency call to combat a Xaphan-snaring operation on a drab, backwater world would see the end of all that.

Perhaps he should have listened more closely to Countess Monama, that huge woman in black who loved to thump her chest and tell him as a boy that "evil" dreamed of him from afar. Perhaps he merely assumed the evil Countess Monama had seen was simply Princess Marilith—an easy assumption to make. He could not have known that, one day, Princess Marilith was to have a similar vision—that someone, or something evil dreamed of him from afar, and that her vision, like Countess Monama's, held true. Something dark and terrifying would one day come for Captain Davage, Lord of Blanchefort—something with a soul as lonely and wayward as his own.

And there was no running from that.

2

THE SISTERHOOD OF LIGHT.

The Sisterhood was adamant. The creature in the *Seeker*'s brig—the Black Hat—must die. She was all that was left of a dark, invisible party caught snaring a Vith chapel on Poteete, a small planet of on fringes of the League. After a short but fierce battle, the Black Hat was captured. Her guard of Hulgismen had been slaughtered by the 5th Marines in an up-close action, her contingent of two Black Hat Painters savagely slain by the Sisters, their brains scrambled, their bodies crushed. She also should have been killed, but at the last moment, she covered herself in a complex, twisting Shadow tech cocoon, one that took the combined power of the Sisterhood days of exhausting work to slowly unravel. She sat in the *Seeker*'s brig, surrounded on all sides by the Sisters in adjacent compartments.

The Black Hat sat alone ... not moving, not saying a word.

The Sisterhood of Light, powerful and influential, wasn't in the habit of asking the League for anything. They did what they pleased. They were ages old, the League's oldest and most powerful sect and, some said, the real power behind its continued success. In the time of the Elders, the League served the Elders faithfully, faring the stars for them in ships of their design. The Elders, twenty-five in number, celestially huge and powerful, required starlight to survive and their beloved adopted children—the League—located suitable stars for them. And they were kind, sharing the starlight with all. The Elders loved their League children and rewarded them with Gifts—the gift of youth and health, the Gifts of the body, and to a select few, the Gifts of the Mind, turning them into mortal gods.

And then the Elders faded and died and the League was all alone … alone with their mighty Gifts.

The Sisterhood of Light was formed ages ago to investigate the Gifts and determine their potential benefits and possible dangers, and as their knowledge grew, so too did their power and influence. It was said the Sisters were no longer Elder—that they had evolved into something else, something strange. It was said in hushed whispers that the Sisters had a hand in deciding who lived and who died in League society … and in Xaphan society too. Any who lived to see the next day, they say, was by the Sisters leave.

Stories for a dark, windy night, no doubt.

The Sisters and the Black Hats were ancient enemies. Once Sisters themselves, the Black Hats, proud, rebellious—evil—were prone to studying forbidden things simply because they were forbidden. They broke away, laughing in the Sisters' faces, taking all their knowledge and power with them, and became Xaphans. The Black Hats, using the Mass—the infamous Phantom Hand—could kill any they chose to, even millions of miles away. Only the Sisters could turn the Mass, could prevent the Black Hats from killing at a thought. As such, the Sisters and the Black Hats were continually at odds, locked in an unending battle of the mind, their power intertwined forever with the Black Hats, their hated enemy. It wasn't uncommon for a Sister to suddenly die, sometimes in their hidden places, sometimes when they were walking down the street, killed by a lurking Black Hat light years away, unable to fight any longer.

The hatred between the two sides was tangible, palpable.

And so, the Black Hat prisoner sitting in the brig.

In a normal situation, the Sisters simply seized the Black Hat by the mind and mercilessly shredded it, dealing the Xaphan wretch a slow, slobbering death. But they were aloft in space in a Fleet vessel, and the Fleet did not allow executions without Command approval. Fleet regulations normally meant little to the Sisters—they acknowledged no authority other than their own. To them, the Fleet and their Captains were nothing more than transportation.

This particular situation was problematic for them, however. This was the *Seeker*, and its captain was Davage, Lord of Blanchefort. The Sisterhood had a long-standing friendship with the Lords of Blanchefort over the ages, in particular with Sadric, Davage's late father. He was an Elder whom they openly admired and admitted into their counsel. The mighty Grand Abbess of Pithnar, it was said, admired him very, very much. The Sisterhood, not wanting to cause a stir or slight Sadric's son, decided the best thing to do in this situation was to be courteous; they shall "ask" for permission to kill the Black Hat. Besides, the Sisters found that they liked Davage too, as they had his father. They didn't want to snub him or damage his honor.

A small Sister, adorable in her little winged headdress, white robes, and small, light blue cloak, came into Davage's office and speaking through Lt. Kilos, politely asked Captain Davage if she could execute the Black Hat. The Sisters, so awash in their formidable mentality, could barely speak audibly; instead, they communicated with a complex form of empathy and relied on trained Marines to speak for them to non-Sisters. When they did try to speak with their mouths, it was strange and halting, in a rough, unplaceable accent.

Captain Davage's first officer was Lt. Kilos, a Marine of the 12th Division. The Fleet and the Marines were often at odds with each other—the Fleet considering the Marines brutish and undisciplined, the Marines considering the Fleet an arrogant pack of louts with expensive toys. As such, Kilos was the only Marine first officer in the Fleet. Her promotion to the posting created a minor scandal throughout the service, for Kilos was not only a Marine, she was a Brown too—a commoner, a "peasant" in a uniform. She was rather saturnine by nature, being quiet, often sullen and brooding. She carried her trademark Brown cynicism around like an honor badge. She was notoriously slow in making friends, was rather intimidating by nature, and she had a nasty temper, which had led to her being a frequent resident of brigs and work details wherever she went in her early days in the Marines. Her back had seen the most lashings with the sonic whip in recent memory.

An untrained observer, seeing the captain and Lt. Kilos at work together, might well come to the swift conclusion that she was unpleasant and unruly at best, insubordinate and toxic at worst. Such, however, was not the case. There were few firsts in the Fleet as loyal to their captains as Ki was to Dav. They made a great team, their various strengths complimenting each other perfectly. And Ki wasn't a completely dour person—if given the right circumstance, if allowed to flourish in a positive atmosphere, she was a capable soldier, loyal to the end, devoted to her captain, and steadfast in a fight. Given the right circumstances, she opened up like a big, tough Marine daylily and could be funny and mercurial, her brown eyes filling with laughter and delight. She and Davage often bickered about the most trivial of things, sometimes fighting to the extent of settling their issues in the gym. Yet, at the end of the day, they were best friends and shared a familiar bond that few captains enjoyed with their firsts, Davage appreciated her frank gruffness, her "Brownness," her stark, relentless manner of speaking. Dav rarely ever had to issue her an order. She could usually predict what he wanted without him having to say a word.

Kilos was from Tusck on the nearby world of Onaris, and she looked like it—she had the standard "Tusck Look." She was tall, over six feet, with large, soothing brown eyes. Her hair was long and thick and the color of tree bark. If she spent any time in the sun, her hair transformed into a golden blonde and her skin tanned to deep bronze.

Like Dav, she had spent a good portion of her childhood hungry, but for different reasons. Being a Brown, and being from Tusck, her family was destitute beyond measure. To eat, she and her many brothers and sisters, every day, had to go out and find food, work for it, steal it, or sometimes fight for it. Ki was known for being a dead shot with her huge Marine SK pistol. Her skill came mostly from killing birds on the wing with a simple sling as a girl. Ki often brought home sacks full of them, where they went into a stew pot. Each day presented a new series of obstacles and challenges. Dav was a prisoner of his wealth and standing, Ki, a prisoner of her wrenching poverty.

*   *   *   *   *

Lt. Kilos, tall and resplendent in her red, black, and gold Marine coat, white pants, and tall boots, related the Sister's request to Davage. Both the Sister and Kilos expected Captain Davage to hear the request, thank the Sister for her courtesy, and then "grant" her permission to proceed with the execution. Then, smiling, curtseying, the Sister shall excuse herself, go to the brig, and viciously slaughter the Black Hat like an animal.

Davage thought about it. Outside, the stars moved past, the *Seeker* gliding through space effortlessly. The Cyclops eye of the main sensor made a huge beam of light that panned about this way and that.

Kilos and the Sister waited for his expected response.

Davage stood up and went to the window. He stood there a moment, looking at the stars.

"Sister," he said finally. "I am honored that you have taken the time to come here today and offer your request. I am humbled by this unexpected show of courtesy."

The Sister looked at him with her big blue eyes and smiled brightly. She spoke to Kilos.

"Dav, she says the Sisterhood has benefitted greatly from its long-standing friendship with the House of Blanchefort through the years—you and your family are well-favored, and they look forward to continuing that friendship with you, as the current Lord. And she says, as they are guests aboard your vessel, they won't think of executing a prisoner without first informing you and securing your blessing."

Kilos shook her head, unused to the Sisters being so … friendly. "Somebody out there must like you, Dav."

Davage was flattered by the Sister's courtesy, and he didn't want to upset her. He was about to grant the Sister's request and send her on her way.

Looking at the stars, the endless depths of them, he was reminded of Princess Marilith—he always thought of Marilith when he looked at the stars. Marilith, out there somewhere in the dark, empty space, tall, scheming, beautiful—planning his death even as she pined away for him.

His previous conversation with her entered his mind. Her warning, that "something evil" was coming for him, searching for him, calling out to him, rang through his mind.

Could this, this Black Hat in his brig, be what Marilith was talking about? Could the silent Black Hat, sitting there in an evil trance, be reaching out to him for some reason?

He wondered.

He turned and Sighted, looking all the way down to the brig. He wanted to have a look at this Black Hat, at the person he was about to condemn to death.

He supposed he owed it to her.

3

THE GIFT OF SIGHT

The Sight.

Captain Davage had inherited the Sight from his father. Of all the Gifts the Elders had given to the League ages ago, the Sight was the rarest and the least considered. It was a Gift that was hard to have in the first place: it had to be passed down through bloodlines. The Sight also was difficult to master and was seemingly limited in benefit—thus, it was largely forgotten. Other, easier Gifts were much more common and practiced throughout the League: the Cloak, the Stare, the Strength, and the Waft. Even the Dirge, which nobody really liked, was put to use more often than the Sight. It had vanished altogether in large sectors of League society and was thought to be a myth in others. Not even the Sisters, whose eyes were nearly useless, made much of a study on the Sight, not in thousands of years when they declared it a minor, odd, and mildly amusing Gift.

The Blancheforts traditionally had the Sight, it being passed down from Lords of old to the present. Lord Maserfeld, Davage's grandfather, once used the Sight to locate skulkers in villages he'd just sacked and slay them.

Davage had the Sight. He recalled as a tiny boy that his mother, father, and sisters sometimes appeared strange to him—normal one moment, nude, energy-laced, skeletal the next. He recalled playing in the Telmus Grove and looking up at the rising dome of Dead Hill where his family ancestors were entombed, he saw withered, forlorn faces looking down at him. For his sanity's sake, he spent years calming his Sight, controlling it, exploring its secrets, mastering its various intricacies. Certainly it was a given if you had the Sight you could see things in the dark, and maybe see things that were invisible—but as Davage discovered, there was so much more to see. He recalled, as a very young man, looking up from the tall towers of his ancestral castle, up toward the northern night sky, and using his Sight, he could see the small, blinking satellites floating about high above. He could see graceful Fleet vessels cruising in their orbits. He could see the maintenance dry docks as they passed overhead. Fleet dry docks parked at four hundred and fifty miles above the surface, and Davage, with his Sight, could see them like he was right there.

And that wasn't all. He could see through the dry dock, through the girders and hulls and see the people moving about inside. He could see through the people, too, he could see down to their atomic structures. He could see the heat trails that they made as they moved through the hallways. He could see the cold vapor of their iced drinks, and though it once frightened him, he found he could see what the people in orbit were *about* to do; he could see things that they recently *had* done.

The Sight was truly a potent Gift when properly used. Additionally, when he used the wonders of his Sight, his eyes glowed, a profound, mesmerizing golden light. He found his two sisters, Lady Pardock and Lady Poe, became enraptured when they looked at his glowing eyes. His eldest sister, Pardock, was once coming to beat him senseless for ruining one of her favorite Blanchefort gowns with spilled ink and his glowing eyes calmed her enough for him to escape into his mother's protective arms.

The Sight was truly a Gift of many surprises and benefits if one merely took the time to … look.

✳   ✳   ✳   ✳   ✳

Eyes glowing, Davage Sighted from his office all the way down to the brig in the rear section of the ship and the Black Hat sitting within.

The Sister looked at his glowing eyes with admiration.

Lt. Kilos, a Brown, didn't think twice about it. She looked at her fingernails, feeling hungry for lunch.

Davage homed in on the brig, seeing it clearly through all the metal and distance.

There she was, sitting in the brig, her Black Hat mask gone ... her scarlet robe, her face ...

Her face! Creation, her face!

He wasn't prepared for what he saw. He did a double take. He gasped.

He nearly knocked his chair over.

Kilos was startled. She forgot all about her fingernails and lunch. "Dav, what is it?" she asked.

Grabbing his hat, Davage made for the door and offered it to the Sister, who appeared confused.

"Sister," he said. "Before we proceed, I must see the prisoner."

A look of startled shock etched itself on the Sister's face.

"You want to do what, Dav?" Kilos said, incredulous, speaking for both herself and the Sister.

"I want to go in there and see the prisoner. I wish to talk to her."

"You want to interrogate the Black Hat? What for?"

"I have a few simple questions I wish to ask her," he said.

"And you expect a response of some sort?"

"I do not know. I won't know until I ask."

Several more Sisters arrived in short order. They appeared agitated. They spoke silently to Kilos, blasting her with thought. The Sisters, unused to using their mouths to speak, were pumping Kilos full of silent chatter. Such a frantic treatment could often leave a Marine dazed, insensate. After a moment, she composed herself and spoke.

"Dav, the Sisters here are beside themselves. They want to know why you want to go in there, and they want to know when they can execute the Black Hat."

"I want to go in there because I want to see the prisoner. I've some questions I wish to pose. The Sisters may execute her when I am satisfied that my questions have been answered."

Kilos rubbed her eyes—she was growing a whopper of a headache.

"When was the last time the prisoner was fed?" Davage asked.

There was more chatter as the Sisters spoke to Kilos. "It has not been fed. It was not expected to still be alive, Dav."

Davage turned to the Sisters. "It? The Black Hat is a prisoner of this vessel, and as such, *she* is entitled to certain rights and amenities— food and drink being just a few of them."

Davage hit the Com and called for an orderly. In a flash, one arrived.

"Catlin," Davage said. He knew her name; he knew all their names by heart. "Will you please go to the mess and bring a plate of something simple and some water to the brig? Don't go in, just wait there for me."

"Aye, Captain!"

"Thank you, Catlin." She ran off.

One of the Sisters mumbled in her halting, strange accent. "Captain … what you wish proving?"

"Sister, I'm not trying to prove anything. I simply wish to see the prisoner and ask her a question or two."

"Speaking to a Black Hat is pointless and dangerous. We forbid it. We shall execute the prisoner now …" Kilos said, a Sister wrenching her thoughts into her head.

Davage was determined. "I am going there so that I may see the prisoner. You may proceed with the execution if you must." Davage left the office and headed for the brig at speed. The gaggle of Sisters and Kilos followed.

"You cannot be present when we execute her … the backlash will kill you as well," Kilos said again for an agitated Sister, her mouth and voice being controlled like a puppet. She was going to be sick later, she knew it.

"Then, I suppose I will die today. I am going in there."

"Davage!" Kilos said, her head and her thoughts being wrenched this way and that. "What are you doing?"

"I have to see something for myself."

"If you go in there, the Black Hat will kill you on sight!"

"Lieutenant Kilos, we have twenty Sisters here, each one monitoring her every move, her every thought. If she makes a hostile action, then, by all means, you have my permission to execute her."

"And that will be moments after you yourself have been killed. Killing you, a Fleet captain, would be a bold statement. Dav, I have a responsibility for your safety …"

"Because of which I sleep very well at night. Ki, I have no desire to throw my life away. I have every faith in the Sisters, and in you, to protect me."

They strode through the ship and eventually arrived at the outer doorway to the brig—it was a long walk. Catlin, the orderly, was waiting there with the tray of food Davage had requested. Davage thanked her again and took it from her.

The Sisters looked at one another, dumbfounded.

"Captain Davage, I forbid you going in there!" Kilos yelled.

"Is that from them, or from you, Ki?"

"Both."

"So noted—put it in your daily report … Lieutenant."

"Don't attempt to give me that 'Lieutenant' crap, Dav—it's me you're dealing with! And, 'Captain,' I'll remind you that we've disagreed on things before—but never like this. Perhaps we should discuss this further in the gymnasium. No Gifts—no Strength, just you and me solving a disagreement."

Davage smiled. "For someone who claims to be concerned for my health, you seem eager to lay a beating to me."

Kilos jumped front of him, blocking the entrance to the brig. Tears began to well up in her large eyes—that didn't happen often. "Dav, how could I live with myself if I stood by and allowed you, my captain—my closest friend—to come to harm?"

"Ki, we've been in tough scrapes before, you and I, right? And we always come through. Have you no faith in me at all?"

She looked down and wiped the tear away. "I do, Dav, you know that … But this—this is a Black Hat. She'll kill you just to spite the League—to take the life of a Fleet captain. Her life means nothing to her."

"You know that for sure, do you? Trust me now, I promise, we'll be laughing about this later."

Kilos gave him a pleading look and then stepped aside.

One of the Sisters, the first one who had come to see Davage, put her hands on his chest and stared at him.

She said through Kilos: "Please do not go into her presence."

"I must. I must see her."

"I could restrain you. I could keep you from doing this," Kilos said.

"I know that, Sister, and I am asking you not to. I am asking you to trust me ... to have faith in me."

The Sister looked at him, her eyes deep aquamarine. In all his years, Davage had never engaged a Sister in such a way.

"Will you do this for me, Sister? Will you have faith in me?"

Kilos shook her head, the Sister's thoughts overwhelming her. "Dav—the Sister—I can't translate what she's saying and feeling. She's begging you not to do this. Let them kill her."

Davage, holding the tray, looked at the Sister. "Sister, I shall be fine. I simply must see something. I must look her square in the face, one to one ... and know that I saw what I saw."

"What did you see?" Kilos asked.

"I'll tell you when I re-emerge."

The other Sisters threw their hands in the air. "One bad ... movement ... she die!" one of them said.

The first Sister put her small hands to her face and walked away, certain Captain Davage was about to die.

Davage, holding the tray, opened the door and went in. The door closed behind him with a clank.

4

BLACK HATS

The Black Hat Sisterhood ... certainly a scarlet-clad enigma and ever-terrifying vexation of the League.

They were the Devil in the flesh, the Boogey-man and the Riders of Doom all rolled into one convenient yet very-real package. They were the eternal enemy, the plague in the night, the pack of murderers who were the subject of endless stories spun to frighten children into good behavior. Of all the secret Xaphan Societies, they were by far the most powerful, the most dangerous, the richest, and the least beholden to the Xaphans themselves. As the Xaphans spun helplessly around Mirendra, depowered and slowly dying, the Black Hats had the dark power to make all five of them tremble.

It was a long-held belief that the Black Hats were invincible in battle, that to face them was to die. Only the mighty Sisterhood of Light, it was told, could stand before them—their League Light to match the Black Hats' Xaphan Darkness, centuries of hatred standing between them. The check to the balance.

The two opposing sides certainly took a radically different approach to their various disciplines. The Black Hats loved the theatrical, the spectacular. Their Painters were known and greatly feared for their deep Cloaks, their clogged mire of illusion and deception, their ability to snare an area completely undetected and slip away to the dark, their illusion all encompassing. And should they somehow be discovered, should the hated Sisters arrive, they had their Hammers, adept at the Special Gifts, the Point, the Sten, the Mass—all gruesome and spectacular methods of killing an enemy, at mowing down entire forces at a stand ... deaths that will have people talking, have people locking their doors at night and gazing fearfully out their windows.

The Black Hats had their vile henchmen as well—the Hulgismen. Like visions out of a civilized person's nightmare, they were brutal, their filthy mouths slavering in their mindlessness. And, stark naked, they did the Black Hats' bidding and defended them in battle. These mindless brutes were, of all forces known, completely immune to the Sisters' power—it was said that it was their raw brutality and uncivilization that allowed them this immunity. It was said should a stitch of clothing ever touch their bodies, should a comb ever pass through their hair, then they would lose their immunity forever. In any case, they had a singular thirst for the Sisters' blood, and as long as they had an ounce of strength available to them, they relentlessly strained to put their hands around a Sister's throat and end her light forever. In response, the League created the Stellar Marines and their dreaded SK pistols specifically to protect the Sisters from the ravenous Hulgismen. An odd juxtaposition—the naked howling Hulgismen armed with nothing more than Nyked knives and their bloodlust arrayed against the dapper, orderly ranks of Marines and their thundering SKs.

And finally, there was their Shadow tech, ever present, ever dark, a Black Hat specialty, the illegal darkness they flaunted in the Sisterhood's face. In the hands of a Black Hat, Shadow tech could be made to do anything: make snares, make weapons, make Nyked poison, make demons of the night. To be touched by Shadow tech, it was said, was to never be touched by anything again.

The Sisterhood of Light, on the other hand, relied on more subtle Gifts. The "miracles" they could create at will delighted the League and kept it in awe—rightfully so. Their TK was unmatched, as was their use of Hyper Gifts, and they could fry a Black Hat's brain in a psychic grapple without half trying. Also, they were the only force known that could throw aside Shadow tech, detect it, and render it dead and harmless. Only the Sisterhood could de-snare an area rife with Shadow tech traps. Only the Sisterhood could hold back the Phantom Hand.

So, arrayed before each other on the battlefield, the Black Hats surrounded by their naked, blood-thirsty Hulgismen, mindless creatures immune to the Sisters' power, and the Sisters defended by their loving squadrons of Marines, they fought as they had for centuries, each giving the other no quarter within the pre-set and civilized parameters they had set for each other.

No one dared face the Black Hats, and no one dared question the Sisters' authority. Their very reputations demanded a certain fealty from their opponents, a respect and decorum that had not been challenged in known memory.

Nobody willingly faced a Black Hat. Only the Sisters would dare.

Nobody attacked a Black Hat. Only the Sisters could hope to triumph.

And certainly, nobody tried to talk to a Black Hat.

Not even the Sisters …

* * * * *

The interior of the brig was cold and lonely. It was deathly quiet.

Sandwiched in between various bulkheads and other required structural components of the *Seeker*'s rear hull, the brig was a long cylinder, about twelve feet high and fifty feet long, the walls sloping and convex. There were five cells in the brig, each cell guarded by a clear glass door that had been machined into incredible strength. All of the doors were open—there was no need to shut the prisoner in. The guards were all outside, all around, ready to strike, ready to kill.

Slowly Davage moved past the open cell doors.

Finally, in the center, he saw the prisoner—the Black Hat. He couldn't believe what he had seen in his office; he had to see for himself. He had to look her square in the eye and see.

She was sitting quietly on the bench, erect, perfect posture, her small hands placed properly in her lap. Her scarlet robe was a shocking splash of color in the drab ochre interior of the brig.

Her black mask was gone, and her face was completely exposed. Like most of the other Black Hats Davage had ever seen, she was a tiny woman, barely five feet tall. Her face was thin and pretty. Her skin was characteristically pale and blemish-free. Her eyes were big and green. Cheekbones high, her nose was distinctive and prominent.

Her dark red hair was long and wavy. It was pulled back from her face and tied in place with a black felt bow. A black bow ... not something he expected a Black Hat to wear.

And the mark was there—the Black Hat's mark—the black, twisting, ink-vine tattoo wrapping around her right eye trailing down to her cheek bone. A hard patch of black on her pale skin.

Her expression was distant—blank. Her eyes were glassy and doll-like.

Here she was—the dreaded Black Hat, scourge of the League, evil given form ... a tiny, pretty woman with a black bow in her hair and a mark on her face.

Slowly, Davage walked into the cell, his boots clacking on the floor tiles. With measured movements, he placed the tray on the small table to his right and sat down opposite her.

Davage thought, *For the first time in centuries, a Xaphan and an Elder sit together without actively trying to kill each other ... truly a first.*

Her expression didn't change; her eyes were blank, distant.

Davage sat there, leaning forward slightly. He said nothing. His CARG rolled over in its saddle a bit, clanking on the floor.

He looked at her long and hard, taking in her features.

It was true, what he had seen from his office; it was all true. This woman, this Black Hat, looked just like Captain Hathaline ...

"How am I ever to forgive you!"

... of House Durst, his neighbor and lifelong friend, his peer and cohort. Davage had spent his childhood with Lady Hathaline ...

"You have betrayed me! Betrayed me!"

... at his side. And together in the Fleet, they had shared so many adventures and fought countless battles side-by-side.

The more he looked at her, the more of Hath he saw. Everything was there; she was her perfect double with the exception of the mark, the Black Hat's mark. Dear Hath—how he missed her, how he regretted never giving her at least a little bit of what she wanted ... before she died.

No, didn't die—was killed, murdered by Princess Marilith of Xandarr. He couldn't blame Marilith too much, couldn't hate her. It had been a fair fight … and Marilith had owed Hath.

He wanted to talk to her, to this Black Hat. He wanted to hear Hath's voice again. He wanted it like nothing else.

But this wasn't Hath; this was a Black Hat—a Xaphan. This was an enemy of the League, a woman who could kill him with the slightest thought.

He had to be careful.

They sat like that for hours, neither moving, neither blinking. Davage, his instincts for diplomacy inherited from his father Sadric operating in full gear, realized that if this was to work, and consequently if he was to get out of this alive, he needed patience. She had to make the first move. That was the key. He'd sit there forever if he had to.

Silence.

Davage heard the vacuum manifolds that operated life support clunk a few decks above. He could hear the occasional muffled whooshing of a lift moving by and the indistinct droning conversations of passing crewmen, blissfully unaware of the mortal confrontation that was going on in the brig.

He could hear his intestines gurgling.

He could hear her intestines gurgling too.

Then, from far away: *Tap … tap … tap-tap …*

He could hear it, plain as day, all the way from the outer hull, the odd, disembodied echoing knocking sound that happened from time to time. It sounded like a fingernail knocking against the thick duraplate. It was a sound that carried a long, long way. It was just the hull plates cooling, grinding together, Lord Probert had told him once in the stark, sterile way that engineers tend to talk in, but the crew … the crew hated hearing it. They thought it was a bad omen, a sure sign of disaster to come; crewmen were always superstitious. They called it the "Hand of Vith"; other more macabre crew referred to it as "Hathaline's Calling." Captain Hathaline and her lost ship the *Dart* had taken on a rather Flying Dutchman-type mystique since the second Battle of Mirendra, which Dav hated.

Tap-tap … tap … tap …

"*Captain Hathaline knocking on the door, waiting for Captain Davage to love her evermore ...*" so they sang in hushed tones.

And here dear Hath was, returned from the grave it seemed, wearing a Xaphan's Black Hat robes and a mark on her face, a murderer in a trance.

More time passed.

Come on, Hath ... talk to me, he thought.

Finally, almost imperceptibly, her green eyes flicked toward the tray of food and water Davage had brought in.

Now ... now was the time.

"I've only recently been informed that you were not fed in a proper or timely fashion. As captain of this ship, the fault ultimately lies with me, and I offer my most humble apologies. Should you wish to file a formal protest, I assure you your complaint will be presented to the Fleet Admiralty, where, no doubt, an investigation will be conducted at once regarding the matter."

The Black Hat said nothing.

"You should offer your complaint in writing, as is customary."

After a few more moments of silence, her eyes, hollow, glassy, and doll-like, slowly, unblinkingly moved toward Davage, regarding him for the first time. He felt his insides shudder a bit. He could feel her power, her terrible power, coiled, tense, ready to spring ... ready to kill.

It was like being stared at by the Devil himself. The Devil in Hath's beautiful body.

He knew, from this moment forward, that he was in mortal combat with this Black Hat. It wasn't a battle of fists or weapons or starships but of words and ideas.

He knew his life hung on a thread.

Slowly, quietly, she spoke in a malevolent whisper.

"... your name ..."

"My name? Certainly; I am Captain Davage, Lord of Blanchefort. Well met, ma'am. And might I ask your name?"

The Black Hat fell silent, her eyes still regarding him, trying to make sense of this situation.

She spoke again. "... What do you want ..."

Davage smiled. "What do I want? Why, I just told you what I want. I want to know your name."

Silence.

"And I am certain that, should you so choose, you could tell me exactly what I want. You could probably tell me things that I want that I am not yet aware of wanting myself. You are, after all, a Black Hat."

The Black Hat, her eyes fixed now on Davage, rustled slightly. "... I am confident, should I use any of my powers, the Sisters will put an end to me ... Is that not right?"

"The Sisters? Yes, well, they are understandably apprehensive. However, as I have previously mentioned, I am the captain of this ship. There will be no executions here without my authorization. I have authorized no executions so far today."

Davage observed the Black Hat. She seemed puzzled. "You seek information then ... you will receive none ...."

"I do seek information; I wish to know your name."

The Black Hat looked off into the distance again. Clearly, she had no idea what to make of this.

Davage smiled, and he locked his eyes with hers. "I have begun this meeting honestly with a sincere apology regarding the lack of civility shown to you. I then asked you your name, again, as a matter of honest interest. I shall continue to be honest. I have allowed you to live because you happen to resemble a person very dear to me."

He looked at the black bow sitting in her hair. Hath would never have worn such a thing.

The Black Hat now seemed genuinely puzzled. "... I do not understand ..."

"And I suppose that all we know of you are stories—ones we ourselves created. Fanciful tales really and none too flattering—that you are evil, unrepentant, heartless, cruel, and despotic, without an ounce of good in you. That you bathe in darkness, revel in mayhems and destruction, and..."

"Your stories are correct. I am evil, heartless ... pitiless, and live only to spite the League ...."

She paused for a moment and continued. Davage listened. "I have killed thousands in battle, and I have killed thousands more simply because I felt like it, and I am going to kill you, Davage, Lord of Blanchefort .... You will not leave here alive. I feel like killing you ...."

"Indeed ..."

"I know that when I commence to murdering you, the Sisters will attempt to stop me. They will be successful in killing me, but not until you are dead ..."

"Most distressing."

"... and when I am dead, I will seize your glowing, stainless soul and drag it down to hell with me .... We shall spend eternity together ... locked in combat..."

"Hmmm. How are you going to do me in? Are you going to Waft me outside the ship, into the empty belly of space?"

"The Sisters will Waft you back in ...."

"I see. Then you will be dead and for nothing, as the Hospitalers will resuscitate me. Will you then crush my skull with the Mass, break it like a walnut shell?"

"Such an action takes too long. Again, the Sisters shall kill me before I could ..."

"Before you could complete the Mass operation, yes. You could Dirge me to shoot myself in the head."

"The uttering of the Dirge brings the Sisters ...."

"How about the dreaded Point?" he asked.

"No, no .... The Point will take ..."

"Yes, yes, and on and on. It seems you're in quite the predicament. You wish to kill me and drag my soul to hell, where we can fight each other for all eternity, yet most of the more spectacular deaths you could effect upon me take a bit more time than the Sisters will give you."

The Black Hat rustled on the bench. She seemed to be in some discomfort.

"You speak bravely .... Would it be so, I wonder, without the Sisters here to protect you from me .... " Her voice was like whispered ice.

Davage stood up. "Ma'am, I have never said that I am not respectful of your power. I know full well that you could kill me with only a moment's notice and probably without a second thought."

Suddenly, Davage leaned very close to her—close enough to smell her breath. She seemed surprised, mortified even.

"And that's exactly what I wish to discover here—if there is that second thought rolling around in your mighty head somewhere."

Davage left the cell. "Eat, please, drink or not. 'Tis up to you. More will be brought later regardless."

"Exit this chamber, Lord of Blanchefort, and you die ..." she said with a sneer.

She stared hard at him, her green eyes piercing and utterly evil. "You ... sir ... are not going anywhere."

She regarded him for a moment and cracked a small, wicked smile. "You came here, all on your own ... to 'talk' to me ... to 'brighten' my day ... how nice. So, League Fleet Captain ... here I am ... talk! Cheer me up ... and make it good ... your life depends on it ...." Her voice became a growl. "But be warned ... Should you grow stale ... should you bore or annoy me ... the trap will shut ... and you will die."

Davage doffed his hat. "Good meal, ma'am."

"Sit down!" she said in a commanding, wicked voice. "Have some food ... and start talking ...."

Davage, his insides roiling, knew he had to leave—it was leave now or never leave alive. He tipped his hat. "I like that bow in your hair, ma'am. It suits you fine." He then walked from the brig and back outside.

Before the door closed, he heard her say, "See you soon ... love ..."

There waiting for him was an exhausted Kilos and several Sisters. All seemed astonished that Davage was alive. Kilos holstered her SK pistol and embraced him roughly.

"What a bloody idiot you are, Dav," she said into his shoulder.

"Good to see you too, Ki. Good Creation, she looks like Captain Hathaline—have you seen her, Ki?"

"I haven't. Is that why you wanted to go in there?"

"Yes."

The Sisters also appeared to be glad to see him alive; they smiled, chattered silently amongst themselves, and lightly patted him on the shoulder.

Davage looked back at the brig and Sighted through the walls.

"Well, did you discover what you were looking for?" Ki asked.

Davage peered through the walls of the brig. He could see the Black Hat, alone once more, sitting there trying, apparently unsuccessfully, to assess what had just happened. She lightly touched the bow in her hair with her right hand.

She looked at the door to the brig.

After a moment, he saw her scoot a bit closer to the tray of food. Slowly, with measured grace, the Black Hat began eating, wiping her lips with a napkin after every dainty bite.

"No, Kilos … but I think I am close."

Several more Sisters, followed by two Marines, came into the brig's outer chamber. They Sighted through the walls.

They turned to the Marine.

"Sygillis of Metatron," the Marine said dryly, writing it down in his view pad.

"Hammer."

5

BREAKING THE CLUTCH

After a long, strange day and a tiring session of paperwork, Davage finally settled to bed. Not a night owl per se like Lt. Kilos, who was rarely if ever in her rack, he nevertheless usually got no more than a few hours of sleep a night. His duties were ongoing. But today, he was exhausted, his eyelids closing by themselves as he sat at his desk.

He was so tired after his visit to the brig. Sitting there in front of the Black Hat had taken all of his energy. Afterwards, for the rest of the day, he kept seeing things, and that was unusual for an Elder with the Sight. Must be his imagination, he guessed. He saw shadows and indistinct shapes in the corridors, on the bridge, in the mess. He'd see a hand going for his throat and a lurking shape following him, pursuing him—laughing at him.

He'd Sight, his eyes flashing, panning around, and there was nothing there. He Sighted the Black Hat once or twice; there she was, sitting in the brig in a trance with Hathaline's beautiful face pulled back in a grimace.

He finally finished his paperwork and crawled into his huge and oft-neglected bed for a few hours of rest. Sleep quickly overcame him, and he began to dream.

His dream went out of control almost at once.

He dreamt of the Black Hat, Sygillis of Metatron. She stood in front of him in his dream wearing her scarlet robe and her featureless Black Hat sash, her face hidden behind it. Her gloved ebon hands clenched into savage claws.

And then the dream came to life.

"I am here with you, Lord of Blanchefort. Welcome," she said in a malicious voice. "I've been waiting for you."

He looked around. He was in a dark place—a sort of black churchyard with many walls, passages, and alcoves all around. Black spires and steeples clawed their way up to a vaulted, bitter sky of angry clouds. The Black Hat stood there mocking him in the distance.

"What did you think, you arrogant League Lord?" she asked in an icy whisper. "That you could simply come and go from my presence as you please? You foolishly came to me, and I became interested in you, Captain. I followed you back, like a deadly spider sitting unnoticed on your shoulder. I was patient, I waited all day for you, but every so often I gave you a little tickle, just to let you know that I was there. Now here we are, just the two of us."

Davage tried to move but was locked in place. "This is just a dream," he said.

"Yes," the Black Hat said. "Just a dream. You dream, I dream … our minds wrapped together. Here we may have a bit of privacy, you and I. Here our dreams become very, very real."

The Black Hat waved at him with her claws. "And here, in this dreamscape, I am going to kill you."

Davage clutched his head. "I could call the Sisters. I could cry out for them."

"What's the matter, Fleet Captain, are you scared? Scared of a tiny little person like me? This is a game, and I insist we play it to the finish." She bowed slightly. "Therefore, I've an offer to make to you."

Davage turned to his right. A corridor trailed away. Struggling, his legs like lead, he went down it.

"Well?" her voice echoed from behind. "Care you to hear my offer?"

Davage reached a dead end. He Sighted. He couldn't see through; his Sight didn't work. He felt very alone without it. "Fine then," he said. "What is your offer?"

"I offer you your crew, sir. We will fight here, you and I. We will battle to the death, and regardless of the outcome, I will not blow myself up and take half your ship with me. I could do a lot of damage in the brig. You know I could. Fight me, and I will spare your crew. That is my offer. Choose not to fight—choose to seek the Sisters—and your ship sinks in a spray of my bones and my guts. What say you?"

"The Sisters will not allow you to sink the ship."

"I'd not be able to build up as large of a Shadow tech charge as I wish before they became aware of what I was doing, that is true, but still … I'll make a rather large hole regardless."

Davage shook his head. "I do not wish to kill you," he said. "I want to help you."

"Help me? I need no help. A noble if foolish sentiment. Regardless of what you wish, I greatly wish to kill you, and if you do not fight me, I will ruinously damage your ship."

"I how can I trust you'll keep your word?" he asked.

"You cannot … yet, I speak truthfully when I say yours is the only soul I want to claim. Yours is the only life I wish to take. The rest are worthless. Useless!"

"I've nothing to fight with. I am unarmed."

His CARG appeared in front of him, coppery in the dark, and his MiMs too and gun belt on the ground. "Here are your weapons and your Gifts. I give them back to you. In this shadowy place, you can do everything you can in the real world … and so can I. Though this be naught but a dream landscape, to us it is very real. We will face each other, your power against mine. The winner walks away; the loser dies."

Davage strapped on his gun belt and picked up his CARG and closed his eyes. He felt his Sight returning to him, and that made him feel a bit better. "We needn't do this. I was trying to be civil—to offer you a bit of courtesy."

"And I thank you. I will remember you fondly. And never fear, we will be seeing each other again soon in hell. The Sisters will be very angry when they see what I've done to you … when they find you dead. They will tear me apart. They will feast upon my flesh. Ha! Let them—I'll have you, nevertheless."

The sky overhead became turbid and fierce. Davage held his CARG at the ready.

She looked at him and, in a mocking gesture, imitated his guard with a similar stance. So short, clad in her scarlet robe, she looked like an ancient fire plug.

She Wafted in a blast of wind and vanished. He lit his Low Sight and whirled around.

"I was hoping to find good in you," he called out into the air, "to know why you are so angry!" he shouted.

She appeared behind him. He put the horn of his CARG on her neck. Tenderly, she reached up and touched its length with her black gloved hands.

"Anger, sir, is all I know. Hate, sir, is all I feel."

"That isn't how it has to be. What sort of life is that? Let me help you!"

He reached out to her, and she recoiled in surprise for a moment. She tipped her sashed head to one side. "You are such a kind man," she said softly. She ran her fingers up and down the length of his CARG. "So kind …" Slowly, Shadow tech claws grew out of her fingers. Grabbing on, she stroked the length of the CARG. "Let me pleasure you," she said as her claws grew and grew until they were two feet long, their undulating black blades sparking against the surface of the CARG.

"Unfortunately, your kindness is unwarranted, unasked for … and unwanted."

And like he had once been told, Shadow tech didn't make a metallic sound when scraped. Instead it moaned and wailed, like it was alive.

They circled once or twice, she continuing to rub his CARG seductively with her moaning claws. "This…is so unfair," she said moving slowly to her left. "I can kill you at my wish, and all you have is this silly weapon. You must be very frightened."

"Not frightened. I'm disappointed. I truly wanted to help you."

She stopped and stood still. She threw her arms back, her claws rising into the air. "Oh, that hurts, Lord of Blanchefort, that stings—that I've disappointed you. Hehehehe ... go on, try to kill me. I will allow you an open attempt, a free shot, if you will."

She waited, her featureless black sash floating about her head, covering all traces of her face and hair. He thought he could see her grinning beneath it.

Davage smiled and put his CARG down. "I have a demand."

"I see," she said, waggling her claws at him. "State your demand."

She Wafted with a blast of air and appeared behind him, her tiny yet cruel hands wrapping around his chest, the claws interlacing together—an odd, menacing embrace.

"I demand you remove your mask," he said, nonplussed.

The hands appeared quizzical, surprised. "*Hahahahahaha*! Request denied."

"What is the matter, Black Hat? Scared?"

The hands pulled back, and she reappeared in front of him. She seemed puzzled. "Why make such a demand?"

"You were very beautiful, sitting in my brig, where you sit right now. Fine skin, lovely red hair—those shining green eyes. I wish to see it again."

"Think me beautiful, do you?"

"I do. I wish to see your face again."

She stood there a moment. "Lord Blanchefort, I make a counter offer. You are a handsome man. If I didn't hate you so, if I didn't wish to taste your blood, I might find myself rather enamored with you."

She pulled up the lower part of her mask, exposing her mouth, only there was no mouth there. There was a Shadow tech amalgam of hairy female and male parts, squirming, rolling, dripping, reaching.

Davage was horrified. He turned away.

"*Let me kiss you!*" she said in a demonic Black Hat voice.

She approached him. He could smell her as she neared in the dank air.

"*Come here and kiss me!*" she shouted, using the Dirge.

Davage, Dirged, unable to control his actions, began moving toward her.

"Heeheeheheee," she tittered softly.

When he got to her, she put her arms around him, reached up, and kissed him with that travesty of a mouth. He gagged as parts wormed and thrust their way down his throat.

Feeling himself begin to wretch, he hauled back and delivered a crushing head butt to her mouth, sending her recoiling, holding her face. So much for the Dirge. A swollen mouth will hinder it.

Davage tried to go on the initiative. "Again, show me your whole face and be rid of your Shadow tech trappings ... if you are not scared to face me as a woman and not a monster," he said.

The Black Hat stood there for a moment, confused. She suddenly lunged and sent a claw speeding toward his chest. Davage side-stepped and countered, crossing the claw with his unbending CARG. The Shadow tech screamed as it crossed the hard surface of the CARG.

She purred, impressed it seemed. She swiped again and again.

He crossed, parried, met her guard, side-stepped, and thrust. Sparks blossomed and floated from their clashing weapons.

Davage was a master with his CARG. The Black Hat, though fierce and determined, couldn't match his skill, and only his mercy left her standing. She tried an overhead swipe, which Davage met with the full weight of his CARG. It was a heavy weapon, and its mass was too much for her, her claws bent and shattered. He then gave her a shallow cut across the chest, which didn't seem to bother her in the least.

They stopped a moment, both breathing hard. She then came again, her claws regrowing, and seeing her try such a move previously, Davage moved to his left, swept her legs out from under her, and sent her down with a thud.

He put his CARG to her throat.

"Will you yield and listen to reason?"

Suddenly, he felt an iron hand grip his throat. He was lifted off the ground into the air. "Certainly," she said.

TK, she had him in a total full-body TK, and there was no getting out of it.

Gripping him in her TK, she stood and brushed herself off. She regarded him for a moment. She then slammed him down to the ground hard. Repeating the action, she did it again and again, over and over until the landscape spun. His CARG jostled loose from his TK'ed hand, and she kicked it away.

She brought him down very close to her masked, featureless face. She looked at him and caressed his chin with a claw. "Pity ..." she said.

And with a savage cry of victory, she sent her claws toward his chest. Again and again, his uniform shredding into tatters.

Her claws couldn't penetrate Davage, however. She found that his skin, while TK'ed, was rock hard, diamond hard, the angry claws not able to penetrate. They bounced off, the protesting Shadow tech wailing at the feast of blood denied to it.

She stopped and laughed. "Hmmm, pardon me, then, if I simply *crush you!*"

She tightened the TK, Dav feeling his guts compressing up into his throat.

Dav, feeling it all coming to an end, found as she compressed his chest, his limbs began to free up. Quickly, he drew his MiMs pistol, pointed it, and fired.

POCK!

Even in this dreamscape, its report was small and unsatisfying. A tiny toy gun, the MiMs.

She took the bullet in the shoulder. Wincing in pain, she dropped the TK, and Davage fell to the ground.

She formed a massively long Shadow tech whip with a waving cat-o-nine tails at its end and lashed him with it. He felt his flesh sundering at its touch.

He went to his knees, alight in agony. He dropped his MiMs. With a wave of her hand, the tiny, elegant gun vanished.

"Heheheheeeeheee," she tittered.

She hauled back and cracked Davage across the back with the whip, the shaft tearing through clothing and putting an ugly, bloody wheal on his skin. As the whip pulled back, Davage noticed the cat-o-nine tail was actually a grasping Shadow tech hand complete with a full, tooth-filled maw in the center of the palm.

She lashed him again. The hand gripped onto him with its horrid claws, and when she pulled back, it wrenched away a fist-sized bit of flesh.

Davage cringed.

She sent another whip stroke. Davage deftly moved to his left, seized his CARG, and sliced the whip in two. Grabbing the end of the severed whip, he gave it a good jerk, and the tiny Black Hat rocketed toward him. Roughly, he clothes-lined her across the neck. She fell, gagging.

Providing her with a taste of her own brew, he picked her tiny, robed body up and threw her down on her head where she lay on the ground and groaned. She raised her head to look up and he golf-swung his CARG across her face with a thudding, non-cutting blow. A rapidly assembled Sten saved her from a bone-breaking and possibly fight-ending hit. Nevertheless, Stenned or not, she spat out bloody teeth.

She moved the Sten toward him, and he just had a moment to dive out of its way.

He dove into one of the corridors and went around a few bends.

CRACK!

He felt a sting on his leg. Looking down, the whip with the hand was back, wrapped around his right leg. With a jerk he was pulled off his feet and dragged back toward the corner. In almost surrealistic fashion, a set of long Shadow tech claws appeared from around the corner and danced about, waiting to chop him into bits.

"*Hahahahahahahaha!*"

He plunged his CARG into its mouth and tore the hand in two. It let go.

Instead of running from the hideous claws, he charged toward them, and using a cutting stroke, he sliced them through again. He quickly reached around the corner and grabbed the Black Hat, who clearly wasn't ready at this point to be attacked. Again, he picked her up like a tiny red duffel bag and crashed her back down, where she groaned in pain. Her right arm snapped where she had tried to break her fall.

Stunned, bleeding from her MiMs shot, in agony from her arm and her near-toothless mouth, she Wafted away with a blast.

Dav, using his Sight, saw that she was going to reappear down the corridor to his left. He whirled and sent his CARG in a spiraling cutting arc in that direction.

She appeared a moment later, saw the CARG coming, and putting her arms out in front of her to protect her face, made the CARG vanish just as it was about to run her through.

She exhaled in exhaustion and wagged her finger at him. "Enough of that," she mumbled, toothless. She Wafted behind him and sent her claws speeding toward the back of his head.

Dav Wafted, appearing to her right, and socked her square in the jaw, knocking her down.

Davage Wafted again, this time appearing behind her. He put his arm around her throat.

"I am still awaiting the removal of your mask, ma'am," he said.

She struggled for a moment and giggled breathlessly. "Oh, sir, I am enjoying this. You fight well." With a gloved fingertip, she traced little designs on his arm. "How shall I do it? How shall I kill you? The choices are endless."

Davage suddenly grabbed her by the nose and ripped her sash off, exposing her face. He hoped that her little nose will come off with it.

There again was the red hair, the pale skin, the green eyes, the strange mark around her right eye, and a red, throbbing nose. It was Captain Hathaline, her face with a bleeding mouth.

She puckered in rage. In a cascade of Shadow tech, she blasted him off of her. He landed a few feet away, the touch of the Shadow tech galling and unbearable.

She stood, her mouth pulled back in a scowl. Her teeth were a broken and jagged patchwork.

Davage sensed that he was in extreme danger. He Sighted, looking up into the blasted sky.

Sten ... she was creating a Sten field over his head. The Sten was an illegal Black Hat specialty. It was an invisible force field; Black Hats used it to protect themselves from most incoming projectiles and energies. To touch a Sten was a shocking, deadly experience. To touch it for a moment unloaded a massive shock into the person. To touch it for more than a moment or two was utterly deadly. The major drawback of the Sten was that it was very draining to use and somewhat slow to create. Adept Black Hats could create a Sten far away from their bodies. They could move and shape it, turn it into a killing field.

This Black Hat, this Sygillis of Metatron, appeared to be very adept. He could see the Sten field beginning to form overhead in his Sight.

Moving with the speed of a championship athlete, he rolled away, just clearing the edge of the Sten, and it sparked into the ground.

She looked at him quizzically. "Can you see my Sten? How is that possible?"

"Sight," Davage said, wondering if she was now going to take his Sight away from him too. He should have said nothing.

"The Sight does not exist. The Black Hats have proved it does not exist."

Wickedly grinning, she created a small Sten maze and set it over him.

"You are encased in a Sten. I have boxed you in. There is death all around you. Let's see how well you can see it."

"I'll just Waft away."

She smiled. Hathaline's face, alight in evil. "If you do, I'll blow myself up, again taking most of the ship with me. Run my maze, Captain, and your crew will be safe."

"I think you are lying," he said.

"You are probably correct."

His CARG appeared in the center of the maze. "I will even give you your silly weapon back, should you survive to reach it."

The maze was shifting, moving. She created paths and then closed them just as fast. He took a step in the wrong direction intentionally. He wanted to see if she changed the maze, to prolong the torment.

She did. She moved the wall, allowing him to enter. With the way open to his left, he stumbled in that direction. She apparently was enjoying this sad game.

Outside, she was delighted. "I once killed a whole squadron of League Marines with the Sten, one just like this one. I simply swept it across the field and they died, screaming. You should have heard them scream."

Davage tired of this game. He looked at the CARG. It actually wasn't there—just a simple TK paint. His Sight gave it away. He made to reach for it and then Wafted. He Wafted right into her and planted her in the chin with his fist, sending her flying. She hit the ground and, grimacing, fired a sinewy, intestine-like rope of Shadow tech at him.

It wrapped around his throat, its brackish, clammy, stinking substance sticking to his skin like glue. It felt like it was alive, full of crawling, biting, stinging insects. His skin recoiled with discomfort.

Spinning him around, she wrapped him up like a spider packaging its prey for later consumption and then plopped him down.

He couldn't move a muscle.

He tried to Waft, and she laughed. "You cannot Waft through Shadow tech. I am sorry."

She slowly approached and knelt down. "You have fought well, truly. I have fought Xaphan warlords, Marines, League Fleet ships, even the Sisters. You have lasted longer than any of them. You have pained me. You should be proud."

"You cheated. You took my weapons from me just as you were about to perish several times."

She leaned forward and licked him with her bloody tongue on the nose. "And so?" She stopped and regarded him. "Hmmm, how should I do this?" she said. "A pity. If I was capable of feeling such things, I might actually like you."

"You're going to kill me now?"

"Of course I am, and I'll not think twice about it. Perhaps fighting you for eternity in hell, as we soon will be doing, won't be such an unpleasant thing."

She smiled and raised her hand. "Have you ever witnessed a person die by the Point?"

"I've been briefed on its effects."

She shrugged. "You really must see it to truly appreciate it. Usually, people simply explode from the inside out. The Giftless, the Browns, die instantly, but Gifted Blues take a bit longer. Many times Blues explode too, just like Browns, but occasionally powerful Blues, like you, do random sorts of things. I've seen people turn inside out. I've seen bones crack and entrails turn to dust."

She lifted her finger. "I wonder what you will do."

She reached out to Point.

There was a flutter of movement from a distance. She hesitated.

Davage looked at the Black Hat. For the briefest possible moment, there appeared to be two of her standing there, facing each other.

Having no other weapons available to him, he lit his Sight and blasted her. His Sight, aside from being blindingly bright at full, tended to have a calming effect on those looking at it. Maybe it will calm her enough to relax her coils.

She looked at his eyes, mouth agape. She stared, her green eyes glowing like emeralds in his light.

"What is this?" she cried. "*What is this?*"

She smoked in his Sight, plumes of black soot belching away from her as if she were on fire in a stiff breeze.

Her Shadow tech cocoon crumbled, and he was free. He wasn't sure what was going on, but his Sight clearly appeared to be having an effect on her. He approached and continued, hitting her with it as hard as he could. She stood there in the spotlight of his fully lit Sight, smoking.

She fell to her knees, her eyes locked in place.

There was an audible blast, and a cloud of darkness appeared to part from around her.

She sighed and slowly reached out for him. "Lord Blanchefort?" she said in a small, probing voice. "Lord Blanchefort … I …"

The floor to the dreamscape fell away, and she dropped, hanging onto the edge, her broken arm dangling.

Down below a vast, fiery mouth appeared. It opened in a smiling bellows, exhaling fire.

"*DDDDDDIIIIIIEEEEEEEEE!*" it rumbled.

"It's her!" she cried. "It's her!"

She hung on to the edge in the onslaught. "Lord Blanchefort," she said. "Help me, please!"

A long tongue of fire and evil lapped up, tormenting her. "Please!" she shrieked.

Davage crawled forward and pulled her up by the wrist. Standing, he bore her away from the edge, the rumbling and fire passing into the distance. When he thought it safe, he stopped and put her down. Things became indistinct. The dream began to fade.

She stood there looking at him with new eyes.

She faded away, and his dream became his own again, the battle fought and apparently won to some extent.

He rustled in his bed and then continued sleeping.

In the morning he only remembered having a strange dream, a dark dream having something to do with Sygillis of Metatron, the Black Hat. The most vivid thing he could remember was a flash of light and green eyes.

6

"RED"

"Lord Blanchefort, you are an exasperating man!" the robed, headdressed Sister said as she sat in Davage's office.

It was the morning following Davage's bizarre trek into the brig. He'd had that strange dream and been badly sick that morning—either it was nerves or his body reacting to the Black Hat's power. After a few hours of throwing up in the bathroom, he finally felt like himself again, though his skin crawled for some time to come. And he noticed he had several odd, painful welts on his back and chest.

Davage took a drink of coffee. "Sister, either your spoken language skills are getting better or I am becoming more telepathic. I cannot determine which from which."

The Sister turned to Kilos and silently spoke to her.

"Dav, she says she's been practicing up for that remark. And I must say that I agree with her. I cannot, and she cannot, fathom why you are returning to the brig again. Tempting fate again."

Davage put his coffee down and picked up a report. "As I have said, I have not yet had my questions answered. I don't see what all the fuss is about. I was not killed yesterday."

The Sister again filled Kilos's head with thoughts. "The Sister says your implacable cheek probably had the Black Hat discombobulated yesterday. Today she will be more ready to do you in."

Davage considered that for a moment. She was probably correct. He looked at Ki in her Marine uniform. Her long red coat reminded him of a side of beef.

"She could do me in from here if she so chose. Wouldn't that be a spectacle, to make my head explode in my very office?"

"Be serious, Dav."

"I am deadly serious. Sister, may I offer you some coffee?"

The Sister looked at Davage and after a moment, nodded, the wings of her headdress bobbing slightly. Davage got up and poured her a cup of steaming coffee. "How do you like it, ma'am?"

"Black ..." she said herself in her strange accent.

Davage finished pouring and offered her the cup. She took a few drinks.

"Good ..." she said.

"Dav," Kilos said, "the Black Hat needs to be killed. The Sister says she will kill the Black Hat today."

The Sister appeared sad.

"The Sister says she is sorry. The Sister says she does not wish to disappoint you, but the Black Hat will die today. She must."

"The fact that this Xaphan looks exactly like Captain Hathaline gives you no pause, Ki?"

"No, it doesn't."

"Really? Ki, when I say that she looks like Captain Hathaline, I don't mean she bears a vague similarity to her. I don't mean she *sort-of* looks like Hath or that she *kind of* reminds me of Hath. She looks exactly like her, for Creation's sake!"

"Maybe it's a Cloak." A gold thread stuck out of her stiff black and gold collar, catching the light.

"If it was a Cloak then I'd know that, wouldn't I? There has been no Cloak devised that I cannot Sight through. She is Hath's double—her twin, and I want to know why. I must know why. I'll not see Hath die again." He smiled. "By the way, Ki, you've got a thread, just there."

"She's not Captain Hathaline, Dav!" Ki said, whirling around, trying to get at the thread. Ki was very particular about her uniform. It had to be perfect, or she'd go mad.

The Sister, looking anguished, spoke to Kilos again. "Dav, the Sister implores your forgiveness. She wants to know if you will find it in your heart to forgive her when the Black Hat is dead." Kilos got the thread and shook her head. "Boy, Dav—I've never seen a Sister this concerned about how a Fleet captain feels."

"Sister, you need not fear, for I love you like no other. But again, I will be in the Black Hat's presence again today, and I will die right next to her if need be."

The Sister closed her eyes and winced.

"Dav, are you insane?"

"Ki, we are the League. We are the children of the Elders, nurtured with their teachings, bathed in their light. We are supposed to be the good guys."

"We are the good guys."

"Are we? You and the Sister here are spoiling for her blood, without cause, without trial or referendum. Is she, the Black Hat, something to be killed, nothing more? Is that something the Elders teach?"

"Black Hat," the Sister said holding her cup. "Sygillis of Metatron ... murderer ..."

"All I saw was a frightened, starving woman, sitting alone, surrounded by enemies."

"Black Hats don't feel fear, Dav. You're assigning her attributes she doesn't have," Kilos said.

"Black Hats ... evil. Black Hats must die."

"The institution certainly, is evil, I acknowledge that. But the people, the Xaphans ... they are us! They must be capable of redemption."

Davage stood, his blood rising. "Sister, we made a promise to the Elders. We promised to stay in this sector and defend life, defend all we could from the Xaphans. Well, there it is. There is the life to be defended sitting in my brig. In this case, the life needing defending happens to be a Xaphan. Xaphan or not, Black Hat or not, her life is worth defending too."

A tear came to Davage's eye. "Sister, Kilos, are we so familiar in our war with the Xaphans, are we so comfortable in our hatreds, that we can forget the very basic nature of our charge, our ongoing mission? It could very well be that my father was right, after all—that there is hope for our two factions. And ... and should you be correct and she chooses to snuff the life out of me—to kill me, to murder me in cold blood—then I will go to my death doing what I thought was right!"

Davage leaned against the wall and wiped the tear from his face.

A soft hand touched his back. Davage turned. He thought it was Kilos.

It was the Sister, still holding her coffee cup. A tear rolled down her cheek too.

"You ... a good Elder, Captain," she said. "A ... great loss ... you die."

Davage laid his hands on her slender shoulders. "I've no intention of dying, Sister. I am certain I can do this. I am certain I can get through to her. I am certain I can awaken the Elder within."

The Sister, trembling, looked at Davage.

"So, Sister, is the Black Hat to live, or is today the day we both die?"

The Sister turned from him and sat down.

She spoke to Ki. "Dav, she says she wishes to share something with you."

Dav poured himself another cup of coffee and sat down opposite her. "Thank you, Sister, I am listening."

The Sister filled Ki's head. "She wants you to know that the Sisterhood has information regarding the Black Hats, information which is not generally known except in certain ancient texts. She says she wishes to share this information with you, as she truly is concerned about your well-being."

Davage blushed. "I am flattered and most thankful for this information."

Kilos looked down and straightened her red coat. Her huge Marine SK pistol jutted from its holster. "The Black Hats, Dav, are evil. They are surrounded by an invisible wall of darkness. The Sisterhood calls it the Black Abbess's Clutch. She says this wall, this darkness, keeps the Black Hat in a perpetual daze, an endless dream. Dav, she says because of this Clutch they feel nothing but rage and hate. They aren't able to feel anything else. She says all of the emotions that make us Elder are suppressed within them, beaten down, kept in sway. There's nothing left for the Black Hat but rage and hate."

Ki wiped her nose. "Kind of sad, really."

Davage finished his coffee and stood. "Sister, I thank you for this knowledge."

"Sit down, Dav," Ki said. "She also says that this Black Abbess's Clutch is not breakable. There is no known way to break it. It is there, and it always will be there. So, given that, will you please let them kill her? I say it will be a kindness."

Davage put his hat on and straightened his coat. "Sounds to me, given this information, that the Black Hat is not really responsible for her actions, is she? That her foul nature is forced upon her."

Ki stood up and slapped herself in the forehead. "You know, Dav, how did I know you were going to say something like that?"

"I suppose it's because you understand that I am now more determined than ever to assist this wayward soul. I wonder, should the Clutch be broken somehow, what might happen? All of her previously suppressed emotions possibly quick-rising to the surface—bubbling like a cup of boiling tea, all the herbs and flavors, once held in bond within the tea bag, suddenly released and allowed to circulate. I imagine such a thing will be a sight to see."

"You can't break the damn Clutch, Dav!" Kilos yelled. "Who's going to break it—you? The Sisters can't do it, so how in Creation are you?"

Dav looked at Ki and smiled. "Ki, I do believe your face is as red as your coat right now."

Ki pointed at him and looked genuinely angry. "If my face is red it's because you made it red!"

He turned to the Sister. "So, Sister, I am on my way to the brig. If you wish to kill the both of us, I suggest you follow."

The Sister shook her head and smiled.

"Dav," Kilos said, "the Sister says she will argue your case to the Sisterhood. She says she will do it because you ask it of her. If it was anyone else, that Black Hat would already be cold and stiff."

"Thank you, Sister," he said.

The Sister turned to Kilos one last time then left the room. "Dav," she said. "The Sister says she will do her very best to protect you. She sincerely hopes that you will survive this exercise."

"As do I, Kilos."

*　*　*　*　*

Davage entered the brig, again holding a tray of food and water. He had some fruit on the tray, along with assorted smoked meats and a few sweet pastries. He also had a pot of coffee, just in case this session lasted through the afternoon like the last one did.

The Black Hat sat exactly where she had the day before. This time, she watched Davage come in, set the tray down, and sit. She watched him intently, eyes glittering.

"So," she said in a quiet, measured voice. "You have returned to my presence, again."

Davage smiled. "I have. Good morning, I hope you slept well," he said in a cheerful voice.

"I must admit, I was wondering if you had the gall to face me again."

"Oh I've gall a-plenty, ma'am. I've gall to pass around."

"Is it courage or madness that has brought you to me a second time?"

Davage looked at the tray he had brought her yesterday—the food was gone, the water drunk. "You know, ma'am, it's odd how those two concepts tend to combine. I see you ate. I'm glad, and I hope our food was to your liking. If you have a specific request, I will see that the galley prepares it for you."

The Black Hat sat, silent.

"I did not have my question answered yesterday. I am still awaiting your name. Also, I thought I'd share with you that I think I dreamt of you last night, though the details are fuzzy."

"Interesting," she said. "And I believe that I dreamt of you as well."

"Really," Davage said, recalling the Clutch. "Dreamt of killing me, did you?"

"Most probably," she said. "As for my name, I am certain the Sisters have already scanned me, though I still live, have already determined my identity. I am certain they could list out for you all of my various crimes, and I am guilty, sir, guilty of everything I am charged with. I assure you."

"I wish to hear it from you, ma'am."

The Black Hat smiled a shark's toothy smile. "So the victim asks his murderer her name."

She spat with contempt. "Lord Blanchefort," she said in a mocking voice. "You appear to take much stock in stories. Tell me, what do your stories say Black Hats do when they have been detected in battle?"

Davage thought for a moment. "I believe they say a detected Black Hat will attempt to create the most mayhem and damage possible before being killed."

She smiled. It was a slow, ugly smile. "And here you are, a Fleet captain, and one who is well known to us—one who has taken many of our lives, one who has been a thorn in our side for decades."

She leaned forward, her eyes glittering. "And I have already told you that your stories are accurate. So, what do you think I am going to do here in the next few moments? I am going to do now what I should have done yesterday."

Davage knew he was in trouble. He thought fast. He leaned forward. They were almost close enough to kiss. She seemed genuinely put off by this.

"So," he said cheerfully, "you intend to kill me, do you?"

"I do. I have thought of little else since our first encounter."

"Well then, I think killing a Fleet captain shall be a bold statement for you. Consider this, though. I take it you've heard of me in whatever circles and environs you habit?"

"I have."

"Then you'll know that I, like you, have also killed a number of people, though I take no pride in that. But I, unlike you, did not do it by simply pointing at them and watching them explode, or by sweeping them aside with a wave of my hand. No, no. I did it man to man, man to woman sometimes … pretty much right at this distance here where we are now."

Some of the glitter in her eyes faded.

"Yes. Right now, ma'am, you are defenseless. The Sisters have permitted you nothing. You have no Sten, no fields of illusion, you have no Shadow tech shield or snares, you have no Hulgismen to screen you. Right now it's just you and me, and I will wager that my reflexes are vastly superior to yours. I have all sorts of options. I could CARG you in twain, I could pummel you insensate. I could shoot you if I felt uninspired, or I could just snap that tiny neck of yours with my bare hands."

She leaned back. "You will find that I am not so helpless physically. I am strong."

"Indeed," Davage said.

The Black Hat closed her eyes. "Then why do you not proceed with it? Let us fight. I am Xaphan, you League; that is what we do."

"Because I don't wish to kill you, as I have said."

Davage smiled brightly. "Well, now that that ugliness is behind us, I still do not have a name to call you," he said, pretending that he did not already know her name.

"You may call me death, for that is what I am to you—your death, sooner or later. I wish to kill you like I've wished for nothing else."

"Death is such an ugly word to say. Hmmm, may I call you D then? D, for death?"

"You may not."

"Well, I have to call you something, don't I? I'll just call you Red— red robe, lovely red hair. Red it is."

"Refer to me as Red and I will most certainly kill you."

"Well, Red, seeing as you are determined to kill me anyway, I will continue to call you Red. How about that?"

In watching her expression carefully, Davage thought he noticed, for the first time, the smallest hint of a smile cross her face—yet another first.

Davage, for all his bravado, knew he had Red, the Black Hat, right where he wanted her. Denied the use of all her formidable powers by the waiting Sisters, in close quarters with a man who was a superior hand-to-hand combatant, the only weapon left to her was debate, and that was clearly a tool she was not used to using. And here, in the *Seeker*'s brig, she was facing an opponent who was, apparently, not afraid of her—yet another weapon denied.

She began picking at the food Davage had brought her and commenced the battle.

"I believe I understand why you are here."

"I have told you why I am here. I am here because you look like a friend of mine, because I wish to know your name, and because I am looking for goodness in you."

"There is none, as I have said. You are trying to confuse me…"

"I am trying to understand you, to discover the person beneath the robes."

She grabbed a pastry and took a small bite. "Yes, under my robes. You wish to love this body … you …"

She stopped suddenly and looked at the pastry in her hand.

Davage adjusted himself in his seat. "Is something wrong with the pastry, ma'am?" he asked, observing her carefully.

She popped the rest of the pastry into her mouth and grabbed another one.

"I like this," she said quietly.

Davage was intrigued. "You like the pastry? I must admit, I could eat a dozen of them at a sitting."

"You will bring me more of these or I shall kill you," she said in a somewhat perfunctory manner.

Davage smiled. He recalled the Clutch, and what could happen should it be broken—the bubbling up of emotions.

Like tea boiling in a cup, the tea and the flavor bursting out of the tea bag.

Interesting …

Davage, putting this notion to the test, poured himself a cup of coffee. She watched him. "What is that?" she asked.

"This? Coffee, a very fashionable drink in the League. An ancient drink."

She took a deep breath. "It has an interesting scent."

"Can I make you a cup?"

She didn't answer, instead, she leaned forward expectantly. He poured her a cup and she took it, noting the heat. She took a drink, and her face cringed.

"What is this? Poison? You cannot poison a Black Hat."

Davage laughed and took her cup from her. "It's not poison. Here, you simply must cream and sugar it to your liking. See, two lumps of sugar and a bit of fresh cream. That is how I take it."

He stirred the cup and offered it back to her. "Here, take it. Try it."

Dubious, she took it and had a sip. She took another. "I require additional sugar," she said swallowing.

"Certainly." Davage took another lump and plopped it in. She took a sip and then leaned back with it.

"As I was saying," she said, taking another sip, "my body. You wish to copulate with it, do you not? Do you wish me to take my robes off? I am beautiful, yes? Do you wish to have …"

She stopped speaking and started sniffing the air. She sniffed, looked around, and sniffed some more."

Davage watched her carefully. "Red?" he asked.

"What is that smell?"

"That smell? The coffee, do you mean?"

"No."

Davage looked around. Red continued to sniff. He checked himself. "I don't—well, I have a bit of cologne on from this morning. You can smell that?"

She leaned forward and sniffed the air near him. She closed her eyes and took several deep inhales. He couldn't help but feel a little awkward. "It … was a gift from my sister for my birthday some years back, my cologne. One of her sons is a perfumer by trade and made this scent just for me. Do you like it?"

She stopped sniffing and then looked at him. "Of course I do not like it…" she said taking a few more deep breaths. She finished her coffee. "And again," she said backtracking to her previous topic, her thoughts apparently quite disjointed. "You certainly desire to know my body. That is obvious to me. So, how shall we proceed? Shall we set to it right here in the brig?"

Davage realized that she was trying to go on the offensive, to pin him down on a topic and derail his attack. She was beginning to un-button her robes from the top. She was trying to use the classic sex ploy to muddy the conversation, to slow it to a crawl. Though a puerile and childish tactic, it could be effective if allowed to go on for too long. Quickly, he turned it around.

"Actually, I was hoping to escort you to your new quarters," he said finishing his cup."

"My quarters?"

"Yes. The brig is such an ugly, inconvenient place and for a prisoner such as yourself, completely useless. I've ordered guest quarters be prepared for you at once. There you will have access to a proper bed, facilities, and change of clothes. I am distressed to say it, Red, but your robes are becoming a bit … stuffy as the days go by."

Red quickly looked down and as Davage noticed, blushed a tiny bit.

She took a few more small bites of food. "I will say, Captain, you have a knack for changing the subject and keeping me confused. Very well, I will permit you to live long enough to escort me to these quarters you offer. I will expect more of these pastries that I like to be made available there, as well as more coffee. The coffee will be properly treated. If I receive it untreated, if I receive it in its bestial form, I will kill you. And you—you will wear more of your insipid cologne at all times in my presence, understood?"

Slowly, in a stiff manner, she stood. She was tiny, barely coming up to his solar plexus.

Together, Fleet captain and Xaphan Black Hat, they exited the brig and made their way down the corridor.

Davage, in anticipation of this movement, had ordered the hallways cleared. Her quarters were to be in the deepest part of the ship, close to no critical systems. The Sisters were already in place in all adjacent rooms. Though no longer in the brig, her quarters were no less closely watched, no less a prison.

Red moved very slowly. Her movements were stiff, pained even. Davage noted she seemed to be having trouble walking.

"I can feel the fear all about me—except from you."

"Your status as a Black Hat carries with it a fearsome reputation."

"The reputation is earned. We are defilers of the League."

She looked up at him. "Why are you not afraid of me?"

"Should I be?"

"Yes, for I am going to kill you."

Davage smiled. "I'm not afraid of dying. Therefore, I'm not afraid of you."

He watched her slowly walk. "I have argued the Sisters to let you live."

"Then you are a fool, for I am going to kill you regardless."

As they continued down the hall, Red, the Black Hat, began limping badly.

"Red, you appear to be having difficulties walking. Are you wounded?"

"You will mind your own business."

"Fine, fine. It's just, at this rate, we will arrive at your quarters sometime this evening."

"Insolent cur. I have a mind to put an end to you right here and now. My death will be a blessed respite to this—"

Red stumbled and fell with a cry. Davage looked down and noticed she was leaving a trail of blood in small droplets.

Davage reached down and picked Red up; it was like picking up a sack of laundry. Feebly she thrashed around and even tried to strangle him with her tiny hands.

"*Unhand me!*" Red screamed.

Davage carried his struggling, unwilling passenger all the way to her quarters.

7

ENNEZ THE HOSPITALER

"Are you out of your freakin' mind, Dav?"

"My 'freakin' mind,' Ennez? You are watching too many puerile League shows, I'm guessing."

Davage stood in the dispensary, which was little more than a small office with two medical beds and several blinking medical scanners. Tinctures in colored bottles lined the walls. The Elder-Kind, with their robust, disease-free existence, generally didn't need an overly elaborate medical setup. Ennez, the popcorn-haired Hospitaler Samaritan, sat with his feet up on the desk. His silver winged helmet glinted on a peg nearby.

The Hospitalers ...

Second in age only to the Sisterhood, the Order of Hospitalers was a sect of warrior-healers. They were notable for being the only major faction within the League that had Brown, non-Vith roots. They always wore black, accented with silver.

They started their existence long ago as fighting valets to the old Vith Lords. They were the loyal servants, the trusted and beloved companions, always on hand to lend an ear, to offer good advice and give their Blue Lords an added sword in battle. They were always regarded for their ability to fight. Armed with their silver Jet-Staves and magnetic accessories, a good Hospitaler could out-fight a squadron of armed Marines, moving with the speed of a Hulgismen, walking the walls, fighting like a demon.

Then, long ago, on the blood-soaked lands of some forgotten battlefield, a Hospitaler did something unheard of—he treated his fallen Lord's wounds. Elder-Kind, being blessed with eternal youth and no disease or congenital defects, had little if any need for medical arts. Still, the Elder-kind often lived dangerous lives. The blood could be poisoned, wounds could be deep and unfastened, disease could set in if preventative steps were not taken, limbs could be lopped off. Slowly, by trial and error, the Hospitalers began the frustrating and halting quest to expand their medical arts knowledge. The warriors became healers too.

Eventually, they became adept at quelling blood poisoning, at thwarting decay, at closing gaping wounds, repairing broken bones, and stitching lacerated flesh. They became masters at re-attaching fallen limbs and counter-acting poisons. They devised a battery of scanning equipment, developed healthy baselines and case-studies. Eventually, through hard work, this Brown sect became every bit as powerful and sought after as any other. Even the mighty Sisterhood of Light often solicited the Hospitalers services. No other sect could make that claim. The Xaphans, too, were keen for the Hospitalers' services, for almost none had joined them in their Great Betrayal of 00000ax, and many battles had been fought to steal Hospitalers in space and press gang them in service. Not until the flimsy and misnamed art of Xaphan Cabalistry came into being did they have any medical arts skills at all.

And they were known for being a bit cantankerous, a bit insubordinate, and they had no issue saying no when the League Lords, Sisters included, came calling. When one or more Hospitalers were needed, the requesting representative—a starship captain or whatever—had to petition the Order. They then decided if the representative was worthy of the request. They always meted out Chancellors, the lowest Hospitaler rank, but to get one of higher rank, a Caduceus, Mercurian, or a Samaritan, was an honor. To get one of those meant you were well-favored.

And so Davage went to Ennez, his Samaritan, to convince him to examine a Black Hat, the enemy.

"Ennez, it's time to go to work. You've a patient awaiting treatment."

"The Black Hat, you mean. Let her fix herself if she's hurt."

"She cannot fix herself, Ennez. If she uses any of her powers, she'll be killed on the spot by the Sisters. She is in medical distress and needs your help. She can barely walk."

"I've been reading her file, this Sygillis of Metatron. Have you read her file?" Ennez asked. "It's soaked in blood."

"I haven't. I've been too busy trying to stay alive in her presence."

"Do you realize how many people she's accused of murdering?"

"Are you coming with me or not?"

"Do you remember what happened to the 30th Marines a few years back, remember that? She happened to them, Dav, for Creation's sake!"

Davage crossed his arms and shook his head. "Answer my question, please."

"Well, what if we go in there and she kills the both of us?"

"I've been in protracted close contact with her on several occasions. She has not killed me, though she makes frequent reference to doing so. And I don't think that, at the moment, she's in any fit state to be killing anybody."

"Okay, what if we go in there and she lets you live and decides to kill me instead?"

"Well then, Ennez, I guess I'll be petitioning the Hospitalers for a new Samaritan, provided, of course, that I myself survive. Maybe one with better hair next time."

Ennez's strange, poofy hair was a constant running joke between them.

Ennez smiled and stood up; his silver instruments jangled in the pockets of his black uniform.

"Look, Dav, you know I'd never disobey you, right? If you order me in there, I'll do it. Are you ordering me to go?"

"I don't want to have to order you in there. I want you to want to go in. I want you to want to help someone who is in need."

"You want me to willingly subject myself to examining a bloodthirsty, Marine-killing monster?"

"I do. By the Elders, I've already had this conversation with the Sisterhood. She's not a monster, Ennez. She's just a tiny woman, one who's hurt and needs assistance. She wears a little bow in her hair, for Creation's sake!"

"She does?" Ennez put his helmet on. "What about the 30th Marines?"

"I hate to say it, Ennez, but that was on the battlefield, and she fought them fair and square, though the outcome was obviously tragic and gruesome for us. If a whole squadron of Marines couldn't handle one tiny woman, then their tactics appear to have been flawed, and I suppose if she hadn't wiped them out they'd have wiped her out. That's war."

"Might have saved us a lot of trouble if they had. And what about the Sisters?"

"What about them?"

"Being in the position that I am in, Dav, I get to hear a lot more of the Sisters thoughts than most people. They are scared for you, Dav. They are already mourning you as dead. And that makes them sad. They like you—love you even. One of them really seems to like you— almost like she has the hots for you."

"Sisters do not get 'the hots' for people."

"Really—want to tell her that? Do you know on how many ships the Sisters barely know the captain's name? But here you are, cherished by them. What Fleet captain could say that?"

Davage stood there for a moment, not quite sure what to say. "I am truly touched that the Sisters feel that way, though I do not know what I have done to earn such regard."

"You're a good fellow, Dav. People like you—I like you, Lt. Kilos likes you … and the Sisters too, I guess. They aren't so much different from anybody else."

"I suppose, then, that the real trick will be to see if I can get a Black Hat to like me too." Davage paused. "She looks a lot like Captain Hathaline, the Black Hat does. You remember her, Lady Hathaline of House Durst?"

"I do. She was a beautiful woman. Is that what this is about, Dav—some sort of cosmic atonement for the loss of your dear friend?"

"I don't know what this is about, Ennez, I really don't. But I can tell you this. Deep down, I don't think she's as bad as we believe her to be. I've currently no evidence to support that, but that's my gut instinct. And she's a fellow soul who's hurt and needs help. Maybe an unsolicited act of kindness will help bring her around, make her a little less hostile."

"What are you thinking, Dav, that if we're nice to the Black Hat—"

"Red. I've been calling her Red."

"—that if we're nice to Red, then she'll be nice to us? Then everything will be okay?"

"Ennez, perhaps that is exactly what I'm hoping. Has anyone ever thought to consider it could be just that simple? Now, come on—let's you and me go and be nice to her."

✳   ✳   ✳   ✳   ✳

Davage entered the room. It was dark and cold inside. It was a tiny room near the ship's secondary plumbing core; he could hear pipes clanking overhead. He allowed himself the luxury of clear Sight. With it, he saw that Red, the feared Black Hat, was lying on her side on top of the bed, still clad in her robes, which, as Davage had touched on earlier, smelled of wear and sweat. He could see she was awake.

The 30th Marines, Ennez had said. Lost on the battlefield. Dead to a man.

She did it. The loss—all those people dead.

She fought them fair and square ...

Hathaline. She looked just like Hathaline. She ... also dead.

Her body quaked with small tremors; she was in pain.

The Sisters already thought he was dead, soon to join poor Hath.

"Red?" he said quietly.

"Get out," she replied.

"Red, you are clearly wounded. I've brought a Hospitaler. I wish him to attend to you, to determine the problem."

Silence.

After a moment, she stirred. "Anyone entering this room dies."

Davage strode up to the bed. "Red, I am becoming fatigued with your continued threats. So, you have five seconds. Kill me or otherwise be silent, relax, and let us help you."

She regarded him for a moment. "Do not call me 'Red'. My name is Sygillis of Metatron. I am certain you already know that. The Sisters know me. There, I have told you my name. I have opened my soul to you."

Davage smiled. "Very well then, Lady Sygillis. That is very lovely name. May I use it?"

"Do what you must. Then leave me in peace."

Davage went to the door and brought Ennez in. Tentatively, his silver helmet glinting in the darkness, Ennez approached and began scanning Sygillis. Davage noticed his collapsed silver Jet Staff was protruding from his black uniform, ready for use should it be needed. Davage also noticed he was wearing his magnetic bracers and knee gerts. Ennez wasn't taking any chances. He was ready to start walking the walls if he needed.

"Umm, where are you in discomfort, ma'am?" he said, voice shaking slightly.

"I will speak to none, save Davage, Lord of Blanchefort."

Davage threw up his hands. "For Creation's sake, you are stubborn!" he said. "Fine then—Lady Sygillis, Davage, Lord of Blanchefort wants to know where it hurts?"

Before she could answer, Ennez rose up in shock. "Captain!" he cried.

Davage approached him. "Have you found the problem?"

"I have." Ennez put his scanner back into its pocket. Slowly, carefully, he took the hem of her scarlet robes and lifted them past her shins.

"There, Captain. There's the problem."

Davage looked at her feet. "Her shoes, Ennez?"

On Sygillis's feet was a pair of strange black-heeled shoes. Aside from being ugly and unfashionable, Davage at first couldn't see anything wrong with them. They looked like shoes House Grenville ladies wore—singularly unappealing.

"Sight them, Dav, for Creation's sake," Ennez said. "See for yourself."

Davage sighted the shoes ... and was horrified.

These weren't shoes; they were torture devices. The interior, aside from being cramped, was lined with metal ribs, pins, and small blades. Her toes were extended into all manner of hideous exertions and held in place with what appeared to be screws.

And there was blood everywhere inside.

"Dav, she's close to blood poisoning. These things have got to come off. But it's going to be hard, and it's going to be painful."

"Cut them off."

"I can't. They're composed of some sort of dense alloy."

"All right, I will hold her. You pull them off."

Davage approached the head of the bed. "Wait a moment," he called back to Ennez. He leaned down and whispered into her ear. "These things on your feet are killing you. We are going to remove them; however, it will be painful. You must ready yourself. You must keep your thoughts and your powers in check, Lady Sygillis. Do you understand?"

She looked at him and said nothing.

"Do you understand? I'll not go through this exercise only to have the Sisters execute you in the end anyway for fear of your power."

"I ... will try."

Ennez sprayed a mild topical analgesic on her ankles to try and deaden them a bit. Davage hauled her up by the torso and held her like a rag doll.

"Ennez, do it."

With a firm tug and a jangle of tools, he pulled her left shoe off. A spray of blood and the stench of decay came with it.

Davage looked at Sygillis. She did not move. Her mouth opened in a silent scream. Tears came freely from her eyes; she was in agony. She held onto him with all her strength.

A light ballast popped.

A second, then a third ... pop!

Davage couldn't help but feel sympathy for her, for the pain she was in.

Ennez pulled the other one off. His helmet dented and flew off his head. Davage's hat went flying also. His CARG rang.

Sygillis, the Black Hat, without a word, fainted.

Davage looked down at her feet: two bloody, swollen stumps, ragged flesh, the smell of rot profuse.

Ennez got his scanner out and waved it around. "Broken, her toes, Captain ... all ten, and in multiple places. Her arches too. Good Creation ..."

He picked up his dented helmet, popped it on his head, and headed for the door.

"She's going to need a lot of work. I'll be back with my medical cart." Don't go anywhere. Do not leave this room."

"Ennez," Davage said. "Well done, and thank you for not making me order you to come in here."

He clanked his silver helmet and left.

Davage sat there in the dark. The door opened, and Kilos came in, her left hand on the grip of her holstered SK pistol.

"What's going on in here, Dav? The Sisters are—by the Elders!"

She had seen the bloody, stinking shoes and knelt down to look at them more closely.

"What are these?" she asked, horrified. "Eugghh!" she recoiled at the smell.

"They are evil, Lieutenant," Davage said. "Plain and simple."

8

A BOWL OF OOUST

Ennez packed up his equipment. "Her feet will be fine, Dav. The threat of blood poisoning has been arrested. I've repaired the bones in her toes and stitched up her lacerations. Her arches were a bit more difficult to fix and will require some time to heal. She'll need to stay off her feet for a few days."

He straightened his helmet. "Oh, you know she has a fresh wound on her right shoulder that looks an awful lot like a bullet hole, though there's no bullet in it and no traces of powder or scorching."

"Really?"

"It's very small but it goes deep, like a MiMs shot. Also, a couple of other things. She had a broken arm. I fixed it too, and virtually all of her teeth are badly damaged and will certainly rot if I don't take action. I'll prepare my enamels and repair them tomorrow. I'll expect you to be here with me as I perform the work. To stick my hands into a Black Hat's mouth—imagine."

Davage looked at her feet; they were encased in neat white bandages. Ennez did excellent work.

"I guess you were right, Captain. Xaphan and Elder-Kind ... we are the same people."

"Very enlightened observation, sir."

He dinged his helmet again and pulling his medical cart, left the room.

Davage pulled up a chair and waited for her to awaken. Ennez had removed her robes and dressed her in a pair of white pajamas. Her red hair was still tied back with the black felt bow.

Davage mused: a black bow. Hath never put such things in her hair ... her beautiful red hair.

Oh, Hath. He missed her so. He prayed to her for guidance ... to her hero's tomb back on Kana in the House Durst yard, to her elusive ghost.

He received none. Hath's shade was silent as usual.

Marilith—Hath's killer whom he still loved. Is this the person Marilith said was calling out to him? Certainly she had been fairly hostile to this point, but perhaps—perhaps she'd come around.

The Black Abbess's Clutch—could it be broken? Was it already? Had he somehow broken it? Her reaction to the pastry and the coffee and to his cologne was telling.

He watched her sleep. Hathaline ... she could be Hathaline. He wanted her to be Hathaline. He wanted his friend back.

Soon, she opened her eyes and looked at him.

He smiled. "I might ask you what in the Name of Creation you were doing wearing those hideous contraptions on your feet, but I am certain I'd not receive an answer."

Sygillis sat up in bed. Free of the shoes and the pain they kept her in, she seemed a bit more eager to talk.

"Pain," she said. "They are meant to keep us in pain."

"Why?"

"Pain, Captain, is an essential component in the creation of Teneramus—Shadow tech you call it."

"So, you wear these things ..."

"Dora ... they are called Dora."

"You wear these Dora so that you may create Shadow tech?"

"We can create Teneramus without Dora. But with Dora, they are stronger, more potent, more lasting."

"Seems a bit counterproductive, seeing how the Dora just about killed you."

"They are not meant to be worn for more than a few hours at a stand. I had worn them for days in your capture."

"Why didn't you just take them off?"

"I cannot. They are snared. Another must remove them—a safeguard ensuring that we perform our duty."

"Why didn't you ask us to do it for you?"

"We do not ask the League for anything. You are our enemy."

Davage smiled. "I see, and you're welcome, by the by."

He stood and went to the bathroom and poured a glass of water. He brought it back and set it down on the table next to her. "Here, in case you're thirsty and refuse to ask for a glass of water."

She looked at the water and after a moment, picked it up and began drinking. She finished it, and Davage got her another one.

"My Hospitaler also tells me that your teeth are badly damaged. He will be returning tomorrow to perform the repairs. May I expect that you will behave and allow him to repair your teeth in peace?"

Sygillis reached up and felt her teeth. She winced. "You fix them," she said. "I will allow you to repair them."

"I do not know how to repair teeth. He will repair them tomorrow. I shall sit nearby if you wish."

Davage smiled. "Do you realize that we have been talking for several minutes now, and you have yet to threaten to kill me?"

She carefully felt her mouth with her hand. "Oh, I am going to kill you, Captain, make no mistake, at the first convenient moment that I get. I simply haven't decided how, that is all. I haven't decided what will be … fitting for a man such as yourself. I have, however, determined that you have earned a good death, one that will be talked about and remembered in both Xaphan and League Society. You appear to have courage and a bit of wit. I feel you have earned that honor. Rest assured, in any event, my final judgment for you will be spectacular."

Davage puzzled over what she had just said. "Lady Sygillis, was that a compliment of some sort?"

"Yes, the highest I can offer you," she said as if it should have been clear.

"Why should you choose to compliment me?"

Sygillis thought for a moment. "I suppose … because you faced me like a man."

"Has nobody ever looked you square in the eye?"

"No … nobody."

"Then why do you wish to kill me?"

"Because it's my duty. You are the League. You call yourself Elder, and you must die. I have to kill you." She looked up at the ceiling for a moment. "I have to kill you."

"Fine," Davage said. "I'll have something to look forward to then. Why don't you try using the Dora? Just slip them on my feet, and a few days later I'll be dead. Or if you wish it to be quicker, you could just beat me with them and—"

Sygillis, the Black Hat, made a noise, a soft snorting sound that she quickly suppressed. Davage paused, wondering what the sound was.

It was a laugh.

Sygillis had just laughed. Just a tiny, short giggle, but still, a League Elder had just made a Xaphan—a Black Hat for that matter—laugh.

Davage was astonished.

Sygillis sat there in bed and also seemed astonished.

Slowly, his thoughts racing, he headed to the door. "I'll leave you to your sinister contemplations."

Sygillis watched him walk to the door. "Captain?" she said.

He stopped. "Yes?"

"You had mentioned previously that, should I desire anything in particular from the galley, you will have it prepared for me. Correct?"

Davage was intrigued. He stepped away from the door and approached her.

"I did, I did indeed. Is there something that you have in mind?"

"Ooust, I want a bowl of Ooust. With coffee to drink and possibly some pastries for desert. I will require your assistance in properly preparing the coffee."

He sat back down in the chair next to her. He didn't bother to point out that she, a Xaphan, has just asked him, a League, for something—yet another first.

"Hmmm, Ooust—I'm afraid that I don't know that particular dish. However, Lord Ottoman, my chief chef, has a vast knowledge of dishes." He looked up at the ceiling.

"Com," he said.

"Com here, Captain."

"Get me Lord Ottoman right away please."

"Aye, sir."

After a moment, a jolly, beefy voice filtered down through the com. "I'm here, Captain, what can I do for you?"

"Ottoman, my friend, I've just had a special request for a bowl of Ooust. Can you make such a thing?"

"Ooust? That's a new one on me, and that cannot stand. I won't have a dish floating around out there that I don't know. If you give me the recipe, I'll be happy to make a batch. I'll call in the whole staff if I have to. I must prepare this dish, this Ooust, or I shall not sleep tonight. It's a scandal."

Davage turned to Sygillis. "Can you assist Lord Ottoman with the ingredients? He appears most distressed. I am asking for your help."

Sygillis thought a moment. "Well, I believe it has …"

"Speak up a bit, please, so that Lord Ottoman can hear you plainly."

She cleared her throat and spoke up. "I do not know the exact proportions."

"Well, ma'am," Ottoman said cheerfully. "Why don't you just give me the basics, and we'll wing it from there."

"It has a broth of …"

And as she recited the ingredients, Davage realized that he had never heard Sygillis's voice before. No longer an aloof, ugly whisper or a mocking, threatening shout, her voice rang out, clear and true.

And Davage thought it was a beautiful voice … it was Hath's voice. He closed his eyes and listened.

9

THE SEEKER

Davage sat in his office, signing reports, looking over ship stores and crew complements. Outside, through his window, stars soared past. He could feel the thrusters tick as the helmsman on the nearby bridge moved the wheel.

✶ ✶ ✶ ✶ ✶

The *Seeker*, Captain Davage's ship, was fifteen years old. Built to *Straylight*-class configuration, it was a League Main Fleet Starship. It was twenty two decks in all. Fleet vessels were never more than twenty-four decks in height. It went back to the Elders. Their number was twenty-five and the Fleet, not daring to consider itself equal in any way with the Elders, always made sure their ships were decked out a little less than twenty-five. It was a very different philosophy, say, from the Stellar Marines, who made it a point to have twenty-five of everything: twenty-five soldiers to a squadron, twenty-five shots to their SK pistols, twenty-five buttons on their coats, and so on. The first seventeen decks of the ship were twelve feet high, and the last five decks were eight and a half feet, with four and a half feet of inter-deck crawl tubes between each. The *Seeker* was about three hundred and fifty feet tall at its highest point and fifteen hundred feet long. It was designed by the legendary civilian Lord Milos of Probert—the House of Probert being known for generations for their engineering skills. Lord Probert's father, Wadlow, had designed the earlier *Webber* class of ships and his sister Rhondo had created the *Tekel* class of scout vessel, all workhorses of the League.

Outwardly it was a beautiful, swanlike, predatory-looking ship. It was sectionalized into three main components: the head of the ship, the long neck, and the large, winged rear section. The spade-shaped head of the ship contained most of the command sections and crew quarters. The front section was dominated on the outside by a large, circular sensor that threw out a long shaft of glowing light, giving the ship a rather "one-eyed" look. Farther back, the long neck of the ship consisted mostly of structural components. Finally, the rear section of the ship was the largest and the deepest. It was designed in a winged shape, with the wings being cranked or bent in two places to resemble the articulation of a bird's wing. It was topped with a tall tower containing various bays and the main mess.

As a Main Fleet starship, it was built to engage and defeat the Xaphans. It was fully armored with duraplate, which had a high level of resistance against Xaphan cassagrain weaponry. Its hull and superstructure were so rigid and stiff that the *Straylight*s were often known for ramming enemy vessels—the infamous "Slap" that was so feared and dreaded. It mounted a complement of five hundred canister missiles in fourteen different bays. Although nothing more than a guided missile, the Elder technology it contained made the canister the League's "ace" weapon, making them virtually unbeatable. Each League captain swore an oath to never lose a canister to the enemy; its Elder tech was a closely guarded secret. A captain will sacrifice his whole command, crew, ship, and all to protect the canisters.

The *Straylight* also mounted twenty Battleshot batteries. Battleshot was a massive gun emplacement that fired short-range explosive shot. A single Battleshot battery could unleash half a million rounds of explosive ordinance every minute—a withering wall of fire that could sink any Xaphan vessel set against it at a close range.

The *Straylights* were also fast, strong, and maneuverable. They revolved sixteen Stellar Mach coils buried deep in the rear section of the ship. Winding just four of these coils pushed the *Straylight* at blistering, sub Mach speeds, winding ten was standard for a safe Stellar Mach. Winding all sixteen, the ship "blinked" out of existence and re-emerge elsewhere, navigation impossible. For planetary excursions, the *Straylights* had ten gas-compression engines that were very reliable but known for being deafeningly loud. It could also float, submerge, and land like a transport vessel. Additionally, a wheel-helmed *Straylight* could out turn a much smaller Xaphan X-2 craft without much effort. Captain Davage, a former Master Helmsman, was nothing short of a magician with the helm wheel.

Given all that, the size, firepower, speed, and maneuverability, the *Straylight* was unchallenged—their principle enemies, the Xaphans, had nothing to match it. Xaphan ships, the X-2s, Ghomes, and Merci's, were small and poorly constructed. They were designed to be easy to produce in vast numbers and relied on sheer overwhelming hoards to swarm a League ship, their Xaphan crews expendable.

The *Straylights* mounted virtually no science equipment, those things being kept in tight leash by the powerful Science Ministry and their old Vith *Venera* ships. Science, as they say, was for the scientists; let the Fleet do the fighting.

The *Seeker* was the 172nd *Straylight* vessel commissioned. It was laid down in Provst, Kanan shipyards. It had three sister ships, the *Dart, Exody,* and *Redoubt,* whose spars were laid at the same time. As with all ships in the Fleet, its captain, engineer, and boatswain were appointed via the Fleet Admiralty through a long, complicated, and often-times confusing process. In theory, anybody could assume those various roles; all one needed to do was present oneself to the Admiralty and argue one's various merits in open debate. In reality, one needed money, great social acclaim, or highly placed contacts to be appointed. Once appointed, the captain, engineer, and boatswain had to "re-appoint" every four years.

Davage, Lord of Blanchefort, a well-thought of, highly placed individual with a belt-load of command experience, was appointed to the captain's chair of the *Seeker,* though he faced stiff resistance from

powerful Lord Grenville—a man with an inherited familial dislike for
Lord Blanchefort.

As a Main Fleet starship, the captain had a fair amount of autonomy
as far as where the ship went and what it did when it got there—the
Fleet Admiralty issuing only the vaguest and loosest of standing orders,
all based on the ancient Elder Promise by which they were all bound:

> Fight the Xaphans.
> Defend life from the Xaphans.
> Sink, or take as a prize, as many ships
> and crew as possible.

Main Fleet actions were instigated by individual ship captains,
who then issued a call to charge, which was answered, in turn, by other
willing Fleet ships. Major battles were fought often without a single
direct order from the Stellar Fleet Admiralty.

Captain Davage had lots of enemies within the Xaphan ranks, his
most famous adversary being Princess Marilith of Xandarr, and they
were eager to meet him in battle. Those were the heady days of the
League-Xaphan conflict, when swirling, turning ship to ship fights
were common. As a result, the *Seeker* was in near-constant conflict with
them, and as a further result, his victory totals were extremely high. He
sunk the Xaphans, confounded and enraged them, impounded their
vessels and captured their crews, often times without his ship so much
as being scratched.

$$\ast \quad \ast \quad \ast \quad \ast \quad \ast$$

Davage put a report down and looked around his office. Pictures
everywhere, many of the *Seeker* and his crew, many of his family, his
late father and mother—Sadric and Hermilane—his sister Countess
Pardock of Vincent, and his other sister, Lady Poe—a sad, troubled
woman whom he worried about constantly. The gossip around League
Society was that Poe was crazy or possessed by spirits. Davage was
always stung by the gossip, but he had to admit, Poe often times
acted … crazy. Some said Poe will bring down House Blanchefort all
by herself. Mental illness, so rare and unheard of, was a dark stigma.

There were other pictures—of Lady Hathaline of Durst.

Captain Hathaline of the Main Fleet vessel *Dart*, beautiful in her Fleet uniform and hat.

His lifelong friend.

Dead.

He'd known her all his life, she being approximately his age. Their respective castles within eye-shot in the cold north of Vithland, Blancheforts and Dursts had always been friends and allies. Hathaline was the seventh of seven Durst girls. No heirs. The Durst line was headed to extinction. It happened; Great Houses came and went.

She had always liked Dav, always went on and on about how smart a Blanchefort-Durst pairing could be, how they could light up League society together. Dav shrugged her aside; he never really wanted much to do with posh League circles and fancy to-dos, which Hath loved. Dav was coy and slow to respond to her suggestions, but she was relentless. She was certain their union was meant to be.

But then there was the Princess Marilith thing: The Wedding. The event that ruined everything.

Dav's late father, Sadric, society man and diplomat, hatched an outrageous plan to end the League-Xaphan conflict by marrying two Great Houses together. Surely he figured, such a spectacle might bring the two sides as one once and for all—as if centuries of bitter hatred could be so easily dismissed and forgotten. Princess Marilith of Xandarr, a powerful Xaphan House, was selected from their side, and she toured the League looking for a suitable pairing. She and her contingent were all the rage for a while in League Society. Sadric's plan apparently was working.

Hathaline was shocked, enraged, heartbroken when Princess Marilith selected Dav to be her husband. Of all the sons of the various League Great Houses available to her, she had to select Dav—her Dav. This woman—this half naked Xaphan—was stealing the man she intended to marry, and she wasn't going to take it quietly. She wasn't going to let him go without a fierce struggle.

Hath was very potent in the Gifts—the Dursts being of the line of Subra of the Mark always had exceptional Gifts. She could Waft, Cloak like a Sister, she had a minimal Sight, and she had the Stare. She had a powerful Stare—a very powerful Stare. It was a long-hidden

Durst secret that Hath, as a young woman, nearly killed a servant with
it in a fit of child-rage.

There is a rare aspect of the Stare—one that is virtually unknown
outside of the Sisterhood. They call it the Cloud. The Cloud could
muddy a person's psychic signature—could distort a Stare, could make
some things appear more prominent, while diminishing others.

Hathaline had the Cloud to go along with her green-eyed Stare.
She'd learned all about it from the old Vith books in her family's castle.
She made it a point to know everything about the Stare, her specialty.
It was always a powerful Gift, a contentious one. The Stare—to be
able to look at a person and instantly know everything there was to
know about that person. It never seemed right; the lack of privacy was
shocking. To Stare Hard at someone … the pain that it created. The
Sisterhood had once considered declaring it illegal because of all the
bad things it could do, the pain it could inflict, and because of the
deadly Gifts that could be derived from it. All of the illegal Black Hat
Gifts had been based off of the Stare.

Biding her time, Hath knew that Countess Pardock of Vincent,
Dav's older sister, was going to Stare Princess Marilith. Always fiercely
protective of her younger brother, Pardock wanted to have a good
hard look at Marilith, this Xaphan princess, to see what made her tick,
to make sure Dav wasn't going to be put into a bad situation. Lord
Sadric had warned her not to, but Pardock was going to do it anyway.
Countess Pardock had always been a rowdy and fearless woman—a
proud rebel with blue hair and a gown. Some said she was possessed
by the spirit of her raider, brigand grandfather Maserfeld—that he
had been reborn as a woman to plague Sadric of Blanchefort, a son
Maserfeld always felt was too dandy for his own good. Some said she
was the son that Maserfeld had never had. She was every bit as hot-
tempered and unpredictable as her grandfather and ever as ready to
raise swords, fight duels, and rough up League ladies and potential
suitors as her pugilistic mother Hermilane had been. In any event,
Pardock was devoted to her family and especially her baby brother,
and the well-being of his soul was worth more to her than the fear of
creating a huge scandal and public embarrassment for her father—a
man who had gone mad with the idea of this wedding, obsessed with

it. For her brother, Countess Pardock will have crossed into hell and fought the devil himself.

And Hathaline used the Cloud on Princess Marilith at the grand pre-wedding ball. She Clouded her, she Clouded her but good—the arrogant Xaphan princess had no clue what was being done to her, about how her life was about to change forever.

Marilith and Hath glared at each other across the ballroom floor as the dancers twirled and the music played, Marilith smug in the knowledge that she was stealing Hath's man—for she'd been told by her entourage that Lady Hathaline of Durst deeply loved Davage.

"Poor little Hathaline, that silly girl of Durst, her tiny heart in tatters. Do not admit her to the wedding ceremony, for she might try something … unseemly."

And Hath hit her with the Cloud.

Marilith was an ambitious, fairly unscrupulous, fairly unprincipled woman who was planning to take over League/Xaphan society and rule it with Dav at her side. It was a lofty and haughty ambition certainly—but nothing too unseemly, nothing unheard of to be sure. Xaphan princesses always thought big.

But Hath's Cloud amplified those desires and ambitions, turning Marilith's psychic image into a psychopathic, monstrous rant leaving half the League dead. And Countess Pardock, herself a master Starer, saw it. She saw the Clouded image and was horrified. Standing there on the ballroom floor, she dropped her drink, aghast that her brother was about to marry a monster.

Fearing for her brother's very soul, she refused for them to be married. She took that baton and threw it down as the rest of the chapel gasped in shock and pulled him out of there.

As a result, Marilith was left behind, Davage literally running from her, from the dark image Pardock had seen, and in her sadness, she eventually became every bit the psychopath Hath had Clouded her to be, determined to get his full attention one way or the other.

Victorious, with her Xaphan rival out of the picture, Hath waited for Dav, shaken and reeling from this incident, to come to her for comfort—and she being so loving and kind. But Davage never seemed to recover from the Marilith thing, his scarred heart slow in healing, slow to reach out and trust. Dav had loved her. They had Zen-La'ed, their minds had linked. Davage still loved Marilith.

He took to the stars, joining the Fleet, wanting to get as far away from home as possible. Unable to forget him, Hath eventually followed, becoming his navigator and then his first officer. Davage then helped her in becoming captain of the *Dart*. His arguments before the Admiralty convinced them that she was right for the appointment. They soared the heavens together, fighting the Xaphans, fighting Princess Marilith, her sorrow turned to infinite anger.

And just as Davage appeared to be recovering, as his heart healed, as he began seeking a wife at last, Hath, confident in her standing with him, told him what she had done to Marilith years ago at the ball. She wanted everything above board.

He was furious, incredulous.

He got Hath in a room at Fleet, and there he dressed her down, chewed her out, and laid her open like he had never done to anyone before ever.

"How could you be so cruel?" he had said.

"How am I to ever forgive you?" he shouted.

"You've blood on your hands!" he cried.

And Hathaline, Lady of Durst, captain of the Fleet, hat in hand, stood there, listened, and wept.

But being a tough-minded Durst, Hathaline didn't give up. She took to the stars in her ship, determined to redeem herself, to win back Dav's friendship and maybe more. Maybe he'd come around and the "smart match" she had always talked about, always dreamed of, might come to be.

Hopeful and determined, she soared away in the *Dart*, never to return.

Dead. Mirendra. Ship destroyed. Crew lost. Marilith had her revenge at last.

To lose a friend, a life-long friend, after harsh, angry, hasty words had been spoken was a terrible thing. The guilt Davage felt at knowing his friend died thinking he hated her was grinding ... relentless.

He didn't hate her. He'd been angry certainly, outraged, of course. That Hath went to such lengths for him—perhaps he'd never given her the attention she was due ... perhaps his inattention drove Hath to do what she did. Perhaps it was his fault after all.

The regrets ...

Now, here he was, a Black Hat under guard in the rear section of his ship.

A Black Hat who was known for her power—for the multitudes of people she'd killed.

Sygillis of Metatron.

And she looked just like Hath. Just a tiny bit smaller, darker green eyes, and with a Black Hat's mark on her face but everything else was perfect.

Hath reborn as a Xaphan murderer.

How often does one get the opportunity for redemption? How often can one reach out into the cold, earthy depths of the grave and speak to the dead—to say, "I'm sorry," and "I didn't mean it."

Through Sygillis of Metatron he will redeem himself, even if it killed him.

10

THE PRISONER REQUESTS ...

As the days went by, Captain Davage continued his dangerous ventures into Sygillis's quarters. She had become much more agreeable, much more prone to simple conversation, but still, every so often her eyes acquired that glassy, doll-like pose, every so often she threatened to kill him again in an icy voice. Lt. Kilos came in with him once, and Sygillis literally turned into a spitting, raging beast, not calming until Kilos left the room. Kilos, her SK drawn, was certain she was an irretrievable rabid animal and suggested the Sisters be allowed to kill her.

Davage, though, insisted that she was making good progress. He insisted he continue this odd, dangerous game. He was convinced that somehow, some way, the Black Abbess's Clutch, that invisible wall of evil, had been broken, that she was free, and she was awash in new thoughts and feelings.

Besides, he was driven. Something deep down didn't allow him to stop. He couldn't avoid her even if he wanted to. He guessed, even though she seemed to take great delight in threatening to kill him, that he liked her. Despite it all, he thought that she was charming.

And she was so beautiful. Hathaline's face, brought back from her hero's tomb.

He made his way down to lonely, dark Deck 13. He knocked on her door.

"Come in," came a soft voice.

He opened the door and went in. Sygillis's quarters were fairly small, just a space for a bed, a small sitting table, a bathroom, and the ever-present clanking of pipes. Her door was unlocked, but she dare not go out. The Sisters would pounce on her immediately.

Sygillis was not there. The room was empty.

He didn't feel like he was in any particular danger, and apparently, as the Sisters were not reacting, she was here somewhere.

"Hmmm," he said deliberately. It was best to play this as casually as he could.

He low Sighted the room, using as little Sight as he could. He didn't want to give any indication that he was actively looking for her.

In his low Sight, he could see her plain as day. She was crouching by the bed in her pajamas. She was apparently using some mild form of TK—something that masked her image but not alert the Sisters.

She was smiling, a big silly grin, as if she thought she was getting away with something. Any thought he had that something sinister might be happening vanished.

He made his way to the table and sat down. Out of the corner of his low Sight, he saw her sneak around to the other side of the bed.

"Com," he said.

"Com here, Captain," came the Com officer from the bridge.

"Com, please ask the Sisters to check Sygillis of Metatron's room."

"Standby, Captain," the Com said. "Captain," the Com responded after a moment. "The Sisters say Sygillis of Metatron is currently in her quarters. They want to know why you ask. Do you require assistance, sir?"

He could see Sygillis sneaking up on him to his right. Again, she looked excited, like she was about to pull a fast one.

"No, no, I am fine I think, just a routine check. Captain out."

He sat there for a moment and pretended to be puzzled. "I know you're here, Lady Sygillis. Why not come out?"

She crept up to him and did something he never would have guessed in a million years: she blew in his ear and licked his earlobe! She then backed away and tried to make her way to the other side of the room.

Standing up, he followed her, still pretending that he couldn't see her. She stumbled and padded about, trying to get out of his way. She hit her bandaged foot on the side of the bed and fell down.

That was enough silliness. "Lady Sygillis, are you all right?"

She didn't respond. She tried to hobble around the bed.

"I can see you just fine, you know, and for this whole time."

She seemed shocked. "You can see me, Captain?"

"Of course I can see you. I have the Sight; certainly you know that."

"The Sight does not exist. The Sight is a myth."

"But it does. It is not a myth."

"Then I suggest you stop me!" she said, making her way to the door.

Davage didn't want the Sisters to become annoyed. He sprang in front of her, and she bumped into him, kicking his boot with her bandaged foot. She hopped in pain. He put his hands on her tiny invisible shoulders.

"I'm sorry for that," he said. "I hope I didn't hurt your foot."

She stood there for a moment and put her invisible hands on his face. She held them there.

"Is your foot all right?" he said again.

"My foot is fine," she said finally. She became visible.

"Are you through playing 'Confuse the Captain'?" he asked.

"I was simply wishing to have sport with you."

"You didn't think I would be alarmed and call the Sisters?"

"The game we play does not involve the Sisters. This is between you and me. You are man enough to play this game with me, I think."

She still had her hands on his face.

"Why did you blow in my ear?" he asked. "Why did you lick my ear?"

"Because I wanted to. I wished to know what you taste like. You taste good, if you're curious to know. Will you blow in mine—in my ear?"

"No."

"Why?"

"Because Fleet captains do not blow in the ears of their prisoners."

"Am I your prisoner?"

"Yes, you meet all of the criteria."

"I see. And if the prisoner requests such an action, in writing perhaps, as you suggested earlier?"

"The request will take six months to process. At that time, the request will be refused. Such an activity does not fall under the minimum requirements imposed on a ship's captain regarding the maintaining of a prisoner."

"And if I were to protest the decision?" she asked.

"Then a hearing shall be convened to further explore the matter."

"And if the final judgment were to be rendered in my favor?"

"Then I'll select an orderly to do it—a female orderly, of course."

She smiled. "What are you afraid of, sir?"

"Nothing. I am not afraid of you. We have been through this before."

"You are not afraid of me killing you, I will grant you that. However, you are still afraid of me."

"And how so?"

She took a step toward him. Though she was clad in pajamas and her feet were bandaged, she had a commanding presence. "You are afraid that we shall become lovers some day."

"Is that what I am afraid of?"

"Yes, it is."

"And does such a thing not frighten you?"

"Not at all. I await it. I am eager for it." She smiled at him. "As I said, you taste good."

"I have told you that I am uninterested in—"

"It matters not, the lies you have told me. We shall become lovers regardless."

"And why do you wish to become my lover?"

She took a step toward him. "Let's see ... because you are a man, because I find you handsome, because I like the sound of your voice, because I enjoy your company. Shall I go on?"

"You have greatly improved at the art of debate, I must say. I cannot dominate you as I once did."

"I have had a fine teacher."

"Then allow me to put your argument to rest. We shall not become lovers, because I will not allow it—ever. All the morals, ethics, and principles I hold dear make no other choice possible. Is that concise enough for you?"

Sygillis, eager to argue, made to respond, but then her eyes glazed over and became hollow and glassy again. It appeared that she was going to topple over, and Davage caught her before she could collapse. Carefully, he placed her into bed and pulled the bedclothes up to her chin.

She had been becoming more prone to these strange spells as the days wore on. He was becoming concerned, if that was possible. He wanted Ennez to look her over.

She stirred. She spoke, slurred.

"I have had … a vision … of the future … just now."

"I have heard Black Hats can often see the future."

Sygillis's eyes drifted in and out of focus.

"And what did you see?" Dav asked, stroking her red hair out of her face.

"I saw us … standing together … in … Metatron I think."

"Metatron?"

"Yes, I am certain of it. Metatron. We stand there together, hand in hand. Just the two of us. You are telling me something."

"And what am I saying?"

"I am … not certain … but I weep as I listen. What you tell me … means more to me than I can currently comprehend …"

"It's a dream, Sygillis, nothing more."

She looked at him, eyes glassy. "Believe in me, Captain. Do not … be afraid to love me … please …"

She said no more. She did not move; she did not close her eyes.

11

A CRY FOR HELP

<Davaaaage!>

A steel scream ripped through his mind as he slept.

Davage sat up in bed and held his head—a knife had apparently been jammed into it. He rubbed his eyes. Had he just been dreaming?

<Davaaaaaage!>

He doubled over and winced. That was no dream.

The Com cracked to life.

"Captain!" Kilos yelled. Whenever she called him Captain, he knew something bad was happening.

"Situation!" he said.

"She's gone mad, Dav! Berserk! She's tearing her quarters up and screaming your name!"

"By the Elders—what has happened?" Davage Sighted his star-lit quarters and began hurriedly dressing. "Has she used any of her powers?"

"Other than a bit of telepathy, I don't think so, but the Sisters have just about had it, Dav! If you have any hopes of saving that Black Hat still, you better get down there, and fast!"

Cursing, Davage pulled his boots on.

"Ki, I am on my way there now. You tell the Sisters that I have not authorized this execution, and if they choose to take her life then they will have to face me over it and hard!"

"You better hurry!"

Without tucking his shirt in, Davage clipped on his MiMs gun belt and clanking, saddled CARG, threw his hat on, and headed out into the corridor at a run.

When he got to her quarters, quite a commotion greeted him. A company of Marines, their SKs drawn, were stationed on either side of the door. Four Sisters stood there, two of them in their night garments. They looked sleepy and rather grumpy.

There was a terrible racket coming from inside the quarters. The sounds of objects flying and cloth ripping assailed his ears.

"*Davvaaaaaagge!*" came a shriek through the door.

Davage adjusted his hat, unbuckled his MiMs, and went toward the door.

"Captain, you aren't going in there, are you?" asked one of the Marines, his SK pistol at the ready.

"Well, Captain? Had enough … this silliness?" said one of the Sisters, her accent rough and grating at this early hour.

"Captain, please be reasonable," a Marine said for one of the Sisters.

"I am going to kill her now!" another Marine said.

Davage turned to the Sisters. "Sisters, please … she is clearly in distress of some sort. I am going inside to assist her."

One of the Sisters, the one he was used to seeing in his office, came forward and put her hands on his chest. She was wearing a night robe and didn't have her headdress on; her shoulder-length blonde hair was damp, as if she'd recently washed it. Davage couldn't help but notice that she had a pleasing bosom and a comely figure. A Sister … with a pleasing figure. Who would have thought? The fact that the Sister probably knew that he'd just noticed her in a carnal sort of way was … mortifying to say the least.

"Captain," a Marine said for the Sister, "please do not go in there. She is a raging beast and will certainly kill you upon sight. I'll not see you killed."

"Sister, again, I am endlessly humbled that you care for me so, however, I am certain she will not kill me. She cried out for me, not to kill, but to seek aid. I must to her side and help her as best I can."

"Then I will come with you. I will protect you," a Marine said for her.

"Sister, your presence will prove provocative; she might think you are there to harm her. She might think she is under attack. I must do this alone, as I am a harmless nobody, she will …"

The Sister put her finger on Dav's mouth. She spoke: "Not … nobody …"

Another Sister came forward. "Enough—she will die!" a Marine shouted for her.

The Sister shot her a furtive glance, and she backed away. The Sister then reached up and kissed him on the cheek. The Marines appeared amazed.

"I will miss you, should you die," a shocked Marine said for the Sister.

Davage cupped her face in his hand for a moment. This display of love was enough to wrench his soul into pieces.

"Then, for you, I will make it a special point to survive," he said.

Without a further word, Davage opened the door and went in. The Sister, good-looking in her nightclothes, watched him as the door closed.

The quarters had been torn to shambles. The bed was overturned, sheets ripped and tossed. Broken glass was everywhere.

Something dark lay on the floor, amidst the wreckage.

It was her black felt bow.

And then, there she was, standing by a broken mirror, arms extended, head cocked to one side, mouth pulled back, teeth showing, her hair a tangled red cloud around her scratched face—like a vision from the grave.

She was naked, her pajamas ripped from her. The bandages on her feet had also been ripped away. Her feet were raw, throbbing.

She lunged at him, and for a moment, he found himself reaching for his CARG.

She reached Davage and threw her arms around him. She sobbed and moaned into his chest.

"Davaaage … help me," she cried, slobbering.

"Lady Sygillis, what is it, what is wrong?"

"TTTTTeneramusssss."

"Teneramus … Shadow tech?" he said.

Sygillis sobbed, her face was drawn in anguish. "It's killing me, driving me mad!"

"But why, how?"

She was hysterical. "Can't … can't … can't get rid of it. Growing … filling me, *DRIVING ME MAD!*"

Davage couldn't make any sense out of it. "You're saying Shadow tech is somehow growing inside you."

"Sisters … Sisters … won't let me cast … won't let me expel … growing … going to die … *GOING TO DIE!*"

And Davage understood.

"So, are you saying that, because you are prevented from creating Shadow tech, that it is adversely affecting you?"

"Going to die," she wept into his chest.

"And the only way to better yourself is to get rid of it, to cast it?"

She looked up at him. Her eyes, wet, puffy, pleading. "I don't want to die."

"Lady Sygillis …"

"I don't want to die."

"Listen to me."

"*I DON'T WANT TO DIE!*"

Davage pulled her naked body off the floor and placed her back on the ruined bed.

She continued to moan.

Davage took her gently by the face. "Lady Sygillis …"

Her eyes were darting, glassy. Wherever she was, it was far away.

"Do you trust me?"

She didn't respond.

"Lady Sygillis, do you trust me?"

She hesitated a moment and then looked up at him and nodded. "Yes."

"Then trust me now. I understand your situation; you need to expel your Shadow tech, yes?"

Her eyes pleaded with him.

"We will take care of this problem. We will fix this."

"We will fix this," she repeated. She seemed to calm down a bit.

"Can you endure for a few hours more?"

She nodded and wiped tears from her eyes.

"Be strong. I will arrange for you to be able to cast your excess energy today."

Davage went to the door and opened it. Kilos was outside.

"What's going on, Dav?"

"It's all right, Ki. What's our current position?"

"We are mark seven of five AM past Mallets."

Davage thought a moment. "Mallets, Mallets ..."

He had a thought.

"Seetac. Seetac is mark three of five AM from Mallets. It's perfect. Kilos, send to Navigation, plot solution for Seetac 2 and wind for fastest possible speed short of going to Stellar Mach. Understand?"

"Aye, Captain."

"Go now."

Kilos ran down the hall. Davage looked back into the dark, destroyed room.

"Have courage, two, maybe three hours maximum, and you will be able to rid yourself of the Shadow tech."

"Captain?"

"Yes?"

He could see her forlorn naked body sitting on the bed looking at him in the dark. "Could you please stay here with me ... for a bit?"

Davage closed the door and walked back toward her. Using his Sight, he found a fresh pair of pajamas in a drawer and slowly, tenderly, dressed her. He cleaned her scratches and checked her feet. All of Ennez's good work had somehow held.

He fetched a comb and picked up her bow. He then began carefully combing her hair, working out all of the tangles her hysteria had wrought into it.

She looked at him with wonder. "Your eyes ... they glow."

"I'm just using a bit of Sight, so that I may work in the dark. Now do you believe in it?"

She didn't answer, just stared at him as he worked.

"Why are you doing this?" she finally asked, still staring at his eyes. Davage had the distinct impression that, for the first time, she was actually listening to him, actually awaiting his answer.

"Because, as I have said, I am looking for good in you."

She put her hand on his arm as he combed. "And if I may ask as a matter of interest, what are your findings up to this point?"

Davage put the bow back into her hair and knelt down. He was eye to eye with her. "I believe that, under all of the robes and the Shadow tech and the threats and the clouds of myth and fear, there is a person … a person who is crying out to be heard."

He moved a bit closer to her. "And I assure you, Lady Sygillis, I hear you."

Her eyes watered and her mouth pulled back as if she were about to cry but was stopping herself.

"Now I must attend to your arrangements."

Davage headed to the door and it opened. Light from the corridor pooled in.

"Davage, Lord of Blanchefort," she said.

"Yes?"

She looked at him for a moment. "Thank you."

Davage doffed his hat and bowed. "You are most welcome."

Another first.

*   *   *   *   *

"Captain Davage, now you have gone too far."

Davage stood in the meeting room. Seven Sisters sat at the table, each flanked by a Marine. The Sister who'd kissed him earlier sat near the back, dressed in her usual robes and headdress.

She smiled at him and offered a knowing look. She was clearly relieved he was alive.

The other Sisters weren't so charitable. They were angry. It was the Marines who were speaking, but it was the Sisters who were doing the talking. To top things off, the Grand Abbess of Pithnar, one of the twenty-five Grand Abbesses of the Sisterhood, sat at the end of the table. She did not have a Marine. Her exalted presence made Davage a bit nervous.

The Sisters were not happy.

"We have gone along with you to this point, listened to your ravings, allowed this monster to live, but now ... now you want us to allow her to actively create a Shadow tech manifestation? Illegal! Unheard of!"

"Yes, Sister, calm yourself please. She says the Shadow tech is growing within her, that, by not casting it over the last several days, it has grown to dangerous levels—like milk in a cow's udders, I suppose. If she is allowed to release it, then she will be all right."

"And you propose—you propose to set her to shore on some distant planet and allow her to create Shadow tech for as long as she deems fit?"

"Exactly. We are on course for Seetac 2. It is perfect. It's a remote, arid and uninhabited world."

"Captain, the casting of Shadow tech is illegal."

"Sister, she is already a prisoner of this ship ... add it to her list of charges if you must. If we do not allow this, she will die."

"Then justice shall be done upon this Black Hat Hammer. I say let her die in agony."

"Right, Sister, and if she should lose control and her excess Shadow tech blast a hole in this ship and sink it straightway?"

"Then perhaps we should simply execute her now and end her suffering."

"And again, Sister, should she, whilst in the throes of her execution, lose control and blast a hole in this ship, we shall sink just the same. No, we must put to shore on Seetac 2 and allow her to be rid of this menace. She has sought our help in this matter and we, as League good and true, must assist her."

"Captain, allowing the Black Hat to set foot on a planet is the heights of lunacy," a Marine said for a Sister. "She will Waft away the first moment available to her."

"Yes, but this is Seetac 2, Sister; where is she going to Waft herself to? She will be marooning herself in any case."

"Thus freed, she could conjure up an army of Shadow tech followers, horrid and winged, and will set herself up as a queen on a black throne amongst black legions. An unholy, dammed planet she shall create."

Davage shook his head. "Sister, where do you come up with these machinations? Scheme after scheme, each more grandiose and cartoonish than the last. Sister, whilst she is being worshipped by her capering Shadow tech army, will any of these fiends be cultivating her a crop? Otherwise the Queen will be dining on bark off the tree and leaf off the plant, supplemented by the occasional reptile and muddy, stagnant water."

The Sisters looked at one another. A few smiled and laughed. The Sister toward the back gazed at him in an approving manner.

"Sisters, I believe she has made significant progress. I believe I am close to proving that she is not beyond redemption. I believe that the shell of evil around her has been broken."

"Impossible."

"Is it? She is no longer full of anger and hate. I've taught her to like coffee. I've taught her to laugh."

"Captain, you are aware that she is plotting to kill you, correct?"

"Is she?"

"Yes indeed, Captain. She has thought of little else. Her thoughts are riveted on it. Your death is all she wants left of this world. The first two times you encountered her ..."

"The first two times?"

"Yes, she was obsessed with your murder."

"How about lately? Is my killing still at the forefront of her thoughts?"

"Not quite so much, it is to be admitted."

"Ahhh, so there it is. My killing is no longer an obsession for her ... merely a passing fancy. Now, I call that progress. I am certain if you scanned the thoughts of my first officer here, you will find much the same."

A few more laughs. Kilos shot him a look.

"Perhaps she's infatuated with you. Perhaps she fancies a handsome face."

Davage slammed his hand down on the table. "Yes, Sister—now I have you! Is infatuation not, oftentimes, the basis of love? And if she can love, then there is good to be had within her. Redemption is possible. The shell is broken, I am telling you!"

Davage turned from the table. "Sisters, my friends, we will be entering standard orbit around Seetac 2 within the hour, and I will be taking her to the surface where she may, under full chaperoning, discharge her Shadow tech, I suggest you ready your Sisterhood to precede us and prepare the venue to your liking. The only other thing to do is abandon the ship and let her explode."

The matter was settled. Davage had nothing more to say. He stood, still facing away from the table. After several minutes he heard the shuffling of chairs and feet. The room cleared.

"You have missed your calling, Captain. You should have been a diplomat," came a lilting, musical voice."

Davage turned. The Grand Abbess had remained. Apparently she didn't need a Marine to speak verbally. She sat at the table, beautiful, smiling.

"No, Great Abbess, I have found my calling. I am a Fleet captain. I have little skill in matters such as these."

"I disagree, Captain. You have done remarkably well. And please, do not be put off by the unpleasant tone of the Sisters—they are tired, astonished by this situation, and they are concerned for you. No one wishes to see you come to harm. You are our Captain too, and we cherish you."

The Grand Abbess smiled. "Captain, please come to me, I wish to look at you."

Davage walked toward her. Smiling, she stood and put her hands on his face.

"My," she said, "you are the image of your father. I can say you are more handsome. Lord Sadric was a ... good friend ..."

"And what do you think, Abbess? Am I in mortal peril by this course of action?"

"The Sisters' assessment of the Black Hat's thoughts is correct, Captain. She has been planning to kill you—has thought of little else. However, as you pointed out, she has not been thinking of it so much as of late. She seems to be genuinely fascinated with you, Captain, and why not? You are, most probably, the only person who has ever willingly approached her, the only person who has ever looked her square in the eye, and the only person who has ever faced her and not been afraid. It must be bewildering for her, you can imagine. And perhaps the only thing she knows how to do at present is plot murder. But she saw your eyes today, glowing with that wonderful Sight you inherited from your father, and I think she thought they were beautiful—the most beautiful things she has ever seen, and she has not thought of killing you since. And that is cause for rejoicing—a Xaphan Black Hat who is reconsidering killing a prime target like a Fleet captain."

"I was looking for a second thought."

"I cannot go that far in assessing her thoughts as of yet. However, look what you have achieved to date: you have survived several encounters with a Black Hat, you have challenged her, engaged her in debate, provoked her thoughts—you've even brought a smile to her face, and a laugh too. You were kind at the right times, and you were stern at the right times as well. And when lost in the depths of her anguish and despair, look what she did. She cried out for you, and you did not fail her—you saved her life in a number of ways today. I allowed her that little bit of telepathy. A cry for help should not be punished with death."

The Grand Abbess began walking toward the door.

"We of the Sisterhood are powerful, wise ... yet we could not have done what you have accomplished here. If our war with the Xaphans is ever to end, it is for someone else, someone like you, to pave the way for it. We are too close to the matter. It is in your power, Captain, to save her, though, as you already know, the process will be dangerous. Be assured that we will do all we can to protect you, and I will pray for you—and I will pray for her as well. I will pray that she remembers your light even when the darkness around her seems to have no end, and I will pray that you find what you are looking for."

The Abbess turned and walked away.

Davage called to her, pleading. "What am I looking for, Abbess? Tell me, please."

Before she got to the door, she turned one more time. "Your father would be most proud of you. I believe in you, Captain. You will know."

12

"MAY I COME WITH YOU?"

"Now, let's go over this one more time, please."

Davage stood in Sygillis's quarters. He was thunderstruck. The change that had come over her since her fit of hysteria was remarkable to say the least.

Sygillis stood in front of a mirror. It was broken; she had broken it hours earlier.

She was dressed in a black Hospitaler Chancellor's bodysuit with a blue traveling shawl over the top of it. Davage had borrowed the outfit from Ennez—he didn't ask why he had such a thing, a lady's outfit, in his wardrobe. He didn't think it prudent.

Davage noted, with some irritation, that she was fixing her hair in the mirror.

"Lady Sygillis, I need you to focus. Please let us go over the procedures for this shore mission one more time."

Sygillis turned to him and smiled. Not the ugly, malicious smile as before, but a bright, happy smile.

"You needn't preface my name with a title, Captain. I am not royalty, and we don't bother with such silly things. You may call me Sygillis, simply Sygillis. I believe I enjoy hearing you say my name."

How can this be? Davage thought. *Ladies have titles—how could they not?* Kilos had no title other than her rank, but she was a Brown and therefore without title and was thankful for it. Marilith was a Xaphan and had a title, though she was of a royal House. But since Sygillis was a Black Hat, he thought it best to comply, however reluctantly, with her wishes.

Xaphans …

"Fine then, Sygillis," he said, his tongue badly wanting to add a title. "Again, the Sisters are most agitated about this launch to shore and will leave you no quarter."

"Why, Captain … are you worried about me? Worried I'll be killed?"

"Actually, yes, I am. We've come all this way, we're here at last. We might as well do this successfully. And my definition of successful in this case is that everybody returns to the ship alive after it's done."

"You will be there to protect me."

Davage noted the irony of it. "True. However, the Sisters are tired and a little trigger-happy. If you give them any provocation, any at all, it's lights out for you."

"Does that distress you?"

Davage rubbed his forehead. "You know, I think it does, actually. I've had very little sleep in the past week, I've been yelled at by just about every Sister within earshot, my first officer wanted to take me to the gym and beat me up, and I've had my life threatened, by you, more times than I can recall. I will hate to see the culmination of all that effort lying dead, brain-scrambled on the planet surface."

Sygillis laughed. "You are a humorous man, Captain. You make me laugh. I find I like that. I find I like to laugh. I have laughed more with you than I have in my entire life. I suppose that is worth letting you live. Hmmm, was that a threat, do you think?"

"Sort of. So, when the laughs stop, that's when the dying starts, is that it?"

"Probably, and besides, how are we to become lovers if I kill you?"

"We're not going to cover this ground again, are we?"

"We are, sir. I've seen the future; it's going to happen, so why fight it? I'm not. In fact, I'm ready to begin immediately if you are."

"There's nothing to fight. We are not going to become lovers."

Sygillis laughed again. "As you like, sir," she said, bowing. She approached Davage and looked up at him; she was so short. "So that we may take a further bold step in becoming lovers, I will comply with your procedures."

She cleared her throat. "I will not release my Shadow tech in the horizontal. I will confine it to the vertical. I will not combine the Shadow tech into a solid mass. I will not breathe life into the Shadow tech. I will not Waft, I will not Sign, I will not Point, and I will not Devine ..."

"You just made a rhyme. Was that intentional?"

Sygillis laughed again. "You see ... that's why you get to live. You are so funny."

Davage straightened her cloak and noted to himself that she looked spectacular in the black Hospitaler bodysuit. "You seem fine now. Better than fine, actually, you seem—good. Are you sure you need to do this?"

"The Shadow tech must be released. Previously, I did not know how to deal with the situation, and it was overwhelming me. But with your help, Captain, I am better able to control it for now. Still, if it is not released soon, I will die."

"Well then, everything is prepared. Shall we to the surface?"

She began walking to the door, and Davage noticed something. She wasn't wearing any shoes.

"You appear to be missing your shoes."

Sygillis looked at him. "I'll not be wearing shoes."

"The ground will be rocky. You will need adequate footwear."

"I will never wear anything on my feet again."

"Your feet are still healing. You'll hurt them on the planet surface. A practical pair of shoes ..."

"No! I'll wear no shoes. You may carry me if you wish."

Davage stared at her for a moment.

"Captain, may I call you Davage?"

"Of course."

"Davage, I don't want to wear any shoes. The pain from the Dora, it was more than I could endure. The memory of it is most unpleasant. I should feel more at ease, for the time being, without any. Please ...." She noted Davage's over-sized Falloon boots. "You appear to be wearing enough for the both of us."

Davage thought about it for a moment.

"All right, then. I shall carry you on the planet surface. But please, let us proceed."

They exited into the hallway. Kilos was waiting, along with several other Marines. As they walked, Kilos moved in behind Sygillis, her hand on her SK, her large brown eyes fixed on the back of Sygillis's head.

After a few intersections, Sygillis suddenly stopped, turned, and faced the much taller Kilos.

"Boo!" she said laughing.

Kilos, in shock, drew her weapon as Sygillis laughed. Kilos's eyes flared with anger.

Davage waved her down. "At ease, Lieutenant."

Slowly, Kilos holstered her SK. "That—that wasn't funny."

Sygillis looked at Davage. "No?"

"Possibly later, much later, it will be funny, but not at the moment," Davage said.

She looked confused.

"I'll explain it to you when we get back, all right? Now, let's look to the matter at hand. Let us go down and unload some Shadow tech."

They entered the Ripcar Bay and mounted one—ripcar number 4, in this case.

A ripcar was a thin, arrowhead-shaped vehicle used for both planetary and low-orbit actions. Noisy, fussy, and clanking, it was built to be fast, maneuverable, and rugged. As such, the crew compartment was little more than a slight hollow scooped out of the back of the car. The entire crew area was preserved in a containment field, but to the novice, sitting in a precarious hollow atop this bucking, snorting bronco could be a gut-wrenching task. He recalled Demona of Ryel, who was otherwise a courageous woman, was terrified of it.

Davage wondered how Sygillis will do.

Happily, she sprung aboard, Davage again noticing the tight-fitting bodysuit she was wearing.

Kilos, not afraid of the ripcar, but not a great fan either, climbed into the back.

Davage, eschewing the small, insignificant seat, preferred to stand while flying.

He expertly engaged the controls, and in a few moments, the containment field hummed to life. He then rammed the stick forward and the ripcar lurched out of the bay with a clank into open space, the *Seeker* quickly falling away.

* * * * *

The surface of Seetac 2 was every bit as arid and unpleasant as Davage had made it out to be—hot, well above 100 degrees, rocky, and lonely in its lack of obvious life.

Davage jumped down out of the ripcar and carried Sygillis. The ground was laced with volcanic rock; her bare feet would be cut to ribbons.

Kilos jumped down, still eyeing her with an angry note. That "Boo!" thing had put a massive shock into her.

Carrying Sygillis, Davage found a sandy bit of ground about a hundred yards from the ripcar and set her down.

She looked around, sweating. "This will do. Please stand back a bit." She threw off her blue shawl, once again glorious in her black bodysuit.

Davage and Kilos backed up. She still had her gun hand on her SK. Davage jabbed her in the ribs. "Will you get your hand off your damn pistol?" he snarled quietly.

"Not a chance," she snapped back.

"You're embarrassing me, and at this range, if she wanted to kill us, there isn't much we could do about it anyway."

"I don't care!"

Davage looked around. Far off in the distance, just within the edge of normal sight, he could see the Sisters, about twenty of them, spaced out evenly, forming a ring around them. He imagined they must be sweating buckets in this heat.

"Davage," Sygillis called out. "I am ready to begin."

Davage tipped his hat to her. "Let it fly."

"So ... `Davage,' is it?" Kilos asked curtly. "When the hell did that happen?"

"Quiet," he said.

She raised her slender, pale arms into the air, threw her head back, and knocked her fists together.

Nothing happened at first. Then, Davage noticed a black webbing of sorts forming between her fingers. Obviously, creating Shadow tech was a slow process.

Then, like a blast from a cannon, a massive gout of black, twisting material shot into the hot air. The blast kept going up and up until it was thousands of feet high, a raging, twisting streamer of black.

It was a little unsettling looking at it, like a great black cyclone. Davage, even a distance away, could feel his hairs standing on end. The power she was releasing was incredible. The brass buttons on Kilos's Marine uniform began to jump and spark.

At about four thousand feet, the shaft of Shadow tech flattened out and began forming an ugly black cloud of soot that was rapidly descending.

Two minutes, three minutes, four minutes, still she was awash in Shadow tech. Davage could only glimpse her occasionally, her head and torso mostly cloaked in black material. He Sighted her just to make sure she wasn't up to anything. She just stood there, swaying slightly, a look of infinite relief etched on her face. Davage couldn't help but admire her power, the forces she commanded.

Soot from the black cloud came down and settled in dark sheets.

Finally, after ten minutes she stopped and put her arms down. Davage and Kilos were filthy from the soot. Davage noted with some humor that the distant Sisters were also filthy—he guessed, since they weren't killing her, that it was nothing but soot. Sygillis, however, was as clean and pale as ever.

She turned to Davage and picked up her shawl. "Thank you, sir. I am finished. It is all right now."

"Are you sure?"

"Yes. I am clear."

"Feel better?"

"I do. Thank you."

He picked her up and carried her back to the ripcar.

"I am sorry about the soot. Since the Sisters will not let me control it, it will fall where it falls." She gently brushed it off of his face and made a little spit-curl with the bangs of his dark blue hair.

"It's quite all right."

The ripcar was filthy. Davage set Sygillis down, and he and Kilos cleaned the interior as best they could. Finally, they got in and Davage hauled it into the sky.

Sygillis appeared to be enjoying the ride. With abandon, she looked around and peered over the side.

"Show me," she said finally.

"Pardon?"

"You are the famous Captain Davage, yes?"

He looked at her.

"Your friend, Princess Marilith, goes on and on about your skills as a pilot. It seems to both enrage and fascinate her. Show me; make this vehicle do something interesting."

Davage smiled and reached for the throttle.

"Captain Davage," Kilos said in a tart voice. "May I remind you that we are due back aboard *Seeker* immediately so that we may plot solution for our next destination?"

Sygillis stared at Davage.

"Lieutenant," Davage said to Kilos, "you are far too young to be so damn old."

He cranked the throttle and sent the ripcar in a massive series of rolls, slides, and loops. Sygillis leaned back and shrieked with delight, laughing and clapping the whole time.

How different, he mused, from some of the other guests he'd had in it. Demona of Ryel hated the ripcar, was convinced she was going to fall out and white knuckled even in slow, straight flight. Black Hats are truly fearless.

When they got back aboard the ship, Kilos grabbed Davage by his shirt. "Every damn chance you get to play in that damn car, you ..." she said before turning green and getting sick in the corner.

On their way back to her quarters, Sygillis was chattering with excitement. "That was exhilarating, Davage, truly remarkable. When can we do it again?"

"I am not certain, I suppose the next time you are in need to discharge your Shadow tech we could have another go. How long do you think that will be?"

"Oh, about a week or so,"

"Fine."

They reached her quarters and went in.

The room was completely cleaned and repaired. The bed was made, and a bowl of food, cheeses, and fruits sat on the table. "I ordered your quarters repaired whilst we were on the surface."

She sat down at the table and grabbed a piece of fruit from the bowl.

"Sygillis," Davage said. "I must say that I am very pleased by your performance on the surface. You kept your word, you complied with our wishes, and that was a very spectacular display. Most impressive."

She smiled at him and took a bite from her piece of fruit.

"Did you like that? I was hoping to impress you."

"The change in you since just yesterday is, well, remarkable. I cannot tell, at this point, whether you are attempting to lull me into a contented state so that you may more easily kill me or ..."

She laughed. "Davage—Dav, if I may please call you that, on the planet surface I could have killed you and your lieutenant in so many different ways. The thought really didn't cross my mind. Like I said, you make me laugh, you engage me in interesting conversation, I find I enjoy your company, and I think you have pretty eyes. And best of all, we have unfinished business together."

"Back to that again. You are incorrect. We have un-begun business. Business that never was and never will be."

"Tell me honestly that you have not thought about it ... that the prospect does not intrigue you?"

"This is pointless."

"Please answer the question."

"I have not thought about it. The prospect does not intrigue me."

She looked at him with a skeptical eye. "I find it interesting that you are choosing to lie to me right now, Captain. I can tell when you are lying. Debating a Black Hat who has learned to use her tongue has its disadvantages."

"Are you seeking to annoy me with a pointless topic, or does the prospect of becoming my lover actually intrigue you?"

"Yes and very much yes. I enjoy talking you in circles, I enjoy making you blush, and I look greatly forward to becoming your lover. Remember, I have seen the future, so it's just a matter of time. The sooner the better."

"Really ... some bizarre alternative future, no doubt."

"There is no such thing. The future is the future."

"That's not what we say in League society."

"Then you know nothing in League society."

She took her blue shawl off. "Make your eyes glow again for me."

He headed for the door. "Sygillis, really," he said, indignant.

She smiled, feeling victorious. "She was right," she said.

"Who was?"

"Marilith. You are a wonderful pilot. I was very impressed with your skill. I am very impressed with you in general. I am glad I didn't kill you earlier."

"Of course you are. I am Captain Davage."

She held her apple and laughed. She put her feet up and took another bite from it. "May I come with you ... wherever you are going? I wish to come with you."

"You may not."

"Then stay for a bit. Let us make a pot of coffee and share it together."

"Time is short and I must to the bridge."

Sygillis wasn't giving up. "Then, when will I see you again?"

"I do not know. When a moment allows."

"I want you to take dinner with me, as I wish to continue arguing with you regarding the pending and inevitable status of our relationship. I promise, this evening I will not try to kill you, and as you have seen, I can be taken at my word."

"What if I cannot make time for dinner?"

"Then, all previous notions are off. See you tonight." She smiled.

"Perhaps then you will see fit to make your eyes glow for me again. Your prisoner requests it of you."

With that, Davage left the room. Of all the threats she had made so far, this one was the most disturbing by far.

* ✴ * ✴ *

She finished her apple and threw it aside. The great heaviness within her was gone. He had taken her to the surface and allowed her to be rid of it.

He had promised to help her and he did. This man, this Davage—an enemy—had saved her life.

He was a Fleet captain; he was her enemy. Why had she not killed him? That was her duty …

No, not an enemy. What was he? Could he be … a friend? Was that possible?

Why could she not stop thinking about him?

His eyes, in the dark, glowing with golden light, just like in her dream … the old dream. Was it he? Was he the Light? Had she been waiting for him all this time?

To kill him, such a waste. His light … so beautiful.

She was excited. She wished she could leave her room and go with him. He had been right, though. She was still a prisoner.

For now, for now …

She closed her eyes and thought about the future, about the things she had seen.

Metatron.

Just the two of them standing there alone.

Something whispered … something said that had meant everything to her.

She and Davage … making love. He, showing her things she had never thought possible. Her body, small, trembling, lost in his touch …

And something more, something that she was only now coming to understand.

She had seen herself, the subject of a large, gothic portrait. She stood in an ornate chapel wearing a blue gown. Her hair was arranged in some strange configuration. Her face was painted, her Shadowmark highlighted, not hidden.

Her portrait hung on the stony wall, surrounded by other portraits.

There was an inscription on the frame.

It said: SYGILLIS, COUNTESS OF BLANCHEFORT.

The future … it couldn't come soon enough.

13

THE BLACK ABBESS

"If you ask me, Dav, now—now is when this thing gets really dangerous," Kilos said. She took a drink of coffee, winced, and set her cup down. She hated coffee. "I wouldn't go back in there with her under any circumstance."

Davage, sitting in his office, shrugged. "Come now. All she asked was if I would join her for dinner."

"That's what she asked, but that's not what she meant. What she meant was if you don't show up, then she was going to try and kill you again. That's a pretty serious threat. I think she's taking a liking to you. I think that's very clear."

Davage put his cup down. "You really think so? I got the impression she was trying to annoy me with a pointless topic."

"Yes, Dav, I do. I'm not much of a debater, but she wouldn't keep bringing the subject up if it wasn't on her mind. Also, why wouldn't she fall for you? Why did Demona of Ryel, Princess Marilith, Marshall Henbane, and Captain Hathaline all lose it for you and not her?"

"You never did, Ki."

"Oh please, Dav. I like you too much to love you."

"And Demona of Ryel, too?"

"Yes, Dav—open your eyes and look around sometime! All that Sight and you can't see what's right in front of your face. It was pretty obvious. I liked Demona. I thought you two struck a fine couple, if you really want my opinion. Anyway, women just seem to like you—why I don't know."

Davage took a drink and looked at Kilos. "That tiny little man you married, he's a bookworm—I mean a librarian, right?"

"Yes."

"Does he realize what a hostile Marine he married?"

"Yes, he does. It works in my favor."

Davage laughed and took another sip.

"And, Dav, what if, as time goes by, she starts demanding more and more? What if she starts wanting something from you that you're not willing to give?"

"Why would she do that?"

"Listen, Black Hat or not, she is still a female, and is fully capable of acting irrationally. I know, if I had her power, there are probably a few men walking around out there who might be dead right now—you included."

Davage sat down and thought a moment. "I am … noncommittal, as usual."

"You can't be shook up about the Marilith thing for the rest of your life. What is … is what must be, I suppose if I were to wax philosophical. Maybe, when Hath did that thing to her at the ball … what was it?"

"The Cloud …" Davage said with a hint of bitterness.

"Yes—the Cloud. Maybe that's what Marilith was going to become on her own anyway. I think Hath did you a favor. In any event, tread carefully, and do what needs to be done in order to ensure your survival, even if that includes lying down with that Black Hat."

"Ki, don't be crude."

"And by the way, Dav, I also enjoy having dinner with you from time to time. Remember me? Kilos, your first officer, your best friend! We never get to sit in the mess anymore. You're always down there on Deck 13 with the prisoner. I miss my buddy."

"Just doing my part to heighten League-Xaphan relations."

Kilos looked hard at Davage. "Why have you done this, Dav?"

Davage put his coffee cup down and thought a moment.

"Tell me, Dav. I'd really like to know."

"I don't know, Ki. It must be because she looks like Hath—that must be it. It is almost as if I have been granted a reprieve. When I speak to her, it's as if I am speaking to Hath again. I hear her voice, her beautiful voice, back from the grave."

"She's not Captain Hathaline, Dav."

"I understand that, and the more I get to know Sygillis, that point becomes more and more obvious—and I don't mean that as a bad thing, Ki. Hath ... I loved her, but she was so damn Blue. She loved parties and invitations and social circles and gossip. I never wanted any of that."

"Dav, you're the Lord of one of the Bluest Great Houses out there."

"Correct, are you saying that I act like a typical Blue Lord?"

"You know you don't. Why ask me such a silly question?"

"Just to emphasize a point. Hath acted every bit the Blue Lady, and that often gave me considerable pause. I always knew Hath liked me, but I could never truly determine if she liked me for me or if it was just my family name, my standing she coveted."

"Dav, you know my relationship with Captain Hathaline was never great, and some of the things that passed between us I keep private—that was between she and I, and she's not here to offer her side of the story—but I could always tell that she deeply loved you."

Davage thought a moment, remembering his friend.

"Ki, if I am to be completely frank right now, I believe I find Sygillis of Metatron ... charming."

"You find her what? Charming?"

"She's full of surprises, she has a wonderful wit ..."

"When she's not threatening to kill you, you mean."

"... and she's not Blue in the least. I believe I find her perspective on things refreshing. She'll ask me questions about certain topics and take a counter position—she likes to engage in debate as much as I do. We could spend hours bickering back and forth. And I tell you and I'll tell Hath's shade if I ever see her—if she had comported herself as

Sygillis does, we'd have married a hundred years ago. I'm glad that I've had the occasion to make her acquaintance."

Kilos sat down next to him and put her hand on his shoulder. "So, when's the wedding?"

Davage smiled. "Undetermined. I'll make sure that you're there as the best man."

She laughed and mussed his blue hair. "Just, be careful, agreed?"

Kilos looked up suddenly. Her large brown eyes grew distant.

"Ki," Davage asked. "Are you all right?"

She didn't answer.

"Ki?"

After a moment she shook her head. "Dav, you're being summoned."

"I am? Who is summoning me?"

"The Grand Abbess. She wants you to come to the Priory, right away."

Davage finished his coffee. "This is a first. Did they say why?"

"No, they didn't. They sound really serious, though."

*   *   *   *   *

All League starships carry with them a small contingent of Sisters and a squadron of Stellar Marines, whose primary role is to protect them. The Sisterhood, a secretive and somewhat aloof sect, operate in a Priory, a small cluster of isolated rooms and passages designated for their exclusive use in, usually, a remote part of the ship. The *Seeker's* Priory was located in lonely, seldom-visited Deck 7—the bottom of the ship's frontal hull.

The Priory was the one place that no starship captain commanded. It was the domain of the Sisterhood. Davage had never even set foot in it.

Kilos, a Marine and more closely associated with the Sisters, had to guide Davage through the maze of corridors on Deck 7. He felt uneasy. Here he couldn't hear the ship, he couldn't feel its movements. It was like he was no longer on board the *Seeker*. It was like he was somewhere else, locked in place, incense-laced and rooted in stone.

There were Sisters everywhere. Some had faces that he recognized, and some he'd never seen before. They sat and watched him pass, silent, smiling as usual.

He remembered what Ennez had told him—that the Sisters aboard the *Seeker* liked him, cherished him even. He'd never considered the Sisters actually liking him. Certainly they were always kind and patient, but he'd always thought them above having mere affection for an individual. How could they "*like*" someone, after all? They were the Sisters. They had the whole League to think of. He considered the notion and blushed. He certainly didn't want to disappoint them. He thought about the Sister who often came to his office, the one with the figure. She seemed to like him a lot.

They giggled as he passed.

Kilos guided him to the Priory Gates, an ornately decorated series of rooms that led to the interior. There, Kilos stopped.

A Sister, his Sister, emerged, and smiling, she took Davage by the arm and led him in.

"You're not coming, Ki?" Dav asked, a little hesitant.

The Sister looked up at him.

"I can't go any further, Dav—I haven't been invited. The Sister says she will take good care of you."

The Sister led him into what appeared to be a grove. She clung to his arm, small and dainty—but strong. He could feel her strength. He had always heard that the Sisters were strong—powerhouses—but he'd never experienced it until now. Davage was strong, and with his Gift of Strength, he was incredibly strong, but he guessed this tiny Sister was far and away stronger than he was.

He looked around. They walked through a vast maze of plants and old, moss-covered stone. He looked up and thought he saw stars... He thought to Sight the area but didn't want to appear rude.

"We are ... no longer aboard the ship, are we, Sister?" he asked.

She smiled at him and laced her fingers through his. Davage was holding hands with a Sister. He didn't quite know what to think. He could feel a slight tingle dancing around his head. She was talking to him ... speaking in that wonderful empathy, which he couldn't hear. What was she saying, he wondered?

"I am sorry, Sister. I cannot understand you."

She pulled his hat off of his head with her free hand. Then, stopping, she removed her headdress, her hair fell out and she straightened it. Not damp as before, Davage noticed her hair was platinum blonde, almost a brilliant white. She popped his hat on her head. She then pointed at his CARG.

"My CARG, Sister? You wish to see my CARG?"

He unsaddled it and showed it to her. It was a heavy weapon, weighing over seventy pounds. She examined it for a moment and took it from him, its weight not fazing her in the slightest. She felt its length. She noticed it was not bladed; it was smooth to the touch. She was puzzled.

"Not ... sword?" she struggled to say.

"No, it's not a sword. It is the family weapon of my line. My father created this particular one."

She went up to a thick old tree and rapped the CARG against its trunk. She then handed it back to him and pointed at the tree.

"You want me to chop the tree down?"

She nodded.

He readjusted the CARG's hilt in his hand and brought the shaft flush against the tree trunk. "Watch carefully, Sister. This is called Sadric's Cut. Just a novelty, really, but is interesting to be sure. I am told that my father once used this cut to impress my mother, who was known for appreciating a fine weapon's stroke."

The Sister watched. Then, in a quick second, he moved the shaft through the thick trunk and reversed, making a thin cross-section of the stump. The tree shuddered, lost a leaf or two, and then stood.

The Sister clapped. Smiling, she pushed the tree over with a flick of her wrist. It toppled in a noisy heap.

She picked up the cross-section, admiring it. Using her finger, she began carving letters into the fresh wood. When she was almost finished, Davage heard a crack from above, like a thunderbolt. The Sister heard it too, looked annoyed, and tossed the cross-section away. Appearing sad, she gave Dav his hat back, donned her headdress, and again took Davage by the hand, leading him away.

Looking back, Davage saw what she had written on the wood. It said, "Please kiss me."

They continued. Ahead was a huge, domed building draped in vine, and scented plants that loomed into the night sky. They went in.

There sitting inside was the Grand Abbess.

"Welcome, Captain," she said.

Davage took off his hat. "Grand Abbess, well met. Clearly, I received your summons. I am here at last."

"Thank you for coming, Captain. Please, sit down."

Davage seated himself. The Sister who had guided him here stood, smiling. The Grand Abbess gave her a quick glance and the Sister turned and left.

"It seems you have an admirer, Captain. The Sister is saddened that she cannot speak to you directly. Much is lost when speaking through a Marine. So much thought and feeling not properly conveyed."

"Perhaps when time allows, I might persuade Lieutenant Kilos to instruct me. I should be honored to commune with the Sisterhood directly."

The Grand Abbess looked at him a moment. "The Sister should know better—such things as she is experiencing are forbidden."

"Please ... if there is any fault to be doled out, then I am certainly to blame."

"Trouble yourself not, Captain. You have not acted out of turn, and nor has she. These things happen. We are all Elder, after all—we have feelings too. She will be fine. And I must say, I cannot fault her taste."

Davage looked at his hat on the table.

"I am sorry if I presented myself in such a way that presented ..."

"Again, Captain, you are not to blame. You are a fine man, as your father was before you. I remember Sadric well. Many ladies across League Society admire you, so why not a Sister, though she knows she cannot proceed. Perhaps, one day when her time comes, you will delight her and allow yourself to participate in her 'program.' That will make her very happy, I think."

"I shall ... look forward to it. So, Grand Abbess, what can I do for you? This is certainly a rare and unusual honor."

She hesitated a bit. "I have someone who wishes to speak to you, Captain."

"I see."

She looked down at the table for a moment. "Please, do not be alarmed ... and know that I am here."

Davage didn't quite know how to take that statement. He became apprehensive.

At the far end of the table, a twisting, smoky cloud, like a pillar of brimstone, formed. It rose to the ceiling, flattening, spreading out, hissing slightly.

After a moment Davage Sighted a figure inside the cloud, a red, ominous figure, coalescing, growing like a transparent bladder filling with blood.

The top of the cloud split open, and like an ear of rotten corn, a red figure burst out and hovered; the cloud around it continuing to seethe and twist.

It looked like a robed female, small, dainty, with tiny, almost non-existent shoulders. Her face and head were covered with a black sash that floated with ethereal movement. Davage could not see her legs—they were lost in the black cloud. He Sighted; there were no legs there to be seen. Clearly, this was a projection of some sort.

The figure hovered in the cloud with a smokelike grace.

"Captain Davage, allow me to introduce Magravine ... the Black Abbess of the Black Hat Sisterhood."

The figure, Magravine, regarded Davage for a moment. He felt his insides blanch.

"Well, Grand Abbess, this is a surprise," Davage said composing himself. "I had no idea the Sisterhood maintains ties with the leadership of the Black Hat Order."

"Not ties," the Black Abbess said, her voice a crawling, malevolent sneer. "An understanding."

"Indeed, Captain," the Grand Abbess said. "We have no formal ties to the Black Hat Sisterhood. We do, however, maintain an occasional dialog with their leadership. Such an arrangement allows us to ... lay out the groundwork for how our struggle will proceed."

"Every conflict has rules. We are not uncivilized," the Black Abbess said, her voice surprisingly baritone for such a tiny person.

Davage greatly wanted to be elsewhere. "I see," he said.

"The Black Abbess has pointed out that we, the Sisterhood I am referring to, have not followed the rules."

"You have not killed Sygillis of Metatron," the Black Abbess said.

"You are correct, and as far as I am aware, she will not be killed in the days to come," Davage said.

The Black Abbess twitched. "That is not our agreement. There are to be no survivors. They are all to be killed. No quarter is to be given. Sygillis was defeated upon the battlefield, and her life is forfeit. I am owed compliance."

The Grand Abbess spoke up. "That is not quite correct, Abbess. Sygillis of Metatron should have attempted to kill herself in the creation of mayhems after her capture. She chose not to do so."

"That matter is of … considerable concern to us. She is a Hammer, trained to fight. She should have killed Captain Davage by this point, or died trying. He is a prime target in our minds. He is a fair target."

"I was hoping to find good in her, Abbess. I believe I was successful."

The Black Abbess looked at Davage; she paused, and then spoke as if she were speaking to a lesser animal. "She knows nothing but what we have taught her. We have taught her to fight. We have taught her to hate and to kill, and she has done that well and often … up until now."

"Yet, she has not fought me, and on several occasions. She has not tried to kill me."

"Then she has failed. She is dead to us."

"She has not failed, ma'am. Perhaps, with her wisdom, we might one day see an end to our bitter conflict. I was hoping that one day we could reach out and embrace you as our own again. It is a dream I now share with my departed father."

The Black Abbess glared at him. Her voice became chiding, condescending. "That … can never happen. Is that not right, Grand Abbess?"

The Grand Abbess looked down for a moment. "It does seem … unlikely."

Davage stood up. "Well, this meeting has been most pleasant. However, I will not kill Sygillis, nor will I authorize her killing in the near future."

"You have no authority over the Sisterhood, Captain, certainly that has dawned on you at some point. Abbess, I demand the life of Sygillis of Metatron immediately!"

The Grand Abbess sat silent.

"If you or the Sisterhood wish to take her life, I must be passed through first," Davage said.

The Black Abbess cackled. "And you think that is a … concern of some sort, do you, Captain? How large a speck do you fancy you are to the Sisterhood, hmmm?"

"That is enough, Abbess," the Grand Abbess said. "We are not you … empty and cruel. We are devoted to this man, for he has earned our love in heart and in deed. He is an inspiration to us."

"Truly," the Black Abbess said. "See you his father in him, do you not? Your … indiscretions are showing, Abbess."

The Grand Abbess stood, furious. "Not another word, I warn you!"

"Then, give her to me, and I will depart. Nothing more will be said. I will kill her if you've not the stomach."

"Enough!" Davage shouted. "I've no interest in your lies. Sygillis of Metatron will not be killed whilst I've strength to stand guard over her."

"Know you the blood she has spilled? Innocent, screaming League blood."

"That was in another life; I hold her not responsible. She did your bidding as a slave, an automaton, nothing more."

The Grand Abbess turned to Davage. "Captain, perhaps we could …"

"She has requested asylum, Grand Abbess. I will not turn her away or allow her to be led to her death. She is no longer a prisoner. She is now an exile requesting assistance."

"Asylum," the Black Abbess spat. "She'll ask for no such thing …"

"Nevertheless, it has been granted."

"Captain, you are truly as insufferable as your reputation dictates." The Black Abbess grew large and terrible in her black cloud.

"You will give her to me now, Captain. You will meet us in space, and you will give her up."

"I will not."

"You will face the gaze of the Black Abbess? You dare to face our black legions?"

"Any hostile Xaphan vessels in range with a closed fist will be sunk. You doubtless know me; you know what I can do."

"We will give you no peace. We will claw at you."

"I wonder, Abbess, if you wear a bow in your hair as she does?"

"Then 'tis the whole of it. Be advised, failure to either kill or remand her into my custody will result in a call to open war against you."

"I am so advised. Thank you."

"We will not rest until she is either dead or you and your crew are dead along with her."

"Thank you. Again, I am advised."

"Captain," the Grand Abbess said. "Are you certain you wish this course of action?"

"I am. I will not abandon one who has requested my help."

"Then … let it begin. And Captain … were I in your situation, I would not stray too far from the Sister's side, for the Phantom Hand will be waiting, I promise you that."

"He has our protection wherever he may go," the Grand Abbess said, standing. "And I look forward to turning your Mass right back at you. Perhaps you will meet your foul end at last."

"Why, Abbess, I have not seen such passion from you in some time. How many other Fleet captains … the sons of special friends … receive such personal attention, I wonder?"

"I have allowed you free reign for too long, and that is over. If Captain Davage believes Sygillis of Metatron is worth saving, then she will be saved!"

The Black Abbess quivered with rage. "Not for he nor anyone else!"

She raised her hand, and it grew into an ugly claw. She appeared on the verge of hitting the Grand Abbess. Davage Sighted. Most of the Black Abbess appeared to be a mere projection of some sort, but her clawed hand—it appeared very real.

Springing to action, Davage unsaddled his CARG and jumped in front of the Grand Abbess, holding his weapon in the usual Blanchefort guard position.

The Black Abbess, her claw still raised, looked at Davage, incredulous behind her black, featureless mask. She was speechless for a moment, and then she snorted … a wicked laugh perhaps?

She lowered her hand, wiggled the clawed fingers at Davage, then the hand disappeared. Bobbing slightly, she made an odd motion, like she was blowing him a kiss. He could smell brimstone.

"It seems you wish to sit at my table, Captain. Very well, a chair is offered. What began as a mere annoyance now has my full personal attention. You, sir, are fully in the gaze of the Black Abbess."

She thought for a moment. "Perhaps having Sygillis killed is too hasty a judgment—yes, yes, I see that now. You wish her saved, you wish her to smile and laugh and do all the little things little people do—to frolic with you in some green pasture. Then, if only to spite your tiny, insect face, I wish her returned, I wish her a Black Hat again, only this time not in some far-flung temple in Metatron. This time she will sit at my side in the Shade Church where the darkness is stifling. The lives she will take, the terror she will inspire."

She rose into a clutching, choking mass. "You wish to play the game with the Black Abbess, then it shall be played. I will have Sygillis back as a deadly Black Hat. I will see the *Seeker* in flames for this inconvenience, and I will lay you, Captain Davage, dead … dead …*DEAD*, with not even a soul left to swallow!"

The Black Abbess cackled a blood-freezing laugh and vanished.

The Grand Abbess took a deep breath and sighed.

Davage stood there, holding his CARG. He suddenly felt ridiculous for his gallant outburst in front of the Grand Abbess—an ant rising up to defend a lion. What must she be thinking?

He felt humiliated.

"I am sorry, Great Abbess. I did not mean to embarrass you." He began to saddle his CARG, but the Grand Abbess reached out and touched it.

"I remember when your father made this weapon. I was there; I added a few things of my own to its making. I blessed it. Now, the son of that fine man raises it in my defense."

"I will take my leave, and again, I apologize for—"

The Grand Abbess put her hand on his cheek. "You have been troubled, Captain, have you not? Samaritan Ennez told you the other day that we of the Sisterhood liked you, and you were humbled with this knowledge, burdened even. You felt that you unknowingly set a standard of some sort and must now live up to it. You are afraid you will fail us somehow, disappoint us."

Davage looked at the floor.

"You gladly offer your life in defense of one who needs no defending. That is why we cherish you. That is why Sisters from all around clamor to come to the *Seeker* and observe you, if only for a little while. You are a living reminder of why we are here, of what our purpose is. You give of yourself freely, without hesitation. You spring to the aid of a Grand Abbess, or a lowly junior crewman ... or a Black Hat with a bow in her hair."

A tear rolled down her face.

"It is I who am humbled, Captain. If only I had had your courage, once ..."

They embraced.

"I am sorry for this, for all of this," she said. "In the type of battle we fight against the Xaphans, a battle of the mind, there would be none of us left, no Sisterhood, no Black Hats, if we did not agree to certain ground rules. We would all be dead. And she will do as she says—the *Seeker* will be attacked on all sides by the Xaphans."

"Then let them come. Fighting the Xaphans is my duty. I will face them. I will sink them in a fair fight."

"Captain, Sygillis of Metatron is, even amongst the Black Hat ranks, notorious for her power and rancor. She is about as bad as they can get."

"Then there is hope for us, for, with relatively little effort, I have turned her. The Black Abbess said it herself. All she knows is evil. I have created a seed of good in her. I have broken the darkness around her. Will you stand with me?"

"Need you ask such a question, Captain?"

*　　*　　*　　*　　*

The evening bell sounded. The night crew headed dutifully to their posts while those coming off shift wearily made their way to their quarters. Davage excused himself from the bridge. He was tired from a long day.

As he headed for his quarters, he recalled Sygillis asking if he might be by to have dinner with her. It was a little late for dinner, but he wanted to check up on her—see how she was doing. It had to be boring for her, sitting in her tiny quarters all day, nothing to see, nothing to read, listening to the pipes clank. He planned to go to the Sisters soon and insist they allow her a bit of roam under his charge and responsibility.

So here he was, heading to her door, again. He found he couldn't help himself. He found he wanted to see her.

He was, after all, going to war for her.

They were going to be lovers she said …

Impossible!

She had seen the future. Black Hats were known to do that.

In a haze of Shadow tech, that's all. Look what it almost did to her.

She brought it up, over and over again … lovers.

So, what was he doing here? Why not just leave her be?

She was so beautiful …

She was so flattering …

To change the mistakes he made with Hath … To see her smile. To make her happy.

He had failed Hath.

He will not fail Sygillis, Hath's identical twin.

He made his way down to Deck 13 and wound through the corridors, meeting few people along the way. He came to her door. All seemed quiet, though he knew there were Sisters all around, monitoring her every move.

He knocked on the door.

A few moments later, he heard the bumping about of footsteps on the other side, and finally, it opened. Sygillis stood there, still in her pajamas. Her bare feet were starting to look much better. Her hair was messy, like she had been asleep.

She rubbed her eyes and smiled. "Captain Davage," she said.

"Evening, Sygillis, well met. I am sorry I couldn't make dinner as you had requested. The tasks a captain must perform are rather time-consuming. I simply wanted to stop by and wish you good night. I am sorry for the hour. I should have let you sleep."

Sygillis stepped back from the door. "No, no—I was hoping you were going to come. You've walked all this way, please delight me and come in for a moment."

He had hoped she wanted him to come in. Ki had mentioned she thought Sygillis was fascinated with him. She hadn't detected his similar thoughts for her.

All of Hath's beauty and none of her stogy Blueness. He felt something ache deep inside.

"I should allow you to get your rest, and I really need to turn in."

"Please, for a moment only."

Davage stepped into her darkened room. She brought the lights up and poured two glasses of water from her small table. Davage noticed her bed clothes were undone—she had been asleep. Her quarters were so tiny.

"I missed you this evening ... for dinner," she said handing him a glass of water.

"I was indisposed."

She smiled. "I was feeling very sad at your absence. Well, I suppose I can forgive you, though I was very disappointed. I do so enjoy chatting with you. I understand that a captain has—"

She stopped suddenly. She took several short whiffs. She then began sniffing Davage intently, her eyes growing wide.

"I realize that my uniform might be a bit stuffy."

"The Black Abbess," she said quickly. "You have been in close contact with the Black Abbess. I can smell her fire on you!" She dropped her glass. "What were you doing in close contact with the Black Abbess?" Her eyes grew wider and wider—approaching hysteria, glinting with green fury.

"Indeed, I had an unusual meeting today with a spectral woman calling herself the Black Abbess."

"What did she say—what did she say?"

"She said a series of things, none of which were pleasant."

"WHAT DID SHE SAY!" Sygillis screamed, her lips starting to foam.

Davage was beginning to feel a bit apprehensive. Sygillis appeared terrified to the point of madness.

"She said, if you must know, that I am to hand you over to her at once or kill you. She ..."

A seething black rope of Shadow tech shot out her hand and wrapped itself around Davage's neck. Instantly he was lifted into the air. She picked up her glass and broke it on the table edge. She then jammed the sharp end into her leg. The moment she did, the Shadow tech developed a cold, crawling air about it. It was unbearable against his flesh.

"So!" she said shouting. "You hand me clean to the Black Abbess and send me to my death. How cruel. *HOW CRUEL—YOU WOKE THIS BLACK HEART, GAVE IT HOPE, ONLY TO SEND IT BEATING INTO THE FIERY MOUTH!!*"

"Syg ..." Davage croaked, "if you ... will ... allow me to ... finish ..."

"I'LL KILL YOU!"

Tears leaked out of her eyes. "For this cruelty I'll kill you!" she said, mouth drawn back.

She threw him down, lifted him up, and slammed him back down again.

"Syg ... listen ... to me!"

"NO MORE LIES ... DAMN YOU, NO MORE LIES!"

The door to her room opened, and a Marine came running in. "Captain!" he yelled, drawing his weapon.

With a sweep of her arm, the Marine was dashed senseless into the wall, Stenned hard. His SK clattered to the floor.

Davage could feel her Shadow tech working its way into his mind, clawing for information. Beyond his control, the events of his meeting with the Black Abbess began flashing across his head—she was accessing his thoughts, and she was not being gentle about it.

"Kill her ... or give her to me ..."

"Let them come, let them be sunk."

"You are fully in the gaze of the Black Abbess."

"Asylum ..."

A moment later, he could feel the Shadow tech slacken around his throat. She set him down, eyes wide, a look of infinite anguish on her face.

"What have I done?" she said.

Future's end.

She gasped in a racking spasm. "Davage!" she cried. "What have I done! Forgive me!"

The door opened again. A squadron of Marines and four angry Sisters came into the room. They seized Sygillis by the mind and began the slow, wrenching process of killing her.

Mouth open, eyes glassy, she grabbed her head and screamed silently. She slumped to her knees.

The Sisters closed in, not saying a word, their mind-lock a killing cacophony.

Davage recovered. "Sisters," he croaked, "please stop this. T'was a misunderstanding, is all. But it is all right now!"

They ignored him.

Holding her head, Sygillis looked at Davage one last time and closed her eyes.

"F ... forgive ..." she said.

Davage ran to Sygillis, knocked her to the floor, and flopped on top of her tiny, convulsing body. He could feel the chaos of raw thought pouring into her.

"Sisters, stop!"

They continued. "Away, Captain! This ... be ... her end!" they said.

"*Stop!*" he shouted.

The cascade of thought was killing him too.

"Captain," a Marine yelled, his eyes averted. "Get away from her and let the Sisters do their work!"

"*Stop!*"

"Captain!"

14

A HEART SET TO BEAT

In her nightmare, she was a tormenting beast. She hovered and cajoled, sharp knives in her hands.

She tormented a man, a tall, handsome man with dark blue hair.

She wanted to stop; she did not wish to hurt the man. The last thing she wanted to do was hurt the man.

But she hurt him she did, on and on without end, and his pain was exquisite.

Stop …

Knives flashing. The man screamed.

Stop!

Her arm rose and fell … and he died in agony.

Stop!

Sygillis rose in bed. She was lying in a strange place … not her quarters. It was a small room or office with two beds arrayed against the wall. There were computerized monitors and terminals here and there blinking and clicking. She guessed she was in the ship's medical center.

Why was she alive?

Her head was a sopping mass of pain. Every inch of it hurt. It hurt to think. What had happened?

She remembered with painful dread. The Black Abbess—her smell was all over Davage. She panicked, suspected Davage of treachery.

Betrayed, betrayed ... Her heart broke. Davage broke it. His betrayal broke it.

And she attacked him. She was going to kill him for betraying her, for breaking her heart.

Had she given him time to explain ... to say his piece?

No, she hadn't. Her temper came up.

She roped him and threw him to the ground and galled him with enraged Shadow tech. She dug into his mind. She ripped the thoughts out and she saw the Black Abbess.

And she saw Davage. She saw him defending her. She saw him standing up to the Black Abbess.

Asylum ... he lied to the Abbess and said she had asked for asylum.

He defended her. He was true.

She had betrayed him. She had failed him.

Tears came to her eyes. "Dav ..." she sobbed.

Future's end ...

She heard something to her right. She looked, her head in a pain-ridden cloud.

Davage sat in a chair nearby. He sat back, his head propped up against the wall, his hat down over his eyes. His CARG glinted copper at his belt. He was asleep.

Full of longing and shame, she stared at him. She stared at him for an unknown length of time. He had saved her, and she had tried to kill him over it. How could he ever forgive her?

How could he ever trust her again?

His was the Light in the Dark. Here he sits.

Future's end ...

She seethed with frustration.

They were going to be lovers! He was going to show her things she had never known before—wondrous things. The experiences they were going to share—he was going to be her guide, she was going to be standing at his side. She couldn't wait for it ...

The things they will create together...

It was set in the future, needing only the passage of time to bring it to pass.

She had loved to tease him about it, to chide him and watch him blush. Annoying him was an easy way of getting his full attention, which she craved.

For the first time in her long, dark existence, life meant something. She was looking ahead to each new day, to something that was just around the corner.

His were the eyes in the dark—she knew it, she knew it!

Future's end.

He was going to be her lover.

Future's end ...

More than that, they were going to fall in love. This tall, handsome Fleet captain was going to be the center of her universe. She was going to be his Countess, and he was going to be her Lord. She'd seen that too, but had never mentioned it. That shock might have been too much for him. She hadn't wanted to scare him off, to prolong the coming of the future.

Ruined, ruined ...

The adventures they were going to experience ...

All done, all finished ...

The children they will have ... the heirs she will give to him. Wife and mother ...

Gone, gone, all gone ...

Why was she still alive? Why? She'd rather be dead. All the things she wanted were dead and gone ... and she along with it.

She watched him sleep, and she found she dreaded his waking. She dreaded it more than she had ever dreaded anything. Even the Black Abbess ... His power over her exceeded anything she had ever known before.

She was afraid.

She was terrified.

She dreaded facing him. Black Hats were fearless—so why was she afraid? She had never felt such raw fear.

After a while, her head pounding, Davage awoke.

She said nothing ... she just stared at him.

"Sygillis," he said sleepily. "You seem no worse for your adventures ..."

"Why am I still alive?" she managed to say, her voice trembling.

"The Sisters—I stopped them killing you. In near the nick of time too. You must have a searing headache. I certainly do."

"Why did you save me?"

"Because I didn't think it necessary to kill you over a misunderstanding."

"A misunderstanding? Dav ... I was going to kill you."

"Why?"

"Because I was sure you'd given me up. Betrayed me to the Black Abbess."

"Are you still wanting to kill me?"

"No!"

"Why not?"

"Because I looked into your mind. I saw that you protected me, defended me. Lied for me ... You lied to the Black Abbess ... for me."

"Indeed."

"I didn't give you the opportunity to describe your encounter with her. I assumed the worst; I assumed that you had betrayed me. Nobody stands before the Black Abbess. Nobody denies the Black Abbess."

"You panicked, you're saying."

"Yes, and I deserve to be dead for what I did to you. It is better than this ... shame."

Davage leaned forward. "You feel poorly over this incident, do you?"

She looked at him. "Yes, of course ..."

"Why? You are a Black Hat, are you not?"

Sygillis cringed at the name. "Yes, I was ..."

"Is the goal of a Black Hat not to create as much mayhem and chaos as possible?"

"Yes."

"And in killing me, a Fleet captain, and an annoying one at that, you, in death, achieve a great victory."

Sygillis began to cry. "I don't want to kill you, Dav. Not anymore."

"Why?"

"Because you set my heart to beat. What do your stories say ... that Black Hats hearts don't beat, that they rot in our chests—a useless piece of flesh. You freed it."

"And how did I do that? I did nothing but offer you a bit of courtesy."

"Maybe that was enough. Maybe all it took was one brave man and one woman—who had a second thought after all."

Sygillis began sobbing into her hands. "Please, Dav, I'm sorry. I'm so sorry."

Davage stood up and watched her cry for a moment. He reached out and softly stroked her hair. "That's all I wanted to hear, Sygillis. You pass my test."

"Dav ..." she said sitting up and taking his hand. She had a sorrowful, pleading look, her red hair a twisted mess. "Can you forgive me?" she asked breathlessly. "I'm begging you to forgive me!"

He stopped and regarded her for a moment.

"That's all I want ... to know that I have your forgiveness. All else is meaningless. And if you cannot, then kill me. Take your CARG and pierce me through the heart. Pierce it true; it would be an act of mercy."

He had once been asked to forgive someone. He failed to do so. Davage took a cloth and wiped the tears from her face. Her Black Hat mark was wet with them. "There's nothing to forgive. It was a misunderstanding, nothing more, and I consider the matter closed. But if you must hear me say it, then be it so. I forgive you, Sygillis."

It was like a barbed chain had been removed from her chest. More tears. She held her arms out, seeking an embrace.

"These tears," Davage said. "Are they all for me?"

"They are only for you ..."

Davage stepped forward and embraced her. The strength in her arms was more then he could have imagined—it took his breath away.

"Know this," she whispered in his ear. "I will never raise my hand to you ever again. You have my word, my solemn oath. Do to me what you will. I will never harm you again."

"Fine," Davage said.

She released him. "And the Marine that I Stenned, is he all right?"

"He is. He is fine."

"Perhaps when he is better I might be able to apologize to him in person."

"I think Deon will like that."

She lay back down and held her head. It pounded. "And since I'd not see you accused of lying," she said, "I, Sygillis of Metatron, formally ask you, Davage, Lord of Blanchefort, Captain of the League vessel *Seeker*, for asylum. May I please have asylum aboard your ship?"

"Asylum is granted."

Ennez came into the dispensary, his popcorn hair jutting out of his helmet.

"How's she doing, Ennez? How's our lady here?" Davage asked.

He checked his screens. "Fine, fine. I don't see any permanent damage." He opened his cabinets, and after rummaging through a series of colored bottles, poured her a small glass of clear liquid. "Here," he said, offering it to her. "Drink this. It'll help the pain."

She drank it and sighed.

"Captain," he said. "She's going to need rest."

"I don't need rest. Don't go, Dav, please!"

Ennez looked dubious. "Dav, she needs rest."

Davage stood up and straightened his hat. "So, then, I'll be off. Get some sleep."

"Dav," she said, "can I hope to see you later? You'll come back, won't you?"

"Ennez shall have to lock the door to keep me from visiting you."

Sygillis beamed and covered her face with her hands. She had gone from the dregs of fear and despair to sheer joy in a matter of moments.

"Well now, since you are no longer a prisoner of this ship, per se, I shall order new quarters for you. Something bigger, with a view with no more cramped interiors and clanking pipes of Deck 13. Something in the front section of the ship, I think. Now you'll have a spacious sitting room, a small kitchen, a workstation with a terminal, and an adjacent bedroom, and you'll be able to see the stars. I've also granted you access to the ship's library. So, from your terminal, you can read all you want, and catch up on League society, if that sort of thing interests you. I am certain we will share lots of laughs there."

Sygillis smiled brightly. "Thank you, Dav, I look forward to it."

Davage left.

Sygillis of Metatron, a scourge and accursed enemy, murderer, feared by League Admiral and warlord alike, sat in her small bed smiling.

Future's end? Future's beginning—the corner turned.

She could feel her heart beating in her chest.

*   *   *   *   *

In the days that followed, Sygillis made great progress. She discovered that she could go five days in between Shadow tech offloads. On the fifth day she began to feel "twitchy," become forgetful, and be prone to those fainting spells she was suffering from earlier. Instead of putting to shore on a planet as they had done on Seetac 2, they had devised a simple but effective solution to the problem. Davage ordered Ripcar Bay 4 cleared. There, standing against the far bulkhead of the empty bay, Sygillis sent her Shadow tech out of the contained open bay doors. Navigation reported that, during these offloading periods, which lasted about ten minutes at a stand, the ship picked up a great deal of sub-Stellar Mach speed. Intrigued by this phenomena, Davage one day ordered the ship set to stop. He wanted to discover just how fast she could propel the ship. Sygillis then released her Shadow tech, and they were amazed by the results: the *Seeker* quickly accelerated to 0.25 percent of the velocity needed to reach Stellar Mach—a phenomenal rate of speed given the fact the method of propulsion was a living being.

The Sisters also, with the Captain's supervision, tested her abilities with The Gifts. They determined the following:

> The Strength: Master
>
> The Waft: Master
>
> The Sight: Nil
>
> The Cloak: Journeyman
>
> The Dirge: Guild Master
>
> The Stare: Guild Master

And for the illegal Black Hat Gifts:

The Point: Guild Master
The Mass: Guild Master
The Sten: Guild Master
Shadow Tech: Guild Master

Without question, her reputation as a "Hammer," one of the Black Hats especially suited to fight, to battle whole armies at once, was earned.

She moved into her new quarters—it was a much brighter, happier place than the cramped, windowless room she had in the bowels of the ship. As the days moved on, Davage began taking her on walks, showing her various parts of the ship, and slowly introducing her to the crew. She initially got a lot of strange looks from the crew, but with the Captain at her side, they slowly grew to accept her; if she was good enough for Davage, she was good enough for them. One of her first new friends was Lord Ottoman, the ship's cook. When he discovered that all of the novel dishes he had been preparing for her—ooust, caratine pie, zork, and kilfre pudding—were Xaphan dishes and the strange woman he'd been serving was an ex-Black Hat, he lit up the Com-waves with chatter, boasting to his legions of friends that he was the "personal chef" to a Black Hat. He even began serving the dishes to the rest of the crew, designating one night a week as Xaphan Night in the mess.

Davage even gave her a job; she had complained about being so bored during the day when she was confined to her room. The Sisters still did not allow her full roam of the ship. He assigned her a junior stocking position under Pay Master Milke—a man afflicted with *Vithianstromata*, as the Hospitalers called it—essentially he grew old, his face aged, his body bent, and his hair turned white. It was an uncommon but not unheard of affliction to old Vith families that were a little too Blue, a little too close to the hip, so to speak.

Certainly a novelty, it didn't seem to bother Milke. Despite his frail look, he was a vigorous man, and he kept her busy filing, checking up on errors and pay disputes, and issuing back pays.

Sygillis, the Black Hat, had become a part-time junior accountant.

As time passed, Sygillis became a more common sight. The crew, following the Captain's and Ottoman's and Pay Master Milke's lead, began taking to her and greeted her as she passed by.

All the crew except for Kilos, who seemed to badly mistrust her.

Davage began catching wind that the two of them were frequently engaging in loud, chiding, insulting arguments. There was word that they were actually coming to blows in the corridors and in the gym.

Davage tried to visit her every evening after his long shift in the bridge was over. If he didn't he found she would be rather cross and unpleasant in the morning. He also found he enjoyed visiting her. Kilos, in a chiding manner, called Sygillis his "girlfriend," and though he reacted badly to the term, Dav had to admit that that's basically what she was—his girlfriend. They spent a lot of time together, they ate dinner together most of the time, they strolled the ship together, and they bickered endlessly in a good-natured way, debating this and that. She had also requested permission from the Sisters to engage in telepathy with him—a simple non-sympathetic link so that she could talk to him whenever she wanted, which was a lot. The Sisters, after some debate, agreed.

Davage was shockingly bad at telepathy, and though she could speak to him, he had difficulty talking back. Her sessions trying to teach him how better to use telepathy had tested her patience on several occasions. Eventually, he was able to respond back, though it was a halting, gibbering sort of mind-speak.

One evening, as Davage visited her in her quarters …

"Dav, I wish to touch you. May I touch you?"

Davage put down his coffee cup. "Pardon?"

"I was thinking today, back to when I was out of my head with Shadow tech, when I embraced you I began to feel better. And when you carried me on Seetac 2, I recall enjoying you carrying me."

"We are Elder-Kind, Sygillis. We enjoy the touch of another. Here, give me your hand." Davage held out his hand for her to take.

She looked at it, smiled, and threw her arms around him.

"I was hoping for a bit more than just a mere handshake, Dav."

At first, Davage didn't quite know what to make of this. She constantly talked about becoming his lover—it seemed to be one of her favorite topics—but she'd always managed to keep her hands to herself.

Gently, Sygillis snuggled into him, smiling and sighing. "Oh, yes, I like this. It feels so good. It feels so good to touch you, to feel you next to me."

"Did you never hug anyone before? Do Xaphans not do such things?"

"No. I've rarely touched anyone. I didn't realize ..."

She reached up and touched his face, her fingers soft, probing, eager. "I didn't realize what it is like."

Slowly, without even knowing he was doing it, Davage began stroking her cheek and playing with her hair. It smelled good. She sighed with pleasure.

She swung her legs over his and snuggled in further, her bare feet dangling off the floor, rubbing the backs of his boots.

"Sygillis, may I call you Syg?" he asked.

"You may call me anything you want, Dav ..." she said leisurely.

"Syg, then perhaps I should go."

"Why, Dav?" she said quietly. "I just got comfortable. Stay here a bit with me. Let me touch you a little longer."

"Syg, you are a guest aboard this ship, and I am its captain. It is not seemly to behave in this fashion."

"Not seemly ... I'll be sure to ... remember ... that ..." she repeated in a voice becoming groggy with sleep.

"No, it's not. I should maintain a more respectable bearing toward you. Indeed, what will you think of me should I not?"

She didn't answer. Sygillis of Metatron, a Black Hat, a Hammer, was quietly asleep in his arms, lost in his touch.

Davage sat there on the couch and felt uncomfortable. He smelled her hair again—it smelled like rosewood. It was a good smell. He wondered what Hath's hair used to smell like. He'd never smelt it before. He had a small lock of it in his quarters, but it didn't smell like anything.

He tried to roll back a bit and slide out of her arms, but as he did, she, asleep, matched his movements, and he was stuck beneath her. He could feel her warmth, hear her shallow breaths.

Resigned, he allowed himself to relax, to enjoy the smell of her hair and the feel of her touch.

Soon, he was asleep too, lost in her touch as well.

15

HUNTING THE CAPTAIN

"Syg, this has got to stop," Davage said

They sat on the couch in her quarters. She had decorated her quarters with colorful fabrics and self-made trinkets. Her terminal chattered with League programming. Hearty coffee brewed in her pot.

"Aww, Dav, it's just something we have to work out."

"Ennez tells me that he has had to replace four of your teeth."

"Yes, that's true."

"And he says that he's had to replace two of Kilos's teeth and fix four cracked ribs."

"See, it's fine—he fixes us up good as new."

"Why are you two fighting in the gym?"

"Why do you fight with Kilos in the gym?"

Davage shrugged. "Because she's a head case who needs a good knocking around every so often. And I don't knock her teeth out, though she sometimes deserves it."

Sygillis scooted in a little closer to Davage and put her legs across his lap. "Well, there you are. She doesn't like me, and I don't think I like her, so we go to the gym to settle the problem."

"Kilos is a tough lady."

"Sure, she hits very hard, but I'm a better wrestler—I cracked her ribs squeezing her with my legs."

"You did?"

"Yep—remember in the brig when I told you that I'm not as helpless as I look. Shadow tech makes you strong. Real strong."

She leaned up next up to him and put her hands on his chest. "Hey, Dav, wanna wrestle?"

"No, thank you." Davage put his arms around her, and she snuggled in. Anymore, Dav and Syg were quite literally inseparable. Kilos would never approve.

"You sure? Sounds like fun. I'll bet I'll win."

"Look, Syg, I do not want you fighting with Kilos anymore, yes?"

"Why not?"

"Because I am worried about the both of you. I don't want anyone getting hurt."

She laid her head on his chest. Her bow was gone, replaced with a colorful beaded barrette that she had made.

"Why don't tomorrow night I'll take you to the mess, and we can spend the evening hoisting our cups and share some good cheer with the crew. Would you like that?"

"Sounds like fun. Can I sit in your lap in the mess?"

"No."

"Will Kilos be there?"

"Probably. I'm hoping a little good fellowship will help bury the hatchet."

"We'll get into a fight. Also, I don't want to share you. Kilos gets you all day. I want you all to myself in the evening."

She sighed.

"Are you planning to sleep here again, Dav? I hope so. But I'm sick of sleeping on the couch. Let's go to bed, but first you're going to have to take off your scratchy uniform, and you are certainly going to have to take your boots off. You should bring some pajamas or something, or I can go and buy you a pair to use when you're here. I've saved my money working for Pay Master Milke."

"Keep the money you've earned, Syg. I have plenty of pajamas."

She looked down and gave his boots a kick. "You and your boots. I never wear shoes and you're never without them. Take them off."

"No, thank you."

"I want them off! I want you to relax! I want you to stay a while!" Syg jumped off and started pulling on his left boot. Before long, they were engaged in a full-fledged wrestling match, laughing, rolling around on the floor, locked up, Syg determined to get his boots off and Dav equally determined to keep them on. Syg was incredibly strong for a woman her size and could wrestle, but Dav, being extremely strong himself, was, with difficulty, able to control her without having to resort to using his Gift of Strength.

He lay on top of her, and she stared at him with deep eyes.

"You got me," she said softly.

"I don't think Kilos likes me coming here," he said, climbing off of her. "I should return to my quarters and turn in. I'm tired."

"Is Kilos your mother?" she asked, sitting up. "That's another reason why she needs her teeth knocked out. What we do together is none of her business. I only get to see you in the evening, and I'll not have her cutting into that time. Come on, round two—let's wrestle some more. I want another crack at you."

"We've been through this before, Syg."

"That's right, Dav, we have, and we'll go through it again."

She kissed him on the cheek. She'd been kissing him a lot lately, but he never kissed her back—he clung to his coy elusiveness with annoying tenacity.

"You know I love you. I love you so much ..." She pulled him onto the couch and wrapped around him.

Dav said nothing and looked at her in the dim light: coiled against him, strong arms around his neck, lovely red hair, eyes big and green, full of genuine love.

"I've already offered my Zen-La, years ago, to Princess Marilith."

Syg got close and spoke into his ear. "And so," she whispered.

"I am therefore lost. I cannot hope to offer it to another."

"Zen-La is not forever, Dav, that is a myth. Do you still dream of her?"

Davage said nothing.

"You don't, do you? And don't lie to me, because I'll know."

"I have not seen her in my dreams in some time, true enough."

Sygillis looked up at him with her deep green eyes. "I dream of you every night."

"She is my Zen-La, Syg ... though there is no hope for us."

"Yes, yes, so you say. Yet, here you are, with me, in the presence of a woman you know loves you ... adores you. You come almost every night, and almost every night you fall asleep in my arms."

"What if I didn't come? Perhaps I should avoid you."

"Then I will come to you. I'll knock on your door until you open it."

"And why is that?"

"Because I am in love with you. How many times must I say it? I want to be your Zen-La. You can offer it again—offer it to me. Forget Marilith, with whom you have no future. We have a future together, Dav—you and I. Can you honestly say that you don't care about me?"

"I do care about you, Syg."

"But?"

"No buts. I care for you very much, and yes, I feel very comfortable in your arms. Still, I have told you from the beginning that ..."

"That you are unavailable and uninterested ... and you were lying then, and you're lying now. Look how you come to me for comfort."

Davage stood up. "I should go, Syg."

"I have loved you from our first meeting, Dav."

Davage thought a moment. "Our first meeting? When you wanted to kill me?"

"Of course I wanted to kill you—I didn't know how else to express myself! I was a Black Hat, for Creation's Sake! I was wanting to impress you!"

"You were hoping the method of my killing ... would impress me?"

"Yes. But now I know that what I was feeling was the beginning of love."

"Well, I suppose that makes sense on certain levels."

"For someone who claims not to love me, you certainly act like you do."

Davage walked toward the door.

She stood up and ran to him. "Don't go, Dav. Stay here. I'm sorry, please. I make no demands upon you, as always. Let me comfort you."

Later, Davage lay asleep on Syg's couch. She was on top of him, her arms and legs entwined around him.

"Take all the time you need, my love. I'll be waiting for you."

* * * * *

Davage, Kilos, and Sygillis sat in the Bridge conference room. Sygillis and Kilos glared at each other.

Davage signed a report and began. "All right, ladies, I've wanted to discuss the possible Xaphan threat posed to us by ..."

He could feel the ice forming between them.

"Ladies, what is going on?"

"I don't like her, Dav," Kilos said.

"I don't like her, either, Dav," Sygillis said.

"Looks like you might need a few more teeth knocked out," Kilos said.

"It seems you want a few more ribs broken! Perhaps you didn't scream loud enough the last time."

Kilos stood up. "Shall we to the gym for another go?"

Sygillis stood up. Kilos towered over her. "Let's!"

Davage stood. "Ladies, enough!"

Kilos and Sygillis stared at each other down.

"Sit down, please," Davage said in a firm voice.

Slowly, they sat.

"What is the problem here?"

"I don't trust her, Dav," Kilos said.

"I don't like her," Sygillis said.

"And your continued sessions in the gym haven't put the matter to rest?"

"No, they have not. I want to beat her up again."

"You didn't beat me up the first and second time!"

"Ladies, please. You two don't like each other—that's clear. However, I see infinite value in the both of you. Kilos, you have been my dearest friend for ten years now. You remember your first day on the ship?"

Kilos looked down and blushed. "I do."

"As do I. You have more than proved my initial confidence in you. I am not exaggerating when I say that I could not be the commander I am without you. Your service to me and this ship is invaluable."

He turned to Syg.

"Syg, I gambled everything—my life, the safety of my crew, my career—on the notion that there is good in you. You have proved me right, beyond any expectation that I ever had. Look how far you've come in such a short period of time."

"What about when she tried to kill you?" Kilos said.

"*Don't you dare bring that up!*" Sygillis shrieked, turning red. "*Get up! Get your ass in the gym right now! I am going to tear you apart!*"

"Syg," Davage said in a low, commanding voice. "Take a deep breath and calm yourself."

Syg looked at the table and took a few deep breaths. Her hands shook with rage.

"Are you all right, Syg?" Davage asked.

She looked at him and nodded.

"Ki," Davage said, "that was a misunderstanding that is in the past and forgotten, and as you can see, it's a touchy subject. In your various sessions in the gym, has Syg used any of her incredible power against you?"

"No, but she's strong as an ox—way too strong for someone her size. She's got to be using the Strength or something."

"That's not my doing—that's just the way it is!" Sygillis said.

"Ki, the Shadow tech makes her strong. If you want to fight with her, that's just something you'll have to deal with. You're a lot taller than she is; will you fight her on your knees? Given that, will you admit that she has fought you fairly?"

Kilos thought for a moment. "Yes, I'll admit it."

"And will the both of you acknowledge that you are both very dear to me, and that it will make me very happy if you two at least try to get along?"

Sygillis looked at Davage. "I will try, if only for you, Dav."

Kilos crossed her arms and looked at the table. "Oh, don't suck up," she said.

"Ki …" Davage said.

"If she agrees to put some shoes on, I will, Dav. I'm sick of seeing her walking around in bare feet."

"I'll not wear shoes for your sake," Syg said curtly.

Davage rubbed his brow. "Can we agree on something light, a paper shoe with a thin sole perhaps, or possibly a minimal sandal? You won't even know you're wearing anything, I promise."

Sygillis looked at Davage and smiled. "Again, to please you, Dav, I will agree to a light sandal."

"Excellent," Davage said. "I think we've made a bit of progress here." Kilos and Sygillis again locked eyes, like two cats ready to pounce.

Davage stood up and smiled brightly. "Well, before we begin the briefing, what can I get you to drink?"

Sygillis looked at Davage. "If you're having coffee, I'll have some. You know how I like it."

Kilos rolled her eyes. "Narva, Dav—buncked."

Davage poured two cups of coffee, stirred in some sugar, and gave one to Syg. He then went to a bare panel, rapped it twice, and a secret opening emerged. He pulled out a cold decanter and a tall mug, filled it, and gave it to Kilos. She took a few healthy swigs and smiled at Davage.

"Now," Davage said, "let's talk about the Black Abbess."

✳ ✳ ✳ ✳ ✳

"The Black Hat Sisterhood numbers five hundred. The exact number varies a bit, but the usual number is around five hundred. There is no central meeting place, no headquarters, no direct line of communication. We are scattered throughout Xaphan space, each of us sequestered in our temples. Our only direct link to each other is the Black Abbess and her Shade Church. It is there and only there that we come into contact with each other."

"You don't know any of the other Black Hats?"

"I know most of them actually … mostly in name only. Some I have gone into battle with, some I'm not on very good terms with. There are no friends per se in the order."

"You said you operate out of a temple?" Davage asked.

"Yes. Mine was located in Metatron, on Ergos's southern continent. Many of the Sisterhood have moved off the Xaphans, but I never did."

Kilos shuddered a bit, and Sygillis saw it. "Something about Metatron disturbs you?"

Davage answered: "More stories, Syg. Metatron is a place Elder mothers tell their children they'll go to if they don't behave."

Sygillis smiled. "I see. It's not a pretty happy place to be sure, and it's been dark since the defeat at Mirendra 3—no power. My temple was located on the Street of the Damned, a black pyramid rising up five thousand feet to a blasted sky."

"And people came and worshipped you there?" Kilos asked, holding her narva mug.

"No—not like that anyways. All my Hulgismen were there, and occasionally prisoners were brought to me. The shills, the occasional conquered warlord."

"Wait a minute!" Kilos cried putting her mug down. "What did you do to all these warlords and shills?"

Syg looked down at the table. "What do you think I did to them? Must I paint a lurid picture for you?"

Davage put his hand on Syg's shoulder—it was trembling. She was lost in bad memories. "Ki, you needn't be cruel," he said.

"Me, cruel?" she said. "I'm not the murderer here!"

"Ki—enough! We are certainly and painfully aware of what Syg did whilst she was under the sway of the Black Abbess. I've said it before and I'll say it again: it wasn't her fault."

Teary-eyed, Syg looked at Davage, miserable. He tossed her hair lightly. "It's not your fault, Syg."

She tried to smile. "Thank you, Dav."

Ki appeared to not be convinced, and Davage eyed her with an angry note. "Now, Syg, I have a few more questions if you're up to it."

Syg nodded.

"How many Hulgismen did you command?"

"One thousand."

"Where are they now?"

"Probably still at my temple, wondering where I am. I really don't know. When a Black Hat is killed, the Hulgismen also die. It's their fate."

"How?"

"The temple is made of Shadow tech. Each Black Hat makes her own. When she dies or is killed, the temple collapses and the Hulgismen there are killed."

"So, your temple is still sitting there in Metatron, awaiting your return?"

"Again, I don't know. Since I'm now an exile and have no intention of returning, I'm certain the Black Abbess has razed my temple to the ground, Hulgismen and all."

"The Black Abbess said she was declaring open war on us. What sort of force does she command at present?" Davage asked.

"The Xaphan forces, since the Mirendra battles, are close to non-existent. They still have ships floating around, but they aren't warships. I'm not sure what they are."

"Ancillary craft, transports you mean?"

"Yes. Additionally, as I said, since the defeat at Mirendra 3, the Xaphans have little power to spare. Their cities are shut down. The lights in Metatron are off. They have been making extensive use of Black Hat infiltrations to create mayhem to compensate."

"As in the *Triumph* incursion three years ago."

"That was Princess Marilith's doing. She promised a bold victory and a warning. I had heard that Marilith uncovered the Black Hat force before it was ready to depart. She was set to task in the Black Abbess's dungeon for it, where she was to die a slow death."

"What happened?"

"She eventually escaped. She killed several Black Hats in the process. She is very powerful with the Gifts."

"She has a knack for that."

Sygillis looked at Davage warmly. "I am very glad you weren't hurt in that attack, Dav."

Kilos put down her mug. "Oh, come off it."

Sygillis turned to Kilos. "You rather that I'd wish for him to have been hurt?"

"No, but this sappy talk is making me sick."

"Ki," Davage said, "give it a rest, yes."

Kilos grumbled something and took another drink.

"I'm curious, Syg," Davage said, "where do these Hulgismen come from?"

Syg took a sip of her coffee and thought. "You know ... I really don't know. They just show up. I'd never given it any consideration. Always right around a thousand. Black Hats tend to go through a lot of Hulgismen. The dead get replaced very quickly."

"Do you communicate with them at all? Is there any discourse, any give and take?"

"I can command them, but they don't communicate in return. They just scrabble about on the temple floor, in the darkness, until called."

"Are there any women?"

Sygillis laughed. "Of course."

"We've never seen any women, just the naked men."

"The female Hulgismen tend and care for us personally. They are also used as midwives."

"As what?"

Sygillis put her coffee cup down and took a deep breath. "What do your stories tell you of how one becomes a Black Hat, Dav?"

Kilos interrupted: "They say that only the foulest, most wicked of Xaphan females are allowed to join the Black Hat Sisterhood. They say you really have to be bad to become a Black Hat."

"Ki ... that was a very rude thing to say."

"Well, that's what the stories say, Dav."

Sygillis said nothing.

"Are you all right, Syg?" Davage asked.

After a moment she smiled at Davage and spoke. "Well, that's where your stories have it wrong."

"All right, then," Kilos said, "let's hear it."

Sygillis still sat there. Davage moved next to her and took her hand.

"Give her a moment, Ki," he said.

Sygillis stared at the table.

"You don't have to answer if you don't want to."

She wiped a tear away and then took Davage's hand with her other one.

"No, no, I'm all right." She took a deep breath. "The Shadowmark on my face …"

"Your tattoo?" Davage asked.

"It's not a tattoo, Dav, and it's not painted on. It's a birthmark."

Davage leaned forward and examined the mark. Kilos did too. It was a long, curling, ink vine design, starting under her right eye, going up to the bridge of her nose, wrapping up and over the top of her eye just above her eyebrow and then trailing down the other side where in stopped just above her right cheekbone. It appeared to be a very complicated design—a twisting latticework of black intersecting lines.

"This is a birthmark?" Davage asked.

"Yes."

"May I Sight it, Syg?"

She smiled. "You may, Dav."

Davage Sighted the mark. It was a seemingly endless series of straight lines that intersected at various points forming an overall twisting ink vine pattern. He sighted farther and farther. He could see lines upon lines upon lines, down and down until it descended into a dark well that was alive with activity. The whole thing appeared to be alive.

"This can't be a birthmark, Syg," he said

Sygillis was staring at him wide-eyed, smiling brightly. "Your eyes—they were glowing, Dav," she said in wonderment. "Just like that night in my old quarters. So beautiful."

"Yes, the Sight appears to make them do that."

She touched his face. "What a wonderful Gift."

"I still can't believe you can't Sight, Syg."

"No, none of us can—it's the one gift we cannot perform. Some of us don't believe it exists. I didn't—remember?"

She composed herself. "To continue, the Shadowmark is the sign of the presence of Shadow tech. If you have the mark, you have Shadow tech within you."

Kilos shook her head. "No, no, Shadow tech is a product of focused ill thought. You have to be evil to create it."

"Syg is not evil, Ki," Davage said."

Sygillis looked at Davage, bright-eyed, full of love. She then continued.

"That, what you just said, Lt., is what the Sisters believe. Shadow tech is a function of the body, not the mind. The Vithian gifts are not just of the mind, they are of the body as well. The body can be focused and trained just like the mind. The Old Viths could create the *emplosser,* the 'living earth,' as they called it. That, in a very crude and unpolished form, was the beginnings of Shadow tech. But like the Blues, the ability to create it requires a very specific trait that, in our current state of evolution, is rare."

"So, you're saying you have to be born with the ability to create Shadow tech?"

"Yes. It comes in both males and females. However, only females can grow and cast it."

"How common is it?"

"Very uncommon. Only one girl child in a million is born with the mark. In men, it is more common, one in about one hundred thousand."

"But men cannot cast it?"

"No, but it is the men who pass it onto their female progeny. Females cannot pass the trait down."

"Are the men marked?"

"Yes, but it is small and very faint."

Sygillis took a drink of coffee. "The Black Hat Order was created, in most part, to study and pursue the development of Shadow tech. The Black Abbess and her followers performed bizarre and gruesome experiments in its use, in its growth and manipulation—thus the schism that formed with the rest of the Sisterhood."

Davage rustled uncomfortably. "Syg, I don't think I'm going to like this next part. So, a marked girl is extremely rare, yes … then what happens when one is born?"

"They're taken, Dav, immediately, to the Black Abbess's church. There, if the girl child survives, fifty years later she emerges a Black Hat, twisted and evil."

"You went through this 'church'?"

"Yes." Unable to contain herself anymore, Sygillis flew into Davage's arms and wept.

Kilos looked at Syg, and for the first time, her hard, skeptical expression vanished, replaced with a look of sympathy.

After a few minutes of hard crying, Sygillis composed herself and was ready to continue, though she sat right next to Davage and held his hand. "As I said, a girl child with the mark is instantly abducted and taken to the Black Abbess."

"Who abducts these children?" Kilos asked.

"The midwives. Female Hulgismen."

"Naked bestial women abduct newly born children?"

"Hulgismen can wear clothing. That's a silly belief you have—the no clothes thing. When assigned as a midwife to a suspected birth, the midwife is clothed and cloaked deep. Thus invisible, the midwife remains with the mother until the birth. If the midwife sees the mark, she'll abduct it at the first opportune moment."

"That is insidious," Kilos said. "Of course that happens only within Xaphan society, correct?"

"Incorrect. The Midwives often abduct League children too."

"How can this be?"

"Again, the birthings are extremely rare. One or two abductions within the course of a several years is a lot."

"How is it determined that a potential birth is about to take place?"

Sygillis wiped her face. "Invernans—the Shadow tech males. They are sent out into both Xaphan and League society and ordered to impregnate females deemed of suitable stock."

"That cannot be!" Kilos said.

"It is. They infiltrate the area, woo the targeted female, and impregnate her, either by charm or by deception."

"What do you mean by deception?"

"If an Invernan is unsuccessful in wooing the female, they come to them in the night, cloaked, and take them while they sleep. Have you never heard of girls suddenly becoming pregnant and they don't know how or by whom?"

Davage tried to stand up, but Sygillis, with her surprisingly strong arms, held him fast.

"Is the Sisterhood aware of this?"

"Yes, Dav, they are."

"That is not possible!"

"It's part of the rules they have in place between them. They promise not to interfere in the Black Abbess's programs, and the Black Abbess swears that none, other than the select abducted children, will be harmed. In many years, both sides have kept to their promise."

"It's a deal with the devil," Kilos said.

"I agree, it's not acceptable. Therefore, there are five hundred women, both League and Xaphan alike, who have been forcibly indoctrinated into a branch of study and are victims of an ancient struggle and promise."

"What can be done, Dav?"

"We can confront the Sisterhood, we can demand answers. And perhaps when the occasion allows, we can try to save as many as we can."

Sygillis's eyes lit up. "Do you mean it? We will try and save the sisters? Like you saved me?"

"Indeed. How can we allow this to continue?"

Sygillis embraced Davage and nearly knocked the wind out of him.

*   *   *   *   *

"You have your own temple, eh?"

Sygillis, holding a coffee cup, sat down next to Davage. "Yes, it was embarrassing to talk about it." She took a drink. "Mmmm. I've really come to like coffee. It's my favorite drink by far."

Davage looked around Syg's quarters. "You once had a temple, and all I have to offer you is this room."

She smiled and kissed him with her coffee-flavored lips. "These quarters are more than I've ever had and more than I ever thought I'd have. The temple was a black, Shadow tech manifestation. I sat in my throne high above the floor, staring blankly at the walls, the Hulgismen milling about mindlessly far below." She looked around.

"I love my quarters. I love my quarters because you gave them to me. Because I love you."

Davage smiled. "I was very proud of you today. That must have been very difficult to discuss, and Kilos can be a handful."

"We'll probably end up fighting again. I'm sorry, I hope that doesn't disappoint you. I know she's your friend."

"Indeed she is, and in time, I'm certain you'll get past this rough point. Still, progress was made today, and I thought you did well."

She looked up at him and touched his face. "Your eyes today ... your Sight, it was so warm."

"I still cannot believe you don't have the Sight. I thought Black Hats were masters of all the Gifts."

"All except that one. None of us can do it." She scooted next to him. "Sight me again."

"What?"

"Please, I want to feel it again. I want to see your eyes glow. Please do it for me."

Davage sat up, closed his eyes, and activated his Sight.

"Well," he said, gazing at her, "I can see all the teeth that Ennez replaced for you. Have they been hurting at all?"

"No, he did a good job."

"Good. I also can see your left wrist has been broken at some point. What happened there?"

"I ... got into a fight long ago. I really don't want to say."

"Fine, fine, I see. There's your heart, beating nice and strong, lungs, kidneys."

He saw something that puzzled him. "Syg, what's this? There's something silvery flowing around inside you."

Sygillis exploded into a smile. "You can see that too, Dav?"

"The Sight comes in various forms—the ability to see through things, the ability to see things very far away, to see in the dark, to see things that are very small, to see things that are otherwise invisible, and to see things that are about to happen and things that already have happened. I am blessed with the Sight in all seven areas."

"Amazing. That last one ... precognition?"

"No ... well, of a kind. I can see things that will happen a few seconds into the future. Gives me a great advantage in battle."

He calmed his Sight, and Sygillis kissed him. She recalled the dream she'd often have—of a Light in the dark. She wanted to tell him but thought better of it.

"That was beautiful, Dav—beautiful. I wish I could do that."

"Now, what was that silvery material I saw, do you know?"

Sygillis got off the couch and sat on the floor. "Come down here, Dav. I want to show you something."

Davage got down on the floor with her.

She was beaming. "That silver material—what you could see flowing around inside of me—is Shadow tech."

"Doesn't look like Shadow tech."

"Watch."

She held her hand out, and her fingers began to glow.

Davage was alarmed. "Be careful, Syg. The Sisters ..."

"It's all right. The Sisters aren't watching right now."

A small, droplet-size mass of dark silvery material formed on her fingertip.

"Hold your hand out, Dav."

Davage held his hand out, and she carefully placed the drop of silver into his hand. There, it flowed about lightly.

"That's Shadow tech?"

"Yes. See how it's acquired that glowing silver color, and see how it stays combined? Shadow tech usually tends to break up without a lot of concentration. How does it feel?"

"It feels warm, slightly effervescent. It feels nice. How have you done this, Syg?"

She looked at him and smiled. "It's love, Dav. It's everything, my new life, my new friends, and most importantly, my love for you. As I've grown to love you more and more, it's gotten more and more silvery."

"Is it less powerful than 'mad' black Shadow tech? This Silver tech?"

"Silver tech, that's a good name for it. And, no—actually, it's easier to control."

"Certainly the Black Abbess must know that Shadow tech will react this way. Why, then, I wonder, does she force the Black Hats to focus on the negative, the hate and the fear?"

"I don't know. Maybe she likes the control, the power she has over the Order. Mad Shadow tech tends to keep you confused, in a daze, in a perpetual nightmare. The Black Abbess, herself being an image straight out of a nightmare, might be able to completely control us in such a fashion."

Davage sat back down on the couch. "Which brings me to my next thought ..."

Sygillis sat down next to him and snuggled into his arms, coffee cup in hand.

"What are we going to do about the Black Hats, Syg?" He thought a moment. Outside, the stars moved past the window. "How are we going to do this? Certainly, the Black Hats are the most fearsome opponents one could dare to face. Innocent or not, they're not going to come quietly."

"You turned me, Dav. And I was a pretty mean Black Hat."

"Yes, and how many days, honestly, was I in mortal peril in your presence?"

Syg thought a moment and took a drink of coffee. "Mortal peril?"

"Be honest, please."

"Maybe a couple of days there ... maybe."

She kissed him again. "Heh ... Who says you're not in mortal peril right now, Dav?"

"Be serious, Syg."

She smiled and kissed him some more. "I am being serious." She ran her hands up and down his chest. "Right now, you are in a great deal of peril. I'm having difficulties keeping my hands to myself this evening."

"Syg ... you promised me."

"I don't care what I promised. I want to make love. I'm ready. I wasn't ready before, but I am now, and I want you to have me."

Davage tried to ignore her.

"I was wondering, Syg, when was it exactly when you stopped wanting to kill me?"

She closed her eyes and thought a moment. "I think it was ... on the third or fourth day. I'm really not certain. I know that on the night when I was crazy with Shadow tech and you came to help me that I thought your eyes, glowing in the dark, were so beautiful. I realized that if I killed you, I'd regret it. I'd regret it very much. I realized that I loved you."

She smiled at him. "You're not going to side-track me, Dav—like you used to do to me all the time. We're going to make love tonight. You might as well get used to that fact."

Davage tossed her hair, still trying to ignore her. "Hmmm, well, when we start trying to rescue these Black Hats, looks like I'll be right back into peril again."

"Well, next time you'll have something you didn't have the first time."

"And what's that?"

"Me. You'll have me to protect you. We just found each other. I'm not going to let anything happen to you. And I'll pit my Silver tech against their Shadow tech any day."

She looked up at him, big-eyed. "May I request a small favor, since I was good at the meeting with Kilos even though I wanted to fight her bad?"

"Anything."

"May I have a kiss?"

"Syg, must we do this again?"

She put her coffee cup down. "One kiss, what's the harm in that? Please, Dav. One kiss, and I promise I won't bug you anymore about it."

Davage sat up a little. "Fine, Syg."

She smiled and kissed him on the lips. It lasted about a minute. When they separated, she looked up at him and purred. "Was that so bad, Dav?" she asked, breathless. "Was that so horrible?"

Davage looked at her.

She stared at him. "I want you, Dav. I want you because I love you, not because I'm trying to annoy you or because I'm trying to embarrass you but because I adore you, because I know that, if you let it be so, we could mean the world to each other. You came to me of your own free will because you wanted to help me. And you faced all the ugliness and evil that I could mete out with goodness and patience, and in the darkness, you shared your light with me. You parted the clouds and ended the long, terrible dream."

"I have been waiting for you my whole life, waiting for your light in the dark. You saved me ... you saved my soul. Don't be afraid of me anymore. There is so much I want to give you ..."

And without a further word, they kissed again.

Before long, they were in her adjacent bedroom, laughing, sighing, lost in each other, their clothes scattered all about.

The future, Syg had said. There was no escaping it.

16

KILOS AND SYGILLIS

"So," Kilos said, taking a big drink of buncked narva, "Who's it going to be tonight?"

Syg thought a moment. "Well, I think we've covered most of the more notable ones. How about Demona of Ryel—I recall you mentioning her. Tell me about that one."

Kilos laughed. "You certainly love talking about Dav's past flings. Fine, fine, then—Demona of Ryel."

Kilos and Sygillis sat in the noisy, bustling mess, near the far wall—Davage's favorite spot. From here, through the window, the vast expanse of the ship could be seen, the wings, the long neck, and the front section far away. Syg sat back with her narva mug, feet up, her tiny sandals almost non-existent. As usual, she was wearing her favorite Chancellor's bodysuit with her blue shawl rolled up in the front. Recently, she had found one of Davage's old belts in his closet, one with a large buckle that was embossed and painted with his Blanchefort family coat-of-arms—the right side of the shield being composed of lines and symbols, the left side emblazoned with some sort of multi-armed creature. Syg wore the belt all the time now, the buckle slung loosely at her hip—it made her feel close to him. Kilos, tall and lanky in her red Marine uniform, sat near her, leaning forward, drinking her brew.

Passing crewmen hailed them both as they moved by with their food and drinks.

The cold animosity that had lingered between them had largely melted away in the past few days. One could almost call them friends now. The revelation that Syg had been abducted into the Black Hats and didn't "sign up" on her own made a big difference for Ki. Being pushed into something that you couldn't control—that was something she could relate to.

Kilos thought a moment. "Demona of Ryel … She was a ship's captain from a confederation fairly far away. She was a good captain, a commander through and through. Very different sort than Dav— more bookish, more formal, more by-the-rules. Not nearly as flashy or personable as Dav, but she was still brave and capable. I probably wouldn't have been a very good officer for her, though, too by-the-books for me, I suppose. She had a pretty awesome starship called the *Triumph*. It had all sorts of interesting technologies that the Lady Branna of the Science Ministry was drooling over: tach drive engines, a very powerful cassagrain-type weapon called a Sar-Beam, and a type of matter-energy teleporter."

"A what?"

"A teleporter, sort of like a Waft, only done with electro-mechanics. With it, one could teleport hundreds of miles, underground even. The Lady Branna swore to master those techs and incorporate them into future League ships. I also remember seeing Lord Probert admiring the *Triumph*."

"What did she look like?"

"She was short—well, a little taller than you, but still short. She had an aged face. All the men seemed to just love her face. Pay Master Milke, Admiral Pax, and Captain Farr of the 10th Marines were ready to raise swords over her. She had thick brown hair that she wore up in a lock, small, pointy features, big green eyes—sort of like yours. A pretty lady all in all, I suppose, except she had a sort of strange, metallic squeaky voice that I, I hate to say, found a little annoying."

Syg giggled. "Did she love Dav?"

Kilos thought. "She ... I guess so, I guess she did. Dav doesn't think so, but she did. She was a very reserved person. She never did anything obvious in front of us that jumped up and said, "I love you, Dav," or anything. I mean, with you, it's obvious that you care about him, the way you light up and get all sappy when he's around, but I never detected anything like that from her. They spent a lot of time alone together, so I have no idea how she acted then."

Syg looked at her mug. "I don't care for Dav, Ki ... I love him. He's all I think about."

"I think she had some sort of run-in with Captain Hathaline over him. That was all the gossip for a while."

"Captain Hathaline? I think Dav's mentioned her once or twice, and I hear the crew mention her name every so often when I pass by."

"Yes, I'm certain you do. She was Dav's first officer and former navigator when I came aboard and eventually took command of the *Dart*, our sister-ship. She was also Dav's neighbor, so to speak. Their castles are within eye-shot—within Dav's eye-shot, I should say."

"Let me guess ... she was in love with Dav too."

"Yes, she was. It was a very arrogant sort of love, though. Her family, the Dursts, and his have always been allies, and since they knew each other all their lives, she felt like he should have loved her just because—like she was entitled to it. He was very close to her but never returned her love, just his friendship."

"And she took exception to Demona of Ryel?"

"So I've heard. Captain Hathaline was a stern, tough lady. As you can probably guess, I ran afoul of her many times."

"Did you end up in the gym together?"

"She was very Blue and never lowered herself to fight fair with a Brown, so our confrontations never got that far. She just put me to a hard Stare, and that was the end of it."

Syg laughed. "The Stare, huh. I'll have to remember that for next time."

Ki winked at her. "Don't you even think about it."

"Where is this Captain Hathaline now?"

"Dead ... killed by Princess Marilith of Xandarr right before the First Battle of Mirendra 3. That was the first time I'd ever seen Dav completely overcome with grief. They'd had a fight ... and then she got herself killed. Hasty words were spoken, I suppose. Dav was broken up over it for a long time. It tore my heart up seeing him like that."

Kilos looked hard at Syg. "What has Dav told you about Captain Hathaline?"

"Not much. I think he mentioned her by name at some point. Of course, I wasn't doing too much listening back then." She took a drink of her narva.

"I don't know if Dav's ever told you this, but you look almost just like her. By the Elders, you look exactly like her."

"I do?"

"Yes, you do. She was a bit bigger than you are, and her eyes were brighter green, and you wear your hair a bit differently, but other than that, you two could be twin sisters. I mean, at first I didn't think you looked too much like her—you had this creepy expression and all."

"I was a creepy person back then."

"That's why Dav asked the Sisters to spare you ... because you look so much like her."

"He did? He's not said anything in detail."

"He Sighted you sitting in the brig and nearly died of shock. That was when he went on his crusade to save you."

Syg sat there, trying to digest this news.

Ki thought a moment. "Maybe that's another reason I gave you such a hard time before—because when I looked at you, I was seeing her. When I was punching you, I was hitting her too."

Syg sighed. "So, the only reason I'm still walking around is because I look like someone else?" She looked at her narva mug bitterly.

"Maybe at first. He was curious as to why you look so much like her—who wouldn't be? But then, as he got to know you, he found that he liked you, Syg."

"Because he thinks I'm someone else ..."

"You're nothing like her. If I'm being blunt, Captain Hathaline was an arrogant ass. He's made mention of it himself, that as he got to know you he found you charming."

"He finds me charming?"

"He does. He likes you, Syg—obviously. I remember when he used to have dinner with me every evening. Not anymore—he's always with you."

Syg cheered up. "Sorry. I'll have to ask Dav about this Captain Hathaline in further detail. What House was she from?"

"House Durst."

"Maybe I'm a long lost daughter of Durst. Were they missing any children?"

"None that I'm aware of. They had seven daughters, no heirs. The Standing Durst name is done—they've all married off, except Hath."

"Looks like everybody loves Dav. He's just ... so loveable I guess. Tell me, I don't understand Dav's relationship with Princess Marilith. She hates Dav, she spends her days and nights thinking up schemes to kill him, yet she still seems to care for him ... if you read between the lines. And he still cares for her?"

"He does. He loved her—they fell in love. Wasn't meant to be, I guess. It took Dav a long, long time to get over her."

"He's still not over her. She has this annoying hold over him that I can't fully break, no matter what dirty, underhanded trick I try. I'll not give up, though. I'll hear him tell me that he loves me, I swear it."

"Does Dav mean that much to you, Syg?"

Syg smiled. "I'll share something with you, Ki ... something I've never fully explained to him."

"What is it?"

"Before, when I was, well—"

"When you were evil, you mean."

"Yes, thanks. When I was evil, I sat in my temple, lost in a fog. I'd have this vision from time to time. I'd see a misty expanse, and far in the distance I'd see a man—a man with glowing eyes. He'd get closer and closer, his eyes shining in the night, searching." Syg exhaled. "Have you ever seen his eyes glow?"

"Yes, of course. I'm a Brown, Syg, it takes more than glowing eyes to impress me. They're pretty, sure, but..."

"No buts ... his eyes, that's what pulled me out of the fog. Those were his eyes in the dark, in the distance. His was the Light. I think I've been waiting for him my whole life—waiting for him to save me ... so, yes, he means that much to me."

Kilos drained her mug.

"And all because I look like his neighbor." Syg sighed.

The evening bell rang, and crewmen and officers shuffled out of the mess to assume their posts. Ki and Syg were virtually alone in the mess.

"Well ..." Ki said, looking at her empty mug. "You know Dav's father was well known for wanting to make peace with the Xaphans."

"Really, tell me," Syg said, interested.

"Dav loved his father very much. His father, Sadric, dreamed of the day that the Xaphans returned home and we'd be one again. It was his greatest ambition.

"But, Sadric, unlike Dav, wasn't a doer; he was mostly an idea man—and he had little if any notion how to bring his ideas into action. Look what his big thing was—a wedding, a unifying League-Xaphan wedding. As if a stodgy League Society function meant anything to the Xaphans. No, if it's going to be done, it'll be the way Dav did it with you—one to one, face to face, right in the mouth with everything on the line, so to speak."

Kilos lamented her empty mug. Sygillis handed over hers. Kilos accepted it with a cry. Crew coming off their shifts began filtering in. Soon the mess was again crawling with life and chatter.

"Anyway," Kilos said, continuing, "Sadric was heartbroken that the marriage to Princess Marilith didn't work out, and he sulked the rest of his life away, locked in his tower."

"Zoe Tower?"

"The very one. Dav was beside himself, one because he loved his father and two because Marilith, the girl he Zen-La'ed with, turned out to be a bad, monstrous error. I think Dav has been waiting all these years to continue his father's work, and the Sisters gave him the chance to do it. The fact that you look like Captain Hathaline probably helped jump start him."

Kilos drained Syg's mug. "I've been thinking ..."

"You think, Ki?"

"Shut up," she said, smiling. "The Shadowmark, the birthmark ..."

"What about it?"

"I think I finally know why Sadric was so keen on making peace with the Xaphans."

"All right, why?"

"Because I think one of Dav's sisters has it."

Syg was shocked. She almost choked. She sat bolt upright, and her sandals flew off.

"What?" she said nearly speechless.

"Yes, the more I think about it, the more I'm convinced that's the case."

She scooted next to Kilos. "Tell me," she said. "Hurry up!"

Kilos held up her empty mug and shook it. Syg seized their mugs, ran to the bar—red hair bouncing—and soon came back with two frothing mugs of buncked narva.

"All right, spill it," she said with growing excitement, handing Kilos her fresh, cold mug.

Kilos took a huge drink. "Dav has told you that Marilith tried to kill his sister Pardock, correct?"

"Yes, because Countess Pardock wouldn't pass the baton, so they couldn't get married."

"Correct—right there in the chapel, she threw it down. If she could have broken it over her knee first and then thrown it down, she would have. See, with you—you were abducted, you had no choice, it was either be a Black Hat or die, but Marilith, she is who she is because that's who she is … and Pardock saw it. She Stared her right through. Pardock saw that she was a rotten, murderous wretch who was going to lead Dav into a long, dark night. Apparently, Captain Hathaline did something to Marilith's persona … made it look a lot worse than what it really was—but I don't believe it. Marilith is evil. Sadric was blinded by his ambition, and Marilith had charmed him into near insanity, but Pardock wasn't going to let her brother be sacrificed and had the courage to call her out. For that, Marilith was determined to kill her, and she broke into Castle Blanchefort and tried to murder Pardock with her own two hands. The way Dav tells the story, Pardock Dirged Marilith out a high window in Zoe Tower, but if you think about it—that's not possible. Marilith, short of being a Black Hat, is incredibly skilled with all the Gifts, except the Sight. Two Dirgists cannot Dirge each other, right?"

Syg thought a moment. "No, they'll cancel each other out."

"So then, what blasted Marilith out the window? And for that matter, what scared her enough to not try it again? Marilith's usually not one to quit once she has something in her head."

"Are you saying Pardock has the Shadow mark? Are you saying Pardock used Shadow tech and blasted her out the window?"

"Not Pardock ... Poe."

"Poe? Lady Poe?"

"What has Dav told you about Poe?"

"Not much. She's his older sister, and she still lives in Castle Blanchefort. She never married."

"No, she didn't. Pardock married into House Vincent and became their Countess, but she outlived her husband—he was killed at the battle of Embeth—and came back. She came back with some of her younger children to help take care of Poe."

"Why?"

"Poe has always been a daunting enigma, a huge, looming Blanchefort question mark. Sometimes, on nights when I really get Dav talking, he'll relate his fears about Poe, about how he worries about her, about her health and safety. He had wanted to be rid of his castle. The Marilith thing, it holds a lot of bad memories for him there, but he kept it for Poe, so she'd always have a place to stay."

Ki thought a moment. "It's not a good thing in the League to be sick—especially to be sick in the head ... to be mentally ill. Nuts, as we say back in Tusck. Poe has been mentally ill her whole life—or has she been? Maybe she's not been crazy this whole time; maybe she's been afflicted with something else. The locals of Blanchefort, in the shadow of his castle, are afraid of her, though they'll never tell Dav that...they think she's strange, haunted ... possessed by something frightening."

"I believe I see where you are going with this, Ki, but it does not add up. A Shadow tech girl needs constant care, constant training, or the Shadow tech will kill her. The Sisterhood didn't declare it illegal for nothing. Besides, what about the Shadowmark? The mark is a hard thing to miss. Dav's never said anything."

Kilos shrugged. "Poe went away for a long time as a child and young woman. Some say she was in the care of the Sisterhood, some say she was out of her head with madness. Did Dav tell you all that? She was always a little strange ... silent, like she wasn't all there. But other times she was a bubbly, charming lady—think of Dav, only female with blonde hair.

"And, as for the mark, I was at Castle Blanchefort for a ball with my husband a few years ago. Dav threw it to celebrate ten years of the *Seeker*. It was a lot of fun. The whole crew got to go. Even the Sisters showed up."

"You were at his castle with your husband?"

"Yes, I do manage to drag him away from the university every so often. We've been guests there lots of times."

"When do I get to see his castle?"

"I've no clue—ask Dav. Anyway, I was in the bathroom getting sick ..."

"Go figure."

"Then Poe came in. She went to the mirror and stood there, looking at herself. She was sort of in a daze and didn't see me. I seem to recall her waving her hand, and the door locked by itself. She then took this thing off of her face, this type of flexible appliance, and there it was. I saw, reflected in the mirror, a huge black mark on her face near her right eye. I thought she'd had an accident and had been badly stitched up and was hiding the scar out of vanity. I mean, it was *really* big."

"But how can this be—how was she not taken?"

"Don't know. Maybe it's because there were no Shadow tech men involved—what did you call them?"

"Invernans."

"Yes, Invernans. I mean, Dav and his sisters look just like Sadric—there's no question he's their father, so there are no 'hidden genes' at work here, no midnight interlopers. Maybe the Black Hats didn't calculate on House Blanchefort bearing a Shadow tech girl and weren't watching. Perhaps it was just one of those things."

"Maybe ..." Syg thought about her parents, who they were, where they might be.

"So, given that, I think Sadric protected Poe her whole life. I think from the moment she was born he saw this thing on her face, this birthmark, and went to the Sisterhood for answers. He was very friendly with them. Maybe they told him about the Black Abbess's work. Maybe that's why he was so keen on making peace with the Xaphans, for the sake of his daughter."

Sygillis gazed off into space and looked sad.

"You could be right. But what about the Shadow tech? I can tell you firsthand how it feels to let it build up inside you—it's a wrenching feeling. Poe could not go for any length of time without releasing it. Without training and discipline and frequent casting, it will kill you."

"Well, that's the kicker, isn't it, the final piece in the puzzle." Kilos took another massive swig. Sygillis sat there, impatient, her mug of narva untouched.

"I just told you that Poe oftentimes seemed a little out there, yes?"

"Yes …"

"What has Dav told you about his castle … about Castle Blanchefort?"

"Only that it's his ancestral home—an old Vith structure and that it's located in the north by the sea. I can't wait to see it."

"It's a pretty place. There is a strange phenomena that happens at Castle Blanchefort, a weird sort of thing that happens fairly regularly. The locals call it Sadric's Rain. Some call it Marilith's Tears, but that drives Dav crazy. The locals think that the castle is haunted because of it."

"What is it?"

"A strange sort of fog. It starts somewhere near the castle, probably near the Telmus Grove, and glides its way down the mountainside to the village and then into the bay where it hangs for a long time."

"Have you ever seen it?"

"I have, last year whilst the *Seeker* was parked in the bay for a refit. I was drinking in the village bars—"

"When are you not drinking, Ki? Good Creation."

"Shut up. Anyway, it was a cold, clear evening—Blanchefort has lots of those. All of a sudden, I see this strange, clutching sort of cloud billowing up near the castle. It obscured the castle's spires and then worked its way down the mountainside and before I knew it, I was blanketed in it. It didn't feel like fog—it felt strange, warm, crawly."

"Was it black?"

"No, it was gray—like a storm cloud. Now, remember I mentioned that every so often Poe acted like she was in a daze, and other times she seemed fine?"

"Yes."

"Well, that day I noticed that Poe could barely talk and was stumbling around like she'd been drugged. Then there's this weird cloud event, then the next day at breakfast, there's Poe, all bright and cheerful. I like Lady Poe. She's so kind and innocent—it's hard to spend any time with her and not like her."

Syg thought a moment. "You might be right ... You might be right ..."

Kilos finished off her mug. "Well, we should be in Com range of Drelsar by now. I think I'll head to my quarters and drop a transmission to my old man—all your sappy talk has given me the urge to tell him I love him."

"See you, Ki."

"Are you going to wait up for Dav?"

Syg smiled up at her.

"All right, fair enough—stupid question."

Kilos put her Marine cap back on and straightened her jacket. "Listen, Syg—don't worry about this, okay? Dav's always had a knack for attracting the ladies, and I suppose he always will. He's a handsome man, he's filthy rich, and he's a good person to boot, so if you want to be close to him, you're going to have to get used to that to some extent. However, I've made light of your fears, and I didn't mean to. Dav has the best Sight of all; he can see things that no one has ever seen. And he saw something in you, something he thought was worth protecting, worth fighting for—back when me and the Sisters and everybody else wanted you dead. Knowing Dav the way I do, I can't imagine him just throwing you aside because some new star-struck lady happened to show up. He has reacted to you like he has to none other—not Demona, not Princess Marilith, and not Captain Hathaline either."

Sygillis smiled. "You really think so?"

"Yes, I do."

"Thanks ... that means a lot to me."

Kilos left through the wooden doors of the mess.

She sat alone for a while, lost in thought, her mug of narva losing its froth.

She thought of Poe, Dav's sister—a Shadow tech girl who didn't become a Black Hat because of chance and because of a father who had the courage and tenacity to protect her from the gaze of the Black

Abbess. She guessed Sadric was a lot tougher than people gave him credit for.

She thought of the Silver tech flowing inside her, a product of love. She thought of all her Black Hat sisters sitting alone in their dark temples, wretched and terrible in their evil and their ignorance, never knowing what it felt like to be good, to touch someone, to feel love, to turn their black Shadow tech into silver.

Syg guessed that, as far as Dav was concerned, she could be very jealous and very vindictive, and that was a dangerous thing. She figured she'd become another Princess Marilith, heartbroken and spurned— forever on the outskirts, on the fringe, forever harassing Dav—forever giving him no peace.

She thought about Dav—the man she hopelessly, deeply loved. She wondered why she didn't try to kill him in the beginning; she wondered what had stopped her. She had killed many people over the years—enemies, League, her own Hulgismen by the score. She'd even killed other Black Hats—ones who'd angered her, crossed her, all without any hint of hesitation or remorse.

So, why did she spare Captain Davage?

Certainly the threat of being killed by the Sisters wasn't in play— she had cared little for her own death at the time.

It must have been a combination of things. Maybe Dav had kept her off balance, kept her confused. Maybe, deep down, she admired him, admired his courage, his raw nerve.

Maybe, as she once told Dav herself, maybe she'd loved him from the start, from her first good look at him. Maybe, beyond all hope, something inside her had wanted to be saved ... had wanted to be free of her Black Hat sash.

The man with the searching golden eyes. The man who was finally right in front of her.

The maybes could go on forever. Perhaps Dav was the right man, and perhaps she was the right woman. In any event, at one hundred ninety years old, Sygillis was living for the first time. For the first time her life meant something to her.

After a while, a cheer rose up in the mess. She didn't have to look— Dav was here. In quiet excitement, she sat with her small hands on the table, her now warm narva mug in front of her, trying not to look in his direction. A loud chattering followed Dav around the mess as he mingled, talking to everybody, clapping them on the back and hoisting his mug with his crew.

She knew after he had completely made his rounds that he will end up at her quiet, out-of-the-way table and sit down. Then, eventually, they will make their way back to her quarters, where they would talk and laugh, and then make love.

Her heart quickened in anticipation.

After a while, Davage approached her. Smiling, she tried to pretend like she didn't know he was there.

"Sygillis, good evening and well met."

"Why, Captain Davage," she said looking up at him. "This is a pleasant surprise …"

Part 2
THE SILVER TEMPLE

When the Sun refuse to shine …
We defy, we defy …
And the Night refuse to die …
We defy …
And we will face the whole wide world,
For a bit of sun, a bit of shine, and a place
Where our sons may one day thrive …
We defy …

—A Silverian charm against evil

1

AN INSANE PLAN

"You three want to hear my thoughts? I don't think the Xaphans will come at us aloft."

Davage stood by the viewer in the meeting room. Kilos and Sygillis sat at the table. Ennez sat nearby, his silver helmet sitting quietly on the table.

"I'd agree with that, Dav. They have a healthy respect for you, and they don't really have much of a force to send into battle," Syg said.

"My thoughts exactly. So, Syg, with that in mind, where do you think the Xaphans will try to mount an attack?"

"I'm not really big on military strategy, but I'll guess that they'll probably try to snare a planet and let you stumble into it."

"Right—exactly. Ki, bring up a list of all planets within thirty light years of here."

Kilos pressed a few buttons on her desktop terminal and a massive list of names popped up on the screen.

"Hmmm, quite a few. I think it's safe to say that we can rule out all of the gas giants on the list. Ki, take them off."

She pressed a few more buttons, and about three quarters of the list vanished. Davage surveyed the smaller list. "Excellent. Now, I don't think that the Black Hats will inconvenience themselves by snaring a very inhospitable planet, one that's very hot or cold, and I'm certain they will avoid planets where life support will be required. Ki, take them off."

Again, the list shrank, this time down to fifteen names. Davage looked at it.

"Yes, yes ... this will do. Syg, how long does a usual planetary snaring take?"

"Depends on how elaborate the snaring's to be. I wasn't a Painter, though. I did the fighting, remember?"

"Be creative for a moment. If you really wanted to pull out the stops. If you really wanted to make a statement."

Syg thought. "About a week and a half, possibly two. That's a lot of Shadow tech to be throwing around."

Kilos looked at Davage. "What are you thinking, Dav?"

Ennez spoke up: "You aren't thinking of raiding a snare operation, are you, Dav?"

He surveyed the list, chin in hand. "I am. I'm thinking we still have time to crash one of these snaring parties. I'm thinking we can snag another Black Hat and turn her."

"Are you insane?"

"What about it? They won't be expecting us. We just swoop in, grab a Black Hat or two, and be off."

"I don't know, Dav," Syg said

"Listen to Sygillis, Dav!" Kilos cried.

"The Sisters won't like that, Dav," Ennez said. "Watching Syg here 24/7 just about gave them aneurisms. Have you ever tried caring for a grumpy, headached Sister, Dav? It's not a pretty thing."

"Hmmm, you might be right, two is too many. We'll grab one for now."

"And just what are we going to do when we get her here? She'll be a hissing cobra just waiting to spit venom," Ennez said.

"What if she blows herself sky high once we get her aboard?" Kilos asked.

"Oh, that's a myth," Dav protested. "Syg—you never thought about blowing yourself sky high, did you?"

"No—I was too busy trying to figure out how to kill you first—then blow myself sky high."

"See, Ennez," Dav said.

Syg winked at Dav and blew him a kiss.

"Then, if it'll make you happy, we'll have to grab her hard and incapacitate her. Syg, can we somehow drain them of their Shadow tech?"

"Yes, but it will be very painful. She won't be happy about it."

"Syg," Davage said, "I thought you were all ready for this."

"I am, Dav, but I just don't want anyone to get hurt—you especially. Abducting a Black Hat might not be a good idea. She'll be too hostile to reason with. She'll have to be killed before she takes the whole ship with her."

"But if we relieve her of her Shadow tech, then she'll be much less of a threat, no matter how cross she initially is, yes?"

"Yes, I suppose so."

"What about her guard of Hulgismen and any other Black Hats who might happen to be around? Just how cross do you think that lot will be?" Ennez asked.

"Again, this is supposed to be a surprise movement. All the Black Hats I've ever seen operate pretty independently. True?"

"Yes."

"So, what's the problem?"

Syg looked down at the table. "I don't know. I simply don't want you to get hurt."

"I'll be fine. You will agree that this life is a bit better than that of a Black Hat?"

"Need you ask me that?" Syg said, incredulous.

"Then I think it's worth a try. Can you detect the presence of Shadow tech from a distance?"

"Yes, and so can the Sisters."

"Then here's what we'll do. We will tour several of the planets on the list. If we detect Shadow tech, we'll Sight them from orbit, see what they're doing, and come up with a quick plan."

"How are we going to do that?"

"I can Sight them from orbit. So can the Sisters."

Syg's eyes lit up. "You can do that?"

"I can."

"Oh, your Sight is the best Gift of all!"

"Syg ... you're going to make me ill here, please," Kilos said.

"You don't think that the Black Abbess hasn't thought of this already, Dav?" Ennez asked. "I mean, she's not an idiot."

"I don't believe she'd ever think we'd have the temerity to seek out and disrupt a snare operation."

"Why not? We had the temerity to steal one of her Black Hats, right? Whatever she's got in store for us, it's going to be a whopper, and it's going to suck, and it's going to be on grand display."

"I agree with Ennez," Syg said. "She's going to want to make a statement. The usual operations probably won't do."

Davage thought a moment. He looked at the list. "I think we'll still head out. I see Calendor is a possible candidate. We'll go there and see what there is to see."

2

FACES IN THE DARK

Davage woke in the dark. As usual, he was in Sygillis's bed. She was asleep, having a terrible nightmare. She thrashed and whimpered.

Davage tried to wake her.

She began crying.

"Syg, wake up."

She screamed.

"Syg!"

She awoke finally and sat up. She looked around; she didn't appear to know where she was for a moment. Finally she looked at Davage and appeared relieved.

"Dav," she said. "I just had a bad dream." She pulled herself into his arms, her naked body up against his. "I dreamt of my temple, in Metatron."

"Your Black Hat temple?"

"I dreamt that it turned silver, just like my Shadow tech. I dreamt that the Black Abbess came to destroy my temple ..."

"And what happened?"

"Somebody inside the temple fought back, fought the Black Abbess."

"Who would do that?"

"My Hulgismen. I could hear them, crying out for me, crying out for help." She looked at him. "They called me mother, Dav!"

She embraced Davage and wept into his naked chest. "They called me mother."

"Syg, it was just a dream."

"It was so real. I could hear their voices. I could see their faces."

Davage wiped her tears away and kissed her.

"Dav, do you think that my temple might have converted itself to silver too, that the Hulgismen within were reborn, just as I was?"

"It's possible, I suppose. The Hulgismen, though, shouldn't they just move on to another temple?"

"No, Hulgismen from two different Black Hats tend to not get along."

"The city of Metatron is on Ergos, correct?"

"Yes. South, in the Fernath region."

"Well, we've plotted solution of Calendor to check for suspected Black Hat snaring activities. How about the moment we're done, we'll plot solution for the Mirendra system, go to Ergos and have a look."

"Do you mean it, Dav?"

"Certainly. We can survey the situation, and if your temple has, in fact, turned to silver, then I imagine we'll just improvise something from that point."

Syg beamed and kissed Davage. "I knew there was a good reason I let you live! I'm joking—I'm joking!"

Detecting a snare operation was much more of a chore than Dav had first thought. They had gone to Calendor, as it was one of the planets on Dav's list of potential sites hosting a large Snaring Op. Calendor, a fairly pleasant world of a mostly agrarian people, turned out to be overflowing with Shadow tech, but not from a specific Snaring operation—it was everywhere in small, metered amounts. People, items, animals, buildings had it on them. It was in the air, soaked in the water. Not much, just bits here and there, but it was enough to make simple detection very complicated. Shadow tech appeared to be more common than he could ever have imagined.

In the end, though, the grand, sinister snaring operation that Dav had imagined was not there. The masses of Black Hats just waiting to be scooped up like red and black sugar cubes was not to be.

Score one for the Black Abbess.

He wondered, though, what the Black Abbess was cooking up—what sort of twisted plan she will try to unleash on them.

He had come to realize that the Black Hat Sisterhood was, at its core, a political organization pretty much like any other and, as such, public opinion figured greatly in its activities. People, both League and Xaphan, saw them as evil, fierce, and unbeatable, and they had to labor to maintain that image. They had to be just that.

Turning Syg—taking a Black Hat Hammer and a self-professed "mean Black Hat"—caused the Black Abbess, among other things, a PR crisis. People might look at this and say, "Why, the Black Hats aren't as bad as we thought," and she couldn't have that.

She was going to have to do something; she was going to have to respond in kind in a manner that will have people shuddering again. Her plan, whatever it turned out to be, was going to be a lot more subtle and insidious than he'd first thought. He was used to enemies like Princess Marilith—a straight-up, over-the-top bad guy who fought him, as such, straight up. She was easy to fight, and she was easy to predict, though he could never fully "get her" in the end. He knew she didn't know any other way to fight him other than full bore—all out. That was a fight he knew he could win every time.

The Black Abbess, though, will probably spend as much time setting the stage, creating a spectacle, as she would actually fighting. The stage and the political message, and effect it will have on those watching played big in her plans. Davage, sitting in his office, had to acknowledge that he didn't have a great deal of skill in this particular area. His father probably had a better head for this, for scheming and political maneuvering. The fight itself will be almost an afterthought—the fall, though, that's where the detail was.

He wanted to make sail for Gioma, another planet on his list that he thought might be entertaining a current Black Hat snare operation. Gioma was promising, as an old League hero, Lord Veltro of Goima,

once annoyed the Black Abbess, but as he promised Syg that he will
first stop at Mirendra and check in on her temple, he had to live up to
his word. Gioma had to wait.

She dreamed of her temple, that it had turned to silver. She only
had it once or twice, but the dream was full and unforgettable. She
couldn't get the thought out of her head.

So, they'd make a quick stop and have a look.

Syg—a mighty, powerful Black Hat in her day—abducted into
their ranks, ripped from her mother's arms. She crawled in the dark,
she said, in the Black Abbess's church, through passes too short to be
able to stand. She scrabbled for food—starving, she was bled of her
Shadow tech. Pushed into a foul pit, she was forced to fight a fellow
trainee—a fight to the death, Syg emerging victorious, but her wrist
broken.

And she fell into darkness, into an everlasting evil dream where she
killed and did unspeakable things for years and years.

The Black Abbess, a cruel black stain.

He wondered, though—were the Sisters any different?

It was considered a great honor and rare privilege when the Sisters
came calling. Davage had the honor seven times previously—four at
Castle Blanchefort, two aboard the *Seeker*, and one on his old ship
Faith.

The stage was always the same.

A small contingent of Sisters arrived and politely announced
that he had been "selected." They then asked if he was agreeable to
participate in their "program." Smiling, soft spoken through their
Marine translators, wearing their winged headdresses and light traveling
cloaks, it was hard, if not impossible, to say no to them. It was hard
not to love them, to adore them.

He always agreed; most "selected" gentlemen agreed. It was an
honor, after all. One never wanted to disappoint a Sister, to send them
away, to say no.

The next day the Sisters arrived. Again they thanked him for
participating and then showed him to a closed door and invited him to
go in, where, inside, a Sister waited.

He never recalled seeing the Sister in the room. She was always in
bed, the bed covers pulled up to her eyeballs.

Those eyes, fixed on him.

She then, almost immediately, gently took him by the mind and led him into green passes of bliss and harmony, a symphony of delightful sound. There, hallucinating, enraptured, he lingered for hours and the Sister, unseen behind these lovely veils, was seeded by him.

In the morning he awoke and the Sister would be gone.

Sometimes he recalled a dim memory of slender arms around him, of small, shy kisses on his face and neck. He could sometimes recall hearing "I love you ... I love you ..." in his mind.

He would then dress and go outside, where the contingent of Sisters, for a final time, thanked him, and took their leave, their mission accomplished. Two years later, in the Old Vith chapels and hidden cloisters of Valenhelm, Pithnar, or Belle, a girl child would be born—a Sister from birth. His daughter—but owned entirely by the Sisterhood. Occasionally, when a contingent of Sisters passed him in the streets, one might give him a second glance and smile in a shy, knowing way. He, in return, doffed his hat, wondering if they had ... ever been in arms.

Did she have any choice, this girl child? Though not abducted as a Black Hat, not chained, not forced to crawl, not forced to fight, was she any less a prisoner?

He wondered; he wondered.

3

MIRENDRA

The Mirendra system, on the boarder of League/Xaphan space, was fallen down, sad, dark, and starving for light. Mirendra, once a massive blue giant star, the "Eye of the Cat" in the Mertens constellation as seen from Kana, was sucked down to a dull ember. Sucked dry by the Xaphans—all five of them.

The Xaphans—it was easy to blame everything on them.

They had first come at the end of the age of the Elders. At that time, The League served the Elders, roving the heavens, looking for stars that might nourish them. Joyous, the League fulfilled is role, guiding the Elders to new stars, and there the Elders fed, taking just what they needed, causing no harm.

But then the Xaphans came. They were creatures very similar to the Elders—huge, planetary in size, powerful in the extreme, and hungry for starlight. But where the Elders shared, the Xaphans hoarded. Where the Elders gave, the Xaphans took. They attached to the star, bled it dry, and quickly reduced it to a small, cold spark.

And that wasn't all. They liked a bit of suffering to go with their meal of starlight. They liked the fear and the dying that went along with it. The more populated a star system was, the better.

Some said in hushed tones that the Xaphans were in fact the Elders, soured and corrupted into another form, that five of the original twenty-five went bad. That's what some said.

Gaudy and utterly evil, the Xaphans clouded themselves in endless illusion and glamour. They came to the League in the last days of the Elders, as they weakened and died, and presented themselves boldly. Appearing as rich, pompous Elder-Kind, they arrogantly entreated the League to serve them, to come to the Xaphans and cast aside the Elders. The rewards, they promised, would be beyond measure.

The remaining Elders, growing weak and pitiful, implored the League not to listen. They begged them to instead fight the Xaphans, to forever make war upon them, for the suffering they would create will be horrific. The Elders exacted the Promise from the League: that they will fight the Xaphans, that they will defend all life from the Xaphans, and finally, that they shall not kill the Xaphans either.

And the twenty-five Elders died and passed into legend, their Promise binding the League and their progeny for centuries.

The Xaphans, though, were relentless. As the years rolled by, their promises of decadent pleasures and Gifts beyond imagination began to sway the League. Eventually, twenty Great Houses, mostly old Blue Vith Houses from the north, fled and joined the Xaphans, living on them, flying their small strange ships, looking for stars for them to swallow and life forms for them to kill.

Thus the League and their betrayers, now simply called Xaphans right along with their masters, made war upon each other for centuries, the Xaphans wishing to take life, the League struggling to defend it. And the League, with their superior Elder technology and their Promise binding them, were victorious time and time again.

Such was the Golden age of the League/Xaphan conflict. The League was strong, and the Xaphans were strong. There was a clear enemy to fight, a clear purpose to uphold.

Eventually, as with the Elders before, the Xaphans became more and more irrelevant. The Vith that went to them during the Great Betrayal were mighty in the Gifts, and enduring loss after loss to the

League, one failed scheme after another, had enough. They began to strike out on their own, their grudge with the League now an old and personal one. The sects they formed were powerful enough to inflict great damage on the League, and they left the Xaphans in droves.

Desperate to eliminate the League and restore their credibility, the five Xaphans listened to Princess Marilith of Xandarr. She had a bold plan to destroy the League, and they gambled everything on it, spending their last great resources to launch a vast force in a place called Mirendra 3.

There, the Xaphans would settle their ancient score with the League.

There, Princess Marilith, on a twist of Fate, settled a personal score of her own … with a lone, wandering, vulnerable Captain Hathaline of Durst who stumbled into her grasp.

Initially successful, the Xaphan attack left the League bloodied and battered, ship after ship lost. Nevertheless, the League rallied and laid a massive defeat on the Xaphans in a second battle of Mirendra 3—thousands of ships on both sides in a confused, twisting, turning fight. The Xaphans and Princess Marilith could not recover—they had no resources left to draw on.

Now, there they spin, stuck around the dying star Mirendra, forlorn, abandoned, starving … waiting for it all to end. The Xaphans: Ergos, Loviatar, Zust, Lethin, and Deluum, wondering how such a thing could have happened to them.

4

"ARE YOU HAPPY, SISTER?"

Davage sat in his office. Far away, through the window, the dull yellowish light of Mirendra began to grow in the distance. There, they'd take a quick look at Ergos, at the city of Metatron to see if Syg's temple had turned to silver.

A Sister sat in his office drinking a cup of coffee. The usual one. The one he'd noticed in her nightclothes. The one who liked him.

"Sister, thank you for coming," he said.

She put her cup down and smiled at him.

"I wanted to thank you."

Confused, she tilted her head to one side. Kilos was not present, so she could not communicate back. She gazed intently at him, trying to understand. Davage continued.

"I am certain, with this whole Sygillis matter, that you believe me to be either crazed or suicidal. Such is, of course, not the case, and I wanted to thank you for indulging me ... for allowing me to proceed ... for defending me."

The Sister smiled. She finished her cup, stood up, bowed slightly, and made to leave.

Davage stood up. "Sister?" he said.

The Sister turned, approached him, and lightly put her hand on his lapel.

"I was wanting to ask you, though I know you cannot answer me in a way that I will understand," Davage said.

Looking up at him, she cocked her head to one side, awaiting his question.

"Are you ... happy, Sister?"

She appeared confused.

"We of the League enjoy endless freedoms—freedoms that you help make available to us."

The Sister stared at him.

"And I should think it ... a shame, a great shame ... if you, as a Sister could not enjoy those same freedoms yourself. And so, I am asking, does being a Sister ... make you ... happy?"

The Sister continued to stare at him. Without realizing it, the Sister had backed him into the corner of his office, her hand still on his chest.

Suddenly, she burst into a huge smile, her eyes big and blue, and gazed at him with kindness and love.

She nodded after a moment.

"I'm glad, then, Sister. I am sorry for my childish question."

The Sister kept him stuck in the corner. He began to feel a bit awkward.

"I ... wish ..." the Sister said, struggling to talk, her ill-used voice raspy and difficult to hear.

"Pardon, Sister?" Dav said.

She shook her head and tried to speak again. "I will ... request ..."

Dav couldn't understand.

The Sister appeared frustrated. She closed her eyes and then ...

She hit him with her thoughts. They barged into his mind in a rush, filling him, overwhelming him. He was not trained for this.

The room spun. His mind shouted in confusion. His thoughts, under her power, bounced, raved, approached perfection, and then crumbled to mindless chaos. The Sister looked a little different to him as his mind gauzed over in random, disrupted veils. Her eyes appeared unnaturally big, and they had changed color, to an odd bluish-violet. She appeared strange and hunched, ancient … intense.

Her thoughts pounded his mind:

WAAAAiwantyouAAAAAAAAAAAAAAAAAAAAAAAiloveyouAAA
AAAAAAAAAAAAAAZZZZZZZZZtouchyouZZZZZZZZZZZZ
ZZZZZZZkissyouZZZZZZZZZZZZZZZZZWAAAAAAAAAA
AAAAAAAAAAAAAAAAAAAAAAAAAAAAAAAAAAAAAAAAA
AAZZZZZZZZZZZZiknowyoufoundmeattractive,andifindyou
attractiveaswellZZZZZZWAAAAAAAAAwhenmytimecomesagain,
captain,iwillinsistuponyouAAAAAAAAAZZZZZZZZZZZandiwill
showyoupleasureundreamedof.howiloveyouZZZZZZZZZZWAAAA
AAAAAAAAAAAAAAAAAAAAAAAAAAAAAAAAAAAAAAAAA
AAAAAAAAAZZienvysygillisZZZZZZZZZZZZZablackhatcan
courtyou,icannotZZnotfairZZZZZWAAAAiwillhaveyouwhenmy
t i m e c o m e s a n d s h e w i l l n o t p r e v e n t m e A A A A A A A A A

She stopped the thoughts, and Davage slipped a bit, the tiny Sister effortlessly holding him up. Once he was free of her power, her appearance returned to normal, but she still had that odd, intense look to her.

She kissed him, and not a gentle peck on the cheek. She gave him a long, passionate kiss on the lips.

She then turned and left, giving him one last look as she walked out.

And Davage tried to compose himself as Mirendra grew bigger and bigger in the window.

5

THE BLACK ABBESS STRIKES

The *Seeker* rocketed into the Mirendra system a short time later.

The last time Davage was here, he grieved over the body of Captain Hathaline, his life-long friend. Her death, and the information she carried, meant life and victory for the rest of the League.

Captain Hathaline, in death a hero.

How Syg looked like her ...

He remembered spending all night long out on his balcony, over four thousand feet in the air, sending signal lights into the cold night, waiting for the dim blue response in the distance—Hath. He remembered jumping off the balcony with her and Wafting down to the bottom. He remembered wrestling with her on it. The loser was the one who got thrown off first. He usually won because Hath was so tiny, but she was always game to try again. How she had loved him, expected him to love her in return, felt entitled to his love. Perhaps that's why he didn't give it—out of principle, not because he didn't think she was beautiful. How angry he'd been at her when he learned what she had done to Princess Marilith at the wedding ball. How he told her he would never forgive her, a lifetime of friendship betrayed.

And she went away in her ship, heartbroken—determined to redeem herself, determined to win his friendship back.

And then she was dead, their last words spoken in anger.

Hath, dead—pushed into an escape pod by her crew, kicking and screaming. Her crew soon dead at the end of Marilith's guns. And soon she followed in an airless coffin, Cloaked by a terrified Sister.

Dav—weeping at her tomb in the quiet, lonely Durst graveyard, begging forgiveness from her silent, empty shade.

Mirendra.

There they met the Xaphans, their forces proud and strong.

There they beat them and the Xaphans, betting everything and losing, festered, the light of Mirendra unable to support them all.

All five orbited the dying star. They themselves now dying, those Xaphan minions who could flee having long since gone.

He could see them on the screen, depowered and naked—like a courtesan stripped bare and deprived of her make-up.

The Admiralty had been clear after the battle: We will not kill the Xaphans as we promised long ago, but we will not save them either. Let them wither and pass away …

Zust was reddish and quiet.

Loviatar, a mottled red ball, wailing in despair.

Ergos, lopsided and ochre, the biggest of the lot.

Deluum, black and lifeless … dead already.

Lethin, blue, a few weak lights shone here and there.

There they were; the Xaphans, the enemy, once great but now weak and helpless.

He remembered the exact coordinates where he came upon the debris of Hath's ship—the *Dart*, the burned metal, the floating bodies—crew, Marines, even a Sister, which almost never happened. And the little life pod, airless, with Hath's body in it.

Open, exposed, humbled in Mirendra … both he and the Xaphans—lost in grief.

He pitied them and secretly wished for the old days when they were mighty and fearsome, an enemy worthy of respect.

Still, this was the Black Hats' backyard, and a few of them still used the Xaphans to operate from. Syg did.

Quickly, through this sad gallery of Once-Was, the *Seeker* made its way to Ergos and the city of Metatron to see if a silver temple was there lighting up the darkness.

The bridge was alert but not overly tense. Mirendra was a pretty clear sector since the battle.

Davage ordered to make orbit around Ergos's equator and scanned for contacts—nothing. He had a mind to beat to quarters, but thought better of it. No need to cry wolf until the beast was in sight.

Ergos was dark and sad. Dav always recalled him being gaudy, light-strewn, like a piece of cheap jewelry, his surface not seen at all.

Here he was, drab and yellowish, not a light in sight. All his finery gone. No proud boasts ... nothing but fitful silence.

Slowly, the *Seeker* descended into a standard parking orbit of 450 miles north of Ergos's equator.

He ordered the helm to drop the nose a little and get a bit closer. The usual smoke and flames as the tough ship began to enter the upper atmosphere.

"Watch out for Drops, Helm," he said to Saari, the smallish, blue-haired crewman manning the wheel—Lady Saari, of the House of Fallz. She had strong ties to the Science Ministry, as her mother was the Lady Branna, one of the League's top scientists. Normally in a tight situation, he took the wheel himself, but as Saari was fairly new, he didn't want to wreck her confidence by taking over and shoving her aside for no reason.

She adjusted her stance and pulled back a bit, the helm wheel being quite a bit bigger than she was. Lady Saari was doing just fine.

The viewing screen filled up with the dull amber light characteristic of a dry-light star—in this case, Mirendra. Davage could feel the sickening tug of Ergos's gravity in addition to the ship's artificial gravity. It took a moment to get used to.

He walked to the front of the bridge.

"Anything on sensors?"

All of the crewmen manning the sensing ports reporting nothing.

Something was wrong, he could feel it.

"The Ops screen is clear, Captain," Kilos said from her station, careful about protocol when on the bridge. "Do you sense something out there?"

"Not sure," he replied.

He lit his Sight. He Sighted everything, from the darkness of space to the horizon, where the red ball of Loviatar was rising, to Ergos's pocked, ugly surface.

Nothing.

He looked down, far away, through the weak amber atmosphere to the dark scab of standing water and rock that was Metatron far below. He stared hard.

"What do you see?" Kilos asked from her station.

"Sure enough, I see something large and silver down there in the greater part of Metatron, amid all the dark stone. Something that shines. Something pyramidal in shape."

"Is it Sygillis's temple? Was she right after all?"

As Davage Sighted in farther, something passed his view. Something big, yet hidden. Something indistinct.

Something Cloaked … something in a deep, deep Cloak!

Davage concentrated, Sighting hard.

And there they were, Xaphan ships, everywhere. Ghome 7 transport ships, one hundred plus, in a hard, interlocking Cloak—the most devilishly crafted he'd ever seen.

And they were mounting weapons, huge, unwieldy cassagrain cannons strapped crudely to their lumpy backs.

He looked up. They were there as well, closing in, drawing the net tight. Cassegrains heating …

The *Seeker* was boxed in.

"*BEAT TO QUARTERS! WE ARE AMBUSHED!*" he yelled.

Claxons rang, and crewmen began jostling about, taking their positions.

"Captain, Fore Sensing, no contacts!" Sasai said.

"Captain, Aft Sensing, no contacts!" Dieter said.

"Captain, Ventral Sensing, no contacts!" Vert said.

He Sighted a hail of incoming cassagrain fire. "Hold tight, everyone."

<Dav!> came Sygillis's telepathy. *<What's going on?>*

Concentrating, he tried to answer. *<Syg, get yourself to the deepest part of the ship. Go to decks four or five and stay away from the exterior!>*

<I'm coming up there!>

<No! You say you love me, then you'll do what I ask now. Get to safety and stay put!>

The *Seeker*, hardly ever touched in battle, was pounded from tip to top with cassagrain hits peppering the hull, the neck, and the huge wings. The hardy ship rocked and groaned—the strength of the *Straylight* design, Lord Probert's masterpiece, was evident once again. The ship plummeted through the upper mesosphere in a shooting gallery with a gaggle of Ghome 7s hot on its heels.

"Captain!" Kilos screamed. "Hull temperature spiking at twelve thousand degrees!"

The hull couldn't take much more. Davage Sighted—he saw something, a slim chance. "Port Battleshot units, fire and maintain!" he barked.

The ship trembled with vibrations from the Battleshot units and cassagrain strikes.

"Captain, Port Sensing: Xaphan Ghome 7 transport ships falling out of cloak and sinking toward the planet surface!"

Davage looked. The Battleshot barrage had opened a small but very real hole in the Xaphan ranks. He saw a chance for escape.

"Helm!" he barked. "Make six arcs of 2:00, bearing 1:00 of midnight. Go now!"

Saari, the blue-haired junior Helmsman holding the wheel, looked horrified. "A-Aye, Captain, six arcs of 2:00, bearing 1:00 of midnight!" She rammed the wheel as hard as she could in the extreme movement Davage had just ordered, and the ship, protesting all the way, responded.

It worked. In a gut-wrenching movement, the *Seeker* had plunged into the hole and was cork-screwing violently toward the surface far below, screaming all the way.

Davage Sighted about. He was pleased; this might turn out after all. The *Seeker* was well ahead of the bulk of the Xaphan force, and they being mere transports, he outgunned, out-toughed, and out-legged the lot of them.

Looking back, he Sighted.

To his horror, they were hot on his tail.

They were now flying backward, using the mounted cassagrain cannons as a sort of rocket assist. Obviously, they were spoiling to ram the *Seeker*, to batter her into a shapeless, sinking mass.

And they were closing fast—much faster than he had anticipated only moments earlier, the rocket assist giving them a huge speed boost.

Davage needed the *Seeker* out of this dive, but the sky was full of Xaphans hell-bent on his destruction. He could simply order all head full, take his lumps, and meter out, firing through any ships that got in his way, but that will leave the ship crippled, broken, listing. He will have to pass through a gauntlet of fire. If he could double back and chandelle to his right, firing the whole time, they will then be able to make a clean run for open space, where they could gun down these embarrassingly slow transports at his leisure.

He saw how to do it. A hard pull to the right on the wheel, followed with firm trim and a lot of redress will do the job. It would be a wrenching, ruinous movement, and the *Seeker* will, no doubt, require servicing, but they will be clear.

It was time. It was now or never.

"Helm," he yelled. "Make ten arcs of 9:00 PM, minus four of 6:00 AM!"

They needed to do it soon; they were running out of room.

Saari looked terrified. She clearly couldn't understand what Davage had ordered. She held the wheel with white knuckles. "Um ... 9:00 arcs of ... 10:00 PM?"

They were out of time!

"TEN ARCS OF 9:00 PM, MINUS FOUR OF ..."

Too late. The *Seeker* was devastated by several terrible impacts.

BOOM!

BOOM!

BOOM!

BOOM!

Four Xaphan ships had successfully hit the ship. Three in the rear section, one in the neck.

CRACK!

Davage heard the heartbreaking sound. The main spar in the neck, the back-bone of the ship, had collapsed. He could feel the ship beginning to torque helplessly.

<Dav! What's happening?> came Syg's telepathy.

"We're sinking! We're sinking!" Dieter yelled, and the ship listed in a long, deadly spiral toward the surface.

Davage agreed with Dieter's assessment; however, he wasn't quite ready to give up just yet.

"Engineering, all ahead full! Helm, pull out of this dive Z-minus nine thousand degrees port of yore. That will keep pressure off of the main spar. All batteries and canister, open fire and maintain until we are clear of this rabble!"

In a long, smoking arc, the smashed *Seeker*, gunning down everything in its path, roared past the transports, sinking many of them in smoky heaps, but taking a massive amount of hits in the process. At the bottom of the arc, the muddled sprawl of Metatron came into the viewing screen. There, amid the spindly towers and black, shapeless, buildings straddling standing pools of murky water, was a tall silver temple shining in the night.

The *Seeker* climbed, roaring and bucking, higher and higher, the Xaphan transports far to the rear clawing back into low orbit.

Then, in the lower pressure, *Seeker* began to fall apart.

A long, zipperlike tear formed in the neck near the cracked spar. Holes and tears began forming randomly as the hot hull cooled too rapidly and twisted and turned, spar-less.

"Containment breach, deck ten, section 42!"

"Breach, deck nine, section, 12!"

And on and on.

"Captain!" Engineer Mapes, Lord of Grenville, yelled over the Com. "Containment is overloading!"

"I want those breaches sealed, Mapes, now—no exceptions!"

"The ship is torquing itself into pieces!"

"This ship is sailing away. Now look to your systems and get those breaches contained!"

Ennez came into the bridge. "Captain," he said, "I've wounded all over on—"

With a bang, a breach opened in the front section of the bridge, a huge twenty-foot hole, outside a thin black sky.

No containment—they were going to depressurize.

Sasai at her Fore Sensing location was quickly lifted off her feet toward the gaping hole.

Davage, like lightning, caught her by the ankle. He too was lifted, and his hat was sucked out. He latched onto a metal pier with his boots, crossed them, and held fast.

"Captain!" Sasai shrieked. "Let me go, I'm over!"

"You are not yet dismissed, crewman!" Davage yelled.

The pier he was holding onto with his legs bent as he pulled her into his grasp.

Ennez, using his magnetic pads, walked the walls and fighting the pull, reached out to Davage but could not quite get to him.

The pier groaned and twisted.

Davage, using his Strength, tossed Sasai into Ennez's grasp. He then thought to Waft away to safety, but found he was blacking out; the lack of air was leeching into his brain.

"Containment in thirty seconds!" Kilos yelled.

Davage barely heard her.

"Lieutenant!" he yelled. "I ... order you ... get the ship to safety. Get ... *Seeker* out of the area immediately. Understand?"

Kilos looked at him dumbly.

"DO YOU UNDERSTAND? I EXPECT THESE ... ORDERS ... CARRIED OUT!"

"Yes, Captain!" she yelled, tears in her eyes. "I understand. Waft, Dav, Waft away!" she pleaded.

With that, the pier broke.

"Dav!" Ennez shouted. Sasai couldn't look and buried her face in Ennez's uniform.

"*DAVAGE!*" Kilos cried.

And Captain Davage, Lord of Blanchefort, was sucked out of the hole into the bleak sky.

He was gone, as though he'd never been there.

The *Seeker*, groaning and twisting metal, grieved at his loss.

* * * * *

When the ship began falling apart, Sygillis was on Deck Four, roaming the corridors. Crewmen and Marines were running around all over. She had wanted to be on the bridge, but she had gone to Deck Four instead.

Because he had asked her to go there.

She wasn't supposed to be on the bridge. Command and control areas of the ship were still off-limits.

That hadn't stopped her before.

The Sisters had grown tired of watching her all the time, and she had proved that she wasn't going to hurt anyone, so they had lapsed into long stretches when they weren't watching.

She could tell when these times popped up, usually when she was working in Paymaster Milke's office, and she took advantage of them. She waited until the white-haired fellow fell asleep behind his desk and then Cloaked herself and Wafted up to the bridge. There, she saw Dav and Kilos and the rest of the bridge crew hard at work doing this and that. She frankly had no idea what they were doing. Oftentimes she stood there and listened to Dav command. It sounded impressive, whatever he was talking about. She had lots of questions, but obviously, she couldn't ask them. On those rare occasions when he sat in his chair, she playfully blew in his ear, and sometimes she'd kiss him lightly. She had to be careful; if he Sighted her, he'd probably be pretty mad. She'd probably have a lot of explaining to do.

She was only there because she missed him—that's all. She meant no harm.

She could feel the muffled thuds coming from high above. Something was hitting the ship. A trap—the Black Abbess had finally attacked. If Dav was letting the ship get hit, there must be a lot of ships out there.

Crewmen and Marines started locking in. "Lady Sygillis," a Marine said, "you should brace yourself. The Captain's going to set the *Seeker* to rocking in a moment."

She had always heard about how Dav could fly a ship. She'd been amazed by what he could do with a ripcar, but the *Seeker* was a huge vessel—what could he possibly hope to ...

The ship pulled hard to the right. Everyone in the corridor strained to hold on. Syg Stenned herself into place. She stood fast even as the ship rolled and plunged in a stomach-churning ride.

Then came the crashes, the loud, thick *booms* as the *Seeker* was rammed.

The crew looked around, terrified.

There was a sickening grinding of metal, and then the ship seemed to acquire a floaty, twisting sort of movement, like it was no longer whole.

"By the Elders, our back is broken!" one of the Marines cried out. "We're going to sink!"

Someone screamed.

Getting a bit concerned, Syg sent Dav a quick message via telepathy.

She wanted to be on the bridge. She wanted to be with Dav.

The ship gave a long, steady groan and then the end of the corridor, near the exterior of the ship, breached. A long, cold rip opened. Girders twisted and rolled, and like a row of rotten teeth, Syg could see open space past the girders.

The decompression pulled on all the people locked into their handholds. They were lifted off their feet.

The corridor began to crumple up under the pressure.

She loosed her Silver tech, coating the walls and ceiling in a thin layer. She then extended and flexed it—gave it strength, and the corridor resumed its former shape despite the pressure.

A white-shirted crewman let go of her hand hold; she could hold on no longer. She slammed into a Marine, and he let go too. They were headed for open space.

Stenned into place, Syg stood fast. Without thinking about the Sisters, she flooded her other hand with Silver tech and let it fly. Quickly, easily, she caught them with her Silver tech ropes and pulled them back.

Another person let go—again she caught him.

Extending her arm, she blasted out a thick blow of Silver tech. It covered the breach and sealed it. It stretched slightly as the ship continued to torque.

But it held. It held firm.

She un-Stenned and released the crewmen. "Is ... is everyone all right?"

They ran toward her and embraced her roughly.

"Thank you, Lady Sygillis! Thank you!"

Soon she was buried under crewmen and Marines wanting to thank her.

In a mound of people, she desperately wanted to be on the bridge.

6

FALLING OVER METATRON

It was an undignified thing, to awaken from unconsciousness, frost-covered CARG whistling, falling through the air, but such it was for Captain Davage.

The dull, amber air of Ergos had thickened enough that he could breathe almost normally. His mind, oxygen starved, slowly came back into focus.

He was falling—he had been sucked out of the hole in the *Seeker*'s bridge, and he was plummeting fast. He'd been able to save Sasai; using his Strength, he roughly threw her into Ennez's arms. The pier he was holding onto was giving way, and he was able to order Kilos to take *Seeker* out of the atmosphere and into the safety of space before he was sucked out. Containment had failed—the ship, its back broken, was torquing too much. The Sisters will come and plug the breaches, or Syg could do it with her Silver tech. He didn't care which.

He'd given Kilos a direct order to get the ship out of the area. It was probably ripping her up, but he didn't expect that she would disobey him; still, he whirled around and looked. The *Seeker* was not in sight. He looked down at the surface and Sighted. If he had time, he could have made an extensive scan of the heavens, but it wasn't necessary. He didn't see its carcass anywhere, only sundry flaming Ghome wreckages pocking the sullen landscape, burning in colorful chemical fires.

Good, good. He knew Ki wouldn't disobey him, though it was probably breaking her heart.

He also guessed that when Syg found out, she'd probably be quite cross with Ki for leaving him behind. He imagined they might have another confrontation. They might even end up in the gym again, beating each other senseless.

That's fine, they can fight each other all they want as long as the ship was safe.

Ki, his trusted friend.

Syg, his "girlfriend," powerful and dangerous.

Now to it—what was his situation?

He was falling. He guessed he was still about twenty miles from the surface. Looking down, the mottled brownish-gray surface was a curved, indistinct mass. Far below he began to make out the hints of clouds, and beneath that, the dark ugly sprawl of Metatron, tinged with black water—a place League mothers warned their children about.

Metatron was dark—no lights. Ergos, the mightiest of the Great Xaphans, was starving in the shared dry light of Mirendra and could no longer afford the gilded dream of illusion. Only the dirt and stone was left. The city was built on a flat shelf of land over a shallow inlet of water. The tall buildings were built up to great heights, buttressed by innumerable cobbled slum buildings and railed causeways lining the waterfronts.

His clothes were covered in frost. The whistling air was biting cold. His CARG was a coppery icicle. But he was a Blanchefort—cold meant little to him. Cold he could handle.

Bang! His CARG, caught in the massive draft, hit him in the back of the leg, shattering ice layers, its intricate saddle holding fast at his hip. Wincing, he rolled over and grabbed its coppery, whipping shaft and held it steady. Yet another indignity—to fall holding one's CARG in place. What would they say back at the Fleet? In such a situation, something smaller and more compact, like the CEROS of House Probert, made better sense.

A humming began to form in his head.

<Captain Davage ...> came a booming voice in his head.

He had wondered what had taken so long. Apparently, Ergos, his great black bulk getting larger and larger beneath him as he fell, wanted to talk.

Time to have a conversation with the world.

"Ergos," Davage said in reply with his wind-whipped mouth. His ability to use standard telepathy was shockingly bad. Syg would certainly not approve, and Kilos might laugh. "Well met, sir."

<But is this not a sweet and toothsome surprise? I did not think to expect you.>

"I suppose your dreary skies filled with cloaked, armed Xaphan transports was not an indication that I was coming."

<I should rephrase. I did not expect to see you alive.>

"Please ... A sky full of transports is something of an embarrassing insult."

<Your ship's back was broken clean by those embarrassing transports, Captain—I watched the whole thing. Very poor helmsmanship on your part.>

"I wasn't at the helm at the outset of your sneak attack, sir, but thank you for that."

<My sneak attack? No, no, Captain. I had nothing to do with it. I am simply an unwilling host. It is the Black Abbess who has authored these proceedings. It seems she wishes you dead. So, how shall we go forward? Shall I capture you, hold you for ransom? Perhaps I can assure my skies free of your damned Fleet for a time. Perhaps a new star will be offered up in your stead.>

"I'll not be captured, sir. I will await my rescue, which will be, no doubt, forthcoming."

<Evading capture could be quite dangerous, Captain. Metatron is crawling with Black Hats and Hulgismen. They are clamoring for your blood. They are here against my wishes. I apologize for earlier using the word "capture," sir. I should have said "shelter." I could shelter you, offer a bit of hospitality whilst we await the arrival of your Fleet.>

"I am fine. Yes, excellent, I was hoping to run into a Black Hat or two." The air whistled through his mouth as he tried to talk.

<Indeed, I've heard. Got yourself a Black Hat pet, a girlfriend. You intend to add another, create yourself a harem of adoring Black Hats? I must say, you have dash.>

"Thank you."

Steadying himself, holding his CARG, Davage looked down and Sighted. Far below, through the smattering of clouds and the dead dry light of Mirendra. He saw the craggy layout of Metatron in clear sight.

And there, as he saw clearly from orbit, was a silver pyramid rising up amid the black, windowless buildings, huddled alleys, and dreary byways of the central town overlooking a dank body of dark water.

Sygillis's temple. Five thousand feet high. Turned to silver.

<Do not approach the Silver Temple unless death is what you seek. That place is out of my control. It is under the gaze of the Black Abbess. Bear you west, and I will meet you with food and safe lodgings.>

"Excellent, I was looking forward to seeing her again."

<Again?>

"Yes, I found her most pleasant the first time."

<Though you be my master and accursed enemy, I find I like you, Captain. You are a man I can deal with.>

"Really, and what sort of deal would you like to make?"

<I am certain you can pre-determine what I want.>

"And I am certain you can pre-determine what my answer will be."

A layer of icy clouds whizzed by. Davage, without needing his Sight, could now clearly see the Silver Temple and the towers of Metatron surrounding it. It was a hard thing to miss. He could also see there was a great mass clamoring at its base—a dark army trying to breach its walls.

He Sighted the mass. There, mixed in among the seething darkness, he saw ten Black Hats scattered about, their red robes standing out clearly in his Sight.

He saw black Shadow tech giants pounding its sloped silver sides. Black spiders, dripping Shadow tech venom, bit into the walls.

They'd brought the band, he guessed, for this massive attack.

And then he saw something strange. The black spiders appeared to have punched a hole though the walls of the temple. As they began to climb into the hole, he saw a barrage of silver bolts come out of the temple's interior, throwing the spiders back. Then he thought he saw silver things emerge from the hole, flying, like specs of silver dust. They then went back through the hole and it sealed behind them.

He hadn't properly Sighted the event, but he was sure he'd seen it.

He suddenly felt his insides blanch. He remembered that feeling—when Syg had first looked at him with her doll-like evil eyes. Strange, how differently he felt when she looked at him now.

He was in the gaze of a Black Hat; he could feel it.

<You are attacked, Captain.>

Davage looked. He could see a twisting black streak heading right for him with speed—a blast of Shadow tech from one of the Hammers, roaring up through the heights.

No time for courtesy or modesty, Davage was going to need all of his Gifts, though he hated using them. He felt it a rude thing to do, but this was no time to be demure.

He Wafted away about a hundred feet farther north, and the Shadow tech blast sailed past. He Sighted down and saw the Black Hat who was attacking him. She was standing alone near the far end of a dark platform, south of the temple. Several Hulgismen stood near her—naked and filthy. A dark waterfall rumbled into a canal nearby. He could see her Sten field shimmering. He saw through her black sash—once again a small, pretty girl with pale skin. Her hair was fawn-colored and cut into a rather roundish shape. She had high cheekbones, and small brown eyes. The usual Shadow mark darkened her right eye. A little mole stood out on her left cheek.

She was without a doubt a Hammer, ready to fight, ready to kill. She seemed rather businesslike as she proceeded with the attack.

Here we go again, he thought. He was going to be one on one with a Black Hat, only this time he was in open combat and at a distance—right in her killing field.

He thought of Syg. He sorely wished she was here at his side, and not because of her fearsome power but because he simply wanted her. He wanted to be in her quarters, in her arms. The smell of her skin. The smell of coffee in the air. The feel of her tiny body next to his. Would that make her happy, he wondered, that she was slowly coming to dominate his thoughts?

The Black Hat moved the towering blast of Shadow tech, trying to envelop him in its deadly darkness. Like a living tornado, it roared toward him again.

Again, he Wafted. It passed by.

Davage's plummet was entering its tenth minute; he guessed he was only a few miles above the ground now.

<Captain,> Ergos said again in his mind. *<Allow me to help you. Let us bargain before you are consumed—before I can help you no more.>*

"No bargains, Ergos," Davage said, again Wafting to avoid the Shadow tech.

<You cannot stand here. There are ten Black Hats in the immediate area and hundreds of Hulgismen in defense, along with an army of Shadow tech beasts.>

"Watch and be educated. I am about to make a bold statement here."

And so it began.

The Black Hats maintained a fearsome reputation and were considered by most to be invincible in battle, that only the Sisterhood could equal them in a fight. It was a belief that Davage himself once harbored.

But in his various "battles" with Syg, turning her from an evil, remorseless creature to the smiling lady she was today, he had learned a great deal about Black Hats and how to attack them.

He now knew they were far from invincible.

The Black Hats were truly daunting opponents, and Hammers, like the one attacking him now, were fully capable of battling whole legions at once. The problem was that Davage wasn't a legion—he was one man, one lone opponent.

He was one lone opponent who wasn't going to play by their rules, and the rules were everything.

The column of twisting, roaring Shadow tech came again, and again Davage Wafted away from it. Such a thing could surely annihilate a mass of people, an army, a large ship, but it could never hit a single person who could simply, leisurely Waft away. It was too big, too noisy, and too slow. Some sort of winged, fanged Shadow tech beast would surely do much better.

He Sighted the flailing column and observed its interior.

In watching Syg discharge her Shadow tech, he had learned a great deal about it as well. A full, powerful charge of Shadow tech moved with fluidic life; it frothed like the bubbling head of a good buncked mug of narva. But as the charge wound down, as its presence became less and less within the Black Hat's body, its consistency changed, became more airy, more indistinct, like a storm cloud.

He noticed that this blast of Shadow tech was, certainly enough, becoming more and more cloudlike. She was running out …

Perfect, perfect. It was time to fight. It was time to save this Black Hat whether she liked it or not. Davage's ancestors, the Vith, with their Gifts of the Mind, were often called mortal gods, and it was time for him to lay all modesty aside and show what he could do. It was time to fight. With a whoosh, he unsaddled his CARG and long Wafted out of sight.

7

BETHRAEL OF MOANE

He reappeared about twenty feet in front of the Black Hat. He landed catlike, on all fours, his CARG laid out flat on the grungy brown surface, the heights of the silver pyramid rising up in the gloom behind him, its silvery light making the lightless black buildings near it appear rather olive in hue.

The Black Hat stopped her Shadow tech blast and looked at him a moment. Again, Davage had the advantage. Black Hats, it seemed, never expected to be attacked, to be met in battle by any save the Sisters. She expected Davage to either be in full flight or be on his knees, begging.

Not this, not this at all. She hesitated, confused.

Time to give her another shock. He Wafted again, only this time he appeared right in front of her, just past the end of her Sten field, which he could see clearly.

"Well met, ma'am. Captain Davage at your service," he said.

The Black Hat took a step back, flabbergasted. She extended her Sten field, hoping to catch him in its shocking embrace, leaving him senseless.

Davage, fully able to see the field, Wafted through it. Now he was in close with the Black Hat—oh the things that must be going through her mind.

And Davage knew where to hit her; he knew where it hurt. He reared up with his long, heavy CARG and slammed it down on the instep of her right foot—right into the Dora.

She let out an audible cry and fell to the ground, dropping her Sten field.

Then, there were the Hulgismen … ten of them, in a fury. The first to approach was CARGed from head to naked groin, his steaming remains slopping in a hideous mash to ground. The second was shot between the eyes from Davage's drawn MiMs pistol. Still, as far as raw bestiality goes, the Hulgismen were superb—fearless, brutal, fast, and strong. The third picked Davage up and threw him to the filthy ground, knocking away his MiMs, the small, elegant gun with its enameled surface standing out in the dust. He picked Dav back up to dash him down again, but Dav, forced to use his final gift, the Strength, brought his fists together on the Hulgisman's uncombed head—his skull collapsed in a spray of shattered bone and brain pulp.

A group of five came directly at him, hoping to overwhelm him in numbers.

Time to use another weapon—the secret weapon. Davage had noted that the direct glowing gaze of his Sight always seemed to have a mesmerizing effect on both Black Hats and Hulgismen alike. He recalled Syg's reaction, the wonder that she had for it. Hath also found his glowing eyes enchanting. His Sight seemed to take the starch out of any who beheld his glowing eyes.

He Sighted them, and they stopped, transfixed.

Davage didn't wait. He swung his CARG with a broad cutting stroke—it made the usual high-pitched whine characteristic of a killing swing. All five were cut in two, lost in his Sight … now dead. Blood again mingled the dry, dusty ground.

With two raging Hulgismen left, Davage saw the Black Hat rise, limping slightly on her right foot.

Just then, the sixth aspect of Dav's Sight began to take hold, the rarest aspect of all.

With it he could see several seconds into the future.

This aspect took him years of practice and study to master. It was a confusing thing to exist in the present yet see things that will shortly happen. It was dangerously easy to get lost in one's own Sight. But as its master, he had a tremendous advantage over his foes, and it was an advantage he was going to put to use.

He saw the Black Hat, furious, sweeping the area clear with a wave of her arm and a blast of Shadow tech.

Dav, waiting for the precise moment, Wafted away.

The sweeping blast came, killing the last two Hulgismen and leveling several dark buildings beyond. They came down in a noisy heap, black dust and soot rising, shattered blocks of stone splashing into the shallow water.

Davage reappeared next to the Black Hat to her right, intending to knock her in the foot again. This time, though, she was more ready. Quick as lightning, she roped him about the neck with a Shadow Tech brand. The dark material, fully enraged and in agony, was hideous to the touch and unbearable. He recalled when Syg had roped him that night in her old quarters—oh, that was a sore topic. You never brought that up. It was, obviously, a very painful memory for her, one that she had no interest in reliving.

Stuck in this horrid embrace, Davage knew he only had moments to act. Lighting up, he Sighted the Black Hat fully in his gaze. As before, the Black Hat stopped what she was doing and stared at his eyes, trying to comprehend what she was seeing. He could feel the power of the Shadow tech falter a bit.

The Black Hat gasped.

With a whistling crack, he slammed his CARG down on her wrist with a non-cutting blow, shattering it and her forearm as well. She screamed in agony and released him.

Whirling around, Davage, with full Strength, laid a double back-fist to the side of her face and temple. What might people say, he wondered, hitting this tiny woman with a full strength blow that he wouldn't feel good using on a much bigger, tougher person, like Kilos?

Still, he had to be sure; he needed this Black Hat out of the picture.

She fell in a heap and did not stir. Saddling his CARG, Captain Davage stood triumphant over her—not in recent memory had a Black Hat been defeated in battle by any other than a Sister.

Looking down, he Sighted: heart rate and blood pressure greatly reduced, breathing shallow—she was unconscious, no faking. Her right arm was a disaster, he noted with a bit of shame. More alarmingly, he saw her head was in bad shape. Her skull was cracked, her temple was bleeding internally, and her jaw was broken. She would need medical attention and soon.

"I am so very sorry, ma'am," he said, gently picking her up. "I hope you will forgive me later."

He took a moment to survey the situation. Most of the dark forces in the immediate area were still focused on the Silver Temple in the distance. They clamored up its sides and pounded on it with huge black fists. Many of the Black Hats were concentrating on controlling their creations—concentrating on the attack.

He looked back to the shattered buildings beyond that the Black Hat had destroyed, soot, smoke of crushed stone. He saw no survivors in the wreckage. Such was life in a Xaphan city, standing tall one moment, wreckage the next.

So, here he was, ignored for the moment, in Metatron. What should his next course of action be? He knew the *Seeker*, with its spine broken, needed to dry dock for repairs. It could not re-enter the atmosphere without breaking in two. They could send a landing force in ripcars, but that will be dangerous, and the Black Hats will pick them off en mass. What they should do is patch up and Stellar Mach to a nearby outpost—Fretlocke would do nicely. There, they could call in a fleet and return battle ready—Arrow Shot, Marines, Sisters, the whole works.

He guessed such an activity will take two, possibly three days.

He scanned the bleak amber sky …

He looked down at the tiny Black Hat, the lady he had almost killed in battle. He wondered if she had that long.

Far away, Shadow tech blasts rocked off of the Silver Temple.

*   *   *   *   *

"Give me one good reason why I shouldn't knock every damn tooth out of your mouth right now!" Sygillis yelled.

She was standing in Davage's office. Kilos sat behind his desk, a load of report viewers in front of her awaiting signature. The Com panel was lighting up. Kilos was busy tapping buttons.

"Lieutenant, Engineering," a voice came, "We are 97 percent positive containment."

"I want 100 percent within the hour," Kilos barked.

"Aye, ma'am!"

Kilos looked up from her work at Sygillis, annoyed. "So you want to fight, do you? Back to the gym for another go? If I wasn't so busy, I'd take you up on it. I feel like hitting something right now."

"How could you? *How could you leave him?*" Syg shrieked.

"I had my orders. They were clear."

The Com again. "Lieutenant, Navigation. We are listing hard a-port and venting."

"Containment will be restored within the hour. I want a counter flood to compensate, mark fifteen of 4:00 AM, understood?"

"Aye, Lieutenant! We are moving .25 percent Stellar Mach away from the Mirendra theatre and stable only in the positive."

"Maintain bearing and slow once Engineering has effected re-spar."

Sygillis, losing patience, slammed her fist down hard on the desk—it shuddered. The Com jumped.

Kilos stood up. "I disobeyed him once. I swore I'd never do it again. He ordered his ship made safe, his crew. I carried his orders out; otherwise we'd be sunk."

"When will we be returning to Metatron to rescue him?"

The Com again. "Lieutenant, Boatswain's Mate. Ma'am—we are losing life support on Deck 10, section seven. Too many breaches!"

"Evacuate the area and seal."

"Aye!"

Kilos turned back to Syg. "We're not. We'll be taking Stellar Mach to a convenient outpost once we're resparred. I recon Outpost 77 at Fretlocke is the best choice. There we'll call in a—"

Sygillis seethed with frustration. "So, you're a gutless coward are you, Ki?" Syg said curtly.

That was it—she had had it. Kilos threw down the report she was holding.

"DON'T YOU—DON'T YOU … FOR ONE MOMENT! HE IS MY CAPTAIN, MY MENTOR … MY DEAREST FRIEND … AND FOR A HELL OF A LOT LONGER THAN YOU'VE BEEN AROUND! HE'S SAVED MY LIFE MORE TIMES THAN I CAN RECALL!"

Kilos took off her Marine coat. *"IF YOU'D LIKE TO FIGHT, SYG, WHY BOTHER WITH THE GYM … RIGHT HERE SUITS ME FINE!"*

Sygillis threw her blue shawl aside and kicked off her sandals. She lifted her fists and assumed a fighting stance.

They began to circle.

The door chimed and came open. Ennez walked in.

"Lieutenant Kilos," he said, "I've got a problem needing tending, immediately," the popcorn-haired Hospitaler said.

"Not now, Ennez," Kilos snarled.

"Yes, now," he said. He stepped aside, and with a gentle motion, pulled Helmsman Saari into the office.

Saari was a wreck, crying in wracking spasms, her face red and puffy, her blue hair a tangle.

Kilos looked at Saari. She remembered her struggling at the helm right before Dav got sucked out. "What is this?" she asked Ennez.

"Lieutenant, you need to talk to her," he said.

"I'm busy …" she said looking at Syg, wanting to sock her one.

Ennez stared at her hard. He wasn't going anywhere; she could see that. She sighed.

"Crewman!" Kilos said "You are at attention. Snap to!"

Slowly, Saari came to attention, tears streaming down her face onto her Fleet crewman's uniform, a simple white shirt, black, stripeless pants, and black boots.

"That's a bit better," Kilos said. "Now, what's this all about?"

Saari, lips trembling, spoke. "My fault … my fault … My fault he's gone. I couldn't … I couldn't turn the wheel … I didn't understand …"

Kilos looked at Saari, and her hard, angry heart softened a bit. Davage had given her an order, and she couldn't carry it out. Now the ship was smashed, now he was gone, and the guilt was consuming her.

What would Dav do ... what would he say? Here was Helmsman Saari, a green kid from a Science Ministry family, a basketcase because she couldn't fly the ship like Dav could, and since Ennez was here, she was probably suicidal.

What would Dav say? Frankly, she had no idea.

Kilos thought a moment.

"Crewman, how long have you been a helmsman?"

"T-two years, Lieutenant," she sobbed.

"And if I am correct, you are of the House Fallz? The Lady Branna is your mother, yes? Lady Branna of the Science Ministry?"

"Yes ..."

"Indeed, I can see her face in you. A fine Science Ministry line. Why are you a Fleet helmsman and not an understudy in the Ministry, if I may ask?"

"Be ... because my mother told me of the Battle of Mirendra 3. She told me stories of Captain Davage and how he flew. I wanted to do that ... I wanted to fly like he does. I wanted to turn the wheel."

"Crewman, Captain Davage has been turning that wheel for over a hundred years. He can do things with it that none, besides himself, could ever hope to perform."

"I ... I ... I failed him ... I failed the ship."

"I seem to recall that you successfully followed all of my subsequent commands."

Saari sniffled and listened.

"I seem to recall that you flew the ship out of the atmosphere with a broken back and with enemy ships all about. That's no small task. If there is blame to be handed out, then blame Captain Davage. He always tries for the clean escape, the impossible maneuver that nobody other than he could perform, and he should have ordered you something more manageable and accepted the glancing blow."

Saari seemed to cheer a bit.

"And I will be depending on you when we return to Ergos."

"Return?"

"Of course. We need to save Captain Davage, don't we? You don't want to leave him there in Metatron, do you?"

"He's not dead?" she said, hope glittering into her voice.

"Of course he's not dead; don't be silly. What's a long fall to a Blue Lord who can Waft? He's probably creating so much chaos down there right now that they'll be glad to be rid of him once we effect his rescue. And just imagine his pride as he looks up into the sky and sees the *Seeker* soaring into view, to his aid ... with you at its helm. He's going to want to know who that fine pilot was, and I will be happy to tell him."

Saari wiped her face. "I ... I will be ready, ma'am. You can count on me."

Kilos smiled. "Your mother will be most proud. Now, go freshen up, agreed?"

"Aye, Lieutenant!"

Ennez nodded and followed her out.

Kilos sighed and sat down on the edge of her desk. She wiped a tear from her face.

Sygillis approached and sat next to her, her bare feet dangling where Ki's firmly touched the ground.

They sat in silence for a while.

"I'm ... I'm sorry, Ki," Syg said quietly after a moment. "I didn't mean to be so angry ... to add to your troubles."

"You needn't apologize, Syg. You simply want him back as much as I do. It's frustrating, it's maddening, knowing he's down there, all alone, struggling for survival."

Her Com began chattering again. Kilos looked back at it. "I can't do this ... He makes it look so damn easy."

"You did an excellent job with the Helmsman just now. And like you pointed out to her, he's been at this for a good long while."

"I suppose so. Thank you. Look, why don't you head to your quarters and get some rest. I'll call if anything comes up."

Syg choked up and began crying into her hands. "I can't go to my quarters—because he won't be there."

Kilos put her arm around Syg, and they sat in silence for another moment.

"So, what are we going to do?" Syg asked. "How are we going to get him back?"

"I don't know. Everything I previously told you is true … our back is broken, we need support. We can't save him in our current condition. We might need rescuing ourselves if we lose anymore systems."

"What's broken, what needs fixing? Tell me."

"We've got broken containment everywhere, we're listing a-starboard, we've rocketed out of the system, out of control for the most part, and our main spar is snapped clean in two. We can't make sail and navigate without tearing ourselves apart."

"Well, I do not rightly know what you just said, but maybe I can help."

"How so? Are you wanting to became a boatswain now?"

"No, no—I don't know what that is, but show me what needs fixing and I will repair it."

Kilos looked at Syg. "And how are you going to—"

Sygillis lifted her left hand and made a halo of Silver tech.

"Come on," she said jumping off the desk, "let's fix this ship and let's save Dav!"

*   *   *   *   *

Davage had taken the fallen Black Hat and hidden in a dark alcove between two dismal buildings. There, in momentary safety, he removed her black sash. Her face was small and serene. She almost appeared to be asleep, her little mole standing out in the dim light. He noted the Shadowmark around her right eye was a very different shape than Syg's, softer and more gentle. He found a tuberous piece of Ergos nearby and splinted her arm with it.

He carefully removed the horrible Dora shoes and threw them aside. Her feet were certainly swollen, but they were in no way as bad as Syg's feet were. He tore some strips of cloth from her robe and wrapped her feet as best he could.

When he finished, he noticed she had regained consciousness. She looked at him not with the evil, murderous gaze that Syg had, but with small, fearful eyes.

She looked terrified. A Black Hat scared?

"Please, ma'am," he said as he worked. "Rest easy."

"My head, my arm …" she said, lisping slightly, her jaw broken.

Davage took her by her good hand. "Don't try to move. Your arm is broken, and I've hurt your jaw. I am sorry. I will get you medical attention as soon as I am able to do so, I promise. I will not abandon you."

"You … faced me in battle. You defeated me. You bathed me in a strange light. Why am I still alive?" Her little mole stood out on her face.

Davage, ever ready to draw his CARG should it be needed, stroked her sweaty brown hair. "This might seem a bit odd to you, ma'am, but I am trying to help you."

"Help me?"

"Yes. I am sorry I had to do what I did to you. Perhaps someday you will see fit to forgive me. I look forward to that day."

He wiped the sweat from her brow. "What is your name?"

"B-Bethrael of Moane."

He was quite shocked at how compliant and forthcoming she was. Maybe, as Syg had previously mentioned, she had been a pretty hard case.

"Well met, Bethrael of Moane. I am Captain Davage, of the League Main Fleet Vessel *Seeker*. I am pleased to have made your acquaintance …"

Her eyes rolled back in her head, and she fell into unconsciousness once again. She shivered. Davage picked her up and tried to warm her.

In the distance he could see the Silver Temple, still under attack from the black hordes. As before, he saw a small hole open in the side of the temple at its heights. Again, silver sparks flew out and then the hole closed.

Davage and the fallen Black Hat were no longer alone in the alcove.

<Well now,> Ergos said, *<I am impressed. That was a spectacular display, Captain, as you promised.>*

Ergos stepped out of the shadows—a projection of his mind. He assumed his usual guise—the fat fop, bald, in garish clothing.

<I had no idea you could be so bloodthirsty and vicious, Captain. This Black Hat had no chance.>

"I did what I did—I take no pleasure in it. She had to be quieted. I'm glad she survived."

<She appears to be in poor shape, Captain. She will need medical attention soon if you are to add her to your growing harem.>

"I am not acquiring a harem, sir. I am simply trying to help this woman. I am trying to assist her in becoming an Elder."

A second entity joined them in the crowded alcove.

< To help a Black Hat find herself? You are the height of wit and lunacy, Captain.>

Davage looked. An image of Demona of Ryel stepped out of the shadows. Her crisp uniform was as black and tidy as ever. Her brown hair was tied up.

"Loviatar," Davage said. "This isn't you usual guise."

<No, but I know you are fond of this form,> the image said.

"What do you two want? I am, most certainly, busy."

<We want to bargain, Captain. We starve here. Can you not see that?>

<Deluum has died. My poor Deluum,> Loviatar moaned.

Davage picked Bethrael up and headed to the edge of the alcove. "Yes, and how many friends did I lose at Mirendra? Perhaps you should have thought of that before setting yourselves in a final attack against us here. Perhaps you should not have listened to Princess Marilith."

<What do you expect of us? We want to live.>

"We offered you a star … one of our own creation. But you wanted dying to go along with it. You betrayed us, and now here you are. Deluum dead."

<We realize our mistake. We will agree to your star, provided it is of the correct composition. Make one for us. Make it bright and true and we will live there, by your leave. We will dream again. Our cities will light up again.>

Davage thought a moment. He felt for Deluum, despite himself. "Should I survive this ordeal I will take your proposal to the Admiralty and argue on your behalf. I promise you that, though I cannot predict their response."

Loviatar's Demona image approached Davage and gently touched his shoulder. *<Then, as a sweetener, let us assist you.>*

"I do not need your help. As I have said, the Stellar Fleet will be here shortly."

<To that,> Loviatar said. *<Allow us to bring you up to date, Captain. You will be pleased to learn that your first officer was successful in getting your vessel out of orbit. However, your vessel is in a bad state.>*

Ergos continued. *<Your engineer is unable to contain all of the hull breaches due to the torque pressures on your twained spar. They cannot assume Stellar Mach, nor can they change course.*

<They are essentially dead in space, hundreds of years from the nearest outpost without the benefit of Stellar Mach. Additionally, without your expert leadership, the Fleet and Marine factions onboard are beginning to grate upon each other. In short, nothing is happening on your vessel.>

Davage listened and could hear the truth in what they were saying. He had always been able to work well with the Marines—his first officer was a Marine, after all. His engineer, Mapes, Lord of Grenville, could be an arrogant man if not properly motivated and tasked. He was certainly a Grenville, but he was a good engineer. He wondered if he would accept orders from Kilos, a Brown Marine lieutenant. A person of no social standing at all.

His heart sank.

<All is not lost. Allow us to offer you this tip. Your salvation lies beyond, in the Silver Temple,> Loviatar said.

"I recall your warning against approaching the Silver Temple."

<Indeed,> Ergos said. *<But you chose not to listen to us, and here you are, out of our grasp and in the gaze of the Black Abbess. There's nothing for it at this point but to complete your foolish journey and enter the Silver Temple. We cannot lift you away, for the Black Abbess is watching. We cannot cross the Black Abbess.>*

Davage thought he could hear a roaring sound.

<Avast! You are attacked, Captain! The Silver Temple—we will speak again there.>

A column of Shadow tech slammed into the buildings surrounding Davage and the fallen Black Hat.

The alcove exploded in a raging funnel of black.

8

LORD MAPES OF GRENVILLE

The man in the massive engineering bay was wearing a Fleet uniform, the usual elaborate blue coat with gold ivy, frilly shirt, boots, black pants, and large triangle hat. He wore the scarlet sash for the Engineering Division decorated with devices and Fleet ribbons. Syg had come to associate the uniform with Davage, though his sash was black. She loved the uniform. She loved the way Davage looked in it.

But this man wasn't Davage.

He stared at her with prying gray eyes, looking her up and down, regarding her, calculating ... coveting. He made no attempt to disguise the fact that Sygillis, still in the habit of wearing her black Hospitaler Chancellor's bodysuit, was very much to his liking.

On the way to Engineering, Kilos had warned Syg about him: Commander Mapes, Lord of Grenville, Chief Engineer.

"He's a marvelous engineer, Mapes is, but he's certainly a Grenville, the younger brother to Lord Sixtus Grenville."

"That means nothing to me," Syg had said.

"It means he can be a pompous ass and makes it a point to be so. Five years ago when our old engineer, Commander Penderline, took command of the *New Britain*, Mapes was appointed as the new Chief Engineer—a surprise move knowing how the Grenvilles can't stand Dav, his castle, or his family to boot."

"How did that happen?"

"Blue maneuverings—social stuff, politics. Ask Dav, I try not to bother in such things."

"I would love to ask Dav something, anything right now."

"Anyway, the end result was that Dav was stuck with Mapes, brother of his archrival. It was gossiped that Lord Grenville was trying to take control of the *Seeker*. But Dav being Dav, he was able to win Mapes over to some extent, and it worked out in the end. Mapes is a talented engineer."

"Dav is able to control him?"

"He is. But we don't have Dav right now, do we? Remove Dav, and he's prone to arrogance and insubordination. He will, doubtless, challenge my command as first officer because I'm a pathetic Brown, and he'll see you as nothing more than a beautiful woman to make trophy out of."

"He may say what he pleases, as long as we achieve results. I am anxious to get Dav back as soon as possible."

When they entered Engineering, there was a great bustle of people moving about here and there. The smell of burning metal filled the air.

Mapes, resplendent in his Fleet uniform, stood by the rails and surveyed the situation. Becoming aware of visitors, he slowly turned.

"Ah, Lieutenant Kilos of the Stellar Marines, I was wondering when you would be arriving down here."

"What is our current status, Commander?" she asked.

"Status? Is it not obvious?"

"Please answer my question."

"Status, if you must know, is not operational. Life support is maintained, breaches controllable as long as the ship does not alter course. Any movement or pressure on the spar and we will go into breach afresh."

"When will we be re-sparred and fit to travel?"

Mapes shook his head. "We will not be re-sparred. The spar is in twain, and we've not the materials on hand to dock it. We must send word to the Fleet and tow to dry-dock."

"We must re-spar, Commander. Otherwise, we will not be able to effect a rescue of the captain on Ergos."

"I'm afraid the captain is lost. We will not be re-sparred without a proper dry-dock and a team of craftsmen in attendance."

"Mapes, I have brought Sygillis here to—"

"I do not care a moment's notice who you have brought, Marine. We will not be re-sparred, as I have said. You are lucky we have managed containment thus far."

"I am in command on this vessel, and I am ordering you to—"

"Issuing orders are you? If you have an ounce of sense available to you, you will lay down your claims to command and allow the Fleet to attend to our situation."

"I am the first officer of this ship, Marine or not, and you will accept my orders in the captain's absence or I will have you clapped in irons."

A passing group of Marines heard the conversation and moved in behind Kilos. They were fuming.

Mapes regarded them with scorn. "Get your frothing rabble out of my engineering bay at once, Brown-head!"

The Marines muttered to themselves in a low growl.

Kilos's right eye twitched with rage at the insult. "You are about to be knocked on your Blue backside, Grenville."

"That is Lord Grenville to you. You should know your place."

A few Fleet crewmen lined up behind Mapes.

It appeared the peace Davage had so easily kept over the years was about to fall apart in a bad way.

Sygillis stepped forward. "Lieutenant, Commander, please," she said. "This bickering is a fruitless waste of time. We've a ship that needs repairing, and we've a captain who needs immediate rescue. I am certain it is in all of our mutual interests to recover him as soon as possible. Please, Lord Grenville, we have come to assist in the repairs required to make this vessel whole once again."

Mapes looked long and hard at Sygillis. His eyes moved up and down her small, fit frame. "Well met, madam." He bowed. "You must be Lady Sygillis, our captain's esteemed guest."

His eyes smoldered beneath his large hat. He seemed to take notice of the Blanchefort belt Syg was wearing.

"The captain has done me a great disservice. I had no inkling that you were such a … handsome … lady of standing. I am sorry that you have been smothered up to this point by the captain … the Blancheforts, you see. I assure you that much more tasteful company abounds."

"Sir," she said, "time is of the essence. We have come to assist you in repairing this vessel. Please, could you—"

"And how could a, lovely lady such as yourself, assist me in the serious repairs ahead, hmmm?"

"I am wanting to fix the problem, the what is it—the Main Spar?"

Mapes doubled over with laughter. His crew followed suit.

Syg and Kilos looked at each other in disbelief.

"Sir," Syg said in a dangerous voice, "I am most certainly not joking. I intend to repair this ship, for it seems that you cannot or are unable to do so."

Mapes stopped laughing and stood bolt straight up—he towered over her. He fumed.

He went to say something.

Sygillis spoke over him, the Dirge hard in her voice. "*Now*," she Dirged, "*You will be good enough to show me this spar machination, and you will show me and Lieutenant Kilos exactly what needs to be done to correct what ails it.*"

Her Dirge voice banged around the bay, fierce and strong. Mapes's crewmen, enraged, made to advance on Syg, and she was quickly surrounded by the Marines in a defensive combat box, just as they did for a Sister in their charge. They were ready to defend Syg to the death. The irony.

Mapes, Dirged, began walking, his staff eyeing Syg angrily. The Marines stared them down, ready for a fight.

"You have set the Dirge to a Lord of Grenville," he hissed on the march. "I'll see you executed for this, Lady Sygillis," he said, his body moving of its own accord.

Sygillis snapped back, her mastery of the Dirge allowing her to talk and hold it at the same time. "And, if anything happens to Captain Davage as a result of this childish delay, Mapes, I will kill you myself as many times and in as many ways possible. Pray you, sir, that he returns to my arms safe and unharmed, for woe to you should he not. *Lead the way, sir, and you need not speak until we arrive.*"

In a shuffling mumbling mass, they exited the bay.

∗   ∗   ∗   ∗   ∗

Davage seized the limp form of Bethrael of Moane and Wafted out of the alcove. A whirling fist of black Shadow tech shattered it, grinding stone into dust and making the ground shake.

He re-appeared about a hundred yards south of the alcove on a flat plain, approaching the temple.

He was panting, winded. Wafting while holding another, even a tiny person like Bethrael, was an exhausting labor. He needed a moment.

Looking back he saw a Black Hat approaching his position. He noted, even at this distance, that she was a good deal taller that most of the Black Hats he'd ever seen—she appeared to be almost as tall as Kilos.

His Sight began to take over.

He saw himself and this Black Hat in hand to hand combat. He saw a huge black battle axe.

She seemed to have no Hulgismen, for none were in the immediate area, and she seemed much wiser as far as fighting with a lone opponent.

And that will make her his most dangerous adversary yet.

She raised her hand, and a scintillating black battle axe formed. It was huge. When she raised her arm, it seemed to tower over her, thirty, forty, fifty feet in the amber air. With her other hand, she formed a withering black whip that cracked and hissed.

She was going to fight him one to one. He wondered, given her power and apparent skill, if he would survive.

He laid Bethrael down and un-saddled his CARG, stretching it out to a manageable fighting length of four and a half feet.

Further underscoring this particular Black Hat's skill, he noted that she was moving around. Most Black Hats tended to stand still when they fought. Obviously, their Dora were a painful impediment. This one closed in, moving easily, gracefully, ignoring the pain she was in.

She raised her battle axe; it climbed to towering heights.

It came down in a whistling arc.

Davage rolled to his left and felt it bite deep into the dirty plain behind him, lifting dirt and rock and bits of Ergos into the dull air. He lunged forward and swung his CARG around. It impacted with a heavy thud against her left foot—the Dora again.

The Black Hat didn't make a sound and didn't fall. Instead, she hauled back and lashed him across the back with her black whip. As he recoiled in agony, she picked him up using a simple TK and mashed him into the ground. Again, her skill at in-fighting was superb. She ignored the usual Black Hat Weapons, the Point, the Mass, the Sten and so on, and used the things that worked—quick, easy TKs, Shadow tech weapons, and her bare hands,

In an instant she was on him. She cast aside her unwieldy battle axe in these close quarters and slammed him in the kidneys with two Full Strength blows—her fists having the characteristic "stony" feel to them. He could hear her grunting as she hit him. She then reared up and drove the heel of her right Dora into his shoulder. Searing pain ripped through him as she twisted it around.

Reveling in the moment, she dropped her TK and tried to rope him with her Shadow tech whip—too slow, Davage pounced. Rolling to his left, he hooked her legs and sent her rocketing, robe and sash, to the ground. Using his own Full Strength, he smashed her across the throat and then followed up with a solid thudding blow to the jaw, sending her reeling.

Time for the Secret Weapon. He saddled his CARG, jumped on top of her, and lit his Sight, waiting for her to become lost in it.

She was ready; she must have been watching him fight Bethrael. She covered her eyes and blasted him off of her with a brutal Sten—the fastest he'd ever seen created.

Stenned hard and accordingly stunned, he flew back and landed in the black dust near Bethrael and didn't move.

*   *   *   *   *

The angry, muttering contingent of Fleet and Marines entered the half-moon-shaped maintenance bay in the "saddle" of the neck—oaths, curses, and insults being exchanged back and forth as they went. Nobody other than Fleet engineering members came here. Kilos had never even seen the place.

"Here, damn you," Mapes said, thoroughly enraged, his voice echoing through the chamber. "Here's the damn spar."

Sygillis looked around. The bay was long and dark, full of access panels, terminals, nodes, and bulkheads. It was all so bewildering for her, all this stuff. She allowed herself to momentarily admire Mapes for fully grasping all of this.

She looked up. Overhead, high above was a long series of stout metal bars and struts all linked together into an intricate, semi-solid mass. It gave her the impression of a backbone—the monstrous backbone of some huge, ephemeral creature.

It looked strong—unmovable. How could such a thing be broken?

"Is this it, Mapes? Is this the spar you mention?" Syg asked.

"It is," he spat, still locked in her Dirge.

"What is wrong with it?"

"It's broken, snapped in twain."

"It does not appear broken," she said, looking at it, trying to understand.

"Not here, Nimrod!" he shouted. "At Js 7 and 8, the next compartment forward."

"*We shall go there, then, and you will show me,*" she Dirged.

Mapes began moving. He looked terrified.

"We can't go in there—that compartment's breached, open to naked space. You'll kill us all," he shrieked on the march.

Syg's heart sank. She had a momentary mind to let him keep going, to march Mapes right in there and allow him to be sucked into space.

"*Stop,*" she said finally. Dirged, Mapes stopped walking and looked relieved.

She looked up at the spar again and followed it forward with her eyes. It disappeared beyond a bulkhead and apparently continued on unseen.

This thing was Dav's salvation, she thought. She mustn't give up.

THE LEAGUE OF ELDER

"So, through there is where the repair is needed, correct?" She pointed forward.

"Yes, tis as I have said. Now, release me at once!"

She took a deep breath and took off her blue shawl. She let it fall to the floor.

Again, she could feel Mapes eyes all over her. She didn't like it. There was only one man she wanted looking at her, and he was far away, possibly struggling for life—clawing for it.

She mustn't fail him.

She reached up with her left hand and let fly a small, tentative streamer of Silver tech. It floated merrily upwards, hit the various cross members of the spar, and began coating it with silver.

"What are you doing?" Mapes asked.

Ignoring him, she continued coating the spar. She increased the flow of her silver, and soon, the entire length of the spar, its strong intricate construction, was covered.

Syg closed her eyes and smiled.

"There, yes—yes I can feel it, in the next compartment, the broken pieces of the spar, the hanging metal, the coldness of space."

"You can feel that, Syg?" Kilos asked.

"Yes—there's a great deal of metal missing, many broken sections. Yes, yes I've bridged the gap—I can feel the spar continuing on past the other side of the gap."

"What are you doing?" Mapes asked again.

"I'm fixing the spar," she said vacantly. "I'm doing your job for you."

"It is not possible to fix the spar in space. There is too much material missing, and the torque pressures…"

The ship gave a groan—of twisting metal and grinding girders.

"What are you doing?" Mapes shouted. He looked over to one of his Fleet crewmen. "Magyart, man your console there."

Magyart ran over to a terminal. He looked at the screen and tapped some buttons. "Sir, Z axis stability … is returning. It is still 150 percent below minimum stability, but it is climbing."

Mapes looked at the spar, now coated in silver. He watched Syg with an open mouth, no longer mocking or arrogant.

Sygillis added more silver to her stream. She grunted and strained. Again, the ship lurched.

"Sygillis…" some of the Marines began to chant, becoming excited in the moment. "Sygillis …"

"Ninety-seven percent of minimum and climbing!"

Mapes stared at Sygillis. "Magyart," he barked, "is it straight and true?"

"No sir, bent to the starboard at fifteen minus two Y axis."

"Lady Sygillis," Mapes said, "you must true the spar, bend it to your right and up a bit. Listen to Magyart, and he will guide you. Magyart, provide her with constant updates!"

Sygillis closed her eyes and strained. The ship gave a loud clank.

"Seventy-two percent of minimum! Eight minus two Y axis!"

"You're getting there," Mapes said. "Continue bending to your right and up."

Something appeared to break, and a huge breach opened high overhead.

"Breach!" one of the Marines yelled.

Hardly giving a second thought, Syg, with her right hand, threw up a blob of silver and plugged the hole. It flexed and held fast.

"Thirty-two percent of minimum! We are reading straight and true!"

"Lady Sygillis, stop bending. Now concentrate of shoring up the spar!" Mapes said.

She raised her other hand and joined its silver. More complaining from the ship.

"Minimum stability reached! We are straight and true and climbing to max hold!"

"Sygillis … Sygillis!" the Marines shouted.

The door to the bay opened and several Sisters came in. They looked at Syg.

One of the Marines spoke up. "What is this?" the Marine said for her.

Mapes turned to the Sisters. "Sisters, let her continue. She is correcting the spar. I know not how, but it is being done."

The Sisters watched Syg launch her silver. They were clearly confused by what they were seeing. They'd never seen Silver tech.

Magyart turned from his screen. "We are 100 percent max stable. Straight and true."

Sygillis stopped and staggered. Kilos caught her.

Released from the Dirge, Mapes went to the console and looked over the readings himself. He then took off his hat and looked up at the now-silver, shining spar, mouth open.

"Remarkable," he said.

"Are you all right, Syg?" Kilos asked.

"I'm fine ... just a little winded."

"Will this hold? Do you have to maintain it?"

"It will hold on its own."

Mapes strode toward her. "Lady Sygillis, let me assist you."

"I'm fine," she said in a harsh voice, not wanting him anywhere near her. He stopped.

Kilos turned to Mapes. "Mapes, I want this vessel sounded from tip to top and I'll expect your report at the top of the hour. If, at that time, you determine we are fit to travel, I want mark set for full revolutions back to Ergos, understood!"

"Aye, Lieutenant!" he said.

With that, Kilos, Sygillis, and the Marines left the bay. The Marines, always a boisterous lot, cheered Syg's name the whole way.

The Sisters stood about, looking up at the silver spar, arguing silently amongst themselves, debating whether such a thing was legal or not.

Mapes watched Syg leave, his eyes never leaving her. No Blanchefort was worthy of a woman like this, he thought.

*　*　*　*　*

He had one of those dreams as he lay there in the dust—one of those dreams that fully unfold and play out, yet last only a moment.

He dreamt of Syg and his castle in the summer—still a cold place in the summertime, but very bearable for the non-Blancheforts. They sat in the Telmus Grove, amid the flowers and the old Vith splendor, ready to enjoy a meal. His sisters, Poe and dear Pardock, were there, all smiles as usual. Poe was having a good day; she seemed almost normal, her affliction held at bay for the moment. Kilos and her husband were also in attendance—Mr. Kilos, the small librarian and professor from Tusck, a man whom he liked very much but rarely got to see. Kilos was out of her Marine uniform for once, lovely in a colorful summer dress.

And Syg sat next to him, her green eyes full of happiness and love.

He said something to her.

He said, "I love you ..."

<Captain, you must awake!>

The dream was over. He was pulled back from the happy scene at Blanchefort Castle to the dull, dreary, pain-filled landscape of Metatron.

What happened? His mind was lost in fog.

<Captain!>

Metatron—someone was talking to him.

Ergos, Loviatar ... or both at once?

<Your death is upon you!>

Davage opened his eyes and there, charging toward him at a howl, was the tall Black Hat, her battle axe once again in hand high over her head. She was ready to pull it down in a sickening death stroke, cleaving him in twain.

This was it.

Fully awake now, he did the only thing he could do—he lit his Sight, golden light flooding out of his eyes for possibly the last time.

Again, as before, the Black Hat covered her eyes to avoid his maddening, hypnotic gaze.

Her battle axe hitched in mid-swing.

He had a moment—a sharp second in which to act.

He un-saddled his CARG.

With both hands and an agonized shoulder, he sent it whistling upwards, a heavy coppery wave.

Copper CARG and Shadow tech battle axe met ...

9

THE CARG OF HOUSE BLANCHEFORT

The CARG had been the ancestral weapon of House Blanchefort for hundreds of years, since the time of the Elders. A novel thing, it squarely belonged to a family of weapons called LosCapricos, being of those weapons conceived in the heady time of the Elders not necessarily for functionality but instead for uniqueness, to bear a symbol for the House that created it. Each Great House had its own LosCapricos, for better or for ill. There were hundreds of them. They were afforded a special place in law. No murders could be committed with LosCapricos weapons, only noble killings, and because the Elders had a hand in their creation, they were always spelled using upper-case letters.

It was said that the CARG had originally been designed by Lennibus, Lord of Blanchefort, and it had met with the approval of the Elder Nylax himself—a rare and lofty honor.

There had been many CARGs created through the centuries, all forged by Blanchefort hands. Though the metals used and the devices varied, all CARGs were generally of the same configuration. It was a hilted, extendable, hollow metal tube, with a radius of about two and a half inches. It was usually adjustable from a fully collapsed length of two and a half feet to nine feet at full stretch. The end of the tube was always capped with either a sharp point or a gilded horn. Except for the hilt at the bottom, it was ramrod straight, like a pole, and indeed, the word CARG came from the old Vith word *cargengian,* which meant simply: long pole.

To the novice, to the unfamiliar and untrained, the CARG was nothing more than a collapsible, cylindrical metal pole with a pretty hilt at the bottom. To the touch, it was perfectly smooth, like the slippery, cool surface of a water pipe. To move it about in one's hand offered nothing more—cool and smooth.

Certainly, if used as a bludgeoning weapon, like a club or heavy bone-breaking metal bar or spear, the CARG could be thought of as an effective weapon—even a deadly one. There was no question of that.

But, place it in the hands of a master, a Blanchefort with years of training, the CARG assumed a much more deadly pose.

The apparently smooth surface of the metal tube was micro-facetted, covered with millions of tiny indentations—a Blanchefort trademark and specialty. When moved in just the right fashion, those facets engaged and severed anything they came into contact with. When moved correctly, the CARG "sang"; the frictionless cutting stroke made a whistling sound that was unforgettable.

In short, the CARG, wielded by a master, could slice through solid rock.

There were certainly a great number of the LosCapricos weapons that were so strange, so bizarre, that they could never really be considered anything more than a ceremonial weapon and symbol. The GRAMPA of House Vincent was a beautiful five-segmented axe that could be more dangerous to its wielder than to the enemy. The VERDIS of House Fallz was a bladed, jeweled net that, while elegantly macabre, was virtually impossible to use.

The CRANIMER of House Durst was not really classifiable as anything in particular, weapon or not. A collection of tubes, metal balls, and wire—no one recalled its lore. Lady Hathaline of Durst, Captain of the Fleet, often told her childhood friend, Captain Davage, that if she ever figured out how to use it, he would have to marry her—that he'd promised her. She wasn't joking either, but unfortunately, she never did solve its inscrutable mystery.

Others, though, were brilliant and quite deadly. The CEROS of House Probert was a small handheld device composed of sharp, interlocking metal arms. When thrown, it took on a life of its own—it became almost as energy and always returned to its master's hand. The BEOL of House Conwell was the famous "Wind Cannon" of old that had won many battles. The elegant VUNKULA of House Grenville was a type of belt equipped with a long, segmented tail. When the belt was worn, the tail, through means unknown, sprang to life and unerringly follow its master's commands like a third arm. The tail could be fitted with any number of attachments and could strike like lightning—Sixtus of Grenville was deadly with it. It was said he was rarely without his gold and silver VUNKULA, hidden deep under the folds of his garish clothes—never used but always ready to strike. It was said he maintained a number of hidden pockets in his coat full of powders and substances that his VUNKULA could dip into and strike for a variety of effects.

And the strangest of all: the NIGHTMARE of House Monama was a large hair pin embedded with a dark stone that was said to be able to alter reality itself.

The CARG was always considered to be in the latter category, a brilliant, deadly weapon, but for years, it seemed destined to go the way of the GRAMPA and the VERDIS and the CRANIMER—a charming, odd fixture of the past.

Sadric, Lord of Blanchefort, had learned CARG lore from his father, Maserfeld, a burly, brutish, and somewhat barbaric man who had the unfortunate but well-earned reputation for being a raider and a brigand. Always raging that his son appeared to be a bit more of a dandy than he hoped for, Maserfeld relentlessly rammed the CARG lore down Sadric's dainty, powdered throat, hoping to wrench the man from out of the silken linens and fancy shoes. Despite himself, despite his apparent frailty, Sadric learned its lore and became the CARG's master.

Sadric went one step further. He eventually delighted his father by creating the strongest CARG ever built, the King CARG, the Masterpiece CARG. He created it not because he really wanted a CARG for himself, but because Maserfeld swore to disinherit him and give everything to Herdie, Lord of Grenville, Maserfeld's archrival if he didn't. It was better, he said, to heap his wealth and titles upon an enemy than to give it to a CARGless, good-for-nothing son.

Maserfeld's CARG was a singularly ugly weapon made crudely from iron and obsidian. He'd named it "Bathilda" and never cleaned it—refused for it to be cleaned; years of gore and punctured flesh had built up on its shaft like an awful varnish.

If Sadric was to have a CARG, it would be a fine, shining, beautiful weapon. It will be something that shall look lovely saddled at his waist at a party.

It took five years to forge. On a "mission," Sadric acquired the metals for it from exotic locations. He stole the core metal for it from the Borune Mountains located on the Xaphan Loviatar, which, he had heard, was known for its great strength and best of all, pleasing color. The taking of this metal was a slight for which Loviatar swore everlasting vengeance.

More metals were needed. Sneaking into a grand Grenville ball dressed as a dark, mysterious woman, he "acquired" the hard, unyielding tip and final seven segments from Herdie of Grenville's VUNKULA and threw it in for good measure—a slight that was said to have ratcheted-up the Blanchefort-Grenville feud in earnest, for Herdie had been "smitten" by this tall, beautiful "mystery woman." More followed.

Loviatar's metal, an elegant, heavy, coppery alloy, took years to heat and properly forge. The Sisterhood of Light, with whom Sadric was very friendly, prayed over the forging and blessed it, adding strange materials of their own design. Once made, Sadric's CARG was heavy, solid, sharp, and nearly indestructible. The Grand Abbess of Pithnar, a close friend of Sadric's, placed an enchantment on it so that he could lift it with ease—to anybody else trying to pick it up, it was a monstrously heavy seventy-seven pounds.

It was beautiful. It had an odd X-shaped hilt, as the shaft of the CARG was circular, Sadric reasoned it didn't have a top or bottom. He dedicated each arm of the X to a different season. For its horn, he was inspired one evening at a wine party and created the tip of his CARG as a twisting cork-screw.

Indeed, it was that beautiful coppery CARG that first attracted the attention of Lady Hermilane, the blue-haired fourth daughter of

House Hannover, its glinting light and cork-screw catching her eye as she danced about the ballroom floor with Marist, Lord of Grenville, Herdie's son. Hermilane was one of the few ladies of standing who was a LosCapricos master in her own right—she being a master of the GEORGE WIND, a small, floating sword. Excusing herself, she went up to Sadric and inquired about his glinting CARG in earnest, forgetting all about the red-faced Lord Grenville. She, one day became Sadric's wife and bore his children—and all begun because she liked his weapon. More fire on the Blanchefort-Grenville hatred.

The King CARG had an additional quality that no CARG previously had—it could be thrown. Whirling perfectly balanced in a heavy arc, it relentlessly thudded into its target. Maserfeld roared with delight as Sadric demonstrated what it could do. You certainly couldn't throw Bathilda and expect to hit anything. It could even be thrown with a cutting stroke, a lop-sided, bouncing, cavorting arc that buried the shaft to its hilt.

It was said Maserfeld went to his grave smiling—his dainty, foolish son had created a kick-ass, flying, woman-enchanting CARG that will have their ancestors cheering and mug hoisting in the halls of the dead.

If Maserfeld had had his druthers, Sadric would have used this deadly CARG to lop off a few heads, bury it up the asses of a few cretins, and sack a few villages. Such, though, was not to be the case. Sadric never sacked any villages, never loped off any heads ... none of that. He was no warrior, no killer.

He'd only ever used it in battle once, after the birth of his second daughter Poe, when those strange, savage people came from the darkness, from thin air, and tried to take her newly born and wailing from Hermilane's arms. In that instance, he used his CARG, in that instance he fought like a lion. And those savage people fell before it.

After that, his CARG became nothing more than a ceremonial show piece. He, at his many parties, loved to delight his guests by demonstrating the CARG's power. He showed them that it was a smooth, unbladed tube. He showed them how heavy it was. He then sliced off thin, straight cross-sections of a large petrified tree stump with the CARG, the cutting stroke making its usual high-pitched whistling sound. And his guests clapped and laughed.

When his son and heir, Davage, was born, Sadric thought not to teach him how to use the CARG at all. He wished his son to be more like him, a suave society man, a man who appreciated social functions and invitations and gossip, and he felt the CARG had no place there except as an obscure decoration and coat-of-arms motif.

As Maserfeld had wanted Sadric to follow in his bloody, brigand's footsteps, so Sadric wished the same from his son.

Such, however, was not to be the case.

Davage had a lot of old Maserfeld in him—a rugged toughness and adventurous spirit, sans the lout and the brigand—that Sadric could not squelch or deny no matter how much powder and wigs and cloth finery he threw at him. Davage yearned for action and adventure, and he got it in sometimes novel places. He learned to fist fight from his sister Pardock, of all people; she also had a bit of rowdy Maserfeld in her. It was said that Davage and Pardock often snuck in disguise to the village by the bay and brawl in the bars with the locals. It was one of their favorite things to do.

His mother taught him the GEORGE WIND lore, Hermilane being deadly with it. In later years, Davage often mused that some of the most savage and desperate sword fights he'd ever been involved in were with his mother.

But Davage wanted the CARG lore. He wanted it like nothing else.

Sadric told his son that, when he could lift it, he may be trained—Sadric thinking its great weight would put a close to the matter. Unfortunately, when Davage was fourteen, he lifted it off its display stand and presented to his father. And so, Sadric relented, and in the old Vith halls of Castle Blanchefort, he taught his son how to use the CARG. He hoped that he never had to raise it in a fight. He hoped it would remain a simple party favor.

Now, on the dirty amber plains of Ergos, it would be the strength of that CARG, the King CARG, the LosCapricos symbolic weapon of House Blanchefort that was once used to delight elegant party guests, that guarded Davage's life, Sadric's only son…

* * * * *

CCCCLLLAAANNNGGG! from the CARG. AHHHHHHHH! from the Shadow tech.

CARG and black battle axe met in mid air, metal ringing and Shadow tech screaming, and both combatants were knocked off balance with the force of the blow. Panting, the Black Hat regarded Davage for a moment, astounded that this man was still alive, that his weapon had been equal to hers.

Davage Sighted; he saw her coming again.

The Black Hat plowed her battle axe through the ground in a vicious up stroke.

Davage met it and turned it aside.

She swung back around and over her head in a cleaving down stroke.

Dav met it again and turned it aside.

She stumbled with the force of the turn.

She was wide open. He could send his CARG right through her heart if he wanted.

He had it in his head that he wanted to save this Black Hat. He wanted to make another Syg—he wanted to wake the Elder within her, to watch her grow into a person, watch her learn to smile and laugh and appreciate the touch of another.

For Bethrael, lying unconscious beyond, he figured she wouldn't be too difficult to turn; she had seemed remarkably docile so far.

But this one, this tall Black Hat, she was savage and dangerous and eager to fight. Would he be taking too much of a chance with the lives of his crew if he brought her aboard? Will she blow herself sky high the first moment she got?

Should he kill her and be done with it?

She tried hooking his CARG with her battle axe, trying to rip it from his grasp.

He turned the CARG and sliced through her battle axe, the huge blade spinning off widely and turning to soot.

Before she could form a new axe, he put a brutal non-cutting shot into her ribs; he heard some of them snap. She doubled over.

He then butt-ended her in the face with the pommel of his CARG. She collapsed.

Seeing victory in sight, he lifted her head and tried to give her the Sight; perhaps that will calm her down.

Again, she covered her eyes and head butted him; her head was like stone.

The area swam. Davage tried to clear his head.

She balled her fists together and slammed him in the chin, sending him backwards.

Again, they stood a few feet apart, both trying to catch their breath. They'd been fighting for five minutes, and they were exhausted.

The Black Hat turned her head and gazed at the fallen form of Bethrael lying some feet away. Davage could feel the malice pouring out of her.

The Point. Davage saw the Point.

She was going to kill Bethrael. She was going to end her life and deny her the possibility of redemption out of pure meanness.

And even though she was a Black Hat "in training," so to speak, Davage had already accepted "Beth" into his family. He felt certain she will convert and be saved and become a happy, smiling Elder just like Syg. Maybe she'd pursue a career of some sort, fall in love with some lucky fellow, pass the baton, and have children. Perhaps she will become a lady of standing of some Great House. Maybe she will want to join the Fleet. Whatever, it didn't matter. All she need do was pick a star, and he and Syg will take her there. He wanted it for her—he wanted it badly.

And all that was about to be put to rest at the end of a Black Hat's Point.

She lifted her arm and extended her finger. In a few moments, Bethrael will be dead.

Davage sprang. In an instant he brought his CARG down on her wrist, and this time he didn't use a banging, bludgeoning blow. This time he sliced her hand off clean. He even jabbed it a bit, so it snagged a nerve and un-docked it, creating pain like nothing else: Maserfeld's Cut it was called, a cruel and torturous thing to do to an enemy that created excruciating agony until medical assistance could be administered.

It was something he had never done to any of his opponents— something he had never even considered doing.

She looked at him, indignant for a moment.

Something then came out of the stump and slopped to the ground, Davage thought it was a large gout of blood.

The Black Hat then began wailing in agony hideously. She clutched her stump, bouncing up and down, whirling around like a child, her dirty robes swishing on the ground. Vomit leaked out of the folds of her black sash. She picked up her hand and held it to her breast, cradling it. She moaned and slobbered in misery.

Davage felt pity for her at that moment. He regretted what he'd done. He thought about slicing off the end of her stump. That will remove the activated nerves and provide her with at least a bit of relief.

He saw something then. The bloody, dirty mass that had come out of her stump moved. It stood up somehow in a gory clump and jumped back onto the Black Hat's chest. Quick as Creation, it crawled across her chest, up her arm, and then back into the stump.

Instantly the Black Hat stopped screaming. She regained that hideous stance, that evil demeanor.

What had he seen? Was she somehow controlled?

There was nothing for it. He was going to save this tall Black Hat too.

Davage flew into her, kneeing her in the stomach; he felt her ribs floating a bit under him. He then smashed her in the face with a full strength punch.

Sitting on top of her, he ripped off her black face-covering sash.

Underneath was a pale, blonde-headed girl. Her face was long and sallow, her blonde hair, corn-colored, was braided and pulled back. She was covered in vomit. Her blue eyes were watery and doll-like. They reminded him of Syg's eyes, how they were during their first meeting—glassy ... evil.

Davage saw those eyes in his nightmares every so often; he dreamed that she turned back into what she was. They were horrible dreams.

She closed her eyes, anticipating the Sight.

With his thumbs, Davage wrenched them open and blasted her with a full lit Sight.

Forced to look, she stared at him and sighed. Her expression changed.

Davage then reared back and head butted her square in the forehead. She gave a yelp and went out cold.

It was done, the fight was over. Davage had triumphed. He felt like picking her up and throwing her down again but stopped himself.

Saddling his CARG, he Sighted her to make sure she was out. Again, heart rate, blood pressure, and breathing all indicated she was unconscious.

Something dark moved past his Sight. Looking around, he caught something lurking inside her.

It was a small man-shaped black blob—like a blood-clot with arms and legs. It seemed to know that Davage was Sighting it. It waved and bounded out of his gaze.

He looked around and found it again in her leg. It seemed to want to avoid his Sight and continued down until it was cornered in her foot.

He Sighted it hard. It was a small but massively concentrated piece of Shadow tech—of a type and complexity he'd never seen before. It had no heart that he could see. Clearly, this was the work of the Black Abbess.

It shuddered and roiled in his Sight. Making a break for it, it darted past his Sight and back out her stump. There, in the dirty ground, it began growing to man-sized.

"*Daaaavvvaaaagggggee* ..." it hissed. "*IIIII heeerrreeee forrr youuuu* ..."

It lunged at Davage. He dove aside and again, got his CARG out.

He sliced its leg off.

Bounding, it came at him again.

Its head flew off and splatted in the dust.

Swing. It could no longer be considered male.

Moving like a demon, it seized Dav by the shoulders, reared back, and plunged his head into the open, oozing stump of its neck.

Davage was overwhelmed with foulness. He could feel the horrid, viscous matter surging up around him, constricting his throat, entering his mouth.

Moments from death, Davage lit his Sight. Instantly, its rank interior charred and shriveled. It roared in agony.

It spat Davage out and buckled, falling into the dirt.

Davage recoiled and shuddered—the touch of this horrid creation was truly appalling.

Davage saw something.

The creature's cleaved nether parts were making their way to Bethrael's prone body. With sinuous movement and evil intentions, it crawled up onto her chest.

The captain pounced.

He flew toward her, grabbed the thing, and hit it hard with Sight. He felt great pleasure as it withered and perished into soot.

He turned to the rest of it. He was going to Sight this travesty into oblivion and good riddance!

Shrieking in fear, the remaining pieces, head, and main body of the thing collected itself and tore off with speed toward the main mass of Black Hats and Shadow tech beyond.

From the towers, horns sounded. A flock of black Shadow tech birds took flight and teemed in his direction, blotting out the feeble, dry sun.

<*The hordes are upon you, Captain. You must to the Silver Temple!*> Ergos's voice boomed out.

Davage saddled the CARG and picked up the tall Black Hat and put her hand in his pocket. He then ran to Bethrael and picked her up as well. They weren't particularly heavy, but after so much activity, he was tired, winded.

Panting, he sprinted across a bridge toward the Silver Temple, about two hundred yards distant. He could hear the black hordes flapping, leaping, and bounding behind him.

He Sighted the temple. He could see through its outer wall, but what he saw didn't make any sense. It made no sense at all.

He saw bleak landscapes and dust. He saw crude silver structures. He saw advanced cities and light.

(*Sygillis—wide-eyed ... evil.*)

He saw Hulgismen, naked, barbaric. He saw people wearing silver clothing, tending silver, seal-like beasts.

(*Syg—happy, eyes loving.*)

He saw a Black Temple ... a high throne, someone twisted and terrifying sitting alone at the top. He saw a Silver Temple, eyes opening, throne empty.

(Sygillis ... evil—hands ready to choke ... eyes alight with hate.)
(Syg ... full of love ... arms held open for a loving embrace ...)
("I am going to kill you ... ")
("I love you ... ")

He looked away; the images of Syg frightened him. He couldn't bear the thought of her as she once was, an evil automaton.

It was as if time was in flux with in temple, as if it existed in many places at once.

He didn't want to go in there. Anywhere but in there.

Panting, he approached the side of the temple—it towered overhead. There was a large moat surrounding it—a moat of black tar.

Horns again. Shadow tech beasts began bounding down from the heights above.

They were surrounding Davage; he had no place to go.

Poof! He Wafted into the Silver Temple.

When he re-appeared, he was still outside, Shadow tech beasts all around.

He couldn't Waft through the walls of the temple. How was that possible? A Waft-lock—was the temple protected by a Waft-lock, just like the Sisters did on board his ship to prevent invaders from boarding?

There must be something like that.

He landed back down near the edge of the moat, stumbled, and dropped the tall Black Hat, and she hit the ground and did a half-somersault. He was about to drop Bethrael as well but made an extra effort not to.

The hordes were all around. He set Beth down and unsaddled his CARG again.

He Sighted them and could see their red hearts, beating hard in anticipation of the kill.

He shattered the heart of one demon with his CARG, then another, then another. The creatures staggered and became indistinct for a moment, but he knew they will be back. Getting rid of Shadow tech for good was a job for the Sisters.

BOOM!

He heard a huge explosion overhead. He looked up.

High overhead, the Spiders had made another hole in the side of the temple, debris raining down. Again, he could see silver lances dart out of the hole. More silver specs floating about. He could see the bright silvery interior of the temple. The spiders, legs waving, caught one or two of the silver specs and devoured them.

<Captain! Now is your chance!> Ergos said. <You must inside the Silver Temple!>

"I don't want to go in there," Dav panted.

<You must!>

Davage cleared out a few more beasts, then, still holding his CARG, picked up Beth and the other Black Hat.

Poof! He Wafted upwards.

He reappeared in midair, about seven hundred feet off the ground—his heart was pounding. It was so hard to Waft carrying someone.

Poof!

Once again he reappeared in midair, this time about two thousand feet off the ground. Looking up, he saw he was about a hundred feet short of the hole.

He couldn't feel his arms ... everything was fading.

There were black spiders, crawling about. There were men mounted on strange silver beasts, carrying bright lances. They fought the spiders, pushing them back.

The hole began to get smaller.

The mounted silver men retreated back into the hole.

<You must inside the temple!>

Near total exhaustion, near death, Davage Wafted one last time.

Poof!

He re-emerged in a cool, quiet silver space.

He had no idea where the Black Hats were. He thought his CARG was still in his hand, but he wasn't sure.

He fell and fell ... a waiting silver far below.

* * * * *

"There it is, just like Dav mentioned," Kilos said in Davage's office looking at the viewer logs of the *Seeker*'s plunge near Metatron.

Syg sat next to her, leaning over, straining to see.

There on the viewer, amid the amber dullness of darkened Metatron, was a shining silver pyramid.

"Is that your temple?"

"Looks like it," Syg said. "Of course, it wasn't silver the last time I was there."

They gazed at the grainy, indistinct images of the viewer. The *Seeker* certainly couldn't see like Dav could.

"Look there," Syg said. "There's a whole Shadow tech army trying to knock it down. There must be at least five Black Hats down there to create that much, probably more."

"How come it's still standing? I would have thought it would be leveled by now."

"I don't know."

Syg thought of Dav, down there, surround by all that. She pushed the thought from her mind and went to the window. Outside, the stars streaked by.

"When will we arrive there?"

"About three hours."

"Can't we get there any faster? Go to Stellar Mach perhaps?"

"No, Stellar Mach is not good for short hops—we'd shoot right past the system and end up farther out than we are now. We are currently at the mark."

"What?"

"We're at max revolutions, Syg. We're going as fast as we can."

Syg sighed and put her head on the glass. She felt helpless.

"I know how you feel, but truly, what I told Saari before is probably correct—Dav's no doubt creating a nightmare for them down there. He can handle himself. He has his Gifts, and if I really thought he was in life-threatening danger, I'd be pulling my hair out with worry right now."

"You think so?"

"I do—and he'll probably have a Black Hat or two with him when we get there."

Syg turned from the window, furious. "If he's risking his life down there for the sake of saving a Black Hat—if he's not fighting with all his strength, if he's not fighting to kill—then I'll kill him myself as soon as I've covered him in kisses."

"Well, I suppose you're probably going to have to be cross with him—knowing Dav the way I do, he's going to try and save a few. That's Dav—stubborn."

Kilos, still looking at the viewer, saw something odd. "Syg, look at this …"

Syg came over, and Kilos ran it back. On the screen, as the ship soared by the Silver Temple, something happened to it—an explosion at its heights.

"Look there, it appears the Shadow tech beasts were successful in breaching the temple's outer wall."

"It was just a matter of time, I guess," Syg said.

"But watch … watch this …"

On the fuzzy viewer, slowed to a crawl, they could see something coming out of the hole—something bright and silvery. Silver bolts.

"What is that?" Kilos asked.

"I'm not sure. In my dream I could hear my Hulgismen calling out to me."

"Hulgismen don't speak."

"But mine were. Could it be that the Hulgismen within the temple are somehow fighting back?"

"With what?"

"I don't know, I really don't. In my dream it seemed like the Hulgismen were evolving—growing, becoming more than what they were."

Kilos looked at the screen, at the frozen image, at the silver bolts shooting out of the hole. "Well, I suppose we'll know soon enough."

"We are going to be under heavy attack. The Black Hats will try to shoot us down. And they are more than capable of doing it."

"We've the Arrow Shot. I'm sure you've seen them before. Fast transports loaded with Sisters and Marines. We blast them down from mid-orbit to the surface en masse. We'll take casualties, of course, but usually we find success if we launch enough of them."

"I'd rather we not lose anybody."

"It's part of the job. We all understand that."

Syg thought for a moment. "Ki, can you take me to the Sisters?"

"What?"

"I've a plan, but I'll need the Sisters' help."

10

THE SILVER TEMPLE

When Davage opened his eyes, he thought he was in a great silver ocean, surrounded by it. He could feel it all around him—silver and a great, booming quiet.

He rubbed his tired eyes and looked around.

He was on a huge, multi-stepped dais, shining and silver. His CARG lay a few feet away, a copper log in a silver fastness. He picked it up and saddled it.

The dais went up and up about a hundred feet more and stopped. High overhead, the pointed ceiling of the Silver Temple was far away, indistinct. Soft white light shined down from it. He could hear muffled thuds coming from outside.

Davage looked down. He was about fifteen hundred feet from the ground. The dais, getting slightly bigger with each step, continued down until it reached the floor. There was some sort of glittering silver lake down there. Everything else on the ground level was covered in dense mist. Ahead in the distance, poking out of the thick blanket of mist, was a thin silver spire almost as tall as the dais itself, adorned with blinking lights. Syg's temple was certainly colossal in size. He thought to Sight it, but his eyes were so tired. He'll Sight it later.

He could see the tall Black Hat lying still on the steps of the dais about fifty feet down. He checked his pocket—yes the squishy, dirty hand was still there. He found a handkerchief in another pocket, wrapped the hand, and put it back—oh the things he was subjecting himself to for these Black Hats. Bethrael was near her, about sixty feet down. She was crumpled up in a little ball.

He went to go down and collect them. Something splashed as he stepped.

He was standing in a shallow silver stream—silver flowed past his boots and continued down to the silver lake far below. He knelt down and dipped his fingers into the silver. It was warm, slightly bubbly to the touch. Just like Syg's Silver tech that night in her quarters.

He looked up; the stream appeared to be originating at the top of the dais.

He carefully made his way up, splashing as he went. As he approached the top, he could see somebody standing there—somebody with arms outstretched. This must be where Syg used to sit when she was a Black Hat. Sygillis of Metatron ... Hammer. Here, alone at the top of this dais is where she sat for years in smothering darkness. He recalled the image of her he'd Sighted from outside: evil, eyes glittering ...

Here she was a heartless murderer. Here she committed crimes. Here she was a monstrous, terrible Black Hat snared in an endless nightmare ...

Here she sat, dreaming of a light in the dark. His light, she had said as she touched his eyes. Here she dreamed of him. He thought of Countess Monama, the huge woman in black who had been concerned about him, who had told him of what was waiting, and how he had given her no proper regard or thanks. She had been right all along; she had seen this place true enough.

He got his CARG unsaddled and continued.

He got to the top.

It was Syg standing there—an image of her, perfect in every detail, with the exception that it was silver. She had her head thrown back a bit, eyes closed, hair tossed in an unfelt breeze, mouth open in a bright smile. She was even wearing her favorite Hospitaler bodysuit and shawl. She was even shoeless …

It was a good Syg, a happy Syg … the one that he loved.

Loved …

He had never told her how he felt, how she had taken control of his soul. Perhaps he liked the attention and fuss she made over him. Perhaps it was flattering to be coy, to be pursued by such a beautiful, interesting, loving, and yes, slightly dangerous lady. He knew she wouldn't try to kill him or anything of a sort … but her temper was certainly spectacular, certainly something to behold. It was all part of the package—part of what made Syg Syg.

Here she was, an image of the Syg he loved. Where once there was evil, good now prevailed.

Her hands were open, palms up. Silver, in a slow but steady stream, gurgled from her hands. It splashed to the dais and continued down.

As he stared at the image, he thought he could hear sounds coming from far below, a collage of talking and chanting, hammering, and animal noises all mixed together, like the strange, confused murmurings carried on a night wind.

He went back down and collected the Black Hats. He checked Bethrael, making sure she hadn't been injured further in the fall. She appeared no worse off than before.

He continued until he got to the bottom. There was a broad silver pool surrounding the dais. It was about fifty feet from the edge of the pool to the dais and about three feet deep. It was fed from the small but steady flow coming from high above.

Carrying both Black Hats, he splashed through the silver.

He couldn't see the distant edges of the temple; he was in dense mist hanging on the ground that he'd seen from above. Wincing, eyes tired, he Sighted through.

In the distance he could see a dense cluster of buildings laid all around the perimeter of the temple near the walls … all huddled under the whitish light coming from high above. The buildings seemed to bear distinct differences in make and workmanship. He could see some that were barely huts—thrown together crudely. Others were better built, changing from small shack to lodge to house to ornate modern structure—all composed of pure, stainless silver. The spire he Sighted rose up out of a gothic, cathedral-like structure.

He could see a mass of people moving toward him, coming through the mist. They moved easily, like they assumed that they were sneaking up on him. They, perhaps, thought that the mist covered them.

He set the Black Hats down carefully.

"Identify yourselves, please," he said in a clear, loud voice, which, in the cavernous open space of the temple, reverberated back to him amplified.

They were clearly startled. They jumped and bustled about in the mist.

They leveled weapons of some sort at him.

"I wish you no harm and am eager to avoid any conflicts here. However, if attacked, I shall defend myself and these two whom I protect."

Slowly, cautiously, the people emerged from the mist.

They were all rather large, fit people, the men being tall and strong-looking, the women a bit shorter and slender. They wore armored garments fashioned from silver. They wore large silver helmets that went all the way down to the middle of their backs. The helmets covered their eyes—lensed goggles were built into the front giving them a rather bug-eyed look. They carried long silver weapons, like thick spears. His Sight told him they crackled with energy within.

Some of the men were mounted on huge, bizarre-looking silver creatures. They looked aquatic of a sort, seal-like, standing on large bent flippers, easily fifteen feet tall. Davage recalled seeing them high above the temple, flying.

The creatures had a solemn, almost intelligent look on their whiskered, seal-like faces.

"Who are you?" one of the men asked cautiously.

"I am Captain Davage, Lord of Blanchefort. Well met. And you are ..."

The man hesitated, then: "Durman, the Silverian, of the Silver Realm."

One of the women leveled her weapon at Davage. "You are a liar!" She pushed her helmet up and out of her face. "Drusilla am I! Maiden of the Silver Pool," she said. "Captain Davage is of our lore. Captain Davage of the Golden Sword is beloved of our Mother and is a god!"

"Sygillis you mean, your mother. Yes, I know Sygillis, and yes … I do love her as well."

The people seemed shocked. They muttered amongst themselves.

"Yet you are not a god, but living man," Drusilla said.

Davage put his CARG down and leaned on it. "Yes, well determined."

One of the seal creatures came forward and spoke in a strong, clear voice. "And," it said, "you carry two Black Hat females with you." He paused, as if for effect. "Carahil am I. I will point out that it is they who attack us, kill us, breach our walls, give us no pause, and hold us to the ground. You claim to protect them; therefore, you must be our enemy."

"I am not. I fought these Black Hats beyond the walls of this temple, and I defeated them in fair combat. Now, I intend to save them, to turn them from the darkness … as I did for Sygillis, your Mother. She too was a Black Hat, right in this very temple."

The crowd became angry, restless.

"Liar!"

"Fiend!"

"Blasphemer!" they cried.

They advanced a bit, and Davage raised his CARG. It glinted in the light.

They stopped and looked at the weapon, at its coppery surface. It was, other than Davage's blue uniform and hair and the Black Hat's red robes and black gloves, the only color other than silver in sight.

"You bear a weapon from our lore. The color is true," Durman said.

"'Tis as I have said."

"Then, sir, prove it! Prove who you say you are!" Carahil the seal said.

"How so?"

"Our Mother's image, atop the sacred mountain. It is said she will move when her love approaches."

"Yes, yes, she will move," others repeated.

"Folklore?" Davage said. "Folklore is not an accurate method of testing."

"She will move if you are who you say you are."

"And if your folklore is in error and she does not move?"

"Then, regrettably, you will die."

Davage laughed. "I hardly think you here have the means to kill me, when all the hordes outside could not."

"Then why not submit to the test, if we cannot harm you?"

"Will you swear you will not harm the Black Hats? Will you swear to that?"

They looked at each other for a moment.

"Yes, we will swear not to harm the Black Hats *until* you fail the test," Drusilla said.

Davage thought about it for a moment. He figured, should this situation go bad, that he could Waft down and defend them quickly enough.

"I will agree, then."

The men brought one of the seal-creatures forward.

"Please, you may ride Carahil to the top. It is a long climb on foot."

Davage mounted the creature. It had the same feel to it as Syg's Silver tech. Silver tech flowed through his huge, powerful body.

He set his flippers and soon Dav was aloft, carried high. Two other creatures accompanied him, both mounted by armed men. They circled the top of the dais.

Davage hopped off in the airy heights.

"Off you go," Carahil said. "I'm truly sorry—I have no wish to be your enemy. You seem a good person to me."

"Have a bit of faith, I have learned that sometimes faith is enough."

Davage approached the statue of Syg.

She stood there, still smiling, still happy. Not moving.

"You expect something to happen, do you?" Davage asked from the heights.

"You claim to be Davage of Blanchefort, you tell us!" one of the men shouted back.

He stood next to the image, his boots in the flowing silver.

Nothing, she didn't move.

"You, sir, are a liar! Our Mother does not move!" one of the mounted men said.

"Have a care," Davage replied. "The test is not yet over."

Davage had a thought. He stepped forward, reached out, and touched the image, his hand on her cheek.

And she moved; she moved her head a bit, nestling it into his hand. She sighed audibly.

"She moves!" one of the men shouted down, nearly falling off of his mount. "For the Ages … She moves!"

Davage felt a tear come to his eye. He missed Syg so. Without thinking about it, he embraced her as he normally did.

And the image embraced him back, her silver flowing down his coat.

Carahil joined Davage atop the dais and rearing up, began joyously making an "Earp! Earp! Earp!" sound.

A cheer and a clamor erupted from below.

Weeping, Dav looked the image in her silver eyes. "I love you, Syg …" he said.

The image blossomed into a huge smile and tenderly held him by the chin, catching his tears. She kissed him on the cheek; her silver lips were warm.

Other seals came up to soar in the heights. Mounted men shouted with glee and waved their weapons in the air. Men and women bounded up the stairs to witness this event … this miracle.

Perhaps their prayers had been answered after all. Perhaps there was hope.

11

DRUSILLA

They brought Davage down from the dais in a clatter of armor and adulation. It was something of a dangerous, jostling trip as the Silver People struggled to see him, to touch him, to touch a god. If one were to fall off the dais, it was a long way down.

Davage insisted the Silver People take care of the Black Hats, and they responded without hesitation. They did what they could for Bethrael. They set her arm with silver splints and were concerned about her head. Her temple continued to hemorrhage. Here, as with the League, the medical arts were somewhat neglected, since the Elder-Kind were engineered to be healthy. They could not stop her bleeding; the clock was still ticking. She needed a Hospitaler and soon.

For the tall Black Hat, they bound her in Silver, where she sat quiet, broken, and empty without the dark thing within her.

Soon, he was whisked into one of their elaborate structures.

He was led to a silver room, the floor covered with thick silver rugs. Durman and Drusilla came in with him.

They bade him sit and then began removing pieces of their armor, Davage assumed they were wishing to make themselves comfortable.

He was amazed, shocked even, as they continued removing items of armor and clothing until they were down to stark naked. They wore nothing but jeweled silver necklaces.

Apparently, a few old Hulgismen traditions died hard, he mused.

They both flopped down on the rugs and sighed.

"Will you free yourself of your clothing, Captain, and be comfortable?" Drusilla asked.

Davage sat down. "No, no, I am at ease, thank you."

Free of their silver raiments, Davage again was shocked: the pair of them were the spitting image of Syg—red hair, green eyes, large nose—it was all there. Drusilla, in her nakedness—the nape of the breasts, the turn of the hip—could have been Syg, with the exception that she was a bit taller and had no Shadowmark.

"You are the image of your Mother," Dav finally said, composing himself.

Drusilla smiled. "Truly?"

Indeed. I'll be seeing her again soon, if all goes well. You can see her as well. It will be like looking in a mirror. I am certain she will like that."

Drusilla and Durman looked at each other, and their faces grew dark.

"Have I said something wrong?" Davage asked.

"We need to share some things with you, sir, if you will hear us."

"I am yours. Please proceed."

"We have much to tell you, though I will try to be brief," Drusilla said. "I shall skip through the usual lore and legends. We know that we once existed in this place as mindless creatures—that this place was once dark as pitch. We scrabbled about in the dark, and our mother sat atop what is now the silver mountain. She was a demon, evil and terrible, and we lived in fear of her. We were her slaves, and she killed us at her whim."

"And then?"

"And then she left, she went away, and the darkness parted and all became as you see now. Our Mother returned to the mountain a short time later, became silver, and she bled the sacred blood—our life's blood."

THE LEAGUE OF ELDER

"Can you tell us what happened when our Mother left? Do you have any knowledge in that area?" Durman asked.

Davage smiled. "You're doing fine so far. What do your stories tell you?"

Drusilla spoke up. "They say our Mother went out one day to do evil, and the Lord of Swords—yourself—saw her from heaven and fell in love with her, even though she was evil and heartless.

"And the Lord—you—dragged her, screaming, into heaven and tried to turn her. At first she would not listen, she wanted to kill the Lord, but you were kind and patient. You looked at her with your glowing eyes and the darkness in her soul fell away. Our Mother became good, and she fell in love with the Lord of Swords. Now they live together in heaven," Drusilla said. "I have seen these things. I have experienced them as our Mother has."

"Regardless of Drusilla's authorship, I am certain our stories are silly, Captain," Durman said.

"Not at all. Very accurate, truly remarkable, I must say. And I will not burden you with the banal mundane truths. The only exception that I can offer is that your Mother—Sygillis—is no demon, and I am no god. I am Elder-born and nothing more."

"You have the sword," Durman said, looking at Dav's copper CARG.

He unsaddled it and showed it to him. "Not a sword—it's called a CARG. It's the family weapon of my Line."

Durman scooted forward. "May I, sir?" he asked, holding out his hands.

Davage handed it to him, and he almost fell forward. He was not expecting the weight.

"By the Mother," he said, "it is heavy. You wield this in battle?"

"I do. It has saved my life on endless occasions."

Durman marveled at it. "Drusilla, hold this … feel its weight."

He gave it to her, and she gasped in surprise, her naked muscles flexing to hold it. She noted with her hands its smooth surface. "It's a club, then? I feel no edge."

"It is sharper than any mere sword—one needs great skill, though, to properly use it."

Drusilla handed it back to Davage. She gazed at him; she was so like Syg. He thought he could almost read her mind. She looked at him fiercely, like Syg did in the evenings, when she wanted to make love and wasn't going to take no for an answer.

"Then, your eyes," Drusilla said. "Is that portion of the story also true? I recall you could see us clearly through the mist."

"I have the Sight true enough, and yes, your Mother likes it very much."

"May I see?" Drusilla asked, not taking her eyes off of him. "Is that a seemly thing to ask, Captain, to see your eyes?"

"Well, it's normally not done, but I can make an exception for you, ma'am." Davage shrugged. He lit his Sight and looked at them.

Drusilla gasped and jumped, with the agility of a tiger, naked into his lap, her hands on his face. She stared at him with wonder.

Davage turned his Sight off, and she sat there, staring at him. He thought for a moment that she was going to attack him.

"I'm sorry, Captain," she said finally, climbing off. "That must have been quite rude of me. I couldn't help myself. I've never seen such a thing."

"No pardon needed, ma'am," he said straightening his coat.

"Now, I have a question for you, if I may?" Davage said as he watched Drusilla climb back to her spot. "You were, of course, Sygillis's Hulgismen, yes?"

"We do not know that name."

"You served Syg, did her bidding, went into battle with her?"

"Yes."

"Then you were her Hulgismen. Now Syg—Sygillis I mean—did not know where you came from, she said you simply arrived here in the temple. Do you know where you come from?"

Drusilla and Durman stood up. "Come with us, Captain. We shall show you."

They took hold of their silver necklaces and in a moment, their clothing and armor changed into an airy molten form, flew through the air, and formed back into armor and cloth. In an instant, they were fully dressed. Davage was impressed.

Drusilla approached him and took him by the hand.

They made their way out of the building. Outside, under the silvery light above, was a bustling village. Davage noted homes, schools and smithies where strong men and women hammered silver into various things. There were small barns where the seal-like creatures grazed on liquid silver and tended silvery young hatched from silver eggs. There were chapels and theatres, cemeteries and workshops, all seemingly dedicated to, wrought from, and sustained by Syg's flowing silver.

He saw red hair all over the place, green eyes in quantity. All bigger, markless Sygs running around everywhere.

And as Dav had noted earlier, the make and style of the buildings changed as they made their way to the perimeter. The closer to the wall they got, the more crude the structures became.

As they passed an alcove, Drusilla, still holding his hand, pulled him, with great strength, into it. There, momentarily alone, she pushed her helmet back, her red hair flowing out, and kissed him, her armored hands greedily feeling every inch of him.

Davage had to fight to remember that this wasn't Syg—it was Drusilla, a Hulgisman.

She was so like her, though—her lips, her taste, even the way she kissed was the same. The only difference was that he didn't have to stoop quite as much to kiss her.

Davage stood up after a moment, and Drusilla could no longer reach him.

She stared up at him, her green eyes greedy, taking in everything. She pulled her gloves off.

"I'll not apologize for that, sir ..." she said as she tried to work her warm hands into his shirt. "I'll not apologize for how I feel. I have seen you in my thoughts, my visions since the darkness lifted. I have seen you through our Mother's eyes."

"Drusilla, please ..." Davage said.

"Love me," she said kissing him on the neck, "as you do our Mother. You say I am like her in every way. Pretend I am she if you must. But love me, please sir!"

Davage, for a moment, allowed his arms to go around her. She unstrapped her greaves, stepped out of her boots, and began, with amazing dexterity, undressing him.

"Drusilla!" came Durman's annoyed voice from a distance.

Davage pulled away from her, fixed his clothes, and continued. After a moment, Drusilla caught up to him and, again, took his hand.

They at last arrived at the temple's wall; it was silver and sloped its way in an easy angle toward the distant top.

Drusilla pointed at the wall. "Here," she said, "here is where we came from."

Davage knelt down and looked at the wall—his eyes hurt too much to Sight. It had a knobby, organic look to it.

"I don't understand," he said.

<Yes, inscrutable, is it not, Captain?> came a voice.

Davage turned. There, standing in the silver was Ergos and Loviatar.

<Welcome to the Silver temple, Captain,> Loviatar said, still in her Demona image. *<We are glad that you were not killed in the onslaught outside.>*

Durman and Drusilla shook their heads.

"I take it you know this lot?" Davage asked.

"They are thieves, Captain. They steal our power," Drusilla said.

<Thieves? Have we not been gracious hosts?> Loviatar asked, hurt.

<Yes, consider what we take—a bit of rent and nothing more,> Ergos said.

"And what do you provide to earn this rent?" Davage asked.

<We have information. We have knowledge—knowledge that you seek.>

"Right," Davage said. "Let's test that." He pointed at the wall. "What is this?"

<That is a birthing wall, Loviatar said. *<The Black Abbess removes a portion of the Black Hat's—in this case, Sygillis'—eggs in an ovarian harvest and seeds the wall with them.>*

"And the fertilization?"

<The Black Abbess clones a percentage for the females and uses Invernan seed for the males.>

<And, before you ask,> Ergos said, *<time is accelerated in measured sections of the wall, the supplying the Black Hat with a steady supply of Hulgismen throughout her life. Hulgismen advance from seed to fully grown in only a few days. Remarkable technology.>*

Loviatar approached the wall. *<And now, here we are. Thanks to the charms and guiles of the handsome Captain Davage, Sygillis has awoken, and her Shadow tech turned to silver. Now time courses here uncontrolled. In a short while, the Hulgismen have evolved from mindless beasts to what we have here now. Even the vermin that once swam through the bilge and crawled the floor picking the bones of those Sygillis chose to slay have evolved, their bodies coursing with silver, their eyes full of light.>*

There was a great *boom* from the far wall high above.

<The Shadow tech creatures again break through the walls.>

Durman shook his head. "Our reserves of Silver Blood run low. The hordes give us no peace. We cannot withstand this for much longer; we weaken with each new breach."

"Is there nothing that can be done, no bargain that can be struck?" Davage asked.

"We have a dream, Captain," Drusilla said holding Davage's hands to her heart. "We dream of leaving this place, of taking to the stars, of finding a home where we can leave the Silver Realm in peace, discover new friends ... take husbands and wives, and have children. None of that is possible here. We are all brothers and sisters."

Durman pointed to the silver spire in the distance. "We have converted the temple. We can launch it into the heavens, controlled from there, the Spire."

Ergos smiled. *<The Silver Temple is held in place, Captain. The Black Abbess has slit her wrist and poured out her blood. The temple will go nowhere should she lose face.>*

Davage recalled the moat of black around the temple.

<Additionally, Captain, the Black Abbess seeks to lure Sygillis here, for in the temple with time amok, she will revert in time and thus return to the darkness. She will become a Black Hat again—again making a statement, forever a Black Hat.>

Davage stood there, horrified.

Ergos's eyes grew wide. *<Ah, you see, we have earned our rent. Such knowledge is valuable to you. You wish not to lose a valued member of your adoring harem.>*

"We already knew such things," Drusilla said. "We know we can never see our Mother again. We know the darkness will fall upon both her and us should that happen. The Black Abbess wishes us dead, if only to prove a point to our Mother—that there is no escaping her. We are … of no consequence."

"As am I, and my ship and crew. All of our deaths shall serve as a further punishment for your mother—a further statement."

Boom!

"To the walls!" Durman cried. "Drusilla, to the pool with your Order!"

Durman began running toward the silver dais. People began clattering about, dropping what they were doing.

"May I help you, Durman? May I assist in the defense?" Davage asked.

Durman looked back at him, awe in his face. "You will help us? Ride with us into battle with your golden CARG?" He seemed astonished.

"He will not, Durman! He will stay with me here! Captain, come to the pool with me," Drusilla said.

"We could use his sword, Drusilla!"

"I DON'T CARE!" she shrieked.

Davage broke away from her grasp. "I am here to serve, sir."

"Then come with me!" he shouted, running off.

Drusilla took his hands again. She gazed at him with "that look"—the same one Syg gave him in the mornings as he headed off to the bridge for his shift, the look that silently said, "Don't go." She reached up and kissed him again.

"To touch a god …" she said. "Please stay with me."

"I am no god, Drusilla. I am needed above."

"Then, to adore a fine, brave man … for you are certainly that and more," she said, voice shaking.

Davage followed Durman through the complicated streets and alleys until they burst out into the open area. Ahead, ten of the seal-like creatures were being assembled and mounted. One of the creatures, seeing Davage, approached him and bowed, whiskers twitching.

"Are you to assist in the defense, sir?" Carahil asked.

"I am."

"Then, may I carry you? To make amends for my doubting you previously."

"No amends are required. You were correct to doubt. You had no certainty that I was telling the truth."

"Then, may I be so honored to carry you aloft?"

"The honor is mine." Davage climbed aboard. Carahil was firm and strong, his skin smooth and warm, the Silver tech flowing through him. He recalled Loviatar saying he and his kind were vermin, once swimming and crawling about, eating the dead bodies that Syg had made in her evil. Once medium-sized scavengers, now they were huge, their eyes awash in silver. Could it be possible that such goodness, such shining spirit, could come from the depths of such darkness?

Someone handed Davage a long silver pole of the same type that they had leveled at him earlier.

"I have not been instructed how to use this weapon!" Davage shouted as Carahil began loping ahead.

"Will it to fire, Captain!" he said.

To his right, Davage noticed Drusilla and ten other armored women approach the silver pool. They stopped at the edge, pulled off their boots, and waded in.

"Drusilla!" Durman shouted. "We will need this breach sealed quickly!"

She responded: "The levels are low, Durman! We will do what we can!" She was talking to Durman, but was she was looking at Captain Davage.

"I will await your return, Captain, and perhaps we will have a moment alone together to continue what was started!" she shouted. She and Syg—they just didn't give up!

Carahil laughed as he bounded into the air. "Be warned, Captain. Drusilla usually gets what she wants—and that, apparently, is you!"

Flapping and grunting, the gaggle of beasts and armed men took flight and rose upward. They approached the area where the breach would soon be. The silver was cracked—shafts of dirty, dry light pooled in.

Boom!

More light. Skittery, indistinct movement beyond.

"FOR THE CHILDREN WE WILL ONE DAY FATHER, FIGHT WELL!" Durman shouted.

Boooom!

A huge, jagged chunk of the wall caved in. Black legs and fangs awaited beyond.

At full speed, the silver warriors surged through the hole, energy lances blazing, out into the amber light.

Syg sat alone in the mess in Dav's favorite spot. She had a cup of coffee in front of her, but she didn't drink any. She didn't want it.

For the last hour she had been in the presence of the Sisterhood, arguing a plan that she had—one that she thought might work well in Metatron. She knew nothing of ships and battle tactics and all of that, but she knew the Black Hats, she knew the Black Abbess, and she could guess what would be waiting for them there in Metatron: more Cloaked vessels, lots of Shadow tech and lots of Black Hats.

The Sisterhood of Light and a former Black Hat Hammer both trying to cook up a plan to save a League Fleet captain—the ironies.

The Sisterhood had listened, but they committed to nothing.

The silver things she had made were perfect … perfect in every detail. Her plan will work; she knew it. A lot of people were going to die soon, in the skies over Metatron, and all because of her, because of her dream.

She began to wonder if the dream of the Silver Temple wasn't a plant, a Painted Black Hat snare set to lure her back to Metatron; not to kill her, but to capture and possibly re-convert her. The Black Abbess, losing face, needed to make a statement, a loud one, that nobody—nobody—leaves the Black Hats, ever.

Re-converting her before the black stage of Metatron, sending the *Seeker* to a spiraling, fiery grave, and killing Dav, author of all of this, would do the job nicely.

The thought terrified her.

She wondered how she will do it, how she will end her life. If Dav was dead, she shall kill herself, plain and simple. She wanted nothing more to do with life if Dav was gone, if he was not here to share it with her and be her guide. She will die with Silver in her, as Sygillis the Elder.

She wondered if she'd earned a place in heaven, if all the evil she'd done could be excused, forgotten. She wondered if she would see Dav there.

Outside, she could see a dull, yellowish star begin to grow large in the distance.

Mirendra.

<*Syg*>, came a telepathic message from Kilos—Giftless, yet infinitely better than Dav at telepathy. <*It's near time. Come up to the bridge.*>

Standing, she walked out of the mess to whatever awaited.

✴   ✴   ✴   ✴   ✴

The chaos outside of the Silver Temple was mind-boggling. The Shadow tech spiders and beasts that once lightly peppered the side of the temple now covered it all the way up to the top, legs and fangs waving, a moving mass, an appalling carpet of black.

The Silver Warriors, using their energy lances, pushed them back from the edge of the hole, dispersing their sooty material, but Davage knew there was no getting rid of them for good without the Sisters. They'd be back, and in no time.

Glancing back a moment, he could see the edge of the hole mending—Drusilla and her Order, standing in the silver pool far below, were repairing it, but slowly, oh so slowly.

Ahead a spider lunged into view, waving its legs.

Eyes aching, Davage Sighted it, saw its red heart, and blasted it with his lance. Energy crackled out and seared the spider. Carahil had been right; all that needed done was to wish for it to fire and it did.

The spider's heart stopped beating, and it retreated. Unsaddling his CARG, Davage put it right through the heart, shattering it. The spider drifted into smoke. *Recover from that one,* he thought.

Elsewhere, the fight went poorly. There were simply too many beasts and spiders to push back, and as Davage looked around, only nine riders fought where there were once ten.

A spider skittered into the hole, and then another. He thought he could hear screaming from within.

A leg came up and hit Carahil's hind quarter, and with a cry, he was out of control. Colossal fangs waited.

"Jump off, Captain! Jump!" he cried, seeing his life coming to an end.

Davage put his arms around Carahil's large neck and did the only thing he could do—he Wafted.

Poof!

He re-emerged about a hundred feet from where he previously was, and Carahil was with him. He felt no strain, no heart-pounding exhaustion he expected to feel trying to Waft such a huge creature along with him. The Silver tech, he thought, it flows through his body. It must have properties favorable to Wafting.

Thoughts began to flood into his mind; possibilities began to unfold.

He looked down far below. He could see the black Shadow tech hordes, but nothing else. He Sighted. There standing in his Sight were five Black Hat Painters, calmly controlling their hideous creations as though they were simply watching some sort of horrible theatre. No Sten, no nothing—wide open, confident in their illusion's invincibility.

"Carahil!" Davage shouted. "It's time we impose this fight upon the pupetmasters instead of the puppets! Are you game?"

"I see nothing but the dark masses below!"

"They are there, hidden under a Painted Cloak. Will you stand with me?"

"I will go where you will! I stand with you, Captain!" he shouted, ready.

With that, Davage Wafted.

He emerged about twenty feet from a Black Hat. Again, she stood there, unmoving.

In a moment, Carahil was upon her.

Davage swung his CARG. The Black Hat fell headless. Davage had just killed her. He had no choice; the Shadow tech had to go.

Another Black Hat, standing there shocked by this development ...

Another swing of his CARG. Another Black Hat fell. The Painted Cloak came down, its creator now dead.

A third, enraged, lifted her arm to Point.

Swing, dead. Three Black Hats dead in as many seconds. He looked to the heights. A great many of the Shadow tech creatures were capering about, insensate. Many stumbled off the side of the temple;

others were blasted off with silver. Some separated into a smoky mist and drifted to the ground.

In a moment, a wall of Hulgismen sprang as if from out of nowhere and Carahil flew right into them, knocked to the ground in a living tangle. There was a confusion of slashing arms and legs, and soon he was standing once again on the flat dirty plain of Metatron in a mass of people. Sighting and swinging his CARG, he fought with all of them at once and none at the same time. He recalled his lance and let it fly.

Hulgismen fell. He knew not how many. He could hear Carahil, roaring somewhere behind him, battling the Hulgismen.

Where were the last two Black Hats? He had to engage them. He could not give them pause to regroup, to recover from this shocking indignity, and improvise a plan.

For the people in that temple, they had to die.

The Hulgismen were taking their toll on him. They clawed and pummeled, and they slashed him with dirty blades dripping with Shadow tech Nyke poison. He guessed he was probably Nyked hard, fatally so.

A few more Hulgismen fell, and a few, bloody and mangled, were tossed forward by Carahil who faced their fury with a fury of his own. There, standing a few feet away, were the other two Black Hats, and what they were doing shocked Davage to his core.

They were retreating, hobbling away. With no clear lines of battle, no Sisters, no fealty from their foes, they had no idea what to do, how to fight. A moment later, in a blast of smoke, they Wafted away and were not seen again.

Elsewhere, farther down the battlefield, three more Black Hats, the last on the field, stood like three red statues.

Davage readied himself to Waft to them.

In a flash, the remaining Silver Warriors, eight in all, and a riderless seal following Davage's example raged down on them, fighting close, giving them no space.

Silver flashed; a Black Hat fell. The last two then Wafted away, leaving their Hulgismen and their black creations to their fate.

They were beaten.

Before long, the remaining Hulgismen were dead and the Shadow tech creatures made unsubstantial, though their combined cloud lingered around the temple as a sooty fog.

Davage stood there on their plain, the pain of his wounds aching. Soon the Silver Warriors were all around him, roaring with ecstasy, discharging their weapons into the bleak sky, shaking their gauntleted fists

"Look to Captain Davage, there, I had said from the heights!" Durman shouted. "Look how he fights! Now we have victory!"

Amid the clamor, he looked up at the Silver Temple. The hole was gone—sealed. Instead of retreating back inside, the Silver Warriors chose to stay outside and fight. He couldn't help but admire them.

A large door opened in the base of the temple, and Drusilla and an armored contingent of females came out, all holding weapons.

Durman told Drusilla what had happened. She ran to Davage and embraced him, knocking his CARG from his hand and sending him into the dust with her on top. The Nyke in his wounds was starting to work; he was losing strength.

"You are truly heaven-sent!" she cried.

"The Shadow tech that entered the temple, what came of them?" Davage asked.

"They threatened the central village, and we held them at bay for a brief time. Then they simply faded into smoke," she said.

From high overhead, a long lance of energy hit the temple walls with a crack.

Cassagrains, from the cloaked Ghome transports.

Davage Sighted. He could see about twenty of them, blundering about.

He then saw something else, something far away in the sky but rapidly approaching.

He smiled.

Behind him, in the streets of Metatron's lower quarter to the south, came an ugly roar.

He turned.

Rising up into the empty sky was a monstrous thing—a roughly man-shaped creature that looked like it was composed of mud and clotted blood. It grew and grew until it stood head and shoulders taller than the surrounding buildings, at least three thousand feet tall.

The Dark Thing that had come out of the Black Hat's arm, the thing he had fought, beheaded, and neutered. There it was, now huge and terrible—fully formed again.

Davage looked up at the towering black monster. It swayed in the dull heights. It began greedily looking around. It trawled the craggy streets and alleys of the city beneath it, apparently not interested in them for the moment.

It spied something and roared with evil delight. It reached down and grabbed, clutching with its terrible hand. It then rose, something held fast.

Curious, Davage Sighted it. Clutched in its disgusting paw was a tiny, struggling bit of red.

A Black Hat, one of the ones who fled the field.

The black creature had its priorities—first, punish the Black Hats who had been defeated and make them suffer. Time enough to deal with the Silver Rabble later.

It needled her for a moment in his palm and then devoured her tiny form. Davage had the feeling that that wasn't the end, that she will live in its belly, tormented.

It began trawling the streets again, looking for the other three, homing in on their darkness. It walked to the west, smashing all in its path as it did so, a rising plume of dust and crushed stone trailing it. It found another Black Hat, clapped her in his hand to stun her, and then threw her tiny body up into the air. Several seconds later she came back down and splashed into the shallow waters of the bay. Searching for her, he picked her dripping body up, shook it, and ate her.

Davage had seen enough. He knew what was about to happen here. He stood up. Drusilla stood and picked up his CARG with both hands.

"Drusilla, you must to your control tower, engage your engines, and suffer this place no more."

"We cannot break free of the darkness. It will hold us fast!"

"Leave that to me. I will break the hold, and you must away."

Drusilla stood there, holding hiss CARG. "Are we to never see you again, sir?"

"You've the heavens to explore, Drusilla. You've your dreams to make real."

"And if, in the landscape of my dreams, I see nothing but you?"

She pushed her helmet up and away from her eyes. "Come with us. Think of all we could share together—what we could create, the two of us! Think of what we could mean to each other!"

"I cannot, and you know that. But, rest assured, I will never forget you."

Drusilla stood there with his CARG, giving him "that look" again.

"I will tell your Mother of what I have seen here, of what was wrought with her blood, of the courage and honor that was nurtured from her light. I will tell her of her children and how they stood here in this place, all alone, and turned back all the vileness the Black Abbess could muster."

Tears dripped from Drusilla's eyes. "And you, no longer a creature of myth and lore … not a god, but a living Elder-born man, brave and true. And how the lore of the god pales before the truth of the man."

Another cassagrain hit the side of the temple.

"Hurry, Drusilla."

With that, she took one last pleading look, dropped his CARG, and ran toward the temple, holding her face in her hands.

Carahil was still at his side. He could see Davage was in distress, the Nyke building.

"Are you all right, Captain?"

"I'm fine. You should get yourself inside and make ready to launch, my friend."

He was not fine, the Nyke … He looked at Carahil for a moment, concerned that he might be Nyked too. He seemed fine. The Silver tech within him must have counteracted it.

Carahil sniffed him. "I can smell poison within you, Captain. Please, come into the temple and let Drusilla help you."

"There is no help for me here, my friend. Only the Sisters can save me. Go, return to the temple and make ready to depart."

Carahil regarded him with those large, bright eyes. "I've no words, sir … for this day. I … never believed in answered prayers, but here you are." He shuffled his whiskers, his big, bright eyes appearing sad. "Fare thee well, god who fell from the sky and became a man, who became an honored friend and then became a god again," he said finally.

"Speed well, and please—tell Drusilla she is her Mother's image, in both body and spirit, and tell her that, should circumstances have been different, I would have gladly shared her dreams with her," Davage said, patting him on the back, and Carahil was gone, flying at a high speed back into the temple.

He watched the transports blunder about in the sky, slowly circling the temple, taking pot shots at it. The sheer size of the temple minimized the damage, but still, eventually the shots would take effect. To the south, the Dark Man rumbled about in a racket of destruction, chasing down the remaining Black Hats—his echoing laughter filling the night.

The walls of the temple began to thrum and flash. The ground began to tremble. The temple was readying for launch.

He had promised he would free them. To do that he needed the *Seeker*, which he knew was ready to soar into view any moment now. He'd seen it … He'd seen it.

12

LT. KILOS

Kilos stood at her station on the bridge. Even though she was in command, she still stood near her familiar OPS panel, though a crewman manned it—she felt most comfortable there. Syg was nearby, sitting sheepishly in Dav's chair.

Ahead in the viewer, Ergos's lopsided bulk grew larger and larger.

Dav was down there. Her mentor and Captain. Her friend.

Dav ...

She remembered how it all began, almost ten years ago.

*   *   *   *   *

She stepped off the old shaky transport *New Providence* holding her Marine duffel bag, and spilled, with all the other chattering, disembarking passengers, into the village of Blanchefort—a craggy, colorful seaport squeezed in between the sea and a frighteningly steep range of spiny mountains that spread into the vast interior of the continent. She was wearing her Marine uniform, red coat, thick white pants, tall black boots, and black cap, yet she shivered. She had heard Blanchefort, situated way far to the gray Kanan north of Vithland, was a cold place—cold enough to chill you to the bone if you weren't ready for it.

And she was cold—real cold.

She was from Tusck, a city in the warm sunny south of Onaris. Tusck was a dark, mouthy, urban bit of stone surrounded on three sides by a continent's worth of golden fields and farms, warm sands and rural simplicity.

She was a Brown, all of her family was Brown, her whole town was Brown.

What was a Brown? A Brown, in the traditional sense, was an Elder with virtually no Vith, Remnath or Zenon heritage—Onaris tending to have a higher concentration of Browns than Kana, the traditional home of those three favored tribes. People from Tusck tended to have large, soothing brown eyes and thick brown hair that easily faded to a golden blonde in the sun. Browns, having no Vith ancestry, had no Gifts. They were Giftless and were accordingly looked down upon by the Bluer Elders. They were generally poor. They rarely owned land, and they never had titles in front of their names.

Her hamlet was under the fealty of a Blue Lord, the House of Pittsfield of the Calvert line. He was a man who was rarely there in his manor on the hill near the sea. It stood unoccupied. He rarely interfered in their lives or caused them distress, but he rarely showed any interest in them either. His usual feudal duties were left undone or charged to poorly paid Brown clerks who were backed up in red tape by the years.

She was the eleventh daughter of a crowd of twenty-three brothers and sisters. Having little else, Browns often had huge families. A litter of twenty-three was actually a modest load. Ki was a smallish, pretty girl as a child, but her golden, smiling face hid a rough, quick temper—a feature that reared up and plagued her throughout her life. She frequently got into dust ups with the urchins and weedy lot that frequented her country hamlet in the shadow of Tusck. A boy about her age from down the lane often assisted her in these child-to-child brawls. They became friends, went to school together, and swam in the blue streams and creeks. Even as the boy stopped growing at a smallish size and Kilos continued until she was head and shoulders taller, they remained constant companions. Eventually they married in a small private ceremony in the Brown tradition.

Itemless, penniless, they struggled to make a life for themselves, often moving from place to place tending fields, picking the coffee that was all the rage in Kanan League society, cobbling roads, building walls, or doing whatever was available. Her husband dreamed of going to school, to the big university in Tusck. They had no money to pay for the schooling, and as Lord Pittsfield was never around, they could not receive a Letter of Honor, a merit grant on the credit of the Lord to attend for free for those students who showed promise, and Ki's husband appeared to be a born scholar.

And she so wanted to send her husband to school, to make his dreams come true. Drastic measures were required.

Being married, she couldn't join the Hospitalers—a sect always eager to accept Browns. Having little other choice and being a tall, strong girl, Kilos did the only real thing she could … she joined the Stellar Marines. She wanted to send her husband to school, and though it meant they would be apart for long stretches of time, she was willing to do it.

The Marines were her third choice—all things being the same. With the first choice unavailable to her, her second choice was to join the Stellar Fleet, learn a trade, and who knows from there, the Fleet often being a well-spring of opportunity for Blues and Browns alike. But, again—no Lord Pittsfield, no Letter of Recommendation, no Fleet. So, with tears in her brown eyes, she said good-bye to her husband and shipped out of Tusck port to become a Marine.

Being a standard-issue Marine could either be very, very good, or very, very bad. If you served well and if you were assigned to a prominent ship duty—or best of all, if you were selected to serve a squadron assigned to protect a Sister, then being a Marine could be an exciting and profitable experience—penniless Browns who joined could, if things worked out, retire fairly wealthy. And like all Marines, Kilos was taught to speak to the Sisters. It was a wonderful, unique way of speaking, full of thought and feeling, light and sound. It was no wonder the Marines loved the Sisters like no other.

But if you weren't assigned a ship and you weren't assigned to a Sister, being a Marine was a dreary, humiliating, and often-brutal experience.

And so it was for Kilos. Assigned to a weary garrison in Bustoke, she toiled for several years, breaking up fights in the towns, chasing down petty criminals, even digging trenches, her beautiful red Marine uniform soiled and torn.

Why did Ki have such a hard time? Was she being singled out and shunned for some reason?

Nope—again, her rotten temper and quick fists got the better of her time after time. She punched out her commander while in training. She punched out her jailer while she was in hack for previously hitting her commander. She spent time in the brig for hitting a fellow trainee on Howst during a mercy exercise, of all things. She could never get anything accomplished, never finish anything without a visit to the brig, or worse, to the yard for a session with the sonic lash.

She was decertified for …

She was put into Hack once again for …

And on and on …

She'd lost count of the number of times her usual bravery, strong back, and fairly sharp mind got her out of toil, and then her temper put her right back in again. She lost count of the number of times she had to Com her husband after a promotion to tell him she'd lost it again, that she was back down to nothing … again.

So, there she was, in a work detail—this time, for the last six months, in the green forests outside of Armenelos on Kana. The local Lord wanted to perform some redecorating, and as usually was the case, there were the Marines to perform the hard labor, little more than slaves. He even paid them in Burl—an old Remnath tribe tradition, where, instead of money, she was paid in food and lodging. The food was very good and as much as she wanted, the lodging very comfortable and lacked for nothing, but she'd rather have been paid in money. She'd rather have had something to send home to her husband.

She'd been moderately curious when she was called to the Commander's office that one day. She'd not been in any recent trouble—not that she could recall. She went into the large office and the Commander, a large, formidable-looking woman named Marshall

Henbane, and a garishly dressed gentleman—no doubt the Lord of this Holding—were waiting for her.

The two of them looked at her for a time, as if they were sizing up a show animal.

Finally, Marshall Henbane spoke. She told Kilos of an opportunity that had just come up, one that might hold great promise for her.

She was to leave the work detail immediately, rekit with a fresh set of uniforms, and be assigned to the 12th Marines, a shipboard squadron. She was to be the squadron adjutant to the Fleet captain.

Adjutant? Fleet captain? Ship duty?

She couldn't believe what she was hearing at first. She was about to go from a dreary, unpaid work detail to a fairly cushy position aboard a Main Fleet starship of all places.

She had to be dreaming. This couldn't be true.

But as the conversation continued, the dream faded to a genuine nightmare. The things the Commander and the Lord said gave her great pause.

"Keep your eyes and ears open," they said.

"Report back should you hear or see anything … interesting," they said.

"Feel free to … ingratiate yourself with the captain, be pliable, and report his … indiscretions back at once."

Ki knew exactly what this was. Two Great Houses, two Blue Lords, had it in for each other, and obviously, this man—this Lord—was wanting dirt and embarrassing gossip on the captain to take back to the Blue society he no doubt inhabited and cause a stir.

And he was going to use her to get it.

Blue families—that's how they fought with each other, with gossip and humiliation, with loss of face.

And then the conversation got even worse, if that was possible.

"You will do nothing to compromise the safety and operations of the ship," they said.

"You will betray no secrets to the Enemy," they warned.

"You will be executed if …"

Execution. They used the word. If, while she was digging up dirt on the captain, something bad happened, anything at all—even if she had nothing to do with it—she would be executed as a saboteur.

A disgraced Blue Lord was much better than a dead one, and this Blue Lord wanted his dirt, but he wasn't going to take the fall should anything happen; she would. That's what she was there for.

She was ready to stand up and thank them for this opportunity and say she wanted nothing to do with it. She'd rather keep on digging trenches.

"We will make it very much worth your while," the Lord said.

He said a Letter of Honor had been penned for her husband so that he could go to school at no further expense. All the Lord had to do was sign and circulate it. And money, there will be money. All she had to do was humble a Blue Lord.

As soon as the Lord had a few good tidbits, the letter will circulate, the money will flow. What was the harm in a little gossip?

She thought about it for a moment.

She accepted. She would do it.

Carrying a duffel bursting with brand-new uniforms, Ki boarded the ugly old transport *New Providence* and headed to wherever— she wasn't even told. She'd been given a folder regarding her new assignment and a sealed folder she was to give to the captain once she arrived there. As the transport meekly stumbled into the air, she read her folder over.

The ship she was being assigned to was the *Seeker*, a Main Fleet Vessel of *Straylight* configuration. Even though she was going to be a spy, a rat, she was excited—a *Straylight*, the top class of the line. A real heavy-duty starship.

The captain of the *Seeker* was a man named Davage, Lord of Blanchefort. So, here was the man she was supposed to rat out, humiliate, and scandalize. Her conscience began to settle as the long ride progressed. She wasn't really hurting the man, after all. It was all Society nonsense, and he was a Blue, so he probably had it coming to him anyway. He probably bought his way aboard that ship; he probably had friends all over the Admiralty.

She looked at his record—Blue or not, bought or not, this Captain Davage had earned his merit.

Over a hundred different engagements with the Xaphans.

Four hundred plus enemy vessels sunk.

Two hundred plus enemy vessels seized.

Ten thousand plus enemy combatants captured. She was impressed.

When the transport landed, she couldn't believe it. Instead of a shipyard or Fleet holding ground, they were in a small village—the cold village of Blanchefort, the pilot said. Obviously, this Captain Davage thought the *Seeker* was his private chariot and berthed a Main Fleet Vessel in his village to please his own vanity. He was probably throwing a party. He might have a lady of standing to please.

Blues ... she wondered why she had felt so bad to begin with.

She made her way to the docks, through the crowds of bustling people. There, parked in the half-moon shaped, frigid bay on pylons, was the *Seeker*. Ki had never seen a *Straylight* up close. Even though it was mostly submerged, it was huge, the large, spade-shaped frontal section of the hull rising out of the water like a great white bird's head. She could see its hull plating, its closed gun ports, its decks and could make out the tiny forms of people moving about on top of the front section. She could see the tower rising up in the rear section far away. An incredible vessel. Grace and strength perfectly melded together. The closest thing to a starship she'd ever been was to a rusty old *Webber* that she had to fumigate for fungus before it was scrapped.

A *Straylight*, battle-tested.

The dock in front of the *Seeker* was a crowd of noise and activity. There were small shops and colorful vendors selling items from carts. There were pubs and cafes, inns, tailors, artisans, sportsmen, exotic animals, and no doubt, courtesans plying their trade. The *Seeker's* crew—a mixture of Fleet officers and crew, Hospitalers, Marines, and civilians—milled about shopping, eating at the cafes, drinking at the pubs, and sightseeing.

Behind the village, rising steeply to a lofty precipice, was a huge Vith castle perched in the mountains above the cloud-line. A solitary switch-back road led up to the top. Must be Captain Davage's castle. Beautiful, huge, but sort of scary looking, like a chaotic red pin-cushion of towers and tall spires. She tried to count the number of spires but gave up after thirty; vendors selling various goods and snacks kept interrupting her, and she'd lose count.

It hit her that the villagers of Blanchefort made a busy and very good trade having the *Seeker* here, where, otherwise, the village would have been hopelessly remote and ill-traveled. At first, she naturally assumed the *Seeker* was here merely out of vanity to serve a Blue Lord's whims, but now, she had to wonder. Was the captain, in one simple and elegant stroke, thinking of his people? Was he using his station to enable them to make a fair and honest living?

If that was the case, then this Lord Blanchefort was certainly no Lord Pittsfield.

Ki found herself wandering around in the maze of shops, and she even saw a few things that caught her eye—a ring or two for her, some interesting books she thought her husband might like. But she had no money.

A short time later she made her way onto the ship. She was overwhelmed with it—the complexity, the size. The places this ship had been to, the action it'd seen. She was due to see the captain soon but found herself hopelessly lost in the vast interior of the ship.

She came across a maintenance tech who was waist-deep in an open panel.

With a dirty arm, he groped about for an intricate tool that had, so far, defied his grasp.

"Miss," the man said, "would you be so kind as to hand me the torque bit there?"

She stopped, knelt down, and handed him the tool.

"Much obliged," he said.

She thought a moment. "Sir, I am here to see the captain, but find that I am quite lost. Could you point out his direction?"

The tech pulled himself out of the panel. His head and frilly white shirt were covered in a clingy sort of black soot. He must be an officer of some sort. He wiped his eyes and looked up at her.

"My," he said, "you're a tall one. How tall are you, if I may ask?"

"I am, using League measurements, six feet, one inch."

"Goodness," he said, "six-one. Remarkable."

She remembered the time. "Sir, I am in a bit of haste. Could you point out where I may find the captain?"

The man stood up. He was taller than she was by a good two or three inches. That was something she wasn't used to—to be shorter than somebody.

"I'm headed in that direction. I will show you the way."

Relieved, she waited for him to put the panel back in place. A moment later they were striding through the twisting passages of the ship, the man, chattering, pointing out this and that. She felt slightly intoxicated by all this. Not two days prior she was waist-high in dirt and landscaping materials, now she was walking with orders through a *Straylight*. The possibilities, the adventure—it was so exciting. Maybe she could do this. Maybe she could gather something stupid and harmless here and there, appease the Lord, get the Letter of Honor, get paid, and manage to stay aboard ... to go where this great ship goes.

Maybe she'd actually like the captain. Maybe they'd get along. Maybe they would become friends.

They went up a few decks and then were there.

A small wooden door sat innocently at the end of the passageway with a brass plate reading: "Captain Davage."

The man knocked on the door and waited a moment.

"Come in," came a soft voice from inside.

"Thank you for showing me the way, sir, but I think I can ..."

The man opened the door and held it for Kilos. She nodded and went in.

Inside was a fairly smallish office, a large desk, Com panels, two chairs, and several windows. Ki could see the carnival of lights from the village and the big Vith castle looming in the distance. The walls were lined with pictures of the *Seeker* and various elegantly dressed people—must be the captain's family.

A woman dressed in a Fleet officer's uniform stood by the desk. Her hair beneath her triangle hat was long and dark red. Her shirt was white and frilly. Her coat was tailed and deep blue and woven with gold ivy. Ki loved Fleet uniforms. The woman's jade-like eyes were set and stern. Her boots were placed on the rug as if bound in stone.

Was the Lord of Blanchefort a woman after all?

Ki squared herself and snapped to attention. "Captain, Sergeant Kilos, 12th Marines, reporting as ordered!"

The woman said nothing. Her eyes were a glowing green, and they were fixed on Ki, fierce and inscrutable. Even though Ki was a fair amount taller than this woman, she felt infinitely smaller. Those eyes, those green eyes, could melt lead.

After a moment, she spoke, her voice as cold and icy as the climate outside. "You are joking, no doubt. Know you not Fleet rank insignia, Sergeant Kilos?"

Ki was confused. She looked at her uniform: blue coat with ivy, black pants, tall black boots over-sized in the Fleet style, large triangle hat, black Command sash decorated with numerous ribbons—certainly looked like a Fleet captain's uniform, but she wasn't really up on it. She didn't know what to say.

"Well?" she demanded, those green eyes catching fire.

After a moment, the sooty man made his way past her and sat down behind the desk.

What was going on?

He smiled. "Lieutenant Hathaline, is that any way to welcome our new adjutant to the Marines?"

Kilos was mortified. This man with whom she had chatted so casually was Captain Davage?

"She cannot even identify Fleet rank, Captain."

"Well, Hath, I'd say you certainly look the part, all stern and frowning all the time."

He turned to Ki. "Sergeant, well met. I am Captain Davage," he said cheerfully. "I am sorry that I am out of dress a bit, but I love working on the ship with my own two hands when I can. She is my great pride."

She squared herself with him and again snapped to attention. "Sir, I am sorry for this confusion."

"It's nothing to be sorry over. Please be at ease and sit, be comfortable."

"Sir," she said holding out a folder. "Here are my credentials."

Davage thanked her and accepted the folder. Marshall Henbane had given her the folder. She didn't have any idea what was in it; the folder had been sealed. He sat back and opened it, thumbing through the pages.

"Hmm," he said, "very impressive. You served aboard the *Midnight*. Captain Graves gives his compliments. You also had a stint in Fleet Command, I see."

Hathaline rolled her eyes. "Captain, I have her real file here." She stood and held out a blue file. The Captain took it and opened it, leaning over his desk as he looked it over.

Hathaline was furious. "How stupid does Lord Sixtus of Grenville think we are?" she said in an ugly voice to Kilos.

Kilos closed her eyes and felt her heart sink. She had allowed herself to hope for a moment. She stared at the floor in shame.

Hathaline was all over Kilos. "I think I should Stare you off the ship, Brown-head!"

Davage's eyes flashed and snapped toward Hathaline. She looked at him and backed away, his silent warning to her understood loud and clear.

"I am sorry for that remark, Sergeant, it was uncalled for," she said quietly.

The captain continued reading the file. After a moment he closed the folder and set it down on the desk.

"Shall I escort her from the ship, sir?" Hathaline said in a quieter tone.

Davage sat silent. "Sergeant, will you please look at me for a moment?" he said finally.

Kilos looked up, and their eyes met. He had kind blue eyes. Dark blue, Vith blue.

He smiled.

"Sergeant, tell me, you have never been aboard a starship, yes?"

"No, sir, I haven't."

Hathaline seethed, regaining some of her former anger. "She is a spy and an incompetent to boot!"

The words stung her.

"Sergeant," Davage said in a calm, soothing voice, "have you been trained in espionage?"

"No, sir."

"There, Hath—she's not a spy."

Hathaline stood up. "Dav, she was sent here on orders from Lord Grenville, no doubt to dredge up information that he can use against you for any number of sinister purposes, including the subverting of your upcoming reappointment with the Admiralty! You might not choose to be thoroughly enraged over this matter, but I am! Someone has to concern themselves with your social status. If it's not you, then it will be me! You ought to marry me for this endless work I do for you! I don't see why you don't."

Davage ignored her. "It says in your file—the real one—that you have been working in Armenelos for the last six months. May I ask what you were doing there?"

"I ..." she could feel Hathaline's eyes boring into her. "I was digging trenches for the Great Lord, sir."

Hathaline just about pulled her hat off and took a bite out of it she was so mad. "That Blue, Remnath scoundrel! He sends an incompetent, unqualified ditch-digger to infiltrate the *Seeker*? That is a slap, Captain—a slap on your face, and I'll not have it! I believe he almost wanted this ... person ... to get caught just to see how you would respond! This is a test, and it's a test you had better pass, Dav! I've a mind to go to Armenelos myself and Stare him down, the fancy git!"

"Hath, must you react so? Yes, I'd heard Lord Grenville was wanting to add a country cottage to his manor grounds and was digging up the landscape. A pity really. Armenelos is a beautiful area."

"What do you have to say for yourself, rat, I mean ... Sergeant?" Hathaline yelled, standing up again.

Kilos didn't know what to say. She just sat there in misery.

She had so wanted this.

"Cat got your tongue? Captain Davage is a great man and in my mind, the Fleet's finest captain, and here you are—a rat, with orders to pull him down, humble him, and lose him his command. Were he not such a kind man, were it not for his sake, I would be turning you inside-out right now, Sergeant!" Her eyes shimmered with an enraged light.

"Hath," he said. "That's enough, and I mean it."

Hathaline, giving Kilos one last hateful look, went to the door. "I am going to get security and have her removed, Dav, and she'll be fortunate if I don't Stare her out of the ship after all. Not only is this ridiculous, it's embarrassing as well!"

Before Davage could say anything, she left.

"I am sorry for that, Sergeant," he said. "Lieutenant Hathaline is one of my oldest friends and tends to be rather protective of me, though I know not why."

Patting the soot out of his hair, which Ki noted was dark blue, he grabbed his coat and a long, odd-looking weapon that was made out of gun-metal. He opened the door and peered out into the hallway.

"We'd best be out of here, Sergeant, I think she's serious."

He stepped into the hallway. "Walk with me, please." Kilos stood up and grabbed her duffel. Together they left the office and headed off in some random direction.

After a while they ended up in a large gymnasium.

"Everything she said is true, sir. I was sent here to spy on you," Ki said.

"I think I can imagine what happened, Sergeant," Davage said, his voice echoing around the lofty gym. "Lord Sixtus of Grenville was wanting to renew his attack on me and my family, and in order to do that, he needed a shill, someone whom he could get to do his dirty work for him."

He paused. "You are a Brown, yes."

Kilos looked down at the gym mat.

"You needn't feel ashamed; some of my best friends are Browns. But still, in Lord Grenville's case, your status as a Brown is perfect. He could use you all he wants, and should anything happen, you will take all the blame. I'm certain you were pulled into his office. He found you of suitable stock and asked you to collect as much embarrassing information on me as possible. In such a case, you really don't have much of a choice, do you? You really can't say no to a Great House Lord, can you?" Davage smiled. "Did he mention anything about being executed?"

"He did, sir."

"Yes … certainly brave of him using a ditch-digging Marine to fight his battles and threatening to have her killed to boot. His family and mine have never gotten along. Vith and Remnath—there's a history there. Foolishness really."

Ki felt sick to her stomach. She wanted to be elsewhere; she'd had enough. She turned to the door of the gym. "Sir, I would best be going. It's a long trip back to Armenelos."

She looked around the gym, noting the fanciful painting of the *Seeker* on the far wall. She looked at Captain Davage standing there in his coat and hat. Here was a man she could have worked with, done great things with. She was certain of that.

"I'm sorry," she said. "I'm truly sorry I wasted your time today."

Davage ignored her. "And how should I react to this, Sergeant—this latest attack authored by dear Lord Grenville?"

Kilos stopped and looked at him.

"Perhaps I should be full of indignant rage, rather like Lieutenant Hathaline, and thoroughly punish you for this. That's what Lord Grenville expects that I will do; that's what he would do, certainly."

Ki began walking toward the door again. Davage watched her walk for a moment. "You know what I think, Sergeant?"

"Sir?"

"I don't think you've ever given yourself a chance. I think you've allowed yourself to get the better of you. That's why you're digging ditches. That's why you've been in Hack pretty much your entire time in the service, yes?"

"Sir ... I ..."

Davage took off his coat. "Until you exit the ship, you are under my command, Sergeant, let's not forget that."

She looked at him.

"I am going to give you an order right now, one that I think, given your record, is right up your alley."

"Sir?"

"I want you to knock me down, if you can. You're well practiced with those fists, use them. Knock me down."

She regarded him for a moment. He was tall, fit-looking, and appeared like he could take a punch. "I do not wish to hurt you, sir."

"Look to yourself, Sergeant, and fear not for me. Now, I've given you an order, and I wish it carried out, right now," he said rolling up his sleeves.

Resigned, Ki dropped her bag, took off her coat, and rolled up her sleeves as well.

Ten minutes later, Ki sat on the gym mat against the wall. Her jaw was killing her, she felt a tooth loose, and her right eye was watering, starting to close.

She hadn't been able to knock him down, though she nailed him a few times. And he nailed her too. He could hit—hard.

"You know, Sergeant," Davage said, putting his coat back on, "I think you lead a bit too much with your left. In any event, you hit like my sister—and that's actually a great compliment."

Ki sat there looking at him with her good eye. She honestly had no idea what was going to happen next.

"So, Sergeant, I think I've seen enough. I think you'll do fine."

"You still want me even though I was selected to spy on you."

"Are you still planning on doing that?"

"No, sir."

"Then yes, I want you. I'm sorry you were subjected to the silly entanglements that Great Houses appear to enjoy, but here you are. Lord Grenville certainly expects that, should you be discovered, I will take out my wrath entirely on you—similar to how Lieutenant Hathaline reacted. I cannot imagine a better way to annoy Lord Grenville than to accept you as is and provide you with every opportunity to excel—to finally show your quality. And as I stated earlier, I think you've allowed yourself to remain in the dregs for far too long—and I think, given the right circumstances, you might be amazed at what you can do, at how far you can go. I am willing to give you that chance. I hope as a result of this session here just now that I have earned a measure of your respect."

"You ... were hoping to earn ... my respect, sir?"

"Indeed. How can you follow an order if you've no respect for its source?"

Kilos looked at the mat again. She couldn't believe what she was hearing.

"Lt. Hathaline was correct, this is indeed a test, Sergeant, and why don't we pass it together, what do you say? I'm willing to give it a top-rate effort if you are. Wouldn't it be nice this evening to settle into your new quarters, grab a little something to eat, drop a Com to your husband, and tell him that your first day on the *Seeker* wasn't too terribly bad? Wouldn't that be nice?"

"Yes, sir."

Davage offered her his hand, and he pulled her up off the mat. "I don't think your first officer likes me much, though," she said.

THE LEAGUE OF ELDER 287

"Hath? Don't mind her; she doesn't like me either. Besides, you won't be reporting to her, you'll deal directly with me. I enjoy an open relationship with the Marines here on my vessel, and you will be a crucial component in that continued relationship."

Davage went to the wall, tapped a panel, and a hidden door opened. He pulled out a tankard and two glasses, which he filled.

"Here," he said, offering one to her. "A toast to our mutual success."

"What is this?" she asked, looking at the frothing liquid in the glass.

"Narva."

"That's a fruit drink, isn't it? I don't think I'll ..."

"You've not had narva until you've had it buncked. Try it."

"Buncked ... you mean it's spiked?"

"It is—highly against regulations, I assure you. There—your first bit of dirt on me."

They drank it, and it was good. Ki thought it was really good.

"Oh," Davage said, finishing his glass. "I took the liberty of circulating a Letter of Honor for your husband this morning before you arrived. Yes, I already knew all about you before you got here."

Kilos almost choked on her remaining narva.

"I hope your Lord Pittsfield doesn't mind. When I saw his outstanding school records to date, I couldn't believe he hadn't been offered a Letter previously. It looks very good for a Lord to sponsor such a promising student, and I was happy to do so."

Kilos stood there, dizzy. "Sir, I don't know what to say."

"Also, I found a discrepancy in your records over the last six months. It appears, whilst you were digging trenches for Lord Grenville, he wasn't paying you correctly."

"He did pay me, sir, with the Burl."

"Lord Grenville needs to check up on Fleet regulations. You were officially attached to the 8th Marines, which is under overall Fleet command. He formally requested the services of the 8th Marines and thusly, is compelled to bear responsibility for all pays due the Marines according to Fleet standards. The Fleet does not pay in Burl. I apologize for this confusion and have ordered you receive your full six-month back pay. Your whole company as well. I certainly hope Lord

Grenville's purse doesn't suffer too terribly. The funds should be in your account shortly."

Ki stood there and looked at her duffle. "Sir ... I—"

Davage clapped her on the back and picked up her bag. "Come now, Sergeant, let me show you to your new quarters, and let me be the first to officially welcome you aboard the *Seeker*."

The next day, Kilos flashed home to her husband a big lump of money—more than they both had ever seen. She got him on the Com, and she chattered excitedly about the ship and the village and what had happened with Lord Grenville and about Captain Davage—this Blue Lord who was so much more. She proudly showed him the black eye he'd given her and the tooth that he'd knocked out. It was okay, though, she already had an appointment with the ship's Hospitaler to have it fixed. She was so happy.

She kept a bit of the money for herself. She went out into the village and bought the rings she had liked and the books for her husband she had wanted.

Looking back at the *Seeker* parked in the bay as she stood there with her purchases, she knew she'd finally found a home and a captain to go with it.

She couldn't wait for her adventure to begin.

*   *   *   *   *

Ergos rocketed relentlessly closer and closer.

Syg sat in Dav's chair. Being on the bridge, and being visible at the same time, was a strange feeling for her.

The Sisters were there too, ten of them, each scanning the scene below, looking for Cloaked contacts.

Kilos looked back at the helm. Saari stood there, holding the wheel. She seemed to have composed herself, but Ki wanted to make sure not to push her too hard, so that she wouldn't break. She tried to make sure her orders were clear and easy to follow. This wasn't going to be a turning, rolling Dav-fight; it was going to be a straight at 'em, broadside furball.

The messages the Sisters were hitting Ki with came non-stop.

<There is nothing on the left quarter.>

<There is nothing to the right aft.>

<There is nothing ... >

<There is ... >

Ki recalled how hard Dav had to Sight in order to pick up the transports; they were Cloaked deep, and she didn't think the Sister's could Sight as well as he could.

"Keep trying, Sisters, they're out there in a hard Cloak. Number and composition unknown."

She turned to Saari at the helm. "Helm, report counter flood."

Saari glanced to her right. "Counter flood positive two. Ship is sailing with minimal trim."

"Any pull?"

"No ma'am."

Good, Kilos thought, *good*. "Not a bad job putting the ship back together, Sygillis."

Syg was shocked; she wasn't accustomed to being spoken to on the bridge. She was used to hiding out under Cloak. "Oh, oh ... thank you, Lieutenant."

The Sisters again. *<Cassagrain strike, temple wall, west quarter.>*

"Port Sensing, did you track a Cassagrain strike, temple wall, west quarter?"

"Aye ma'am."

"Transfer data to Canister control, triangulate to source and fire."

She spoke up: "All right, everybody, here we go. I don't think I have to remind you that this action is for our captain—for the man who should be right here, right now—and for all of us, whether you be Fleet or Marine, Hospitaler, Sister, or special guest, he is our man, ours, the beloved head of our family. There's not a person here whose name he doesn't know, whose back he hasn't slapped in genuine friendship. Be you of Great House or not, be you Blue or Brown, Vith or no, his door was always open, and he was always glad to see you. He did all that not because he had to, but because he wanted to ... because he thought it important, because he loves his crew as his own. He's down there all alone, and we are not going to fail him. Here we stand and here we make our family whole again. Understood?"

"Aye, ma'am!" the crew shouted.

With a characteristic "thud," the first canister left the ship and sped off toward its target, tail fire lit bright.

13

THREE SEEKERS

Davage shook his head when he looked up.

There were three *Seeker*s, soaring around at about four thousand feet, lights blinking, canisters firing.

One, of course was the real thing.

The other two were crude, ¼ scale Silver tech dummies that bore only the vaguest of resemblances to the real ship. He didn't even need his Sight to tell which from which.

Syg.

Obviously, Syg had squirted the two dummies out with shaped blobs of Silver tech and persuaded the Sisters dress them up a bit with Cloaked lights and surface details. She even had little Silver tech missiles shooting out, going here and there. She was probably sitting on the bridge right now, controlling them. It must be an odd thing for her to be invited on the bridge. He knew she often snuck up to the bridge Cloaked. She never ever gave his Sight the credit it was due. He didn't mind her on the bridge—he liked it, in fact.

He supposed that they were expecting a vast contingent of Black Hats down here, and that these ridiculous fakes might divert them. He wondered—why didn't they just send down Arrow shot from orbit and flood the area with Sisters and Marines? Kilos, being a Marine, liked to fight up close—she liked raking a target with Battleshot, and she would want to get up close to the Ghomes and sink them hard. Just a different style, a different way of going about it, he guessed.

Or maybe it was something else. Maybe they came in so close because they were wanting to see him, to be able to look down and possibly catch a glimpse of him and know that he was all right. Perhaps they just wanted to be near to him.

His ship, his crew—he didn't deserve their devotion.

He was concerned about the *Seeker* re-entering the atmosphere after the pounding she previously took. She didn't appear to be having any issues maneuvering. Could Mapes have repaired the spar to such a level that they were full in-planet capable? The ship wasn't doing any excessive or fancy maneuvering, but that was probably a result of Ki's straight ahead command style; the ship appeared to be under full control.

It banked gracefully; he could see its dorsal quarter.

No—no, look, the *Seeker's* back was coated in a shiny layer of ... silver.

Syg! Syg had fixed the spar with her Silver tech. Oh that tiny woman—how he missed her. She had fixed the spar, and he could imagine the scene that must have taken place in engineering to get Mapes to allow her to do such a thing—to outdo him at his own game. He guessed a Gift or two had probably been needed, maybe even some illegal Black Hat ones as well.

And then, she had fashioned these crude fakes to try and help save him.

Still, an idiot with one eye and no Sight could figure out the differences. Well, if you're going to come up with a silly, half-baked plan, why not go whole hog?

A canister blasted out of the real *Seeker* and slammed into a Cloaked transport, sinking it hard—more destruction for the good people of Metatron.

He could see the transports struggling to change course to fix their guns on the *Seeker*. The good thing was they seemed to be falling for the bait—they couldn't determine real from the embarrassing fakes as they laid bearings on them as well.

They fired, the *Seeker* returned, and down they went.

The more he looked at Syg's fakes, the more they annoyed him. It was clear that Syg had no idea what the *Seeker* looked like on the outside. Despite himself and the situation he was in, he found it galling, given the amount of pictures, paintings, and models of the ship available to her for reference, that she butchered it so badly; the *Seeker* was his baby.

She was going to get a stern talking to over this, he thought, right after he had properly re-united with her.

A transport fired on one of the fakes.

A canister popped out of the *Seeker*.

Bang, sunk. More wreckage.

Beyond, the temple began to fitfully rise. It struggled into the air, marking its progress in feet and inches.

Beneath it, he could see it was held in place by a thick black rope of Shadow tech, like a tether. And though the tether was stretching, he could clearly see that the temple would never be fully free of it on its own.

And, there was the Dark Man to the south, across the waterway. He stood hunched over with his hands on the destroyed remains of two buildings—like a child looking into a candy store window. He watched the temple struggle to climb into the air. His sinister thoughts were easy to divine: oh, what fun he was going to have, plucking the wings off this buzzing fly. He stepped over the line of towers and lesser buildings blocking his path and splashed onto the waterway. Striding in gore, he proceeded to its location. He was going to ensure it didn't go anywhere. He might just flatten it like an empty can when he got there after he tormented it for a bit.

Not if Davage had anything to say about it. Ignoring his aching eyes, he Sighted the monster, a cone of glowing light rising up into the blasted night.

Immersed in the hated light, it stopped in the waterway and flailed its arms about, fearing the light, despising it. It scooped up handfuls of dark water and threw it in Davage's direction, trying to douse the light; a rainfall of tepid water showered him, but he persisted. It plucked a *Ghome 7* transport out of the sky and threw it at Davage. He Wafted away and reappeared some distance to the north on the vast, flat area near the water. Trying to divert his attention from the temple, he hit the Dark Man again with his Sight. Awash in his golden glow and in misery, it stumbled into the canyons of tenement buildings and rapidly neared, his huge strides covering massive amounts of distance at a step. At last, standing over Davage and his tormenting light, he raised a giant foot and brought it down hard, ready to squash this light, to stamp out this glowing cinder.

Davage saw the foot coming down, blotting out the sky. In his Sight, he saw something rustling around inside the Dark Man—something that enraged him to the very core. Using much of the strength left to him, he Wafted up and away, vanishing from the ground as the foot impacted.

∗   ∗   ∗   ∗   ∗

"What the hell is that!" Kilos shrieked seeing this terrible giant striding through Metatron. It looked like a man-shaped mound of dried blood and gristle, three thousand feet tall, easy

Syg and the Sisters appeared shocked. Syg's hand came to her mouth. She appeared terrified.

<Dark Man, Dark Man, Dark Man, Dark Man ...> came thoughts into Ki's head over and over again.

"What is it?"

Syg sank into Dav's chair, weeping, defeated. "It means Dav's dead."

Kilos looked at the viewer. "What's that then?" she asked.

Syg looked up.

On the screen, as the Dark Man strode toward the Silver Temple, a cone of bright golden light came up from the dusty ground, shining right on him, like a searchlight. It waved its arms, not liking the light. Syg saw it and took heart.

They watched it splashing water, trying to drown the light, then it plucked something from the air and threw it. The light went out as a destroyed *Ghome 7* unCloaked and slammed into the ground, and then the cone of light re-appeared to the north. The Dark Man turned and pursued, splashing through the water.

Then, she saw it raise its horrid foot and stamp down in a geyser of water and broken rock, dousing the light.

Syg screamed.

*   *   *   *   *

Dav emerged from his Waft right in the gullet of the Dark Man. It was a rugose, fibrous dark patch, as if the whole unholy construction was formed of sinew. The interior seemed to wrap toward him, trying to envelop him and pull him into darkness.

He lit his Sight; the coils flew away, giving him space.

He had seen something from below, something that had enraged him like nothing else ever had.

Ahead, in the foul dankness, was what he had seen.

There, four women lay encompassed in black tendrils. They were laid open, guts hanging out, joints cracked and stretched, yet they were alive, fed and sustained by dark tubes forced into their mouths. They were naked, but bits of red cloth gave away their identity—Black Hats, the ones who had fled the field. Here was their punishment, to feel all the pain in the world for as long as possible. Here, in the dark belly, was the price of failure, the price for being afraid and trying to preserve their own lives.

Davage approached them and with his Sight, freed them from the black.

Their faces, their eyes told the tale of the torment they were experiencing.

"I'm so sorry ..." he said.

And he killed them, offering as merciful a death as he could.

His fury then turned to the Dark Man—this beast, this henchman and craft of the Black Abbess. "You wanted me, Abbess—*here I am!*"

He blasted the hardest Sight he'd ever tried, a cone of golden light, and he melted the innards of this thing, this Dark Man. He could hear it roar in pain, and he was delighted. Feel a bit of it, you bastard—taste it yourself!

He blew a hole in its belly, and he could see out into needly cityscape of Metatron far below. He turned his gaze upward, hoping to burrow up into its brain, hoping it dreaded every moment. He could feel it capering about, feeling its death near.

That's when his Sight faded, the Nyke poison inflicted by the Hulgismen robbing him of the strength to use it any further.

*   *   *   *   *

"It stomped on something!" Dieter said from his Sensing position.

"Who do you think it just stomped on?" Syg wailed.

She stood, near panic. "I'm Wafting down!" Syg screamed. "I want down there! I'm going to help him! I'm going to stand at his side!"

"You can't Waft, Syg, the Sisters have Wafting locked so that we can't get boarded. It's standard procedure," Kilos said.

"Then tell them to turn it off!" She turned to one of the Sisters standing near. "Turn it off!" she yelled.

The Sister looked at her dangerously and shook her head.

Kilos thought for a moment that Syg was going to do something drastic; she thought she might hit the Sister. And even though her relationship with the Sisterhood had greatly improved over the weeks, hitting a Sister would be a bad, possibly fatal, move.

Fortunately, events on the surface caught everyone's attention.

The Dark Man began exploding in light—a cone of gold came bursting out of its huge belly, reaming out a large, gory hole. He staggered about.

Dav—he was inside it hitting it with Sight. And it was staggering.

The Bridge cheered—crew, Ki, the Sisters, Syg, and all.

*   *   *   *   *

Davage plummeted out of the hole in the Dark Man's belly and fell to the surface. His strength was nearly gone, the Nyke flowing through him.

He managed to soft Waft down and he lay there, unable for the moment to get up.

The Dark Man blundered about, trying to recover from Davage's attack.

Ahead, the Silver Temple had managed to get about five hundred feet off the ground, the Shadow tech tether stretching but holding. All around, transports occasionally fired, and shortly after came crashing down, blasted by the *Seeker*. Apparently the Sisters couldn't break the Cloak, and Ki was using triangulation to locate them. Effective enough: to fire their cassagrains meant certain death.

The Dark Man recovered and continued on his way toward the temple, and this time Davage had no Sight to confound him with.

He wrung his huge hands, ready to dig into the silver temple.

One of the fake Silver tech ships crashed into him with a splashy thud, sending him reeling. He grabbed it and began trying to pull it apart. It stretched and gave, like silver taffy.

It then exploded, taking half his dark head and part of his chest with it. Syg—good one! The monster fell, again taking a block or two of Metatron with him.

The temple gave a groan. Its engines were apparently beginning to falter. It needed freeing, and it needed freeing now.

He concentrated. He concentrated hard …

*   *   *   *   *

<Free it! Free the Silver Temple! Cut the tether!> came a telepathic blast into Ki's head.

"Was that Dav?" she said, knowing how poor he was at basic telepathy. "Syg, did you get that?"

"Yes. It sounded like him!" she said, excited.

They turned their attention to the Silver Temple. They could see it was aloft. It was slowly spinning, slowly gaining altitude, but it seemed to hang there at about five hundred feet.

A black, twisted cord shackled it to the ground.

"What's that?" Ki asked.

"Shadow tech," Syg said. "A lot of it."

"Canister control!" Kilos yelled. "Fix coordinates on that Shadow tech cord and set dispersion for minimum radius!"

A moment later a canister missile shot out, snaked toward the target, and exploded.

The flash cleared. The cord was still there, still holding the temple in place.

*   *   *   *   *

Davage seethed with frustration. He saw the *Seeker* fire a canister and hit the tether, but to his horror, it was still there, still refusing to release its grip. He could hear the temple's engines starting to fail under the great strain of this protracted gravity launch.

The second fake *Seeker* skittered out of its meandering flight and dived down from the heights.

He saw it. Syg was going to crash it into the tether and explode it. Maybe that will do it. Maybe that will free the temple.

Maybe they will be free. Maybe they will triumph.

Only a bit longer, Drusilla. He could still feel her lips on his mouth.

When it was only a few hundred feet from the target, the Dark Man again!

He had sprung and intercepted the craft.

They watched the Dark Man, like a championship athlete, spring and grab Syg's Silver tech ship out of the air and fall to the ground with it. Almost comically the Dark Man twisted and spun about as he tried to hang onto the buzzing, careening vessel as it twisted this way and that.

"Syg, can you break it free?" Kilos asked.

"I'm trying. He's got it tight."

Kilos turned to Saari. "Helm, bring us down, five hundred feet, holding positive trim. And baffle those exhausts—we don't want to deafen the Captain!"

Saari pitched the wheel, and the ship dipped down. Immediately there was a crash as they slammed straight into a Cloaked transport, which spun down in flames and twisted metal and sunk.

Saari yelped and white-knuckled the wheel again.

"Don't worry about that," Ki said. "You just Slapped your first vessel, albeit accidentally, but no matter."

At five hundred feet, the ship leveled out and Kilos gave the order. "All Battleshot batteries, open fire!"

*   *   *   *   *

Davage watched the *Seeker* roar down from about two thousand feet to a very low, very noisy five hundred, Slapping a cloaked Ghome 7 ship along the way and bringing it down in a burning mass—more tough going to the citizens of Metatron.

At five hundred feet, he could feel the ground shake as the *Seeker*'s Battleshot batteries opened up, raking the Dark Man with withering, explosive fire, making that deafening "Buurrrrrrrrrrrrrrrr!" sound.

A leg and foot—the one he was going to stomp Davage with—flew off. His genitals disappeared in a cloud of exploding shot. What was left of his head stretched out and then vanished, and his hands caved in, releasing Syg's silver ship.

Smoking, the *Seeker* turned to port, stopping the shot, batteries overheating in the long barrage, a swung stump from the Dark Man just missing it.

Deformed by incidental Battleshot hits, the silver ship—Syg's laughably bad attempt to re-create the outer appearance of the *Seeker*— tumbled in the air for a moment, righted itself, picked up some speed, and hit the black Shadow tech tether square in the center, where it exploded in a silver flash.

He cheered. When it counted most, Syg's little silver ship performed brilliantly.

And the Black Abbess's leash snapped with an audible *twang*!

The temple was free.

But his joy was short-lived. The temple still hung there, slowly, painfully clawing for altitude and speed. It rose as lazy as a balloon on a still, windless afternoon.

And the Dark Man wasn't done—not by a long shot. A shot-riddled, beheaded, emasculated relic, he stood up on one filthy leg, rising into the night air like a stinking slag heap. In the stumps of his arms, he held his leg that had just been blasted off. He raised it high into the night, and he was going to use it to club the temple back down to the ground for good. It was right in his wheel-house, where he could really lay into it. There was no way he could miss.

Davage watched in horror.

* * * * *

Ergos appeared to Davage just then, standing there in the plain.

<*We give back what we took, and we hold you to your promise, Captain.*>

He waved his arms, and as if shot from a cannon, the spinning Silver Temple, flush with new energy, rocketed into the sky, shone there as a silver star for a moment, and was gone.

The hammer blow from the Dark Man missed, his leg and foot slamming into a block of dark buildings, leveling them. It rose up in froth; first it shall destroy the dammed starship and then it will flatten Metatron. Nothing will live after it was done. And then it will kill this Davage; slow and hard.

* * * * *

Nobody on the bridge could really believe what they were seeing. Headless, legless, armless, the Dark Man just kept on going. The Sisters were trying to dispel him as they would any they ordinary bit of Shadow tech, but he wouldn't go.

The door to the bridge opened.

"Sisters," came a musical voice, "will you please suspend the Waft-lock for me?"

* * * * *

Someone Wafted onto the plain where the temple had been. Davage watched the person appear, astounded that the Sisters had dropped the standard Waft-lock. That was something they never did for fear of being boarded.

The Dark Man saw the person. Someone small and weak. This person will be the first to die, then the ship, then Metatron, then Davage.

All will die.

All will die.

The Grand Abbess looked up at the Dark Man, utter contempt on her beautiful face.

She listened to it rage for a moment. Without a mouth, its ragings sounding like the pipings of a broken steam whistle stuck open.

"And let it be gone," she said with a wave of her arm.

The Dark Man cried out in surprise and agony. For once in its evil, wretched existence, it felt fear—the fear it had so joyously inflicted on others.

It fell back. It felt itself being torn apart.

It exploded in a cloud of soot. Soon, not even that remained.

14

A VISION COME TRUE ...

Davage watched the Grand Abbess destroy the Dark Man. With a simple wave of her arm, all that darkness was gone.

Always at the last moment, he mused. Who says only the Black Hats have a love of theatrics?

Despite all the things he had learned about secret agreements and abductions and all that, he still felt an unending love and admiration for the Sisterhood. They had earned it.

He felt his strength slip again. He found he could no longer hold his CARG—it was so heavy. How had he ever been able to use this thing?

He dropped it, and it clanked into the dust. The Nyke was getting to him.

The *Seeker* wasn't far. With the Waft lock down he could simply Waft into it—but he couldn't Waft.

All he could do was stand there, alone. Soon, he couldn't even do that. He fell into the dust next to his weapon.

Poof!

Syg appeared in a Waft cloud. In a panic, she scuttled about, her blue shawl flying this way and that, her sandals flapping.

"Dav!" she screamed. "Dav!"

She was so panic-struck, she looked right past him.

"I'm here, Syg," he said weakly.

She turned, eyes a-light.

She flew into his arms. "Dav, Dav!" she sobbed. "My love, my darling, are you all right?"

She covered his face in kisses. "I've been so worried about you!"

He tried to tell her that he needed a Sister, but she was in such a state, she wasn't listening.

Holding him by the shoulders, she looked him over. "Nyked! You're Nyked. Why didn't you tell me you were Nyked?" she said, incredulous.

Dav went to answer but the fluttering Syg cut him off. "Can you Waft?"

"I don't think so."

"I can't Waft two. I will go and get a Sister. Don't move ... don't move!"

She kissed him. "Don't move!" she said again and was gone.

The landscape of Metatron spun. He didn't think he had much longer.

Poof! Poof!

Syg returned, with a Sister—the one who liked him—at her side.

"Here, here he is!" Syg said to the Sister, though she could see him perfectly well.

The Sister approached Dav, sat down next to him, and looked him over. She propped him up and hugged him.

"Ohh ..." she said, startled, detecting the Nykes, and began working on him.

She laid her hands on him, and smoke began pouring out of Dav's wounds, from dozens of them. Dav could feel the Nyke nested in his body, dug in, beginning to fade. He could feel his strength returning.

The Sister, her winged headdress bobbing, spoke silently to Syg. Horrified, she put her hands to her mouth.

"What is it, Syg?" Davage asked. "I'm already feeling better."

"Dav," she said, nearly in tears, "the Sister says these Nykes were set to kill immediately. You should have been dead the moment you were poisoned."

She made to embrace him, but the Sister, still working, kept having to push her away.

After a bit, the Sister smiled and adjusted her headdress back a bit. She put her hands on his face. "You ... tough ... Captain ..."

"Pardon, Sister?" He remembered her hitting him with her thoughts in his office ... and winced.

The Sister turned to Syg, who was pacing about and looked like she was close to hysteria. "She says your Gifts saved you, slowed the Nyke down, kept it from working like it should."

After a few minutes more, the Sister smiled at Dav and kissed him on the cheek.

Syg watched her dubiously.

"Thank you, Sister," Dav said. She kissed him again.

She stood, curtsied, and began walking away, pushing past Syg.

She turned and looked at Syg.

"What's that mean?" Syg asked as the Sister Wafted away. "What's that mean?"

"What did she say, Syg?" Dav asked sitting up.

"She said to remember what she told you in your office because she meant it. What's that mean? What did she say?"

"She said ... to be careful."

Feeling almost like normal again, Dav went to stand up, but Syg tackled him, weeping uncontrollably.

They sat there for a while in each other's arms. Then, Syg reached down and pulled something from out of her sash and tossed it away. It clattered in the dust.

"What's that?" Davage asked.

"A ... knife," Syg choked. "I was going to kill myself."

"What? Why?"

"If something had happened to you. I couldn't go on alone. I couldn't ..."

"Well, I suppose it's a good thing I survived, then."

They stood and looked about, Syg a clingy, kissing mess, but after a few minutes she appeared to gain her humor back. He dusted off his CARG and saddled it again, with any luck for the last time that day.

She looked around at the towers and crampt huddles of buildings, familiar with the area. She looked at the big empty spot where the temple had been.

She saw the two Black Hats lying in the distance: Beth and the tall one, bound in silver.

She turned to Davage, angry. "Those Black Hats over there better be dead."

"They aren't dead."

"What were you doing saving Black Hats?"

"Couldn't help myself. The one on the left is Bethrael of Moane. Do you know her?"

"Bethrael of Moane? I do—she wasn't a particularly aggressive Hammer."

"No, she seemed fairly decent after I badly wounded her. We'll need to get her to see Ennez at once. The other one, the tall one bound in silver, she was tough—the best Black Hat fighter I've ever faced."

"What's her name?"

"Whilst we were in the midst of our mortal combat, the topic of her name didn't come up. I had to cut her hand off, and this thing came out of her ... the thing that grew and the *Seeker* shot at."

"The Dark Man ... it was in her?"

"Yes."

"Then we might as well kill her, Dav. It will be a mercy. If she bore the Dark Man, there will be nothing left of her soul."

"We'll see, I suppose."

As ripcars and transports began pouring down from the *Seeker* to mop up the area, Kilos got out of one and ran toward them.

Again, for the third time today, Davage was tackled into the dust, this time by his first officer. The family was together once again.

Later, as the last of the Shadow tech was cleaned away by the Sisters and their Marines, Dav and Syg stood alone ... away from everyone in Metatron.

"I saw my temple rising into the sky, like a spaceship," she said.

He turned to Syg and took her by the hands. "Syg, let me tell you of your children."

And he told her, he told her everything. He told her of Durman and Drusilla and Carahil, of the light within the temple and the city that was built beneath it.

He told her what would have happened if she had entered the temple and triggered the Black Abbess' trap. The color drained out of her face as he did.

He told her how the Silver Children, young, innocent, bewildered, had steeled themselves and stood fast against the Black Abbess's hoards.

He told her of the stories they sang to comfort themselves as evil knocked on their door, calling for their deaths.

He told her what they dreamed of.

He told her that they had forgiven her, for they knew that she had been lost in the evil nightmare too, just like they were.

Syg listened and wept.

And he told her of the silver image atop the dais. He told her that it had moved at his touch. He told her what he said to the image.

He told her … that he loved her.

They held each other, the knife lying in the dust beyond forgotten.

$$* \quad * \quad * \quad * \quad *$$

A triumph over Metatron. And so, what happened to the Silver Temple?

They wandered for months through the empty dust and lonely bowers of space, their navigation sorely disappointing and wholly inadequate. But as it had on Metatron, the Silver Temple nurtured them, standing against the rigors of prolonged open space. They sang to each other, wondering when they might find a home.

Eventually, they came across a distant green world. They set down, exited the temple that had sheltered them and found the place they were looking for—a kind landscape and gentle sky. A friendly local people. There they built cities and took husbands and wives. There they thrived.

All except Drusilla, the woman who had piloted them to this promised place and wrote their lore. Every night she walked to the top of a distant hill and stared at the stars, waiting for one to fall. Waiting for her Captain Davage, whom she could never forget.

* * * * *

When he returned to the *Seeker*, Davage was greeted with the expected adulation. His crew mobbed him wherever he went. The captain was back; that's all that mattered.

Bethrael and the tall Black Hat both went to the dispensary immediately.

Ennez was shocked and furious at the damage he'd inflicted on them and endlessly lectured Davage as he worked on Bethrael's head.

Dav told him that he had several wounds himself that probably needed looking at.

Ennez said he'd get to them later.

Eventually, griping the entire time, he saved Beth, rebuilt her arm, re-attached the tall one's hand, and mended her broken ribs.

Dav then had the tall one thrown into the brig—he, having faced her fury on the battlefield, influenced by the Dark Man or not, didn't trust her.

The next day, he and Kilos went to the dispensary to see how Bethrael was doing.

Inside they could hear a loud, rowdy clamor.

They drew their pistols and burst in, ready to see Ennez in his death throes at her hands.

Inside, Ennez sat at Bethrael's bedside. They were laughing together—belly laughing, actually, Beth's eyes watering with delight.

"What's so funny in here?" Dav asked, shocked.

"Oh, Captain," Ennez said, "put your pistol away, will you. I was just sharing a funny story I'd heard with Beth here."

Davage and Kilos looked at each other and put their weapons away.

He looked at the bandaged, smiling Beth. "And how are you feeling today, ma'am?" he asked.

Beth wrinkled up her face. "And how are you feeling today, ma'am?" she said, imitating Davage's voice as best she could.

She and Ennez again burst into laughter.

Again, Davage and Kilos looked at each other.

Davage seized the moment. "Listen, ma'am, if this laughing fit has something to do with the shocking state of Ennez's hair, I will have him hauled off and shaved bald immediately. I've been waiting years for this."

Beth wracked herself with laughing. She struggled for breath, waving her splinted arm in the air.

"Captain, will you please leave my hair out of this? It's a sore spot for me." Ennez said, giddy.

"Quiet, Bad-Hair!" Kilos said. "The only person you should be sore at is your barber!"

They laughed again.

Later, after Kilos had to return to the bridge and Ennez to the brig to check on the tall Black Hat's hand, Bethrael looked up at Davage with a serious note.

"You had asked me, sir, if I would ever be able to forgive you, for hurting my head and my arm ..."

"Yes, that is still my hope."

She smiled. "Already done, long done. Things are a bit cloudy, but I remember you, in that horrible place. I remember your eyes glowing and all my anger fading away. I remember you protecting me, defending me, trying to keep me warm. I remember you saving me from the Silver People and the Dark Man. I remember you carrying me even as your strength was nearing its end. You showed me more kindness and devotion than I'd ever seen in my whole wasted life."

She sat up a little. "You are, now and forever, my hero and savior, and I will never forget you."

She took his hand and kissed it. "Thank you, sir."

"Thank you, sir," Davage repeated, imitating her.

They laughed.

15

SUZARAINE OF GULLE

Davage and Syg walked into the outer chamber to the brig. Ennez was there looking over his readings.

"Do we have a name for her yet, Ennez?"

"The Sisters said she's Suzaraine of Gulle, a Black Hat of Hammer class."

"Know her, Syg?" Davage asked.

"I know of her. What was Suzaraine of Gulle doing out there in Metatron?"

"Don't know. How's she looking, Ennez?"

"She's nominal physically, considering the pounding you put to her, the ribs I had to fix, and the hand I had to re-attach."

"I'm sorry for that, but if I hadn't you'd be completing my autopsy right about now. Bethrael's too."

Syg didn't appreciate the joke. "And her soul, Ennez?"

"I don't have a scanner that tests the condition of the soul, Syg," he said. "But her brain is reading normally. It's just that—"

"What?"

"Her autonomic activities are functioning, but not much else. It's like she's in a coma, but she's awake at the same time. It's like she's brain-dead, yet she's conscious."

"It's the Dark Man, I told you. Her soul is gone."

"Explain that, please, Syg," Dav said.

"The Dark Man is a Shadow tech totem. It's horrible, evil. Remember when Kilos said that Shadow tech is created by evil thoughts? Well, she is usually wrong, of course, but in this case, she was right. Certain types of Shadow tech can be created by evil thought, but you have to be next to the devil to do it. Only the Black Abbess and a few others can conjure it. The Dark Man was her handiwork, and he was there to kill you, Dav."

"Syg, please ..."

"You said Suzaraine was a tough fighter, that she didn't fight like most Black Hats and that she covered her eyes when you tried to Sight her?"

"Yes ..."

"Well, there is no way in creation that Suzaraine of Gulle could have done that on her own. It was the Dark Man, and he was gunning for you." She became a little pale as she considered the notion.

"The Dark Man is gone. The Grand Abbess destroyed him."

"The damage is done, Dav. If you bear the pain of the Dark Man, there is nothing left of you when he's gone. She wasn't supposed to survive this."

Dav considered what Syg had said and Sighted into the brig.

Suzaraine of Gulle lay there on the bench, limp, boneless almost, her head lolling long on her flaccid neck. Her corn-colored hair hanging straight to the floor—a distant cry from that tall magnificent warrior who fought him to his last breath on the dusty Metatron plains.

This exercise, he thought, will be endlessly harder than the turning of Syg and the ridiculously easy freeing of Bethrael. This will be nothing less than the recreation of the persona—the re-discovery of the soul.

Davage wondered if it could be done at all.

*   *   *   *   *

"You are not going in there," Syg said after dinner. "I don't want you to work with Suzaraine of Gulle. Find somebody else. Besides, I don't feel anything coming from her regardless. She's alive, poor thing, but her soul is shattered."

"It will be a challenge, but we'll find success with persistence."

"The Dark Man ate her soul. Besides, Suzaraine of Gulle was a terrible Black Hat."

"Oh, indeed—she was a tremendous fighter."

"No, no, Dav, I mean just that, she was terrible—incompetent. It was said that her temple in Gulle was so badly put together, so misshapen, that it couldn't even keep the rain out. She was on the Black Abbess's list—even spent time in her dungeon because of her poor efforts and lack of dark imagination."

"We can't all be good craftsmen ..."

"It's Shadow tech, Dav. I didn't hammer my temple together."

"I suppose I will discover that tomorrow."

"Again, Dav, I should feel more at ease if you assigned someone else to go in your stead."

"Do you want to try?"

"I don't think it will do any good. Her soul has been eaten. She bore the Dark Man, probably as an attempt by the Black Abbess to assassinate you, and there can be nothing left of her soul. I feel for her, but perhaps it's best not to try. Perhaps we should make her as comfortable as possible and let her go."

"I'm going into the brig in the morning, and I'm going to save her."

"I prefer that you did not."

"Why, Syg?"

"Captain Davage," Syg said putting her fork down, "Lieutenant Kilos was good enough to inform me of all the various females you've encountered over the years who have, to quote her, 'lost it for you.' I am here to tell you that I am the last woman who will ever 'lose it' for you. There will be nobody else. *There better not be anybody else!* I would hate to be that woman!"

"Ki doesn't know what she's talking about."

"Oh ... let's see, she was rather specific: Demona of Ryel, Marshall Henbane, Princess Marilith, and that damned Captain Hathaline— what about them?"

"She forgot to mention Jadis Two-Fists, Admiral Scymadar, and Ferd the Younger. And I dispute Demona of Ryel. I don't think she was in love with me."

Syg's head looked like it was ready to explode. Dav fought hard to keep from laughing—these fits of temper from Syg never lasted long and she would, no doubt, be very apologetic later. Syg, in full apology-mode, was a sight to behold.

"All right, fine! More women whom I'm going to have to hunt down! I'll go ahead and take Demona's name off the list, if that makes you happy."

Davage thought about mentioning Drusilla and how she reacted to him, and how he almost had reacted to her. But he thought better of it, with Syg's jealous streak showing mighty green it might not be wise to prod her any further.

"Are you saying that your falling in love with me was some sort of automatic, pre-programmed response? That simply because I was the person you were around the most that you automatically fell in love with me?"

"No, that's not what I'm saying. I'm saying that you, all tall, handsome, and suave, Lord Blanchefort, tend to create an emotional response in women that … could be rather … dangerous for them."

"So, you'd kill such a woman, would you?"

"No, but a humiliating, clothes-ripping public pounding might be in order!"

"Syg, are you jealous?"

"Well spotted, Dav!" she replied tartly. "Yes, I'm jealous—happy?"

"Sygillis, I cannot believe that you would willingly sacrifice the life of Suzaraine of Gulle on the simple notion that you are feeling jealous and for no good reason."

"I am not saying we sacrifice her life. I am saying that, if she is to be saved, *somebody, anybody, other than you is going to do it!*"

Davage headed to the door. "I must to the bridge."

"Where are you going?" Syg shrieked. "You have not asked my leave for you to depart, and additionally, you have not yet kissed me good-bye!"

"Madam!" Davage said. "I will take it under advisement!"

* * * * *

Davage sat in his office trying to complete some reports. His argument with Syg still bounced around in his head.

He'd made up his mind. Syg was just going to have to be upset. He was going in, and he was going to try and save Suzaraine of Gulle.

She needn't worry—he loved her, he will not stray. Also, though it was slightly annoying, he found it flattering that Syg made such a fuss. She loved him, all of her, bad temper, jealous streak, and all.

Still, a woman's life hung in the balance, and he wasn't going to abandon her.

Look at Beth—look at how far she'd come in just a short time, talking, eating, gaining a bit of healthy weight, belly-laughing with Ennez. Her progress was everything Dav had hoped it would be and more. She had already expressed interest in becoming a Hospitaler, of all things. She said she thought the Jet Staff Hospitalers use was "cool." And Dav had to admit, a Hospitaler using a Jet Staff was a cool thing to watch.

Syg had told him that Bethrael of Moane was never considered to be a fierce Black Hat, that her heart was never really in it. Beth herself said that her skills weren't the best—that her temple in Moane was a "shack" in comparison to Syg's, that she was a poor, embarrassing Hammer.

Dav, though, was convinced that, perhaps a good deal of her soul had survived intact from the Black Abbess' church. While the seed of Syg's soul was just that—an undeveloped vessel—Beth's had sprouted on its own and endured the long night. Perhaps, given that criteria, she was probably the toughest Black Hat of them all.

Another thing Syg had mentioned greatly troubled him. Bethrael was a relatively docile Hammer, and Suzaraine was an incompetent bearing the Dark Man within her to kill him. What about the other eight? Were they also poor Black Hats? Were they novices? Were they sent to Metatron because the Black Abbess didn't figure on much resistance from Syg's temple, or did the nut of her plan to re-take Syg and turn her evil render them disposable and inconsequential?

What about the Black Hats he mowed down on Carahil's back? He wondered at the terror, the panic they must have felt.

He thought of the ones he killed in the Dark man's belly ... a mercy killing.

He silenced the thought; the guilt will consume him if he continued.

And so, Suzaraine of Gulle, that tall, shattered woman wasting away in the brig, shall be saved.

There was a knock at the door.

"Please come in," he said. He assumed it was Syg coming to say she was sorry for being so silly.

The door opened and Commander Mapes entered, his large triangle hat in hand.

"Mapes," Davage said, "how goes it? How's my ship?"

"The ship is fine, Captain. Everything is running as well as can be expected."

Davage looked at him—tall, sandy hair, flat, craggy nose, jutting, slotted chin, slightly heart-shaped face, gray eyes—a Grenville certain enough.

Suddenly, Syg sent him a message as she was wont to do. *<I'm sorry, Dav,>* clattered into his brain.

He composed himself and continued with Mapes. "Fine then, and as always, excellent work. So, what can I do for you?"

"It was Lady Sygillis. She mended the spar, truth be told. She is a fine, saucy woman. She ... put the Dirge to me."

<I would like to apologize to you, Dav, as only I can,> came Syg's voice again.

"I see. And did you have the Dirge coming to you?"

"I did, Captain. I was rude and arrogant. And the spar was mended, despite myself. Lady Sygillis was right to do what she did. I fully acknowledge that now."

He paused for a moment and looked at his hat.

"I am to understand, sir, that we have a prisoner below ... one who is in need of assistance. I wish to offer my help in that matter."

Davage dropped his report and stared at Mapes, hard.

"What are you playing at here?"

"Nothing, sir, I simply wish to help as best I can."

Davage sat there and regarded him for a moment.

<When you are ready for your apology, come to me and be prepared to stay a while. You might want to eat something before you come,> Syg telepathied to him.

"And I suppose the fact that this prisoner, this woman you wish to assist, is a Black Hat has made no factor in your mind, has it?"

"I freely admit I admire Lady Sygillis, I admire her power. If this woman—"

Davage allowed his temper to get the better of him. He smashed his fist down on the desk. "This isn't a game, Mapes, a fancy, comely party amusement! This is a woman's life, and it is your life too if you go in there!"

"I know that."

Davage began to fume. The old Blanchefort-Grenville dislike began to bubble up in earnest. Sadric and Mapes' father, Marist, shared an ongoing, mutual loathing, each eternally trying to outdo and humiliate the other. They threw grand balls, extravagant parties just so they could cross the other's name off the invitation list—the ultimate slap. So, here was Davage, having accomplished the novel and quaint act of turning a Black Hat. Now, hard on his heels, here was Mapes, a Grenville, wanting to do the same thing—not wanting to be outdone by a Blanchefort.

"Here on orders from your brother, are you, Mapes? Trying to get in on the latest craze. Look everyone, adopt a wayward Black Hat— teach her to smile, teach her to dance a trick. Watch her fall in love with you. It is easy and fun!"

"Sir, that's not how it is."

"Then how is it, tell me? Do you even know her name?"

Mapes fumbled with his hat. "Her name is Suzaraine of Gulle. Gulle is a small city on the northern end of Zust. Her temple may be found on ..."

"All right, enough ... so you did your research. You've firmly scouted down your quarry, I'll grant you that."

Mapes pleaded with Davage. "Sir, I know how this must seem. We have never been particular friends. I was initially appointed to this post via political stratagems to cloud your command and possibly cost you a reappointment. My brother hates you for stealing his bride—"

"Marilith?"

"—and our families have certainly never been on the best of terms, but you are my captain, and in that role I have always cherished you, always acknowledged your quality. I have done that from near the beginning. This latest incident has thrown into bold relief the full depth of your character, the strength of your courage. You are not only a great captain; you are a great man as well. And I saw how Lady Sygillis looks at you, is devoted to you. I saw, and experienced firsthand, her single-minded determination to get you back, how she would not rest and how she would do whatever needed doing to ensure your return, even if it meant putting a fool like me to the Dirge to do it. I—I want something similar for myself—a woman who loves me to the ends of her soul. I want a woman who will look at me like she looks at you."

"Suzaraine of Gulle is not a toy or a wind-up novelty. Who's to say she won't hate you, try to kill you? She was by far the most potent Black Hat fighter I've ever seen, though that might have been the result of foreign control."

"I am willing to take that risk. For the hope of such love, I am willing to risk my life. There are two lives at stake here, Captain—both hers and mine. I want to make the effort. I want to save us both."

Davage looked at Mapes. He could hear the sincerity in his voice, see it in his face.

"Neither I, nor the Sisters, can guarantee your safety. I will not have a valued member of my crew subject himself to—"

"I am an Officer of the Fleet and the son of a Great House. You are not the only one who has courage, the only one who can put himself at risk. You are not the only man who can save a life. And like you, I am not helpless…"

Davage saw a glint of something moving under his Fleet coat—the VUNKULA, no doubt.

He continued, "For once, Captain, I wish for people to see me, me—not as a commander or the brother of the great Sixtus, Lord of Grenville, but me, Mapes, and I wish for them to say that Mapes is a brave man too."

Dav stood and saw his engineer in a new light. "This is truly what you want, Mapes?"

"It is, Captain."

"Then perhaps I have judged you too harshly. Perhaps, when I look at you, I see only your brother, and I have forgotten that you are your own man. If that's the case, then I am in error, and I apologize. If you wish to do this, and if you are fully prepared for the dangers, the consequences, and the responsibilities that may follow, then I shall not halt you."

"If there be responsibilities, then I look forward to meeting them."

Davage held out his hand. "Good luck, sir."

Mapes took his hand and shook it warmly. "Look at us—a Grenville and a Blanchefort sharing a good moment together."

Davage smiled. "Our fathers are, no doubt, rolling in their graves. But Mapes, this isn't about our families, this is about two men, two Elders, finally opening their eyes and seeing each other's worth fully for the first time."

"And maybe this day marks that end of what was and begins afresh on a new page. I would like that very much." Mapes put his hat back on and made to leave the room.

"Mapes," Davage said, "I will not be happy to lose my fine engineer. I will entreat you to be careful. I will want an exact schedule of when you plan to subject yourself to her. Though I fully acknowledge your skills, I still will want to look in from afar from time to time and ensure that you are relatively safe, and perhaps I could offer some advice on the matter should you feel you need it."

"Thank you, sir. I will, provide the schedule."

After Mapes left, Dav got another message from Syg. *<That was beautiful, Dav. Now come home so that I may begin apologizing to you! I am eager to begin ...>*

Syg had been apologizing to Dav for several hours in her quarters. As he drifted in and out of pleasure-induced hazes, he vaguely suspected that she liked losing her temper on occasion so she could really unload on him later.

Though she had been listening from afar, he related the encounter with Mapes to her in detail.

"Does Mapes realize what he might be in for? Is he seeking a trophy of some sort?"

"That's what I thought a first. But despite everything, he is a good man, and I am convinced he is sincere."

Syg kissed him. "Are you worried about his safety?"

"Of course I am."

"Well, Dav, it can't always be you who's dangling over the fire. Mapes will do fine."

"You didn't find him an overly charming man."

"No, but then again I had other things on my mind, and his chortling was slowing down your rescue. Still, I hope he doesn't get too eager. This is not going to be quick or easy. This is going to be like resurrecting a dead body. She has no soul left."

"I was thinking about that. With you, it was like a fencing match. You were certainly venomous and unpleasant …"

"Thanks, Dav."

"… but you were there. You were an active participant. Bethrael I won't even count. Freeing her was like a big party. This—this could be beyond help."

"He is setting himself up for heartbreak."

"He provided me with a schedule. His first attempt shall be tomorrow right after the breakfast bell. I suppose we shall find out more then."

*   *   *   *   *

The first time Mapes went into the brig, he immediately called for a Hospitaler; he was certain she was dead. Ennez came, scanned her, confirmed her both alive and awake, and left.

There she was, slumped on the bench, dressed in a pair of white pajamas. She hadn't moved in days.

Davage watched with piqued interest from his office—oh but the Sight was convenient.

He tried talking to her at first and then he sat next to her, confused, wondering if he really wanted to be in there with her after all.

After a while, he stood and made to leave the brig. Perhaps he'd been foolish; perhaps the captain was correct.

Before he got to the door, he stopped, thought a moment, and went back to her. Carefully, he lifted her head, moved her hair out of her face, and stared for a moment, looking at her lolled, blank face.

He took his coat off, forgetting about the VUNKULA hanging at his backside. He removed a handkerchief from his pocket and began cleaning her face, wiping away the drool and the crusted material that had built up on her mouth. He then gently picked her up, sat down, and laid her on top of him.

Holding her close, he slowly rocked back and forth. He held her like that for hours.

Davage was impressed.

The next day he tried feeding her. He had a bowl of bland broth and tried to get her to eat.

Nothing, no response. The broth went into her mouth and sat there unswallowed.

And so with the third day, and the forth, and the fifth.

* * * * *

"Dav," Syg said, "this can't go on much longer. The pain was too much for her. It would have been too much for anybody."

Davage sat there in his office and paused a moment. "I have had similar thoughts. Mapes, though, has become attached to her. Failure will break his heart, I think."

"We are inflicting a cruelty on her, Dav. She strides the wastelands, neither alive or dead. We must let her go." She paused. "I've been to see Bethrael."

"Isn't her progress remarkable?"

"It is … it is, and I am glad for her."

"She can wear slippers. How come you can't wear slippers? How come you can't wear a pair of fine Blanchefort shoes?"

Syg looked at Dav and beamed. "Can't is not the right word, love. Won't is better. Anyway, she … still has Shadow tech. It hasn't fully converted yet."

"And?"

"I had her make me this. She didn't want to, but I insisted." Syg held out her hand.

She held a tiny grayish-black knife.

"What's this?" Davage asked.

"It's a Nyke."

"You cannot be serious."

"I'm only thinking of her, Dav, that's all. She still feels his pain. The Dark Man's clutch goes on even after he is gone. One little scratch, quick and painless, and she will have peace."

He looked at the knife and took it from her. The thought of killing Suzaraine, like a pained animal, was offensive to him.

Still ... she was right, this couldn't go on much longer.

*   *   *   *   *

On the sixth day, Davage pulled Mapes into his office. He said he had been watching his progress, told him he was proud of the effort he had put in, that he had been true to his pledge.

But ... time was running out. He told him that she might be suffering, showed him scans that Ennez had made indicating the possibility that all she was experiencing was pain. He showed him other scans—her body was shutting down. She was in the slow, initial stages of death.

Mapes listened, silent.

And Davage showed him the Nyke that Beth had made, explained that it could be the best course for her—to let her go.

Mapes thought about it for a bit. He then begged Davage for one more day. Let him try a little longer, and if nothing happened, then ... then they could put her to rest.

He went in there with fresh energy. He tried feeding her again. He held her, he sang to her; he even picked her up and carried her around the cell.

Nothing.

He shook her, incensed.

Nothing.

After a while he stood there, looking at her, his hat in hand.

She fell over with a thud.

And that was all ... there was nothing left for it.

*   *   *   *   *

The door to the brig opened and Mapes came out, weeping in grief, almost as shattered as the wretched waif within, his heart-shaped face red with anguish.

Davage, Syg, and a Sister waited for him in the outer chamber. He had tried his best, exhausted himself for days, and had failed.

He staggered to the wall; Syg took him and tried to dry his tears.

"She bore the pain, Mapes. She bore it until she could bear it no more. You did all you could."

Davage stood there, listening to the ululation coming from Mapes. He looked at the small knife in his hand. Nyked. One tiny scratch and it will be over, quick and painless.

She will have peace.

He steeled himself and approached the door. He Sighted through it, readying himself for what was within.

He saw something. He stopped in his tracks.

Inside, in the lonely confines of the brig, he saw Suzaraine, feebly, almost imperceptibly, moving. She was reaching with all the strength that was left to her for the bowl of bland food sitting on the floor where Mapes had left it. It was just out of her grasp.

"Mapes!" Davage said. "Mapes, wait! Get back in there!"

Syg turned to him. "You see something?"

"Mapes, hurry!"

Dropping his hat, Mapes, red-faced, tear-streaked, bolted for the door and went in.

Dav watched in wonder. There, inside, he saw Mapes tenderly take Suzaraine into his arms and slowly, carefully, feed her, giving her all the time she needed to take the food and swallow.

Eventually, she ate the whole bland bowl.

Then, still in his arms, she began to weep … quietly at first, then building to a wracking, coughing wail. Mapes, rocking slightly, let her cry, let her toil out all the pain and suffering she had endured.

Eventually, she fell asleep. For the first time since she'd been taken aboard, she slept.

Outside, Davage knew that this was the turning point, that this was the moment when the both of them had been broken down to their barest, most basic of elements, and together, been re-forged.

He knew that it will be all right now. He dropped the knife and turned to the Sister in attendance. "Sister, will you please destroy that."

She looked at it, waved a finger, and it was gone.

And as Davage had thought, Suzaraine began to show marked improvement. She began eating on her own, moving, standing up, and using the hand that Ennez had re-attached. She began speaking, and she had her first smile, her first laugh. Mapes even taught her how to dance—a stuffy Grenville step, but still.

And in their Shadow tech off loads, Syg found that Suzaraine's Shadow tech was every bit as potent as hers had been. Again, her incompetence had been nothing more than a sign that her heart wasn't into being a Black Hat—that it had been her way of defying the Black Abbess.

Unlike the bubbly Beth or the saucy Syg, "Suz" was always quiet and reserved, though Mapes often mused that wasn't how she was behind closed doors—said that she was a regular chatterbox. She was very intelligent and had begun to grasp many elements of basic engineering just by watching Mapes. She was a prolific, thoughtful writer and made many friends in League society via correspondence.

She never spoke to Davage in public, red-faced and shy, she could barely face him without becoming a nervous wreck. But in correspondence, she often wrote him huge letters, detailing her progress, her entry into League society, all the things she was discovering, and her love for Mapes. And though she never actually said it, she was eternally grateful to him for helping her, for not killing her in Metatron.

*   *   *   *   *

And what of their temples? What of Beth's "shack" in Moane and Suz's leaky creation in Gulle?

For them and the Hulgismen within, there was no salvation, no triumph like Syg's temple had seen.

For them was nothing but the full fury of the Black Abbess.

She waited ... waited for their Shadow tech to turn, to become silver. She waited for the Hulgismen's eyes to open and fill with light, and then she struck, and this time with the worst, most evil and bloodthirsty Black Hats she could muster.

They fell on Moane and Gulle and cracked those temples open like huge silver oyster-shells. They pulled every living creature out and killed them all, slowly, terribly. They also killed everybody else, all the citizens of Moane and Gulle who were within close proximity to the temples, close enough to be illuminated in their light; they were to die as well. And they Painted those orgies of pain and destruction for all to see—their fear and torment to be re-lived by any who came near forever.

"Princess Marilith Regrets…" ©2009 Carol Phillips

Part 3
THE FANATICS OF NALLS

1

LORD PROBERT

Syg was triumphant. The past few days had been magical.

First, her vision had come true. She stood with Dav in Metatron, and holding her hands, he told her that he loved her. He loved her!

Second, she was soon to see his castle; the *Seeker* was on its way to Blanchefort to dry-dock and complete repairs. She was going to get to see his castle at last. More things to add to the list that she had gotten to do that many of Dav's past loves hadn't. She was ever competing with this swirling gaggle of phantom women—contesting with a group of women who weren't even there.

She was allowed on the bridge now, and she sat in his chair, quiet, but giddy and excited. Pay Master Milke was distressed to lose his favorite assistant.

On the screen, Kana appeared, a big green and blue ball. The ship entered into orbit, did a lap or two, and slowly plunged into the atmosphere, Dav issuing important-sounding orders. Before long, a gray spur of land and water appeared on the screen, and soon a bay and small village grew into focus. Soon, the helmsman sat the *Seeker* down on pylons in the bay.

She couldn't wait to get out into the sunshine and see his castle.

It took a little longer than she had first thought. Dav asked her to come to engineering with him. She didn't know why; she thought she might be in trouble for something.

Along the way, they came across a small, roundish man in civilian clothes whom Syg had never seen before. He wore a large brown coat, huge plumed hat, and buckle shoes.

The man burst into a smile, and he and Dav hugged roughly.

"Lord Probert!" Dav said.

"Captain Davage—what have you done to my ship this time? I ought to send you a healthy bill, sir!" Lord Probert cried.

They separated, and Dav motioned for Syg. "Lord Milos of Probert, allow me to introduce Sygillis of Metatron, my dear special guest."

Special guest? Why couldn't he just say, "This is the woman I love," or "This is the woman I plan to make my Countess," or "This is the hot babe I've been doing every night as of late."

Men.

Lord Probert looked at her a moment, doffed his huge plumed hat, and bowed.

"Sygillis of Metatron, I've heard. However, you failed to inform me what an enchanting vision she is, Captain Davage."

Lord Probert took her hand and kissed it. "He's really done it to my ship this time, hasn't he?" he said with a wink.

Syg smiled. She found she liked the fellow. He had an easy, friendly way about him.

"Sygillis," Davage said. "Lord Probert here is the 'father' of the *Seeker*, per se. He designed the *Straylight*-class from mere images to the finished item you see here. His father, Wadlow, Lord of Probert designed the older *Webber*-class of ships."

"Yes, yes," Probert said. "I've been wanting you down at the yards, Dav. I've got something new on the blocks."

"You ... you've finally designed a successor to the *Straylight*-class, haven't you?

"Let us say ... I was inspired by the *Triumph*."

"Ohhh, I will wager it's going to be beautiful."

"That's why I need you down there, to help me with some of the details, and to get that harpy Lady Branna of the Science Ministry off my back for a while. Elders, but I am covered with her claw marks."

"Is she wanting to incorporate more energy technology again, shields, warp drives, cassagrains, and the lot?"

"She is, this time from the *Triumph,* and I'll see her dead or in prison first before I allow any of that Bad Gin on my new, beautiful ship."

Lord Probert turned to Syg. "And now, I am here to assess the damages wrought on this fine vessel by your outrageous captain here, but he tells me that the major repairs to the ship were effected largely by you, ma'am."

"Sir?" Syg said

"He tells me that you repaired the spar."

"No need to be shy, Syg," Dav said.

"Oh, yes, sir, I did repair the spar, or so I've been told."

"Well, excellent!" Probert said. "I am eager to see it for myself."

He offered Syg his arm in a gentlemanly way, and smiling, Syg took it. With Davage following, they went into the engineering bay.

The last time she was in this area, she had Mapes Dirged, the Marines and Fleet crew swirling around, ready for a fight.

Inside was a bustle of activity: people moved about, working on this and that. The half-moon-shaped compartment was open to the sky. The cold northern clouds could be seen through a huge, ragged hole high overhead.

And, there was the spar, a coated silver bar, spanning the top.

Lord Probert released her, and Syg made her way back to Dav and took his arm. She looked up, savoring the blue sky. Her heart fluttered; through the hole in the ship she thought she could see the hints of a distant reddish castle spire reaching into the sky. Oh how she wanted off the ship.

Probert took his hat off and leaned back, gazing at the spar high above.

"Lady Sygillis," he said, "did you do this?"

"I did, sir."

Probert went to a terminal, tapped a few keys, and pored over some data.

"All on your own, you did this?" he said again.

"I was eager to rescue the captain here, and I was told this construction, in its previous condition, was preventing that."

"True enough, true enough." He ran his hands through his short brown hair and surveyed her work again. "Captain, were I you, I would make this fine woman your Countess immediately."

"Who says I will have him?" Syg said, smiling.

"Are you available then?" Probert asked, laughing.

"I am—are you asking?"

"Sorry, Dav, it appears that House Probert just stole your Lady."

Dav shrugged. "So, Milos, before we draw swords over Syg here, what do you think? How's the spar?"

He looked up again. "The spar is fine—never better. A fine repair, I must say."

"The Silver tech can stay?

Probert turned to Syg. "My Lady, will this 'Silver tech' degrade or require any maintenance with time?"

"No, no, sir. It will stay as it is."

"Then, Dav—yes, the silver can stay. Be proud of it—I will instruct my craftsmen to build around it. We should re-christen this lady the *Silverback*, if you ask me."

Dav laughed. "We'll leave you to it, then, Milos. I shall expect you for dinner this week, yes?"

"Indeed—will Lady Poe be there?"

"She will."

"Then I shall wash. I must smell my best for her. Err … will the Lady Branna be there as well?"

"I think so. She is a good friend of my sister, Countess Pardock."

Probert shook his head. "Heaven on the one side … and hell on the other."

After waving good-bye to Probert, Dav and Syg left the bay. Alone in the dark hallway, Syg threw her arms around him.

"Countess—I must say I like the sound of that."

Dav looked down at her. "You wish to be the Countess of Blanchefort, do you?"

"I do, gladly. I want it like nothing else. I only await a standing offer."

"Should I drop to a knee and beg you right here in the hallway?"

"The place matters not to me—anywhere is fine. And why bother asking? You certainly know what my answer will be."

"It will happen, Syg, but not here. At a time and place of my choosing."

"I hope the place and time is soon—we've plans to make and I am ready to begin—Suzaraine will be a Grenville long before I am a Blanchefort at this rate."

Dav blushed. Syg kissed him.

"Are we finished here, sir? I am anxious to see your castle. May we go?"

"Go to your quarters and pack a small bag. I have some matters to attend to on the bridge. Once those are done, we can to the castle."

Syg smiled. She couldn't wait.

2

PRINCESS MARILITH

Davage entered his quarters and began to pack. He rarely spent much time there anymore, and he couldn't recall the last time he slept in his own bed. He was constantly in Syg's quarters; that's where he wanted to be. But with rules, regulations, and decorum, he couldn't just move in with her, or she with him, for that matter. It would not do. Syg could not understand that.

He pulled off his shirt and began packing his bag.

The Com chattered.

"Com," he said.

"Com, sir, a message from Fleet Command has arrived for you, marked Blue."

"Aye Com, I'll take it here." He flipped a switch on his Com to disable the screen. Fleet Command didn't need to see him with his shirt off.

"Aye, sir, standby."

The screen opened despite the fact it was disabled.

He wasn't really surprised at what he saw.

It was Marilith.

It had been a while since her last message, when she was desperate to warn him of danger to come. That something "evil" was searching for him.

A lot had happened since then; a lot had changed.

Marilith sat back in the viewer. She wasn't wearing any of the thick makeup she usually wore. She was very beautiful, as she always had been. And her voice—not the usual howl or shriek that she normally had to use, her voice was musical. It was the voice he'd fallen in love with years ago.

"Hello, Dav," she said, sitting up a little on her pouf. As usual, she was draped in light Xandarr veils, leaving little to the imagination.

"Hello, Marilith," he said.

She looked at him for a few moments and smiled.

"I heard about that foolishness in Metatron. Did I not warn you of danger to come?"

"You did, and I thank you. I believe I discovered the thing that you said was searching for me in the dark."

"Oh? So tell me, what was it?"

"A Black Hat named Sygillis of Metatron."

"I know her—very evil, very cruel. Did you fight her?"

"Of a sort. I turned her."

"You turned her?" Marilith smiled and shook her head. "Only you, Dav."

"Now she has fallen in love with me."

A wave of darkness crossed Marilith's face. "I see, and ... surely you do not return this love?"

"I do. It took some time, but I indeed love her too."

"Truly? To love a Black Hat. Are you certain it is not merely a fascination ... an infatuation?"

"No. I am sure. I have Zen-La'ed with her. In Metatron."

"That is not possible. You have Zen-La'ed with me, Dav."

"There is no hope for us, Marilith. And as Sygillis taught me, the Zen-La is not forever."

"The Zen-La is forever, and you have offered it to me!"

"That is simply superstition and talk, Marilith."

"Talk ... If you were here, where I am now, we certainly wouldn't be talking, you and me."

"And where are you, Marilith?"

She paused for a moment. "Somewhere ..." she said in a dreamy voice. "I still love you, Dav. I've never stopped. I still dream of you every night. It harms me that I have to pretend to hate you when we both know I don't. My public persona is ... tiring to maintain. I am ready for you to come back to me. It has been too long. You are my Zen-La, and I am yours ... forever."

Dav sighed.

"And," Marilith continued, "I think this long interruption has actually enhanced my love for you, added a bit of spice."

Davage looked into the screen, at the image there. "And Marilith, if I were to say that I've come to my senses, that I am ready to be your husband, what would your response be?"

"I would be elated, but of course, should you say such a thing, I would not be able to trust you. How could I? As I have always said, you are the only person in the universe who can kill me. You would, no doubt, be attempting to spring a trap of some sort."

She closed her eyes. "I would force you to submit to any number of terms and conditions leaving you naked and vulnerable. I would force you to meet me on some lonely, out-of-the way place. And then, bound and shackled, I would drag you off to some unknown locale, and there we would make love ..."

"No blindfold?"

"Why bother with a blindfold, Dav? What good would it do? Besides, I want you to look at me when we come together. I would have to keep you in chains for years as you proved yourself, though I would be as kind and gentle as I could be." She had a look of longing for a moment. "Are you offering yourself to me? Are you submitting to what must be done?"

"I have told you, I am in love with Sygillis, Marilith. I will marry her. She will be my Countess," Davage said.

Marilith sighed and wagged her finger. "At least you had the good sense to cast aside that old battle axe Demona of Ryel, Dav—a singularly uninteresting person in my mind. Well, I suppose I'm going to have to kill her, Dav, your Sygillis. There is no one for you if not me. You know that."

"You might find that pretty difficult, Marilith. Sygillis was a Black Hat Hammer, and a mean one as well."

"But Dav, it's me you're talking to. You know perfectly well that I've fought Black Hats before, just like you have. Only with me, I just went ahead and killed them. You're so sentimental."

"You'll find that I've thoroughly trained Syg in all the various failings of Black Hat battle tactics. She won't be beat by the simple tricks that other Black Hats fall for."

Marilith frowned. "Oh ... 'Syg,' is it? How cute. Still, Dav, you have never fully given me the credit I'm due. I'm you Dav—simply on the other side of the mirror. I'm just as tough, fearless, cagy, unbeatable, and unkillable as you are. I will find a way to kill her. I will find a way to win. I always do."

"You know, Demona of Ryel never forgave you for that foolish attack on *Triumph* a few years ago. She was determined to hunt you down and make you pay. To bring you to justice."

Marilith brightened into a cheerful smile. "Oh, but wouldn't that have been fun. She wouldn't have lasted mere seconds against me. Will you please admit that?"

"I admit you are a worthy opponent. You feel no remorse for all the death that attack wrought?"

"Should I, Dav?"

"Yes, you should. You see, that's why we could never be together, why we traverse different paths. You say you're on the opposite side of the mirror from me. That small, shiny space is an impenetrable barrier. That is why there was never any real hope for us. You, Marilith, could have been so much to so many people. You could have been a Queen ... and yet look where we are. That is why Pardock threw down the baton. Because you are you and I am me, Xaphan and League."

Marilith sat there for a moment. She wiped a tear from her eye. "You really say some very mean things to me."

"Oh, please. You are fully capable of leaving a mountain of corpses in your wake, yet your feelings are hurt by a few truthful words? Marilith, we've had this conversation before, and I am certain we'll have it again at some point. You ..."

"I must away, Dav," Marilith said, more tears coming from her eyes. "Please tell your Syg that I will be coming for her. Please have the courtesy to tell her that she is going to die. She will not be your Countess. I'll see her dead first."

The screen shut off and went black.

3

THE BALCONY

Syg stood there on the crowded Blanchefort dock, staring at the huge reddish castle high in the mountains for several long minutes. Dav, holding her bag, allowed her to take it all in.

It was like a dream for her, seeing such a wonderful place for herself for the first time.

She finally turned to him, grinning. "All of this is yours?"

"I am the Lord of this principality. These are my people."

She looked at the village, the maze of colorful shops, busy storefronts, eateries, pubs, residences, and the huge mountains beyond, and the fairy-tale castle perched in the clouds.

"How could you ever bear to leave this place?"

"It's hard. I do love these people, but I love the *Seeker* too."

Arm in arm, they began making their way through the crowded dock, the vendors stopping Dav to embrace and visit with him. They'd see Syg there and inquire about her. Dav, not wanting to embarrass her, said she was his special guest and left it at that, but after a time, she began speaking up and introduced herself as "Lord Blanchefort's future Countess—his soon-to-be Countess-in-Waiting." The vendors lit up with excitement—finally Davage was going to be wed and Blanchefort will have a Countess. This was an occasion to celebrate.

Eventually, flush with moment, Syg wanted to stop at every shop she saw and introduce herself, amid cheers and fanfare. She wanted to see everything, to talk to everyone. It took hours to get through to the steep mountain road leading up to his castle.

"I'm going to call for a ripcar," Dav said. "It's a long, steep climb to the top."

Syg looked up at the steep, dizzying heights to the misty top. She took off her sandals and put them in her bag.

"What are you doing?" Dav asked.

"If I am going to be the countess of this land, I want to feel it beneath my feet. And, no ripcar—I want to walk to the top. I want to experience it all."

"You realize it's a walk of several miles and an elevation change of about three thousand feet?"

"Feeling out-of-shape, Lord Blanchefort?"

Dav smiled. "Fine, fine—but there's no turning back once we get started."

Syg, beaming with happiness, took his hand, and they started for the top.

✳ ✳ ✳ ✳ ✳

Of all the places Syg and Dav had ever made love, the balcony in his old bedroom was her favorite by far. It was a small, windswept, precarious stone slab about eight feet long and four feet wide sticking out of his large bedroom window. It wasn't a place for one with a fear of heights. It creaked and shuddered when walked on, the howling wind blowing across its face was strong enough to sweep one away, and only a tiny, two-and-a-half-foot rail was all that stood between the person standing on the balcony and a harrowing four-thousand-foot drop to the crags far below. Looking over the side, the huge *Seeker* appeared as a tiny white spot in the bay.

Syg loved it. Out there, in the wind and the heights no one could hear and no one could see, Dav's tower being one of the highest in the castle, she savagely made love to Dav on it—thrashing, screaming, and tearing all she wanted. On the ship she had to reserve herself quite a bit, lest other people hear. She flirted with the edge, she made the slab rock and bounce, and she allowed her bare legs to dangle over the side. Syg was fearless.

Here, under the northern stars, she thought about allowing herself to become pregnant. To carry Dav's child made her warm with happiness, but she decided it was best to wait until they were properly wed. Then she will give him as many children, as many heirs, as he wanted.

And from the balcony, if she gazed far off to the west and screwed her eyes up, she could just begin to see a castle in the clear, cool distance—white, tall, full of patina-capped spires, but not quite as grand as this one.

Dav, awakening, saw her gazing at it. He pulled up alongside and took her into his arms.

"Can you see Castle Durst in the distance?"

She reached up and kissed him. "Just barely. It's so far away. How could you … Oh, I keep forgetting you and your Sight that I love so much."

She looked at the castle in the distance again. "You can clearly see that? It must be fifty miles away."

"It's more like seventy. On the tall tower, can you see that little plaque near the top, just there?" he said, pointing.

"No, Dav … I can't."

"I barely need Sight to see that, Syg. It's the Durst coat of arms. It even says DURST in old Vith. The castle looks old and down in the weather … just like the Dursts themselves, I suppose."

"I hear tell you and Lady Hathaline of Durst often sent messages to each other."

"We did—from this very balcony. She had the Sight too. Pretty decent with it."

"And now you make love to me here." Syg regarded Dav for a moment. "I understand I look much like she did."

"Yes you do—quite remarkable."

"When you look at me, Dav, is it me you see … or her?"

"You certainly look like her—but you are you, Syg. You and she—nothing alike in spirit. 'Tis you I love."

She kissed him. "Are you certain?"

"I am. Hath was my dear friend, but I never loved her. I love you, Syg."

She looked at the castle again. "Is it possible? Could I somehow be a Durst?"

Dav thought a moment. "Hmmm ... You look the part—look like Hath, I mean, though there's no definitive Durst look, per se. You have the Durst spunk—you have that in earnest. Are you thinking that you might have been abducted from the Dursts?"

"That's what I am thinking."

"Well, I've not heard of anything like that from their past. They had seven daughters—Hath was the youngest. With no males, their line is broken. It happens. They've all married into other houses."

"Are there any gaps in the coming of their daughters? Are there any unexplained absences?"

"No ... none that I can recall. Hath used to tell me everything. She never mentioned anything of the sort."

"But remember, Dav—the Invernians. If a Shadow tech male seeded the Lady of Durst—"

"Evaline ... her name was Evaline. All the Durst women have 'line' in their name, it's a holdover from the Old Vith tradition that they loved. Even the ones who marry into the House get it. She's passed away. Hath's eldest sister, Medaline, is Lady of the house now. She married into House Grimm and became a countess but outlived her husband and came back. Once she's gone, I suppose Durst Castle will simply fall into ruin. Most a shame. If that does happen, I am going to take Hath from their family plot and move her to Fleet Park—where she belongs. I once figured the same thing was going to happen to House Blanchefort ... no heirs ... fallen into ruin."

"I'll give you as many heirs as you want, Dav—as many as we want. I want this House, our House, to last forever. Just tell me when. I'll allow you to seed me tonight if you wish. I'm ready."

"We should wait. Pardock will raise quite a fuss, and that's not a pleasant thing."

She looked at the distant castle again. "Evaline. If Evaline was seeded, then, that is something that is often covered up ... not mentioned out of shame and confusion. Could Lady Evaline have had twins? Could that be the case?"

"I don't know. It's possible."

Syg snuggled into Dav, her long hair blowing in the wind.

"If you like, Syg, we can go there before the week is out. We can visit Castle Durst and see Countess Medaline. Would you like that? Perhaps she'll have something further to tell us."

"Yes, darling, very much so."

"I also have a lock of Hath's hair that she gave to me long ago. We could have Ennez test a small portion, see if there's a genetic match."

Syg turned to Dav and seized him hard. "That's so unromantic," she said, and they began again.

4

COUNTESS PARDOCK OF VINCENT

When Syg met Dav's sister, Countess Pardock, she almost roped her in Silver tech and blasted her. They had come down from the balcony dressed and refreshed and awaited Pardock in one of the many great halls of the castle. She admired all of the old tapestries and decorations as they waited.

Syg was excited; she couldn't wait to meet his sister.

The door to the south wing of the castle opened, and a tall, beautiful blue-haired woman came through, gliding almost in her stiff royal blue House Vincent gown—Pardock being the current countess of House Vincent after marrying Ferddie, Lord of Vincent, who fell at the Battle of Embeth.

Countess Vincent, returned to her ancestral castle to care for her infirm sister.

She had married young Ferddie, Lord of Vincent, over a hundred years prior. The marriage caused a stir, the proud, highly placed Blancheforts wedding with House Vincent, a old, honorable house of Hala stock, yet one with the singular reputation for being … stupid.

Always a Vincent, playing the Vincent—that's what they said in League society. A play on words, a slight on their intelligence.

It was said that Lady Pardock, proud and rebellious, had married into House Vincent because she wished to humble her father Sadric, for he certainly did not wish her to marry Ferddie, whom he considered inferior on a number of levels. Sadric had hoped Pardock would marry Lord Horner of Champion, but Pardock detested him, detested House Champion and the whole Remnath tribe that they hailed from in general.

Ferddie of Vincent; surely she was out of her mind. But such was not the case. Pardock loved Ferddie, simple or not, and so she became his countess. The marriage reinvigorated House Vincent, as Pardock's seven children were certainly not simple-minded. Her son Gath even re-designed the GRAMPA, turning the dangerous, badly conceived LosCapricos axe into a fairly solid weapon.

Pardock approached Dav with a regal manner, her blue hair rustic and jangling in the Hala style, and then, without warning, hauled off and popped him right in the jaw with a sickening smack—one of the best right-crosses Syg had ever seen—knocking Dav's hat off.

Dav doubled over, holding his face.

Pardock, grinning, stared at him expectantly.

Syg pumped her fist, ready to loose a blast. Had Pardock gone mad?

Slowly, Dav straightened up, smiling. "You can still pop, sis," he said.

Pardock beamed as if Dav had just given her a huge compliment, and she embraced him roughly.

After a moment, Dav, bleeding from his mouth, introduced Syg.

"Umm," Syg said, "do you always greet each other so?"

"We do," Pardock said, still holding Dav. "Nothing says 'I love you' like a good punch to the face."

Pardock surveyed Syg from top to bottom. Syg could tell that Pardock had just Stared her. She must be good; her Stare was silent, quick, and painless.

"So," she said. "You are Sygillis of Metatron, the Black Hat who was going to kill my brother."

"I still can, if you'd like me to."

"Nah," Pardock said, "let's let him live a bit longer, shall we."

Pardock took Syg by the arm, and they began walking. Syg guessed, given the friendly tone in Pardock's conversation, that she had passed her Stare test. She obviously loved her brother very much, and that was fine with Syg. She just wanted to see what made Syg tick—and that was also fine; she had nothing to hide ... as far as her love for Dav went.

"Your nephew, Enoch, is very excited that you're here, Dav. He'll be coming of age soon and has expressed interest in joining the Fleet."

"Really? If that's the case then I'd love to have him. I can always find a place for a good junior crewman."

Pardock smiled, and they continued through the lofty Vith halls.

"So, how's Poe?" Dav asked.

Pardock darkened a bit. "Not good, not good at all. I really don't know what to do with her anymore. She seems ... pained. Father would know. He'd know what to do, Dav."

"Countess?" Syg said. "Perhaps I can help."

Pardock looked down and stared at Syg. "Oh?" she said.

"It is Lieutenant Kilos' opinion that Poe is someone like me, and if that's the case, then I can help her."

"Lieutenant Kilos believes that Lady Poe is a Black Hat?"

Syg laughed. "No, no ... that she is a Shadow tech female."

"Do you think that's possible, Syg?" Dav asked.

"From what Ki told me, yes I think it's very possible. It all fits together."

"She doesn't have a mark like you do," Dav said.

"Lt. Kilos says she wears a cover on her face—says she saw it at a party once. Haven't you ever Sighted her?"

Pardock looked shocked. "One does not Sight one's own sister."

Syg blushed a little. "In any event, may I see her?"

Pardock thought for a moment. "Tomorrow. You may see her tomorrow. She is finally asleep."

* * * * *

Syg's heart nearly broke—Dav announced he had to leave her for a day or two. There were some Fleet meetings in Atalea that required his presence. As soon as he returned, he promised he would take her to Castle Durst.

She didn't want him to go. They had never been apart, but if she was to be his countess some day, she will have to get used to occasional departures.

She'd live, though she missed him terribly.

$$* \quad * \quad * \quad * \quad *$$

So, Davage dressed, called down to the *Seeker*, and awaited Lt. Kilos in a ripcar. As it neared, Syg handed him his CARG. He saddled it, kissed her good-bye, jumped out of the window, and landed on the ripcar's hood, Kilos thankfully giving over the controls to him. Rolling the car, Davage sent it into a near-vertical plunge down the sheer side of the Castle and hit the thrusters, Kilos hanging on for dear life.

"Showing ... off ... are ... you?" Kilos cried.

"Absolutely!"

"I'm ... going to ... get you ... for ... this ... some day!" she managed to shout, hanging onto her cap as he laughed.

Approaching the crags and Harken forest, which Davage knew by heart, he trimmed the ripcar to manage the updrafts and pulled up, blasting the throttle, zero G'ing the crew cab and sending Ki's stomach into her throat.

That's when he saw something.

Far below, he saw a hooded figure standing under an overhang at the edge of the forest.

Davage didn't like the look of it.

Whipping the ripcar around, he kicked the thrusters and screamed into the overhang, where he popped the struts and landed in a cloud of dirt and fallen leaves.

He hopped out. Kilos followed, drawing her SK.

"What is it? What did you see?"

"I saw a figure, a hooded figure."

"Could it be just a passing traveler?"

Davage Sighted. He could see the faint heat trail of footprints fading down the path. Davage followed them, Kilos at his side.

"Possibly. But I'm not taking any chances. I had a message yesterday, from Marilith."

"Marilith ... again? For someone who's made a name for herself by hating your guts, she sure loves to talk to you, doesn't she?"

"She said she was coming to kill Syg."

"How's she going to do that, Dav? She's a Black Hat."

"How does Marilith do any of the things she does? I'm not taking any chances."

The trail led to a small stand of trees, where it ended. The figure had Wafted away. Dav whipped his head around, Sighting for it.

It was nowhere to be seen. He hit his CARG in frustration.

Kilos holstered her pistol. "Syg can take care of herself, Dav."

He caught a residual image of the figure as it retreated. He could do that too. Some called it the seventh aspect of the Sight—to see things that once were there. Dav didn't count it as a separate aspect, though. It was simply seeing something that was invisible.

"It was here," he said. "It was wearing a gray robe with a hood."

Ki shook her head as she watched Dav Sight the path, his eyes glowing in the muted olive light. She'd gotten used to seeing his glowing eyes. She still thought it was a wondrous thing but didn't get mesmerized by it like everyone else did. She figured being a Brown sometimes had its advantages. Browns were too skeptical a people to be overly impressed with anything.

"Can you see its face?"

Dav got in front of the image. He saw a man's face, blonde hair, blue eyes, deep within the hood.

"I see a man."

"A man? So, we just probably scared some poor traveler or pilgrim half to death," Ki said, kicking at the carpet of leaves on the path floor. "So much for northern hospitality."

"Wait," Dav said. Sighting harder, he saw the man's face shimmer. "It's a Cloak. A good one too."

The Cloaked face faded away, leaving a dark, cloudy void under the hood. He caught a hint of long blue hair, but that was all.

"We must back to the castle!" Dav said

"Dav, Marilith is crazy, but she's not stupid. Syg is too powerful to take on in a straight-up fight. If she is gunning for Syg, then she's going to take her time, size her up, and devise a plan that favors her. She's not going to go storming into your castle and face a Black Hat

Hammer. And she's going to want you there to watch. If anything, you not being around will ensure nothing happens."

Dav thought a moment. Ki was probably right. He looked at the fading image, the hooded figure, the wisps of blue hair. Either Marilith was going to have to be stopped cold, or for her own safety, Syg would have to go.

Maybe he was the last Blanchefort after all.

5

LADY POE

Syg waved and watched the ripcar fall into a suicidal dive down the side of the castle. She could feel a slight hint of warm air rush up as he hit the thrusters several hundred feet down. She wanted to go with him. She envied Ki for being able to go with him.

She was now alone in Castle Blanchefort with Countess Pardock, her children, and the stricken Lady Poe.

She put on a light dress that Dav had bought for her, and carrying her sandals, she went down to the main hall, her Black Hat sense of direction allowing her to navigate the huge, confusing castle with ease. The place was gigantic. She came across a dark, interesting hall full of portraits as she walked.

Portraits! The Hall of the Ancestors.

She took a few steps and waded into the dim hall. There were hundreds of portraits starting at the floor level going all the way up to the lofty heights of the ceiling.

She made a mental note of its location and would have to come back later. She had seen this place in her visions and was keen to explore it.

Downstairs, she met up with Pardock and a tall, handsome youth, her son—Enoch, Lord of Vincent, Dav's nephew. Her youngest son, Grenwald, was still asleep in his room.

"Good morning, Lady Sygillis," Pardock said. "I trust you slept well."

"I did. I love this castle. It already feels like home."

"Glad to hear it. Well, you wanted to see Lady Poe. She's this way, in the Telmus Grove getting a bit of air. I put her there this earlier this morning." She motioned with her arm, and they went out into the morning sunshine.

Strolling casually, young Enoch a few steps back, they entered a massive grove full of exotic plants, stone Vith vistas, and huge trees. The sky was a deep northern blue, with white clouds rising in the distance. Syg swiveled her head about, trying to take it all in. She wished Dav was here. She wanted to experience this for the first time with him.

"Of course you know I had to Stare you yesterday," Pardock said as they plunged into the green.

"Yes. I hope I passed your test."

"You have a lot in your past, obviously, which I won't go into now with my son present. You have a vile temper, a sharp tongue, and a copious jealous streak … but you truly love my brother and wish him nothing but the best. You wish to be his Countess and bear his children. That is good enough for me. Dav is big enough to deal with your temper and tongue and jealousy on his own, I suppose."

"Would you raise a sword should I have failed your test?"

"Yes. I've done it before. Surely you know that."

"Then, we are in agreement. We both love Dav, you as his sister and I as his future countess, and we both want nothing but his health and well-being."

"Agreed. I will happily pass the baton in this case."

They smiled at each other and continued down the path.

"I will instruct our seamstresses to begin making you your gowns. House Blanchefort doesn't have a single pre-set color, unlike House Vincent with blue all the time—I must say I get a little tired of blue sometimes—so you may take your pick."

"Is wearing a Blanchefort gown a prerequisite to being a countess-in-Waiting?"

"Yes it is," Pardock said with a tone of finality. "The moment he asks and the moment you say yes, you will be wearing a Blanchefort gown."

"I'm partial to black, as I'm certain you can guess."

Pardock shook her head.

Enoch trailed closely behind them. He was a thin, handsome boy wearing blue Vincent leggings. The blue image of an axe was embossed on his shirt. Being so young, he had that typical "unfinished" look that all Elder-Kind youths had, not shedding it fully until about the age of thirty.

Enoch stared at Syg.

"Lord Vincent," she said after a bit. "You appear to have a question. Please, fire away, sir."

He paused a moment. Then he asked, "Did you fight my uncle?"

"Enoch, what did I tell you?" Pardock said.

Syg laughed. "It's all right, Countess. Yes, Lord Vincent, I did fight your uncle, of a sort. It was a fight of good against evil, of light against dark. We fought with words and ideas, with love and patience against vileness and rancor."

"And what happened?"

"Well, obviously, good won and evil fell away. The prize was my heart and my soul. Your uncle defeated me and in the process, he saved me … and I am his forever. I'll fill you in on a secret: I never had a chance against your uncle. It was never a fair fight."

"You don't want to kill him?"

"Only occasionally."

Syg and Pardock laughed.

"I want to fight a Black Hat. I want to win her heart forever, if she is as beautiful as you," Enoch said.

Syg blushed. "You're too kind, sir. Then I would listen to your mother and do as she says, and listen to your uncle, learn from him, become a man like he is, and I am certain you will easily win such a fight."

Eventually, they came to a large courtyard. A tall, thin figure sat slumped on a stone bench near a weathercock.

Poe, Lady Poe of Blanchefort.

Poe the Sad, they said.

Crazy Poe, others said.

"Poe?" Pardock said. "Poe, dear, you have a visitor."

She looked a lot like Dav, tall and thin. She had short blonde hair with wispy blue streaks in it. Her expression was vacant, eyes half-closed in long slits. She mumbled and drooled.

She was wearing a green gown—simple, yet elegant and finely made. A Blanchefort gown. Syg looked at it. She supposed it could be worse. Wearing one of these will be a small price to pay to keep Dav and his sister happy.

As long as they didn't try to make her wear shoes. That's where the trouble will start.

"She is like this often," Pardock said. "And then she is better for a while."

"How have you helped her in the past?"

"Our father left instructions upon his death. He said to take her to the grove on days when she cannot stand, and when she starts speaking in tongues, to leave her."

"And if I am following correctly, Sadric's Rain begins shortly thereafter, yes?"

"Correct. I'm not a fool. I know the Rain comes from her, but I've not witnessed it firsthand. So, you are thinking that Lady Poe's condition and you, as a former Black Hat, are somehow related?"

"I am … and now that I see her, I'm convinced that's the case."

"And you can help her?"

"I can."

Syg approached Poe and slowly sat down.

Gently, she placed her hands on Poe's thin face. "Ah," she said. "There is a cover here." She used a tiny bit of Silver tech and loosened the cover. With one easy motion she pulled it off, revealing a huge sweaty, angry black Shadowmark—a much larger one than Syg's.

"Elder's balls!" Enoch cried. "She's a Black Hat!"

"Enoch, don't be silly—and watch your language, boy!" Pardock said.

"She's not a Black Hat. She could have been one, but she's not. This is a Shadowmark, just like mine. It's basically a birthmark. If you are born with this, then you have Shadow tech flowing within you. Somehow, Poe was born with this and was not abducted into the Black Hat Sisterhood. Your father must have protected her from the Black Abbess, and that was a brave thing for him to do. It's the unmarshalled, uncontrolled Shadow tech within her that is creating this problem. I'm amazed she has lived this long without proper training."

"Can anything be done for her?"

"Yes, yes, certainly, but first she'll need to be rid of this excess Shadow tech. She is rife with it." Syg loosened Poe's gown and placed her hands on her thin ribs. "Can you smell it?"

Enoch leaned forward to smell Lady Poe, and Pardock cuffed him on the back of the head.

"I'll need someone to open her mouth and hold it open."

Enoch came forward again, head still smarting, closely watching his mother, and gently opened Poe's mouth.

"Get ready for some rain," Syg said.

"Will this be safe for my son?" Pardock asked.

"It's metabolized. All of the toxins remain within, and it's safe in this state."

In a moment, thick gray mist came pouring out of Poe's mouth, quickly filling the courtyard and the grove beyond.

They stood in the dense mist.

"You smell that, mother?" Enoch asked, flush with excitement. "I smell it!"

"Quiet, you!" Pardock said in the fog, groping around, trying to find him. "Blanchefort women do not create strange smells. Do not forget that!"

"Is this Shadow tech?" Enoch asked in the fog, unable to contain his excitement.

"It is. Shadow tech, in a harmless misty form ... the poor dear. This will take a while," Syg said.

"Is it ... is it going to change into some sort of terrifying, snorting beast? Mother! Mother! I'mgoingtofightmyfirstShadowtechmonster!" Enoch cried, running his words together.

"Get back to the castle, boy!" Pardock shouted in the fog. "The only thing you're going to be fighting is the back of my hand when I locate you!"

Syg, hearing Enoch's excitement, manipulated some of Poe's misty Shadow tech into a twisting, smiling insect that looped and cavorted in mid-air.

"Do you see that? Do you see that? I'm going to get it now!"

"No you are not, and you will not enjoy the light of day for months after I get hold of you. Sygillis—Sygillis of Metatron, are you behind this?" Pardock yelled.

Giggling, Syg, vanished the insect.

"Awww!" Enoch cried.

Suddenly, Poe began speaking. She spoke in an ugly, sinister voice. "*Sygillis of Metatron. I am coming for you! I am going to kill you! Hahahahahahahahahaha!*"

"Who am I speaking to?" Syg asked quietly.

"*Your enemy! Your rival!*"

"It's Marilith!" Pardock shrieked, frantically groping for Enoch in the fog. "I'd know that foul voice anywhere!"

"*Dear Pardock, do not think that I have forgotten about you. After I have killed her, I will kill you too. It's long in coming! I hold you responsible for everything!*"

Poe tried to rise up, but Syg held her down. "*I'll allow you to run, Sygillis of Metatron. Run away and hide and you may live!*"

"I am not going anywhere. If you are seeking to drive a wedge between me and my Lord, then you have made a mortal enemy today, Marilith. I will meet you wherever you choose, and we will settle this. And be fair warned: only one of us will be walking away when it's over."

"*It will be settled with your death. I will give you no peace. I will hunt you down.*"

"Incorrect. 'Tis I who will be hunting you down. 'Tis I who will be giving you no peace. Let us meet. Let us fight like women."

"*Hahahahahahahaha!*"

The voice faded, and Poe's open mouth gushed fog.

After a time, the fog stopped and Poe opened her eyes. They were Dav's eyes. Syg felt a twinge; how she missed him.

"W-Where am I?"

"In the grove," Syg said.

"Who are you?"

"A friend. Someone who loves your brother. Someone who is like you and wants to help. You needn't endure this alone any further, Lady Poe."

Syg, finding her hand in the fog, took it and placed it on her Shadowmark. "I am going to teach you how to live with this ... the Shadow tech. It will turn to silver, and it is a wonderful thing—you'll see. Today is the last day you will ever be lost in the fog."

"You're ... Sygillis, the Black Hat who wanted to kill my brother?"

Syg smiled and kissed her on the cheek. "Well, I guess it's a good thing I didn't, isn't it? I guess it's a good thing your brother is such a wonderful, charming man. I love your brother very much, and I am going to help you."

Syg helped Poe stand, and together they carefully exited the courtyard, shrouded in fog.

✳ ✳ ✳ ✳ ✳

They made their way back into the castle, Poe following Syg like a lost kitten, hanging on her every word. Syg had suggested that they wait until the next day to begin her training, that she should rest today, but Poe didn't want to. She wanted to begin immediately.

Syg relented and asked Poe to change into something comfortable and to meet her in Dav's tower. There, they would begin her first lesson. Syg changed into her favorite outfit, her Chancellor's bodysuit—she had about twenty of them —and waited for Poe. Enoch wanted to come and watch, but Syg forbid it, told him it wasn't safe. Pardock dragged him off by the ear.

After a bit, Poe appeared, wearing a light red and blue Blanchefort gown. Syg looked at it. The style was simple, yet elegant and pleasing. The style was starting to grow on her. She began forming ideas as to what she wanted hers to look like.

"You aren't going to want to wear that," Syg said.

"Why not?" Poe asked, looking down at her lovely gown.

"Because, as of right now, you are a Shadow tech novice. Shadow tech is very bad for clothing. It eats through it. It creates ugly permanent stains, and I don't want to see your gown ruined. You are going to want to wear something light and out-of-the-way, like what I am wearing. Here …" Syg gave her a spare bodysuit, and though Poe felt shy about wearing such a tight-fitting, stretchy garment, she went into the bathroom and put it on.

"Also," Syg said, "don't bother putting your shoes back on. Shadow tech is very much a thing of feeling, and in order to better control it at this early stage, you are going to need to firmly feel the floor beneath you—and that means bare feet."

"A-all right," Poe said, a little dubious, through the door.

"If you are anything like your brother, then I know that you are probably loath to be parted from your shoes. Getting Dav out of his boots is like fighting a major battle all the time."

Poe laughed and emerged from the bathroom. She was finally dressed to Syg's liking and shoeless, and Syg stepped out onto Dav's balcony, into the wind, and bade Poe to follow.

"I am not going out there, Lady Sygillis," Poe said.

"Why not?"

"Because I am afraid of these heights. Because it is four thousand feet to the rocks below."

Syg smiled. "Lady Poe, here is your first lesson, and I don't want you to forget it, because it's important. Fear is what Shadow tech feeds on. If you feel fear, your Shadow tech will consume it like candy, and you right along with it. The Black Abbess … she made us do … terrible things. She starved us, pitted us against each other, made us crawl in the dark, made us fight—and these weren't innocent wrestling matches either. These were fights to the death, but all that had the effect of removing fear from us. We are fearless, and it's out of necessity. You cannot hope to control your Shadow tech if you're afraid of everything."

She walked out onto the creaking balcony and climbed up on the rail, her hair waving in the strong wind, the long drop yawning behind her. "You must not fear—and if you master your Shadow tech, you'll have nothing to fear, ever again." She paused a moment. "Come out here—feel the wind. Know that nothing can harm you."

Slowly, tentatively, Poe stepped out onto Dav's creaky, lofty balcony, probing its strength with her pale feet. "I-I always begged Dav to get rid of this insane balcony. Our g-grandfather Maserfeld put it here."

"Why, tell me?"

"This tower was once used for guests, so the story goes. Our grandfather put guests he didn't like in this room. He hoped they would become possessed by some Blanchefort ghost and suicide off of it. Dav has always loved this balcony. He and Lady Hathaline."

"What about Hathaline?" Syg said quickly.

"They sat out here, jumping up and down, making it creak and rock, hang over the side, falling off and Wafting down, and sending signals to each other. They'd wrestle on it too. I'm certain they have told you that you—"

"That I look like her ... yes. I suppose I can't help but feel a bit jealous that he was so close to her."

"Well," Poe said, sitting down, not wanting to stand, "He never asked her to marry him. She was his friend, though she wanted to be much more. You look exactly like her, but you do not act her at all, I can tell that already. She was a bit ... arrogant. Very Blue."

"I've heard. Dav promised to take me to Castle Durst when he returns. We are going to determine if I am a daughter of House Durst. I must be."

"Well, you do look just like her—or she just like you, I should say."

Poe smiled. "I'm ... so glad you're here, Lady Sygillis."

"Syg, Lady Poe, just call me Syg. That's what Dav calls me."

"Syg then ... I feel so much better. I feel safe with you here. I know that you're going to help me."

"It's my pleasure. Perhaps you might be able to help me in turn, in preparing my gowns. According to Countess Pardock, I have to wear them."

"Oh, I would love to. I would like to help very much. The countess is very ... insistent ... about certain things."

"Yes, she is. Now," Syg said. "We are going to reach out and touch the ground."

"Touch the ground?"

"Yes. I want you to tell me how it feels."

"How?"

Syg extended her arm and allowed a thin, shiny stream of Silver tech to shoot to the ground—Poe watched the shining stream with wonder.

Syg smiled. "The ground is cold and rocky. Strange, I feel a coarse, low type of grass."

"It's horse grass ... grows well in this cold climate. You can feel that?"

"I can. The Silver tech stream is an extension of my body, and I can feel everything it feels, I can hear sounds around it, I can almost see what it sees. I want you to reach out and grab me a handful of horse grass."

She peeked over the side and shuddered at the height.

"From way down there?"

"Yes, from way down there."

Poe looked puzzled.

"Tip the glass, and your Shadow tech will flow. Pretend you're tipping over a glass of water. Feel it flow. Feel it move. Remember, feel is everything with Shadow tech"

Poe reached over the side and pointed. Nothing happened.

"I am not certain what I should be doing."

Patiently, Syg walked the rail and took Poe by the hand.

"You feel that?" she asked.

"It feels warm...floaty."

"Now, tip the glass. That's all you're doing is tipping over a glass of water. Pretend Dav's down there—pretend you're pouring water all over him, getting him soaked."

Poe giggled and closed her eyes and a thin, brackish gray stream squirted out of her hand, spraying in the wind.

"Good," Syg said, "good. Can you feel that? Can you feel it moving?"

"I can," Poe said, looking at her hand.

Syg released her hand, and the flow stopped. "Now, Lady Poe, do that again, by yourself this time."

It took some doing, but eventually, Poe "tipped the glass" and created her first feeble strings of Shadow tech by herself. She dangled them over the side of the balcony.

"It will be a while before you're ready for more advanced manipulations. Just master the basics first, and then you'll be ready. Now, I want you to practice every day. Not only will that sharpen your skills, but it'll also keep your levels down. You cannot go too long without casting, remember that. If you start feeling tired and confused, you've got too much. Too much is very, very bad."

"You mean to say that by just by doing this, I'll not fall into spells anymore? No more pain?"

"I mean to say. A little bit of casting every day, and that will never happen to you again."

Poe sat there for a moment, trying to take it in. A lifetime of pain, of hiding, of feeling herself a faulted and sick failure … over.

Poe's face burst into a joyous smile. She put her face into her hands. She wiped tears away. Syg paused and let Poe have her moment. As Dav had told her, it was impossible to spend any time with Lady Poe and not immediately like her. She seemed such a good person.

"Also, Poe, make sure you're alone when you're casting. Shadow tech is very poisonous, very dangerous to everybody other than me and you. Do it out in the Grove or up here … and for Creation's Sake, make sure Pardock's children aren't around. Children just love Shadow tech. You saw how Enoch had to be dragged away, yes?"

"Are you leaving? Are you going somewhere?" Poe asked alarmed.

"I'm leaving with Dav at the end of the week."

"You're not going to stay here? A Countess-in-Waiting usually stays in the castle. It's tradition. Pardock will …"

"The countess is going to have to be mad on that point. We'll start a new tradition then. Where Dav goes, I go. I will not be a stay-at-home wife. But don't worry, I'll be back, and Dav told me that Bethrael will be staying here until the Hospitalers pick her up next month. Beth will be a good teacher. You'll like her."

Poe smiled. "So, you love my brother? I can tell that you do."

"I adore your brother. Love is not an adequate word. He is everything to me."

"We had heard that you wished him dead. We were afraid for him."

"You were right to be afraid for him. That was a dangerous thing he did. I was a hideous, evil, angry, murderous woman. And he was man enough to face me, all alone. It seems like that was a long time ago."

"What kept you from trying to kill him?"

"Don't know. A combination of things, possibly. I think I loved him from the start—at least that's what I tell myself. And now look at me … in love body and soul, ready to become his countess, teaching his sister how to control her Shadow tech."

"I am very glad you were able to find each other."

Poe lit up. "Look, Syg … look!" She pulled back her tiny rope of gray Shadow tech and had a bit of horse grass stuck at the end. "I could feel it, plain as day, just like you said. I could hear the wind down there, and I even thought I could see the grass too!"

Syg hugged her. "Excellent job. Soon your Shadow tech will turn silver, and you won't believe what you can do with it."

"Will I be able to make little animals with it? Not monsters, but cute, friendly little creatures?"

"Ah, you've a Painter's soul, I see. Yes, if you like. That takes a great deal of study and practice, but yes, if you commit yourself, you will be able to do that. You can make anything you want and give it a heart and a soul however you please."

Poe smiled and considered the possibilities—such things she will create.

Syg pulled her of off the floor of the balcony and slowly walked her out to the end, the stone creaking and bending slightly as they walked. Poe held on to her tightly, feeling the floor carefully with her feet.

"I understand there's to be a grand dinner here when Dav returns."

"Y-yes," Poe said. "We—we have those from time to t-time. Many people are coming … they wish … to see—"

"They wish to see several ex-Black Hats."

"Yes, they are, understandably … curious and … wish to make your acquaintance. You will … no doubt … be a great hit."

"I am looking forward to it; it'll be my first here. I also understand a certain gentleman will be coming—one who asked for you by name yesterday."

"Oh …" Poe said, brightening. "May I ask that gentleman's name?"

"Milos, Lord of Probert. A wonderful man … a genius."

Poe smiled and blushed. "Milos … he is a good friend."

"It appears he wishes to call on you. I should be most flattered if I were you, such an intelligent, witty man."

Poe giggled. "Milos has always appeared to like me."

"Do you fancy him in return?"

"I—I don't know. I've always been troubled with this ... Shadow tech. I've never been able to plan anything ... to look forward to anything, least of all, courtship."

"Those days are past. You've your whole life ahead of you now."

"I'm already past my Time of Good-byes ..."

"It doesn't matter. The Shadow tech, it will extend your life. There are many Black Hats who are well over three hundred, some over four hundred. When it turns to Silver, I believe it will extend it even more."

Poe smiled and thought ... her whole life. No more spells ... no more agony.

"Poe, look where you are."

Poe looked around. They were standing the very edge of balcony, the yawning drop right ahead of them, the sunshine-filled landscape far below laid out as a mosaic of color, the *Seeker* like a little white dot in the dark waters of the bay. She shuddered for a moment and then was fine.

6

THE DINNER

"Syg, I didn't say we'd be apart forever—just for temporary until I can apprehend Marilith."

Dav had never seen Syg's eyes catch fire like this before.

"Dav," she said in a low, dangerous voice, "I knew you would come up with something like this—I knew it!"

"Syg," he said, "I'm just thinking of you. If you were to come to harm, I …"

"And you want me to go away—to run and hide. Dav, if you think I'm going to allow Princess Marilith of Xandarr to come between us, even for temporary, then you have a few things to learn about me!"

"Syg, Princess Marilith is capable of doing a lot of things. I've been fighting her for eighty years—"

"You don't think I have the power to fight that spoiled Xaphan blue-haired brat?"

"In a straight-up fight, yes, you have more power than she does, clearly. But she isn't going to fight you straight up. She's going to wait until circumstances favor her, and then she'll strike. She isn't going to fight fair."

"You seem to be thinking that I'm going to be fighting fair, Dav! I can be just as devious, underhanded, and sneaky as she can be! And if you think you're saving me by kicking me out, the first thing I'm going to do is hunt her down and kill her! That's right—*KILL HER!*"

"What if she tries to poison you?"

"She can't poison me, Dav. Black Hat, Shadow tech—remember?"

Dav shrugged, went out onto his balcony, and sat down, letting his legs dangle off of the side. Syg slowly sat down beside him.

"Sorry I got mad, love."

"It's fine, Syg. Sorry I suggested we temporarily part ways. That is not something I was wanting to do, anyway."

"I'm never parting ways with you, Dav. This is just the sort of thing Marilith's hoping for—to get you to do her work for her. To drive us apart." She leaned her head on his shoulder and kissed him.

"Are you really going to try and kill her?"

"I am. If she wanted to stay safe, all she had to do was leave us alone."

The wind picked up, and the balcony rocked a bit.

"You and I, Dav, there isn't anything we can't handle. If Marilith comes, we'll face her together. I was just getting used to the idea of having to wear a gown."

Dav laughed. "I won't make you wear a gown if you don't want to, Syg. I'm not overly big into tradition. And if I am to guess, I will bet that you will not be staying here at the castle when I return to the *Seeker*."

"Well, you're right on that one, love. I am coming with you, but I will wear a Blanchefort gown. I'll happily wear one—one that fits me, that is. I want to be your countess. I want to make you proud of me. And the last thing I want is for Pardock to throw down the baton over something as silly as a gown."

Dav put his arms around her, and she snuggled into his lap.

"If Marilith comes, we'll face her together, you and me."

✳   ✳   ✳   ✳   ✳

The dinner the next night was a grand affair. Dav, Syg, and Kilos were there, and so were Pardock, her sons Enoch and Grenwald, Poe, Ennez, and Bethrael. Lord Probert, dressed in his garish best, sat near,

Lady Poe along with an assortment of his craftsmen. Twenty of the *Seeker's* crew were seated at the table, along with ten Marines and two Admirals. Pardock and Poe's friends and various hangers-on rounded out those in attendance, over ninety in all.

Missing, as usual lately, were the Dursts. They were becoming maudlin and reclusive as they aged into oblivion. Pardock was sad; Countess Medaline was once her best friend, just as Hath was with Dav. She ordered their places set and their plates and cups filled, hoping that she would come after all.

Lord Probert clearly wanted to spend time with Lady Poe, he having had a long-standing desire to court her, but her previous infirmity made her shy and sullen. His reverie was shattered, though, when his tormentor, the Lady Branna, Imperator of the Science Ministry, her husband, Lord Timon of Fallz, and her daughter, Lady Saari, appeared at the table.

"Lord Probert!" Lady Branna exclaimed as she sat down and grabbed her napkin, "There you are!" She apparently wanted to continue arguing with him regarding several specs on the new class of starship he was building in Provst. She wanted to incorporate new technology gathered from the *Triumph*.

Captain Davage, though, came to his rescue and sidetracked Lady Branna. He talked about her daughter Saari, his junior helmsman, and praised her for her bravery over Ergos. Flush with pride, she completely forgot about Lord Probert.

Unfortunately, Lord Probert had a number of competitors for Lady Poe's attention. Many gentlemen at the table vied for her time—with the Shadowmark visible on her face. So, she wasn't crazy all these years. She was a Shadow tech female. The stigma of her supposed mental illness was wiped away with one grand dinner. She was now the talk of League society.

Syg was wearing a lovely black dress that Dav had bought for her in Atalea during his conference. She couldn't wait to try it on and wear it to the dinner, but Pardock, her relationship with Syg developing into a good-naturedly contentious one, wanted her in a Blanchefort gown. She didn't care that Syg didn't have any yet, and she also didn't care that none of her old ones or Poe's fit. Syg was way too short. Pardock threatened to stuff her into one and compel her to wear shoulder pads and stilts.

Fortunately, Dav made Pardock see reason, and Syg got to wear her new black dress, relatively unmolested.

As Pardock looked around the crowded table full of Fleet, Marine, and League faces, she marveled. She was sitting at a table with three ex-Black Hats, a formerly ill sister who was now a "cured" Shadow tech female, a love-sick genius, the top scientist in the League ... and strangest of all, an enemy.

The surprise guest of the evening was Mapes, Lord of Grenville, and his Lady-in-Waiting, Suzaraine of Gulle wearing a complicated Grenville gown, which, seeing Syg sitting over there in her black dress, galled Pardock all the more. Thoughts of bodily stuffing Syg into a Blanchefort gown re-emerged in earnest.

A Grenville and his Lady sitting at a Blanchefort table? Pardock expected the undead ghost of her father to come roaring in from Dead Hill at any moment, ready to cross Mapes's name off of the invitation list with fleshless hands and throw him out himself.

With all the various things that had passed between the two Great Houses over the years—the slights, the insults, the deceptions and social vandalisms—Pardock glared at him relentlessly but, as the meal wore on, his actions softened her heart.

He talked and laughed with Dav and Syg warmly. He also doted on his Lady—a tall, beautiful woman whom, she had heard, was an ex-Black Hat recovering from a horrible ordeal—an ordeal with her brother on the flat, dirty wastes of Metatron where they fought, nearly to the death. Yet another Black Hat whom Davage had saved.

Mapes attended to her every need. He helped her cut her food, he helped her when she needed to excuse herself, and he gave her his arm so that she could stand. She appeared so weak. It was clear he adored her. He was very un-Grenville-like in his obvious affections for her.

She was an ex-Black Hat. She and Syg and Beth. Sygillis of Metatron, her brother's soon-to-be countess, Suzaraine of Gulle, a soon-to-be Lady Grenville, and Bethrael of Moane, attached to no one, a bubbly free spirit whom, she had heard, was to be joining the Hospitalers. Sygillis was beautiful and mysterious and spoke in a commanding, courtly manner, yet she was clearly too involved with her future

Lord to be overly sociable. Suzaraine of Gulle, though courteous and intelligent, was too shy and quiet to interest the young men. Bethrael of Moane, however, was going to be huge in League circles. Lithe and beautiful, her outgoing disposition and approachability made her a huge hit. Gentlemen from all over the table were eager to sit with her, share a moment with an ex-Black Hat, ask her questions, and invite her into their various circles. They begged her to reconsider joining the Hospitalers and become a socialite instead. She could have the whole League at her feet, they said. Once again, as before with Princess Marilith, Xaphans were becoming all the rage in League Society.

The dinner went well, and Pardock was pleased. Still, when she looked at the table and saw the empty chairs, the un-eaten food, the sweating cups where Countess Medaline and the Dursts would have sat, she felt sad.

So sad ...

7

CASTLE DURST

The morning after the big dinner, Dav, as he had promised, took Syg to Castle Durst. A waiting ripcar was parked on the grounds. Dav and Syg didn't bother taking the stairs. They jumped off of Dav's balcony and Wafted down. Laughing and cavorting, they made their way to the ripcar, mounted it, and tore off to the west. Screaming with delight, Dav threaded the mountains and gorges that lay between the two castles, hauling the ripcar around in tight turns, sudden reverses, and high-banking climbs.

Syg loved every minute of it; nothing he tried could scare her. He'd certainly have to come up with a new series of maneuvers.

Soon they were there. Castle Durst loomed in the near distance, a white limestone structure like a weathered fossil.

It was rather depressing, seeing the once-lovely yards surrounding the castle fallen into weed and disrepair. The castle itself, a tower-dotted Vith structure about half the size of Castle Blanchefort, looked to be in need of repair.

The Dursts were falling apart ... gone into ruin, their name marking time until it was no more.

They approached the grand main door and knocked. A long time later it swung open. A small, dour-looking servant opened it. Dav explained he was the Lord of Blanchefort and was here to see Countess Medaline. The servant welcomed Dav said he would announce them.

When he saw Syg, he broke into a huge smile. "Lady ... Lady Hathaline!" he said. "Oh, oh ... where have you been? We've been so worried. We thought you dead! Countess—Lady Hathaline's come home!" His eyes were bugging out, and he was slavering.

"Lord Blanchefort, you must please forgive Joules. He is not totally in his right mind these days."

A tall, black-haired woman came down the stairs in a flashy Durst outfit.

Very pretty lady, but she looked sad ... old, if that was possible. One of the last of a long, proud line.

"He, like us," she said, "is lost in madness. Look what we have become."

"We missed you at dinner yesterday, Countess. Though, as always, we set your plates and poured your cups."

"Really ..." Medaline said, disinterested.

When Medaline saw Syg, she did a double-take.

"Lady Medaline, Countess of Grimm, may I introduce Sygillis of Metatron. She is to be my future countess."

"It is my pleasure," Syg said, bowing slightly.

Medaline continued to stare at Syg.

"As you can see, her resemblance to Lady Hathaline is ... remarkable. We are here today, in part, to discover if there is any chance that Sygillis is possibly a Durst."

Medaline thought for a moment. "I don't see how. I have six sisters, five are married, one is dead. There were no other sisters ... and no Lords."

She looked at Syg again. "Actually, now that I look more closely, she does not resemble our Lady Hathaline. Not at all."

"Countess, please. Sygillis is the spitting image of her."

"And how would you know, Lord Blanchefort? You who broke her heart time and time again. All her life she waited for you ... for your sad, sorrowful heart to see her for what she was. She pined for you, went to the stars for you. She went off hoping to please you, and she met her end … and now, now you plan to marry this imposter. This phony! If you had done what was right and married my sister in the first place she would probably be here with us right now!"

She turned. "Please, Lord Blanchefort, go. Let us die and be forgotten in peace."

"Countess, I am sorry if you feel that way. Lady Hathaline was my best friend and if anyone was harmed—is still harmed—by her death, it was me. I wish to pay my respects at her grave."

"I forbid it."

"I am going to pay my respects and honor Hath as she deserves today, and not you or anyone else is going to stop me."

Medaline slumped to the floor and began weeping.

"I am going to ask my groundskeepers to come here every month to clean the grounds and perform repairs on the castle."

"I do not need your pity."

"Then be not so pitiful. You sit here waiting for it all to end. Lady Medaline, you are the Countess of Grimm. You have eight children. Between you and your sisters, you have almost forty children—all flowing with Durst blood. After the prerequisite two hundred fifty years have passed, any one of them or their progeny may declare themselves a Durst, and the House will rise again. I intend to see that they have an ancestral home to return to."

Dav kneeled down and patted Medaline on the back. "We have always been friends, and we will continue, and I intend to make sure that there is a Blanchefort there to welcome them, the New Dursts, when they choose to come home." He kissed her on the cheek.

"I will take my leave and see Hath now. And please, if you are angry with me, if you have issue with me, then confine those feelings to me alone. Involve not my sister, who greatly misses you."

They went outside and walked around the castle, through a small, neglected grove to a large yard surrounded by a tall stone fence.

The gate was locked. "Syg, if you please," he said, pointing at the gate.

Syg filled the lock with Silver tech and turned the bolt.

Inside the yard was a collection of vaults and stones, some ancient and covered with moss. A huge, fairly new stone sat at the end of the yard.

It read:

LADY HATHALINE
SEVENTH DAUGHTER OF SEVEN
CAPTAIN OF THE FLEET
2962ax–3154ax
"A hero rests here. May she soar evermore."

Her image was embossed on the new stone. Syg looked hard at it. It was her face, markless, wearing a lovely Fleet uniform.

Her face ... exactly the same, sans the mark.

And Davage wept. He leaned against the stone and felt her loss like it was yesterday. Syg stood nearby and let him cry, let him have his moment with his friend—her spitting image. After a while, he turned to her, and she held him for a long time.

"I don't know if this is a good time to mention this, Dav, but we both know Countess Medaline was not being completely truthful."

Dav wiped his face. "I know, Syg, that's why I kept this ..."

He held out his hand. There in his palm was a single strand of hair from Medaline.

8

WHO WAS CAPTAIN HATHALINE?

They were sitting in the Capricos Hall, one of many vaultlike, airy halls in Dav's endless castle. This hall was always one of his favorites. There was a long table in the center of the hall, and the lofty ceiling was feathered with Great House flags and banners—a very colorful setup. The walls were lined with strange weapons of all sorts—swords, staves, pistols, lances, clubs, axes—the complete family of LosCapricos weapons, hundreds of them. Most of them were well-made mock-ups and didn't function, but they were still impressive to behold.

Dav and Syg sat at the table. The table was full of food, drinks, and snacks that his staff had put there not long ago. Always recalling starving as a boy, Dav, as Lord of the castle, abolished all of the rules of decorum regarding eating that his father had put into place. Food was always available to those who were hungry in Castle Blanchefort. Syg was sitting there next to him, her lunch picked at. Lt. Kilos roamed around the hall looking at the LosCapricos weapons mounted on the wall, trying to see if she could correctly identify them all.

Ennez and Bethrael also sat at the table with Dav and Syg. Beth, a soon-to-be Hospitaler, was wearing the now-familiar Chancellor's bodysuit like Syg always did. In her case, though, she was actually going to become one soon. She had moved into a commodious room in Zoe tower where she would be staying until the Hospitalers came to get her next month. She was delighted that there was a whole wardrobe full of clothes waiting for her. Dav and Syg had bought them for her, as ex-Black Hats never came with much in the way of clothes. The gentlemen at the dinner certainly tempted her with promises of grand parties and hidden villas, but she still wanted to join the Hospitalers. Nobody said she couldn't be a Hospitaler and a socialite too.

"So," Ennez said, finishing a goblet of wine, "I have the results you were wanting, Dav. I took the hair samples from Syg and from Captain Hathaline that you gave me and compared them with the control sample of Countess Medaline. Beth even helped me. She did a good job."

Beth winked at him and grabbed some food. Dav had heard that they had become part-time lovers, Beth being too free a spirit to linger with any one man, and there were men beginning to clamor at her door from every corner.

"Great," Dav said. "What are your findings?"

"I'm not sure you're going to want to hear this," he said, looking up at the flags high above.

Syg sat there and stared at Dav. She was giving him "the look"— the one that he knew well.

Beth flicked a grape at Syg, hitting her in the face. It didn't faze her.

"Why?" Dav asked.

"Because it's kind of strange."

"It's Syg we're talking about here. Of course it's going to be strange."

Syg slapped him on the shoulder and continued staring at him. She wished they were alone. They hadn't been totally alone since he'd returned from his trip.

<Dav! The balcony—now!> she telepathied to him.

Beth, able to hear the message, giggled.

Kilos approached an odd-looking staff on the wall. "Dav, I can't remember what this one is. What is it?"

Dav looked. "That's the BESSAMER of House Hobby. It's supposed to shoot fireballs, if memory serves."

Ki nodded and moved on.

Dav turned to Syg. "Syg—are you prepared to hear this?"

"Sure ... Dav ..." she purred, still giving him "the look."

"Syg?" Ennez said, trying to get her attention.

"I think she's feeling a little nervous about the results—who wouldn't be? Well, Ennez, what about it? Either you have a match to the Dursts or you do not. I don't understand all the mystery," Dav said.

"Okay, let me put it to you like this. It's a match and it's not a match."

"What?"

<Dav, if you don't take me to the balcony right now, I am going to tear this hall apart!>

Beth whispered to Ennez: "She's about to lose it. Let's start a food fight."

Ennez ignored her. "That's what I'm trying to tell you. Syg—Syg! Will you listen for a moment, please?"

Syg turned to him. "What, Ennez?"

"Do you want to hear this or not?"

She straightened up. "Yes, yes, I do ... please. I guess I am feeling a little nervous, I'm sorry. So, am I a Durst or aren't I?"

"Yes and no."

"Come on, how can I be related to the Dursts and not at the same time?"

Ennez leaned forward and lowered his voice. "All right, Syg, according to my readings, you are not related to the Dursts."

"Well, that is the whole of it then," Dav said. "I am sorry, Syg, I know you were hoping that ..."

"I'm not finished, Dav," Ennez said.

Dav stopped and listened. Beyond, Kilos pulled an odd whip off of the wall with a clatter.

"Watch that ALLYSON," Dav said to Kilos. "That one works, I think."

"House Colt, right?"

"Right."

Ennez continued. "So, Syg is certainly not related to the Dursts—that much is beyond question, but she is related to Captain Hathaline."

"Oh, good Creation, Ennez," Dav said. "What nonsense is this?"

"Dav, Captain Hathaline wasn't related to the Dursts either."

Dav sat there for a moment, trying to process the information Ennez had just given him. Beyond, Kilos was admiring a bronze sword that fought by itself when activated: The GEORGE WIND of House Hannover, Dav's mother's house. Dav knew that weapon well and it, like the ALLYSON of House Colt, worked.

"He checked it three times, sir," Beth said.

"Yep ... three times."

"Beth," Dav said, "are you ever going to stop calling me 'sir'?"

"No, sir." She smiled—she cherished Dav.

He shrugged and continued. "Ennez, I knew Hath from the time we were both children."

"And so? Were you there for her birth? Did you witness it?"

"No—how could I? I wasn't even ten, for Creation's sake!"

"Well then, either the Dursts adopted her or they took her in as a refugee and raised her as their own. In any case, she's not related to them at all. She is, however, related to Syg—a genetically perfect match."

"She's either your sister, Syg," Beth said, "or she's a clone of you."

Syg felt her heart stop.

"This is utter nonsense," Dav said again.

Syg began to cry. Dav took her and held her.

"Sorry, Dav—that's what we found. Did you want us to lie about it to you?"

"No, no, Ennez ... it's just that instead of clearing up this mystery one way or the other, it has been enhanced. I suppose, if I think on it, Hath doesn't overly resemble anyone else in the Dursts. Nobody else had her green eyes or red hair. Of course, that doesn't necessarily mean anything. But if she was adopted or boarded, she never said a thing about it. She was proud to be a Durst."

"You're damn right she was," Kilos said, approaching the table holding the NAS, a small glowing knife of House Albans. "You know how many times she dressed me down, proclaiming her Durstness the whole time?"

"Then she must not have known herself," Beth said. "You said Countess Medaline didn't willingly offer up any samples, you had to lift it. She must have known Hath wasn't her sister. She must know the truth and didn't want it coming out."

Dav dried Syg's tears. "Syg, do you want to continue this, or shall we leave the matter as it stands?"

"I need to know, Dav—something. Captain Hathaline ... my sister ..."

"Or your clone."

"Or my damn clone! Yes, thanks, Beth."

Kilos sat down. "Listen, I told my husband back at the University of Tusck what Syg told us about the whole Black Hat/Hulgismen abduction thing. I also told him about the Lady Poe/Shadow tech female thing, and he became fascinated with the subject and began doing research. Some of the things he found out. I have no idea how he comes up with this stuff, but it applies specifically to this conversation."

"What do you have, Ki?" Dav asked.

"Quite a lot, actually, and I need to know if you really want to hear what my husband found out."

"I do," Beth chirped, already a gossip lover.

Dav looked at Syg. "What do you say, Syg?"

"Yes, go ahead, Ki. Let's hear it."

"All right, don't say I didn't warn you. He found evidence of the abductions, just like Syg said—bits and pieces, a news item here, a bit of correspondence there—and a picture began to form. He thinks the reason Lady Poe didn't get abducted was—and are you ready for this—Sadric killed the Hulgismen that were there to abduct her. He fought and killed them when they tried to take her."

"You're saying my father ... killed somebody?"

"Yes, with your CARG. He defended his baby daughter. Would you have expected him not to?"

"No ... but ... I can't imagine my father killing anybody. The picture just doesn't fit."

Ki looked around the room. "There's more, Dav, if you want to hear it."

"Go on," he said.

Beth poured herself a drink and scooted in, loving the gossip, tingling with it.

Fiddling with the NAS, Kilos continued. "My husband found evidence that the Black Abbess tried to abduct Lady Poe again, years later ... more Hulgismen—more fighting, more killing, and then there was Hathaline, out of the blue."

"My father killed more people? Are you kidding me?"

"No, Sadric was not there for the second attack. He was away sabotaging a Grenville gala. My husband thinks it was either Pardock or your mother who fought them off. Probably your mother."

"Well, I can buy that more than I can my father doing it. So, what are you saying—that Hath was a Hulgisman?"

"Ask my husband. He's the egghead, not me. But there's more. The Dursts already had six children, all girls. Lady Evaline was getting old but got pregnant again with a seventh child, and this time it was a boy—they finally had their heir, their Lord Durst."

"And?" Beth said, fully absorbed, holding her glass.

"He was born dead ... stillborn it's called, I think."

"That almost never happens," Ennez said. "The statistics against that are staggering."

"Well, nevertheless, Ennez," she said, annoyed. "Maybe it was due to Lady Evaline's age—I don't know. Anyway, there they were, grieving over the loss of their Lord, their heir, when suddenly Hathaline shows up."

"Ki, when were you planning on telling me this?" Dav asked, slightly perturbed.

"I only found out a day or two ago myself, for Creation's sake!"

"I don't understand," Syg shrieked. "Where did Hathaline come from then, and how can she be related to me?"

Beth poured herself another glass and grabbed a plate of snacks. She was loving this.

Ki toyed with the NAS. Dav took it away from her.

She continued. "My husband is still gathering information, but he thinks he knows what happened—and I wouldn't argue against him if

I were you. So, Poe was attacked again when she was in her twenties—more Hulgismen, I guess. They tried to kidnap her—to take her to the Black Abbess's church. Either your mother or Pardock fought and killed them. One of the Hulgismen involved in the attack was pregnant and near her time. As she lay there dead, slain, they saw movement in her belly. They cut her open and removed a baby—a beautiful baby girl with striking green eyes."

"How can your husband know that?" Ennez asked.

"I don't know, gossip has a great staying power, gets written down, becomes a matter of public record. My husband can find out anything if he wants to. In any event, when Sadric returned to the castle, he found out about the attack and about this baby girl—a bit of green-eyed detritus from the attack, you might say. Sadric, knowing his friends the Dursts were grieving over the loss of their son, presented them with this baby girl—to slake their pain, I suppose. And they raised her as their own. Nothing more was said."

Davage thought a moment. "Syg, you must have been in your sixties then. You were a fairly new Black Hat, yes?"

"Yes ..."

"Could the Black Abbess have used some of your Hulgismen for an abduction plot?"

"She was always taking our Hulgismen for this and that ... yes, it's possible."

"Then I suppose that could be the correct story. Hath ... was the daughter of one of your Hulgismen. Hulgismen are cloned, so I don't know how one could have been pregnant."

"Female Hulgismen are pregnant all the time. I don't know from whom."

"Well, that would make Lady Hathaline a daughter of your clone—your granddaughter," Beth said with a mouthful of food.

Syg glared at Beth.

"But let's be patient for a moment. Hath couldn't be a Hulgisman. She had the Sight," Dav said.

"Well, she wasn't a Shadow tech female—she didn't have the mark ... so why not have the Sight? It's rare, but it's not unheard of, I suppose. And since she was in close proximity to you, maybe she chose to concentrate in that area, since you could do it. Maybe she wanted to please you."

Dav stood up and walked away from the table. "If you'll excuse me ... I wish to be alone for a bit."

He put the NAS back on the wall and walked away.

Syg stood. "Dav ... Dav!"

She ran after him. "What's wrong? Are you all right?"

He took her hand. "Walk with me, Syg,"

They walked out of the hall into a dark corridor. Syg stopped him. "Dav, what is wrong? Please talk to me. If anyone here should feel upset, it's me."

"I'm all right, Syg. It's just ... Hath was my friend. I thought I knew everything there was to know about her. And now, here she is, a second-generation clone of you. Not a Durst; being a Durst meant so much to her."

"I suppose it's good her surrogate parents loved her enough to keep the truth quiet."

"My mother and Pardock never said anything."

"Would you expect them to? It was in the past and need not be discussed further, until I came along—her look-alike, or I should say, she mine."

"I guess I've known you for my whole life then, Syg. First your clone ... then you."

"Or my ... granddaughter, I suppose."

"Yes, or your granddaughter."

She put her arms around him. "It could be that we were fated to be together, you and me. Someone, somewhere, in a cosmic place, wanted us together, and that suits me fine."

They kissed.

There was movement at the end of the corridor.

They looked. In the darkness, Dav could see someone standing at the end of the corridor in a hooded robe. The figure vanished.

Dave Wafted.

Syg Wafted.

9

THE BATTLE IN THE CORRIDOR

They emerged at the end of the hall where the figure had stood.

Dav lit his Sight. Down in the murky depths of the corridor he saw a figure standing there. It was wearing a robe, tall and thin. The figure appeared strange in Dav's Sight—as though there were many figures standing there, huddled, occupying the same space. He'd never seen anything like it.

Syg jumped in front of him, her expression lost in wonder.

"Dav ..." she exclaimed staring at his glowing eyes.

"Syg," Dav shouted, "not now!"

He Sighted through her.

He saw the figure move. He saw something hurtling toward them.

Like lightning, he unsaddled his CARG and pushed Syg out of the way. With a quick downstroke, he deflected a nasty-looking brass knife, which dug deep into the stone floor.

He made to tear down the hall and engage the figure, but a soft hand on his shoulder held him back.

Syg, having recovered from her short trip into Dav's Sight, brutally caught the figure in a Boxed-in Sten, Syg's control over it masterful.

The figure cringed in surprise for a moment, bounced around in the box, and fell.

Dav and Syg moved down the hall toward it.

"Is this person still alive, Syg?"

"Possibly. I wouldn't intentionally kill anybody in front of you, Dav," she said cheerfully as they arrived at the fallen body.

In the dim lighting, Syg could see a tall, thin man in a thick, heavy robe. His hair was cut short and spiky and dyed an angry color of red.

"Hmmm," Syg said, "spiky red hair. That is vaguely familiar for some reason."

Dav Sighted the body to make sure he was out.

The man was dead … the Boxed Sten, the brutal embrace, was too much for him. But he saw something further … something strange. He saw many people inside of him, struggling to get out.

"Syg, back away!" he said, pulling her from the man.

"Why?"

Suddenly, they saw Princess Marilith, face painted, long blue hair, and colorful veils, come climbing out of the fallen man, from out of his robes.

Growling, Syg fired a blast of Silver tech, enveloping her in it. She savagely pulled her out and slammed her down head first. She then constricted the Silver tech with relish, and Marilith screamed in breathless pain, her ribs and bones snapping in the silver embrace. Syg began unwrapping the dying Marilith; she wanted to throttle her with her own two hands.

Dav Sighted something … something terrible.

Another Marilith came crawling out of the fallen robed man. She drew a large brass knife and sent it rocketing toward the back of Syg's head.

"*SYG!*"

Dav whipped his CARG around and just barely was able to clip the knife with the cork-screw end of his weapon up into the lofty heights, where it stuck in the stone ceiling.

Dav brought the CARG down into Marilith's head, splitting it in two. She fell back into the fallen man, as if he was some type of endless hollow space, her arms waving in a blood-splattering death frenzy.

Dav Sighted again. He led Syg away toward the wall of the corridor.

"Get your Sten up and keep it up!" He was feeling a little shaken after almost witnessing Syg's death.

"Stay close, love!" she said and lifted a quick Sten around them. Dav could see it shimmering in the dark.

Mariliths began pouring out of the fallen man.

Two.

Four.

Eight.

Sixteen.

Thirty-two.

The leering group of Mariliths gathered around the edges of the Sten, confident and arrogant, and looked at it for a moment, fully able to see it, apparently. They lightly prodded it with metal-capped fingers that seemed to counteract the Sten's shocking power. They made laughing, chiding faces at Dav and Syg, certain they were in complete control of this situation. They were going to enjoy this.

Syg didn't wait; she extended the Sten, trying to push them into the far wall.

They held it fast, leaning against it, their metal-capped fingers sparking on the vibrant surface of the Sten. They howled with condescending laughter.

A few other "Mariliths" drew handfuls of little colorful trinkets from their pouches and began scattering them on the floor; there were little frogs, cats, pink birds, and an assortment bouncing, multi colored balls. The balls, in a flurry of bouncing motion, appeared to be reacting with the Sten, draining power from it, and they grew in size steadily as they bounced.

"Dav—I think I'm going to pass out!" Syg cried.

Dav kissed her. "Pull it back close to you, and keep it up! Do not let it drop!" With that he Wafted through the field, right into the mass of leering, cavorting Mariliths.

With CARG whirling, Davage engaged them.

"Oh, look at this, he wants to fight!" one said.

"Truly—we've got a fighter on our hands," another said.

"Oh, he's handsome. Let us leave his face intact so that I may kiss him once he's dead!"

In a confident, condescending manner, they drew all sorts of knobbed, bladed, and projectile weapons and responded in kind, and soon the corridor was a buzz saw of movement.

"I think I'll cut his—urk!" a "Marilith" said as she fell headless, her weapon clattering to the stone floor along with her quivering, headless body.

Syg, behind her shrunken Sten Field, had no idea what to do. She had never been in a fight where she was actually concerned about anyone but herself. Her Sten having been somehow counteracted, she would have normally scoured the corridor clear with a Shadow tech maelstrom, and nothing in that hallway would be alive afterwards— but she couldn't with Dav in the middle of all of them.

What was she supposed to do?

A Marilith fell in two pieces and roughly bounced off of her Sten, a victim of Dav's glinting CARG. Instantly Marilith's guise fell away, and she reverted into a short, homely girl with spiked red hair, the look of shock and surprise indelibly etched into her now-dead face.

She tried a TK. Quick, easy to use, and powerful, TKs were an oft-overlooked staple of any Black Hat's arsenal. In her many battles with the Sisterhood, she'd seen them do amazing things with it, TKs being not flashy enough for a Black Hat. She tried to pick a Marilith up with TK; she was going to toss her about a bit, use her like a club against the others. As she did, a flock of little pink bird trinkets, scattered about on the floor by the Mariliths, took flight and happily chirped about the corridor. The Mariliths joyously laughed. Somehow the birds absorbed and diverted her TK energy.

The TK was defeated in a flock of pink birds.

Syg tried to Dirge. "*You there!*" she Dirged, picking one out of the crowd. "*Fall on your own knife!*"

The Mariliths laughed. A toy frog resting on the floor amid the various trinkets began speaking, mimicking Syg's Dirge, somehow muffling it, rendering it harmless.

Her Dirge was defeated.

Not knowing what else to do, she Pointed. She felt a bit shy about using such a gruesome killing Gift such as the Point with Dav around—she didn't want him to see that particular aspect of her—but what could she do? They were in a serious, no-quarter fight, and she had to help out. The "Marilith" she'd picked out recoiled in pain as the deadly Point energy wrapped around her. Reaching into a pouch at her waist, she pulled out a small blue flower. The flower began growing, began taking in the potent Point energy. She quickly advanced on Syg, holding a long, cruel knife in the other hand. She reared back and lunged.

The knife came through the Sten like it wasn't even there.

Syg, Stenned in place, couldn't move her legs, but she could still duck, and the blade missed—barely, biting into the wall.

"Marilith" reared back for another attack.

Syg Pointed with her other hand—a deadly Double Point. The flower began growing at a much faster rate. A second later, at capacity, the flower exploded. The person in the image of Marilith looked at the ruins of the flower in her hand and had just enough time to begin to scream before she exploded, her body ripping apart and spraying the corridor in sundered gore, her knife, covered in blood, dropping to the floor.

A "Marilith" pulled out of the twisting, roiling group and leveled a long projectile weapon at her. Before she could fire, Dav sliced the weapon in two, opening himself up for a cutting attack, which he barely rolled away from in time.

Syg watched Dav for a moment and admired him; she had never seen him in action before, fighting with his CARG. He was nothing short of incredible. He was surrounded, outnumbered, and in close quarters, but he was holding them back, even pressing the fight and methodically thinning their numbers, his CARG wheeling around in a blur. Her Dav could fight. Thoughts of the balcony momentarily re-entered her head.

Syg felt helpless. What could she do? She was used to the direct, heavy-handed approach to fighting, to erase lots of enemies quickly and thoroughly, but these people, Cloaked to look like Marilith, seemed to somehow have an answer to most of the things she normally used. She recalled Dav mentioning to her that the most effective thing, he thought, in the Black Hat arsenal was a Shadow Tech monster; autonomous, tough, and virtually impossible to fully defeat, Dav had said if the Black Hats he met in Metatron had used those instead of Blasts, Points, and Stens, he probably would have been killed there, either by Beth or by Suz.

Somebody's bloody arm flew past her Sten, and then a veiled leg.

The problem was, creating a Shadow tech beast was extremely difficult. You couldn't just produce the Shadow tech, wind it up, and send it on its way—you had to bind it, combine it, give it a heart, give it a soul, and give it a purpose. A good Black Hat Painter could produce a fully task-driven beast in half an hour. A Black Hat novice, however, took months to create a small, feeble creation

She wracked her brains. Dav couldn't keep this pace up for much longer. He needed help—she had to help him.

Wait …

She remembered all Painters had what they called a Familiar—a small, simple Shadow tech monster that they practiced conjuring many times. A Painter could dial up a Familiar in a matter of moments. It was meant to be used in a pinch.

What had she done before? She hadn't created a Shadow tech beast in years—except for …

She had the answer and created a large blob of Silver tech. It floated out of the Sten and then began twisting and changing in mid-air, like a silver storm cloud.

*　　*　　*　　*　　*

Davage parried a blow from a large, heavy knife. He knocked the knife loose. The "Marilith" in front of him wasn't expecting his CARG to be such a dense, heavy weapon and couldn't hold onto her knife. Without another thought, he put his weapon through "Marilith's" chest. He had initially been fighting to wound, to incapacitate, but after they began attacking Syg behind her Sten, he realized that these people had infiltrated his home and were threatening the lives of all within: Syg, his friends, his sisters, his nephews, his house staff … everybody, and their lives were therefore forfeit.

These people, whomever they were, fought well and fiercely, but they weren't fighting masters by any means. They had begun the battle supremely confident, armed with cruel weapons and strange trinkets. They were certain that they could easily handle him—that they might even have a bit of deadly fun at his expense, reducing him down in a slow, torturous exercise to a pleading, quivering mass.

Suddenly they were falling, sliced in twain, headless, armless, legless, fatally cleaved, and their demeanor changed to angry, determined … frightened. They realized they faced a very dangerous, very capable opponent who was not to be trifled with. They set themselves to the task.

Even though he was badly outnumbered and surrounded, Dav was fully in control of this fight, his Sight laying the near future out for him in a vivid tapestry, allowing him to anticipate and counter any thrust or movement he considered dangerous.

Every so often he Sighted one leveling a weapon at Syg, and he instantly took care of them.

It was a strange fight to be sure. He'd badly wounded a "Marilith" at the beginning of the battle, and a nearby toy cat resting on the ground seemed to take the blow for her, Marilith's wound being somehow greatly lessened by the presence of the cat. Davage went ahead and took her head off, for which the cat had no suitable answer. He thought he saw Syg trying a TK, and a flock of pink birds took flight in a commotion. Every so often, one happened to fly into his CARG and shattered in a puff of feathers and an odd lavender smell. He also recalled Syg trying a Dirge and a toy frog, in a mocking voice, squelched it. These people, whoever they were, had style. He had to give them that.

He kept glancing over to Syg, making sure she was still safe behind her Sten. She looked pained, sick even. He could tell she didn't know how to fight like this—she couldn't clear the corridor with him in it. He thought about Wafting away and giving her a clear shot, but he wanted her to struggle, he wanted her to be creative. She would need that little extra edge in battle when and if she ever met up with the real Marilith.

She suddenly appeared inspired and cast out a large glob of undulating Silver tech, which floated in the air.

Curious, he watched it form for as long as he could. The "Mariliths" also watched. Eyes glittering with delight, they began digging through their pouches.

The silver formed into the image of the *Seeker*, about four feet long and one foot high. Dav was amazed. This time she did a pretty good job, unlike her first two attempts over Metatron; it had a head, a long neck, and a winged rear section—it even had a little light-emitting version of the main sensor that panned about throwing a silvery beam of light. A very decent attempt.

He guessed the "stern" talking to he gave her paid off.

The Mariliths laughed at the sight of the floating *Seeker* and pulled little green flowers out of their pouches. They brazenly presented them to the ship.

Dav watched as a miniature silver version of the port Battleshot batteries opened up. Instantly, three of them and a whole bunch of fluttering pink birds vanished in a hail of silver shot and smoked feathers scented with lavender. The survivors appeared utterly shocked as they took a second glance at the silver ship and their green flower totems—clearly they had been expecting Shadow tech, not Syg's Silver tech. They utterly lost their previous confidence and began scattering in a messy panic. Reaching into their pouches with grasping fingers, they produced little black vials, unstoppered them, and began splashing the contents about the corridor; a distinct smell of jasmine filling the air.

The remaining frogs, cats, birds, and balls began growing, growling, deforming, and attacking.

The monsters hit Syg's *Seeker* in a heap, clinging onto it with claws, biting with tooth-filled maws. They stuck in, but the little silver ship, much as the real thing, kept flying and attacking.

Another blast from the tiny silver Battleshot batteries—another group of "Mariliths" went down. A gaggle of hideous frogs also met their end, with the smell of mint.

This battle had quickly gone to shambles, and the Mariliths appeared to have no more stomach for it, they either dying under the silver guns of Syg's *Seeker* or by Dav's screaming CARG.

They ran back toward the robed man—their portal, their point of ingress and egress—eager to make their escape. One, having already halfway disappeared through him, suddenly fell—shot through the head with a League pistol.

Kilos, Ennez, and Beth appeared.

The remaining Mariliths spread out to engage them instead of Syg's Silver *Seeker* and Dav's wickedly fast CARG. Birds, balls, frogs, and cats joined them.

Beth stopped and Pointed the nearest one; again, "Marilith" drew a blue flower from her pouch, and it began growing, absorbing the Point energy. With her other hand, she produced a large brass knife, and in a froth of fear, she charged.

Ki shot the growing flower out of her hand with her smoking SK.

She regarded the shattered remains of it in her hand for a moment with horror.

A second later, she exploded.

A cat, lunging, fell dead, shot, reeking of rosemary.

Another cat got TKed to death by Beth … crushed. Score one for Bethrael.

Three Mariliths advanced on Beth, but before they got within five paces, Ennez put twenty blows on one with his whirling Jet Staff. She fell a hopelessly battered mess. The remaining two advanced on Ennez, and he did the same thing to them, these people apparently not knowing it wasn't wise to engage a Hospitaler up close.

They also seemed to be completely unprepared for an armed Marine with a fully loaded SK; Ki gunned down Mariliths and animated trinkets mercilessly, and they just stood there and let Ki shoot them.

Beth tried to blast a Marilith with Shadow tech, hers still not fully changed to Silver tech. The Marilith produced a green flower. The Shadow tech was drawn to the flower, and Beth screamed in agony.

Ki shot the flower-wielding Marilith in the face, her triumph with the green flower short-lived.

Several balls managed to clamp onto Ki's shoulder, getting a mouthful of Marine coat. Ki's SK put a hole through one, and Beth's TK popped the rest like over-ripe grapes with a smell of pine-needles.

A flock of birds went down in a chirping, feather-laced pile, seemingly all at once by Ennez's hyper-speed Jet Staff.

The *Seeker* finished up the remaining five or six Mariliths, and soon all were dead. None would be taken alive.

The thick smell of burnt shot propellant from Ki's SK mixed with blood, lavender, jasmine, mint, rosemary, and pine trees. The corridor smelt like a spice rack.

10

THE FANATICS OF NALLS

Dav took a deep breath. "Syg, are you all right?"

She dropped her Sten and ran into his arms, her Silver tech *Seeker* forgotten. It lazily bounced off of the walls and slowly descended, shrinking and fading. He held her tight, still thinking of the knife speeding for the back of her head.

"Is everyone all right?"

"Fine, sir," Beth said, always calling Dav "sir."

"I'm good, Dav," Ki said, reloading her pistol with a new cartridge and lamenting the ragged hole in her coat. "We heard the commotion."

Ennez nodded and didn't say anything.

"Ki, I need you to call down to the *Seeker* and have Com send for the Magistrate. You also might as well summon the Sisters; I'm sure they're going to want to see this. The rest of you, let's go check on Poe, Pardock, and her children."

Ki pulled her communicator out and went to find a window.

They went to the other side of the castle and found Pardock and her sons. Dav told her what happened, and Enoch was mad that he had missed it. Dav suggested she take Poe and go to Castle Vincent for a while until this Marilith thing blew over.

Pardock said she wasn't going anywhere. Poe neither.

They then went back to the corridor and awaited the Magistrate and the Sisters.

"So, do we have any idea who these … individuals are?" Davage asked.

"I remember the spiked red hair from somewhere—can't quite place it, though," Syg said.

"I think I know," Beth said. "I remember my Hulgismen getting into an occasional dust up with a rowdy group of red-headed tuffs tarrying near the base of my temple. They were a group of disaffected roughnecks and urchins from Nalls, which is near Moane. I think they were calling themselves the Fanatics of Nalls."

"The Fanatics of Nalls—yes, I've heard of them. An upstart sect from the dregs of Xaphan Society. I heard they were hoping to make a name for themselves, that they were wanting to move up in the ranks and even challenge the Black Hats."

"Well, there's no doubt for whom they're working," Ennez said, kicking one of them slightly.

"Since Princess Marilith is 'on the quits' with the Black Hats since the *Triumph* fiasco, working for someone like her, no doubt, has a great appeal for them," Beth said.

Davage picked up one of their pouches and rummaged through it.

"Their tactics did seem to favor a direct assault—something Black Hats might find difficult to deal with. And they have an assortment of novel accessories here with them that were very effective in countering the Sten and the Point."

"And TK and the Dirge," Syg said.

"And Shadow tech, too," Beth added, still smarting.

"They were surprised by my Silver Tech," Syg said. "They didn't seem to be prepared for it."

Ennez grabbed a pouch. He pulled out an assortment of colored flowers, little balls, frogs, cats, birds, and a few small items that looked like crude dolls.

"The blue flowers appeared to be effective against the Point, if I recall," Dav pointed out.

"The green one got me," Beth said, painfully

"The birds seemed to draw in TK energy."

"They had some sort of potion that, upon contact, brought all these items to life," Dav said.

"You mean this here?" Ki said pulling a black bottle from a pouch.

Dav looked at it. "The same," he said. Kilos unstoppered the bottle and smelled it. "It smells like jasmine."

Ennez examined one of the dead cats. "Appears to be a construct of some sort. This one is made out of rosemary, oils, and other assorted chemicals. Very clever."

Ennez pulled out a blue flower and looked at it. "Beth, could you Point me please?" he said, holding up the flower.

"I'm not going to Point at you, Ennez!" she screeched.

He set the flower down and walked away. "Now, Point at it."

Dubious, Beth Pointed at it. Sure enough, the flower began to grow in size, absorbing the deadly Point energy. The flower, after about ten seconds, appeared close to bursting.

"Beth, stop the Point, I want to …"

"I can't—that's what I was trying to tell you before."

The flower exploded in a spray.

"You can't stop a Point."

They looked around—dead bodies in all sorts of exertions. In death they were both male and female of various sizes and complexions, all fairly young. All with spiked red hair.

Dav knelt down over the robed man and examined him, looking for some sort of hidden portal.

"They came pouring out of this man, as if he were some sort of gateway or open door. He feels solid enough now."

Beth examined the dead man. "I also heard the Fanatics of Nalls were experimenting with new uses of the Gifts. They bragged about something called the Box, where many people or things could occupy the same space. I also heard that they had discovered the secret of the Hulgismen's immunity to the Sisters power."

"Immune to the Sisters? They are going to flip when they see this, and they are probably going to want every one of these bodies and constructs sent to their research facility in Valenhelm or Pithnar for testing," Ennez said.

"It appears we will not be needing the Magistrate after all. The Sisters will probably kick him right out," Davage said.

*　*　*　*　*

Davage was right about the Magistrate. Ten Sisters and a small squadron of Marines arrived in a matter of minutes and politely informed the Magistrate that they were assuming responsibility for this situation.

The Sisters, always polite, always smiling, yet never challenged. The Magistrate returned to the village and drank himself to sleep.

Davage and Ennez showed them the bags full of trinkets, and they seemed quite disturbed by all of it. They, obviously, had heard little of this Fanatics of Nalls sect.

After a few more minutes, a Marine approached Davage.

"Captain, sir, the Sisters urgently request fealty over all bodies and materials taken from this attack, though they fully acknowledge your skill and bravery in collecting them, express their profound relief that no one here was killed or injured, and are wishing to compensate you any price you deem fair."

A Sister toyed with a blue flower from one of the pouches. Another one tugged on a frog.

"I desire no compensation."

"In that case, Captain, the Sisters request these bodies be taken with all possible speed to chapel Twilight 4 where the Sisters will begin the slow process of examining and discovering all their secrets."

"I see. Twilight 4, way to the south of Remnath, if I am not mistaken."

Syg wandered over to Dav and hung on his arm.

"Correct, sir. On the morrow a procession of three Fleet vessels will arrive to provide escort for these bodies."

"I require no escort."

"The Sisters insist. They feel something sinister is afoot and wish to take no chances. Furthermore, and no disrespect intended, sir, but the fine vessel *Seeker* will not be the lead ship. You will be providing escort to the lead vessel, where the bodies and materials will be kept in safe passage."

Davage shook his head. The Sisters looked a bit concerned.

They pummeled the Marine with thoughts.

"Please, Captain, the Sisters again acknowledge your skill and seniority and greatly desire that your honor be not damaged in this matter. They were simply hoping to provide the citizenry with a grand Fleet display, as in the days of old, and they are certain that, when you see the lead ship for yourself, you will be pleased."

"My honor is not damaged, Sisters, and thank you for your concern. I will abide by your wisdom and look ahead with great interest to this grand procession on the morrow."

The Sisters mentally chattered amongst themselves and appeared relieved.

With that, the Marines quickly collected the bodies and were gone within the hour.

11

A GRAND PROCESSION

The next morning, Davage, Syg, and Ki went down to the docks to await the arrival of the Fleet. Davage had to admit, the Sisters had piqued his curiosity about this procession, and, in particular, the lead ship that was coming.

Ki announced that she was thirsty and headed to a nearby pub. Beth and Ennez followed.

Syg, getting impatient, wanted to know when he was going to propose to her.

Soon, Syg, soon …

Before long the Fleet began arriving, their gas-compression engines screeching through the cold air.

The first to arrive was the *Blue Max*, a fairly new *Straylight* vessel commanded by Captain Wythleweir, a lady of House Conwell. Wythleweir had little Fleet experience. No doubt the vast Conwell fortune and connections came into play during the appointment proceedings for the *Blue Max's* captain's chair.

Gracefully, the *Blue Max* set down in the bay, next to the *Seeker*.

Shortly, the *Caroline* roared down from the mountains. An old *Straylight*, the *Caroline* was captained by Captain Stenstrom, Lord Belmont, in his thirteenth appointment. Light as a feather, the captain brought the *Caroline* down on the other side of *Seeker*.

The villagers were buzzing with excitement. It had been a long time that so many ships had been here at once. They anxiously awaited the arrival of the last ship, a "surprise" that the Sisters had promised.

They didn't have long to wait, soon, coming out of the western sky, a black dot approached.

Dav and Syg looked at it. It didn't sound like a *Straylight*, no roaring, no characteristic whistling, it thrummed with a steady beat.

Dav Sighted it.

"Syg, you remember Ki mentioning a lady named Demona of Ryel and her fine vessel *Triumph* that we all admired so much?

"Yes, Dav—why?" She squinted and strained to see the ship that was approaching.

"Because there it is."

Clear in Dav's Sight was the *Triumph* ... not the ship that was currently speeding Demona of Ryel to her home, but an identical, much larger version built in Provst by Lord Milos of Probert, the first of a new class. It was a long ship with a narrow, elongated upper hull and a squashed, flattened lower section with no "neck" between the two. It looked like two huge teardrops fused together. The engines were splayed flat at either side on sturdy gantries that retracted into the hull, and they glowed with blue light. It put down in the bay and was clearly much larger than the *Straylight*s next to it.

With the exception of being much larger than the original, it was the spitting image of Demona's ship. Syg, in a flap, was pummeling him with questions, but he wasn't listening. He stared at it, lost in nostalgia.

After a time, a beaming Lord Probert and the Lady Branna of the Science Ministry disembarked.

"Well, Captain, what do you think of her?" Probert asked.

"Lord Probert, it certainly looks like the *Triumph* I remember. Quite a bit larger than the original, if I recall correctly."

"It had to be larger, Captain," the Lady Branna said, "as this stubborn old man, and soon-to-be unwilling guest of my dungeon, would not part with his tried and trues. This is the ship of the future, Captain. It is equipped with a fully capable tach drive, along with Lord Probert's beloved Stellar Mach coils, as he would not be rid of them. It is fully shielded and mounts devastating Sar-Beams instead of Battleshot batteries ..."

"An error in judgment that I will see your blue-haired carcass rotting in prison over, I swear it, Lady Branna," Probert said, pointing at her.

She ignored him.

"Canisters?" Dav asked quietly, hopefully.

"Yes," Lady Branna said, "it mounts canisters, though I pushed for deleting them as well."

"I would send you straight to hell first."

"And Captain, it mounts our first, fully functional electro-teleporter assembly. No more need for Arrow Shot; we can now materialize directly from orbit."

"A scandal!" Probert said. "Who ever heard of such a thing?"

"The scandal, Lord Probert, will be when you resort to cannibalism for survival once your rotund backside has polished the stones of my dungeon floor for a while!" Lady Branna replied.

"You'll starve me, will you, harpy! I will ensure you get your three nourishing meals a day in prison, Lady Branna!"

Davage was impressed; Lord Probert and Lady Branna had outdone themselves. He laughed and separated the bickering duo.

"It is a fine vessel, Captain," Probert said. "I already have five more spars laid in Provst. I'll be wanting you in attendance to pick one out. Bring money, as always."

"You would have me set the *Seeker* aside?"

"I wish to see our finest captain set sail in our finest vessel. Do you not agree, Lady Sygillis, that Captain Davage is our best?"

"I suppose he does well in a pinch," Syg said, smiling at him, infinitely relieved that this was not Demona of Ryel's ship.

"It is a fine ship, but to leave the *Seeker* ... we've been through so much together."

"Oh," Probert said, "you Fleet captains, so sentimental. You talk of the *Seeker* like it's a living thing, like it has a soul. If it has a soul,

Captain, it's because you gave it to her. Will your new vessel be any different? It needs a soul too, I suppose, does it not?"

He smiled. "Time marches on."

"Well, then, let's aboard, and I'll show you around."

Probert offered his arm to Syg, Davage offered his to Lady Branna, and they went in.

*　　*　　*　　*　　*

Davage ordered the *Seeker* into the air, the screaming gas compression engines slowly lifting it out of the bay, the massive underside of the ship creating an artificial rainstorm of dripping water. The dock was its usual mass of waving, cheering people watching the giant ship climb away.

Davage always had a sheepish urge to drop the nose and buzz the dock, soaking those in attendance. It was his dock, his town, after all, but as he didn't want to burst the eardrums of every one of his people, he fought the urge off.

Gracefully, he ordered the ship set at station three thousand feet in the air. There, he waited for the other two escort ships and the *Triumph*, whose engines were starting to throb with blue light.

The *Caroline*, performing a slow spin to clear away the water, joined him to his right. The *Blue Max* then began rising in loud, workmanlike fashion, parking at his left.

Soon, the *Triumph* rose into the sky, much larger than the escorting *Straylight*s, but infinitely quieter.

Davage got a Com from the *Triumph*. Yard Marshall Tempus, a yarding captain from Bern, popped into view—apparently a permanent captain had yet to be appointed. In fact, the whole crew were made up mostly of guests, dignitaries, Admirals, and others, all dressed in their finest, with a small squadron of Marines and a few Sisters to guard the "cargo" of dead Fanatics and their baggage.

"Tempus to escort fleet, we are ready to proceed."

"Shall we ascend to a standard cruising altitude of seventy thousand feet and bear planetary revolutions?" Davage asked.

"No, no, Captain," Tempus said. "Let's give the people something to see. Cruise at five thousand feet and make for parking revolutions only. Let's go nice and slow. To Twilight 4 as in the days of old."

Syg, sitting in Dav's chair, looked up. "What's that mean?" she whispered.

"It means this trip is going to take a while … several hours at least."

"Well then," Tempus said, "if the *Seeker* will park to my right and the *Caroline* to my left, the *Blue Max* will bear tail. Keep to a standard formation and let's open the baffles a bit … let 'em hear us coming."

"Aye, Marshall. Helm, you heard him. Collect at four and stay tight."

Crewman Saari, Lady Branna's daughter, smiled, and slowly, the *Seeker* tucked into the starboard of the *Triumph* and the procession began moving to the south … a grand Fleet display not seen in some time.

*   *   *   *   *

The fleet had gone about a thousand miles to the south, and it had taken about an hour to get this far. Syg, beginning to get bored, began sending Dav dirty telepathies.

<*I'm going to my quarters, Dav, to change into something more comfortable. I suggest you wait a moment and then come down to make sure I don't need any … help … changing.*>

She winked at him and left the bridge.

Feeling a bit tied down by this turtle-pace grand procession himself, Dav decided to take her up on her offer. He'd wait several minutes and then excuse himself; he didn't want it to seem that he was going to be dallying with Syg, though pretty much everybody knew that's what he would be doing. Kilos, standing at her Ops station, gave him a knowing look.

12

THE TRIUMPH FALLS

And that's when the *Triumph* heeled over hard to port, dropping out of formation like a rock.

The *Caroline* had to make a severe nose down movement to avoid getting Slapped by the plummeting lead ship. Continuing on through the clouds, the *Triumph* was locked in a steep, brutal dive to the surface below. Davage, intimately familiar with the workings of a *Straylight*, had no idea what might be wrong with this new *Triumph*-class ship—externally, the ship appeared to be functioning normally as far as he could tell.

Recalling Metatron, Davage walked over to the helm and politely, excused Saari, the helmsman. She thankfully stepped back, eager to watch Davage in action. He pulled a pair of white gloves on and lowered the ship into trail. "Let's beat to quarters," he said, wanting the ship ready for action if needed. The claxons went off, and the crew began bustling about.

Very low to the ground, the *Triumph* pulled up, climbed a bit, and leveled, gliding along quietly as if nothing had happened.

"Com, send to *Triumph*," Dav said.

"Aye, Captain," the Com said. "No response, sir."

The silence from *Triumph* was ominous.

Holding the *Seeker* in a shallow dive, Dav leveled up a bit, giving himself plenty of room. The *Caroline* followed suit and shallowed at his flank. The *Blue Max* continued down.

Dav Sighted, staring down through the floorboards and decks, down to the *Triumph*, through its hull and into the interior.

His blood froze. Inside, there were dead bodies everywhere. It was heartbreaking, all these people, elegant, dressed in their best, ready for a grand party—dead, chopped to pieces. Inside, there were no less than three hundred "Mariliths" running about, taking key sections of the ship, including the bridge. The Fanatics of Nalls—they had somehow stowed away. Those odd dolls in their pouches, he recalled—perhaps they had "Boxed" themselves into those.

Davage pulled the wheel back. "I want flanking speed. Com, send to *Caroline* and *Blue Max*, the *Triumph* has been taken by hostile forces and must now be considered an enemy vessel!"

"Aye, sir!"

The viewer clicked on, and suddenly they were seeing the *Triumph*'s bridge. Close up, filling the screen, was Princess Marilith of Xandarr, her face painted for war. There was fire in her eyes and a slight crooked smile on her lips.

This was no Cloaked Fanatic. This was the real thing. He'd know that crazed gaze anywhere.

"Care to play, Captain?" she said with a sneer. "You're going to die today!"

The screen flipped off. And Davage saw what was coming. He rammed the wheel upward to Z plus two thousand feet.

A wailing red Sar-Beam blast came sizzling upward, just missing his rolling belly. Another blast—the *Blue Max* was hit square in the neck of the ship. Smoking, it heeled to port, taking yet another blast in its ventral.

Sight.

Davage whipped the wheel first one way then the other, the *Seeker* standing on its head. A Sar-Beam screamed by.

Enough, enough of this. "Canister control, I want a two-shot stagger fire aimed for the *Triumph*'s stern!"

He heard nothing back.

"Canister control, do you read?"

Before another moment passed, twenty shimmering balls of floating, granular light appeared at various places on the bridge.

Dav had seen this before. Balls of light, just like when Demona of Ryel "filtered" down from her ship to join him for lunch on the surface of Kana.

Matter/Energy converters. Teleportation units!

"We're boarded!" Davage cried, drawing his MiMs.

The Fanatics of Nalls, all Cloaked to look like Marilith, leering, confident, laughing, drew their odd assortment of weapons and sprung to attack.

"Clear the bridge!" Dav yelled, firing his MiMs, the small, elegant pistol making its usual "pock, pock" sound. "Everybody into the conference room, bar the door, and don't open it unless ordered to by me!"

Kilos drew her SK. "You heard him, everybody out!" She began firing, her weapon making a much more satisfying "tack! tack!" report.

The bridge crew, unarmed, quickly made their way to the conference room door, Davage and Kilos covering them with fire. This was something of a maddening situation. The Fanatics, while being eager to fight and initially intimidating, were not overly wise or skilful as they fought. Ki had already dropped four and Dav three, the small MiMs needing two or three shots to kill a person. Dav couldn't clean them up with his CARG as he had to turn the wheel. The *Triumph* out there with its reaching, deadly Sar-Beam fire was of much greater importance.

He Sighted a knife whizzing for his head. He ducked.

He Sighted another Sar-Beam blast. He rolled the ship. The crew, used to a twisting, turning "Dav fight" casually hung on and stood tall as they exited. The Fanatics, though, tumbled and flew screaming about the bridge, many dropping their weapons and at least one being killed with a crushed skull against the ceiling.

The Fanatics were flabbergasted; they'd never experienced anything like it. Some looked miserable, like they were ready to drop their weapons and give up.

Seeing this, the bridge crew stopped running and began fighting. They fought the Fanatics, unarmed and untrained. They fought with whatever they had; Davage saw coffee cups, report pads, shoes, and belt buckles go flying in a cloud across the bridge. The Fanatics, down to eleven attackers, found themselves swarmed on all sides, the bridge crew latching onto them and pulling them down relentlessly. Saari had one around the throat with her belt with her left hand and was beating the Fanatic senseless with a shoe in her right.

A Fanatic leveled a long pistol at her.

Pock—right between the eyes. The Fanatic fell.

Ki's hammering SK, its endless magazine of twenty-five shots, finished the rest of the armed Fanatics.

A final belly roll to avoid another Sar-Beam blast closed the proceedings, and the bridge was secure. A few minutes later the Marines came in to mop up the survivors and declared all key areas of the ship re-taken and secure.

"Is everybody all right?" Davage said as he pulled the *Seeker* into a steep, steep climb.

The crew nodded.

Davage was furious. "Did nobody hear me? I ordered this bridge cleared!"

They stood there and looked at him.

"You could have been hurt, you could have been killed, and I expect my orders carried out next time!"

The crew stood there, many shoeless, one covered in coffee, some, beltless, were holding up their falling pants with their hands. They looked miserable after the rebuke.

"Sir ..." Saari said quietly, shoeless and holding up her pants, "if you are going to order me to abandon my post in the face of the enemy when you are standing at yours, then you will have to court-martial me, sir."

"Me too, sir," others said.

Kilos smiled. "Looks like it's a mutiny."

Davage holstered his MiMs. "Indeed, it appears I'll need to make quick work of this mutiny ... in the mess later on over buncked narva as I toast to my crew's courage. Now, let's get posted."

The crew cheered and returned to their stations.

* * * * *

When the ship started tumbling, Syg was naked in bed. She'd been waiting for Dav, tense for his arrival.

But then, the ship started a pounding series of rolls and lifts, throwing Syg from the bed. Rolling naked to the floor, she Stenned herself into place, the sheets from the bed sparking as they touched it. Through the window she could see the *Triumph* firing on them and the other escort ships scattering.

Marilith—she must be behind this. She and those Fanatics of Nalls.

Always in the wings, always the stalker, Marilith will never leave them alone ... never. And she was probably right over there, in the *Triumph*.

She lowered her Sten, made her way to the closet, pulled out a black robe, and put it on.

She was going to finish this. She was going to the *Triumph* and face Marilith, and she was going to have to kill her.

Resolute, wearing the black robe, Syg went out into the hallway, stopping to take one last look at her quarters.

Just in case.

* * * * *

The scene outside *Seeker* was poor at best. The *Blue Max* was staggering around the sky aimlessly, smoking, every so often after taking a hit from *Triumph*'s guns. The *Caroline* took a direct Sar-Beam blast to the engineering section and was clawing to stay aloft.

That's when it happened. The unthinkable happened.

The *Blue Max* loosed a two-shot canister barrage at the *Caroline*, the missiles hitting their mark, blowing a good part of the port wing clean off.

On fire, in a power dive, the *Caroline* roared down from the heights and passed through the clouds, spinning slowly from ventral to dorsal.

Still at the wheel of the *Seeker*, Davage wanted to Sight it down, but he had other, more pressing worries: the *Blue Max* was laying a bead on him. Sighting, he saw the ship in turmoil, the Sisters and

Marines struggling to re-take key areas of the ship, but the bridge and forward canister bays were under the Fanatics' control.

Worse, on the bridge, he could see Captain Wythleweir on her knees, a few moments away from being executed by the Fanatics.

Dav spun the wheel, and plummeting, he slammed into the *Blue Max's* ventral frontal hull, Slapping her hard. The *Blue Max* rocked to port and veered.

Barely avoiding another blast from *Triumph*, Davage pulled the *Seeker* skyward in a steep climb. He had to get into low orbit. He needed legs to move, his gas compression engines straining to provide lift and speed. He needed his coils to really move, to really turn.

Behind him, the *Triumph* and *Blue Max* followed.

"Aft Sensing, what is *Blue Max's* status?"

"Sir, *Blue Max's* forward canister and starboard Battleshot ports are open."

Dav slid the ship to the *Blue Max's* left, hoping that the port side of the ship was still in Fleet hands and therefore safe.

The *Blue Max* ripple fired four canisters

"Captain, Aft Sensing! Four canisters on flat approach!"

So, Dav thought, *here it is.* He was now facing the canister, the League's "ace" weapon. It could not be out-run, it could not be out-maneuvered, and it had virtually unlimited explosive firepower.

He could return fire with his own canisters now that his weapon bays were retaken—he could destroy the *Blue Max*—but the image of Captain Wythleweir on her knees stopped him, gave him pause. He had to give her a chance, give her and the Sisters and the Marines more time!

Now, to his situation, four canisters on their way. They were coming in flat, all pretty much one after the other.

The canister was a virtually inescapable weapon, but much of its power depended on the skill of the launcher, as the way the canister was programmed depended largely on the damage it did.

And Davage guessed these Fanatics weren't overly skilled.

"Aft canister, pattern Midnight-four. Release!"

There was a "thud," and two canisters shot out of the back of the *Seeker*. They went a short way and detonated in a large, enveloping, mushroom shape. The incoming four from the *Blue Max* flew into this mass of dense, exploding material and were shredded. A good canister launcher would have anticipated something like this and set the missiles to either move around the problem area or pre-explode, sending their warhead into the target anyway.

Not in this case; the canisters simply disappeared.

Davage wasn't going to let the *Blue Max* have another shot. He threw the wheel down, wrenching the ship around in a tight, screaming turn.

He headed right for the *Triumph*, and soon, he was tucked in next to it, just past the edge of its shield rim. The *Triumph's* helm tried to shake him, but Davage was on it like glue, following its moves perfectly. If the *Blue Max* wanted to shoot at him, they'd hit the *Triumph* too.

He Sighted another Sar-Beam and rolled to the other side, but too late. A red, searing lance of energy hit him square in the lower hull, blasting away one of his gas-compression engines. No longer able to keep up with the *Triumph*, the *Seeker* began falling back.

The *Blue Max* loomed large in the screen, its canister bays open.

"Captain, the *Blue Max* is hailing."

On the screen, a wounded, bleeding Captain Wythleweir appeared. She was bleeding from a gash on her forehead and a nasty wound on her shoulder. She was limply holding her MiMs in her left hand. Behind her was a confusion of Marines, crew, and Sisters.

"Captain," she said weakly, "the *Blue Max* stands with you."

"Captain, you're hurt."

"I'll live, sir. That Slap you gave us saved my life, I think."

"Then, if you are ready, let's re-take the *Triumph*!"

*   *   *   *   *

Her heart was turning to stone as she made her way to the airlock. She didn't want to go. She wanted to stay.

How had this happened?

She walked in and closed the door behind her.

She couldn't bear to say good-bye. If she thought about him for too long, she wouldn't be able to do it.

The airlock opened and she flew out, on silver wings.

*   *   *   *   *

He knew the ship better than any, and using all the various crawl spaces, nooks, and crannies, he and his small, blue-haired companion had eluded the invaders to this point. They could skulk about, unseen indefinitely.

But the invaders were so many, and the ship's complement of technicians, inspectors, Admiralty brass, and other assorted guests were no match for them. They were all dead. Even the Sisters and the Marines, taken by surprise, were dead.

The *Triumph* had fallen.

Lord Probert and Lady Branna were all that was left.

They could hear the sounds of battle ringing in from the outer hull. They could hear the brand new Sar-Beams uncoiling in their banks and knowing that those weapons were being aimed at their friends and comrades was enough to stop their hearts. They thanked Creation that they weren't mounting any canisters.

Lady Branna, showing the same courage she had before the Second Battle of Mirendra, wanted to disable the main junction to the Sar-Beam generators, but it was guarded by those people Cloaked to look like Princess Marilith.

All key areas were being guarded.

Another Sar-Beam blast. Explosions coming from outside.

Enough was enough … their friends might be dying out there.

They were going to the junction panel, and they were going to disable it, and if they died in the process, they died.

Lord Probert and Lady Branna were always arguing, always threatening each other. He loved to assure her that she would stand trial for war crimes for all the crazy ideas she had—a trial he will happily testify at—and she vowed that he would know what the inside of her dungeon at Castle Fallz looks like for being such a stodgy mope. But beneath the surface, they knew each other's quality.

Lord Probert: the design and systems man. Brilliant.

Lady Branna: the consummate innovator. Brilliant.

Through the panel, they could see ten "Mariliths" milling about, each holding an assortment of brassy, knobby weapons.

Taking a deep breath, Probert threw the hatch open. They climbed out.

The Fanatics looked at them, grinning, laughing.

"Look," they said, "our mice have come out of their hole."

Probert opened his coat and pulled out his CEROS.

The Mariliths broke into hysterical laughing.

These Fanatics had heard of the silly LosCapricos weapons that were once a great tradition in the League. A whiff of the past ... an embarrassing ceremonial weapon conceived during a drunken, heady time. It probably didn't even work.

Probert held the CEROS prominently in front of him, showing it to them, as was the usual custom.

They began slowly walking toward them, relishing the torment that was to come.

Probert's arm shot out and the CEROS howled. A Fanatic was disemboweled. The disk in mid-flight changed course and returned to its master's hand, disemboweling two more along the way.

Stunned, the remaining Fanatics leveled their weapons and prepared to charge.

Probert threw again, this time sending it off the floor. In a bouncing, cavorting frenzy, it clanged about the hallway in a murderous, cutting cloud.

The Fanatics fell in pieces.

Lady Branna stepped through the grim harvest and reached the panel. Deftly, she ruined the junction panel, removing some components, smashing others.

The Sar-Beams will fire no more.

Embracing each other, they made for the crawl space again, to hide again.

A dark, robed figure waited for them.

∗   ∗   ∗   ∗   ∗

As the *Seeker* and *Blue Max* chased the *Triumph* into the veil of space, the deadly Sar-Beams were an ever-present threat. Finding the *Blue Max* a much easier target, they concentrated on it, hitting her so many times the hull began to glow and vent high-pressure gas through numerous gashes in the hull.

Davage, the senior captain, was about to order Captain Wythleweir to beach her ship when fire from *Triumph* stopped cold. Free to lose, they pummeled it with canisters, being careful not to overly damage the *Triumph*, lest some of her crew still be alive and held prisoner.

The new shields installed on the *Triumph* were good, but several canister shots from *Seeker* and *Blue Max* brought them down anyway.

Loosing a canister, the *Seeker* holed the port warp drive nacelle, darkening it. The *Blue Max* loosed another canister and blew it clean off

Still moving, the *Triumph* made ready to warp away with only one engine. Before Davage could loose the final, crippling canister, the *Triumph* was gone in a flash.

Marilith, as she always had before, had escaped.

Seeker and *Blue Max* trawled the area looking for lifeboats.

<Syg, darling, come back up to the bridge, won't you?> Dav sent to Syg, his telepathy getting a bit better.

As Davage was busy with this and that on the bridge, he failed to notice that Syg didn't answer back. After a few minutes he realized that Syg had not answered.

<Syg, are you all right?>

Nothing.

Becoming concerned that Syg might have been injured, he Sighted down toward her quarters—they were empty, bedclothes tossed about.

He stopped a passing Sister.

"Sister, could you please tell me the current location of Sygillis of Metatron?"

The Sister paused a moment and then looked at him, smiling.

"Ki," Davage said, "what did she say?"

"Dav, she said that Syg's not on board."

Panic suddenly flooded into his mind. Where was Syg, what had happened to her?

"Sir," Sasai said at her Fore Sensing position, "we are closing on an unidentified object, four kilometers full a-beam. Type and composition unknown."

Dav Sighted and felt a wave of relief pass over him. He saw, floating in space, a large silver sphere.

He gave to helm to Saari. "Helm," he said, "bring us alongside the object and pull it in. Lieutenant, you have the bridge. I'm going to receive the object personally."

✳   ✳   ✳   ✳   ✳

Davage made his way to the main docking bay. There, using docking cables, the silver sphere was pulled in.

He walked up to it. "Syg, you gave me quite a start," he said, smiling. "How'd you end up outside the ship?"

The silver sphere sat there.

Davage touched the silver—it was warm even though it had been subjected to the cold of space.

"Come on, Syg, I've got things to do. Out you come."

The silver surface shimmered and disappeared, dumping Lord Probert and Lady Branna to the floor.

"Lord Probert, Lady Branna—we feared you lost!"

They stood up and thanked their maker. Davage noted Probert was holding his CEROS in a shaking hand, and it was bloody.

"All dead, Dav ... they killed them all.

"Are you all right?"

"Fine, fine," Lady Branna said, clearly shaken. "We disabled the Sar-Beams ... Milos, he killed them with his weapon, and I disabled the ..."

She appeared faint, and Davage held her up.

"Are the escort ships damaged? Were any destroyed?" Probert asked.

"The *Seeker* is fine, and *Blue Max* is damaged but serviceable. I ... do not know about *Caroline,* and I fear for Captain Stenstrom."

Probert and Branna looked deflated.

Davage, still holding the faint Lady Branna, asked, "Milos, where's Sygillis?"

"She ... she was on the *Triumph*, dressed in a black robe. She got us to an airlock and put us off the ship, encased in silver."

"Why didn't she come with you?"

"She appeared to be in a daze. She said she had to finish something. She wouldn't come. She wouldn't come with us," Lady Branna sobbed.

Davage felt a wave of agony pass over him. Syg, out there, all alone on the *Triumph*.

"She … she gave me this to give to you, Dav," Probert said.

Probert handed Dav a small, folded piece of paper.

He opened it:

> My Dearest Love …
>
> I have been selfish. I wanted you all to myself. This conflict with Marilith will never end; I realize that now. I must go and finish this. If we are ever to know any peace, I must finish this.
>
> Know that I love you with everything that I am, and it will be your memory alone that shall sustain me through the ordeal to come.
>
> Know that every moment not spent with you is a moment lost forever.
>
> I shall return as soon as I am able to do so, and then I will never leave your side again.
>
> There is so much I want to give you …
>
> S

Tears streaming down his cheeks, Dav Sighted the slip of paper. He saw, deep in his Sight, that, at one time, the paper had been held tightly to her breast.

He stood there looking at it for a long, long time.

13

THE SAD CAPTAIN

The *Triumph* had vanished … gone into the long night of space. Following the battle, Davage escorted the *Blue Max* to sub-orbital Dry Dock 18 for an immediate inspection, the new ship badly damaged and venting, requiring a sharp counter-flood to fly true. Lady Branna's Sar-Beams were certainly much stronger than the standard Xaphan cassagrain.

Also, Davage was relieved to discover that the *Caroline* had safely beached in a field near Tartan, Captain Stenstrom managing to pull the ship out of its howling terminal dive. There, beached and smoking, he, with crew, Sisters, and Marines, fought and subdued the Fanatics.

Back to the area where *Triumph* warped away, he trawled space looking for any clue he could as to its heading and possible destination.

He found no trace. In a near panic, Davage beseeched Lady Branna to look for it with her *Venera* ship, being frustrated by the lack of complex sensing gear on his own ship. She did, gladly, owing her life to both Davage and Syg. She locked onto *Triumph*'s ion trail and followed it as far as Hoban, where, apparently, it failed, the missing port tach drive overloading the system. But, as Stellar Mach was available, they blinked away, their wake already too far degraded to follow further.

He checked with Fleet, but the wires were dry. Kilos inquired with various Marine installations. They had lots of information on the usual suspects—raiders, pirates, disreputables, and the like, but no *Triumph*, no Princess Marilith, no Syg. Ennez checked with the Hospitalers, but they too had heard nothing.

Every ship, every outpost, was looking for *Triumph*, but it, as a ghost, had simply vanished.

Having nowhere else to turn and going mad with worry, he turned to Kilos, to her husband—that wondrous little man in Tusck. He begged Ki to ask her husband to look for clues as to the *Triumph*'s whereabouts. It was against Fleet regulations to solicit a civilian source for information without Admiralty approval, but Davage didn't care. He didn't care about any of that—he wanted Syg back.

He could find out anything, Ki's husband. All Ki had to do was ask.

✳   ✳   ✳   ✳   ✳

The Zen-La …

He tried to sleep, to calm his thoughts. He hoped the Zen-La worked, that he could reach her mind and determine where she was.

And then he will go to her and blast Marilith out of the sky. This time, there will be no kindness, no holding back … this time Marilith was going to die.

This time Marilith truly was his mortal enemy, and he was going to kill her.

So he tried to sleep, tried to reach Syg. As he drifted into exhausted sleep, the Zen-La worked.

And it was horrible.

He saw what Syg was seeing. He saw the Fanatics, all still Cloaked to look like Marilith.

She appeared to be tied down, restrained. They stood over her, leering, taunting, spitting on her.

And then, the knives came out, the instruments of pain and cruelty. The look of glee on their faces.

He saw Syg try to lift her arms to protect herself, but they held her down ... and set to work on her.

The knives coming down.

"*Daaaaaaaaavvvvvvvaaaaaaaaggggggeeee!*" she screamed.

And he could sleep no more ...

$$* \quad * \quad * \quad * \quad *$$

"Dav?" Kilos said, walking into his office.

Davage sat behind his desk, large black bags under his eyes, his screen lit up with maps and charts. He looked thin and drawn.

Syg had been gone for four days. He hadn't slept, and he hadn't eaten. The memory of the Zen-La—it was unbearable.

No word ... nothing. He'd rather he had a corpse to mourn than this emptiness, this lack of information, knowing only that she was in agony, crying out for him ... and he could not help her.

She was gone ... lost to the void.

Kilos sat down in front of him, and he barely acknowledged her presence. Never much for sentimentality, Ki nevertheless felt like crying; she couldn't stand to see Dav like this.

She wasn't around when the Marilith thing happened, but she remembered him with Captain Hathaline. That was bad; that was gut-wrenching.

But this ... she'd never seen him so laid bare, so bereft of hope.

"Dav, are you all right?"

He didn't respond.

"You haven't slept in days, you haven't eaten. Why don't you turn in? Let me help you to your quarters."

Nothing; he just stared at his screens. The Zen-La. She didn't understand.

He was lost in misery.

Ki sat there and stared at him.

"Dav, I just got a Com from my husband. I thought you'd want to know that right away," she said after a bit.

Dav flinched, as if pulling himself from a trance. "Oh, your husband? Has he—has he found anything?"

"Maybe, I don't know."

He rubbed his tired eyes. "Well, let's see it. I trust your husband."

"This is probably nothing," Kilos said, handing him a small file of maps and pictures she'd received from her husband. "I debated telling you about it until I knew more."

He gratefully took the materials and started looking at them, a bit of hope starting to form somewhere in his soul.

"Gelt, Dav. My husband caught wind of something strange recently happening on Gelt. It's a remote, pretty backwards sort of place, and the locals are about as simple and easily startled as they come."

"Gelt?" Dav said. "I've not heard of it before."

"Nor have I."

Dav thumbed through the files, but his eyes were so tired, his mind clouded by lack of sleep, lack of food. He looked without seeing them. His Sight was down to nothing.

"Can you tell me what he's got, Ki? I'm so tired."

Ki got up and came to his side, patiently arranging the files for him on the desk.

"This one here, Dav, says the locals on Gelt are talking about a fiery mountain ... one that came from the sky. They say it came down in a great, flaming heap and hit the ground in a huge explosion.

"Then, this one here states that, the next day, shepherds heading out into the wilderness in an area of seven earthen hills called ... the Seven Wives, I think, and saw a great 'statue' sticking up out of the ground. A gigantic statue."

Ki stopped and swallowed.

"Go on."

"Then they say the shepherds saw hundreds of bodies, quivering, screaming, impaled on black stakes all around the statue, like a great dying forest. The impaled cried out for mercy. And there was a demon, in black, putting more bodies on stakes. A demon that was crying— screaming. The Wailing Demon they called it."

Dav sat for a moment and thought.

"It's all pretty gruesome ... pretty fanciful. I think it's a highly suspect story and ..."

"Com," he said, talking past her.

"Com here, sir."

"Com, send to Navigator. I want solution plotted for the planet Gelt immediately and wind for Stellar Mach by the count."

"Gelt, aye, sir."

Davage weakly stood up and began fumbling with his shirt, trying to straighten it, trying to make himself presentable. Ki moved his shaking hands aside and did it for him.

"Dav, it's just stories told by an easily scared local population. Please don't get your hopes up too much until we know more. We should send scouts."

"It sounds right, Ki. It feels right, and I trust your husband."

Even though the story was a grim one, Davage seemed to brighten a bit; some news, even bleak, horrific news, was something. "Has he ever considered working for Fleet Intelligence, your husband?"

"He loves that old school in Tusck. I guess he's pretty plugged in over there."

"He's amazing, Ki, the things he can do. You should be most proud of him."

"I am, Dav. You know me, though, never one for too much sentimentality."

"I should grant you more time off so you can see him more often."

Ki smiled and finished straightening his shirt. "I love my husband very much, but he is devoted to that old school, and I am devoted to this ship and to you. One day, I know this will all end and I will go home and be his wife and bear him his children. But for now, we are both right where we need to be."

She put her hands on his face. "I will one day tell my children about how I was there, on the *Seeker*, with Captain Davage, the Lord of Blanchefort, and how he was a great Elder, how he was a great Lord in every sense of the word … and how he was my friend."

"There's no 'was' about it, Ki. You will always be my friend—my truest, bravest friend."

Through the windows, the stars heeled around. They looked at the stars, all the tiny points of light. Syg was out there somewhere.

The Com opened. "Com, sir. Navigation reports Gelt is the third planet in the Theta Ferenz system. Solution for Gelt plotted and laid in. Engineering reports we will require three Stellar Mach jumps of ninety seconds, plus four for safe arrival."

"Very well," Dav said. "What is the count?"

"Twenty-two minutes until first Stellar Mach jump."

"Thank you. I'll be there shortly."

"Aye, sir. Com out."

He turned to Ki. "It appears Gelt is quite a ways in the weeds for three Stellar Mach jumps."

He picked up his hat and put it on. "Your husband—I'm grateful to him, Ki."

"Don't be too grateful yet. So, I suppose I'm not going to be able to talk you into getting some rest, am I? You've got twenty-two minutes."

"No, Ki—I'm fine, thank you."

"Well, then, if I can't get you to rest, will you at least eat a little something? Come on, I'll get you a cup of coffee in the mess. It'll make you feel better."

"Will you be having one with me?"

"If that's what it'll take to get you to have a cup, then yes, I'll choke some down."

Together, they left the office and went to the mess.

14

GELT

As the *Seeker* blasted out of Stellar Mach, the lonely world of Gelt loomed ahead, third planet of the Theta Ferenz system. It was a gray, rain-swept, moonless world.

It was about as backwater a place as you could get. Sort of like Mirendra, out in the middle of nowhere, yet another forlorn place where Davage had lost someone dear to him.

The ship settled into a standard orbit and began scanning the surface, the *Seeker*'s sensing equipment being maddeningly basic. Though his eyes were as tired as they had ever been, he wrenched his Sight in focus and scanned the surface himself. It took about fifteen or twenty minutes, but eventually, he Sighted something.

The *Triumph*.

"There, there it is, on the western continent using standard bearings, about eighteen degrees north by west."

"Captain," Sasai said from her sensing position. "Ventral Sensing does not detect anything on the surface in that area."

"It's not on the surface, crewman, it's buried ... about fifty feet down."

"How'd it gut buried?" Kilos asked.

"Don't know, but that's what I'm going to find out. Lieutenant Kilos, you have the bridge. I'm headed to the surface."

Davage went into the lift. Kilos followed him in.

"Ki, what are you doing?"

"I'm coming with you."

"You're staying here. You're in command."

"I called down to engineering and put Mapes in command. He's on his way to the bridge now. I'm coming with you, Dav."

"Ki ... Syg, if she's down there, then she is ..."

"Maybe, and if that's the case, you'll need my help."

"Ki, I need to do this alone."

"She's my friend too, Dav. I'm coming with you."

*   *   *   *   *

The ripcar broke the thick gray clouds; the muddy plain below was dirty and lonely.

Davage dropped containment so that he could Sight clearly without the containment field's shimmering lines of force getting in the way. Sheets of cold rain pelted them square in the face.

"The *Triumph*'s buried under that?" Kilos asked, buttoning her coat against the rain. Looking down, all she could see through the layers of rain was a vast expanse of brown.

Davage looked down and Sighted. Buried about fifty feet in the mud, was the *Triumph*, nose down at a forty-five degree angle, its brand-new hull hopelessly battle-damaged and scorched from a fast re-entry, its port warp nacelle missing—shot away by the *Blue Max*'s canisters. He could even see the layer of long grass that used to be on the surface, now covered for all time.

There, on that doomed ship Syg, all alone, fought Princess Marilith and the Fanatics of Nalls, the fury of their battle knocking the great ship from orbit—the "fiery mountain," the locals called it.

The nearby hills that he had seen on a topographical map, the Seven Wives, were missing.

Ki noticed it too. "Where are the hills? Aren't there supposed to be a bunch of hills around here?"

"Yes," Davage said. "You're looking at them. Down there—pulverized, all that mud." Apparently, they had been leveled and used to cover up *Triumph's* sorry grave.

Ki's brilliant husband had said it.

The locals already lived in terror of this site.

The fiery mountain that fell.

The fields of impaled bodies, quivering and screaming.

The "Wailing Demon" in black that haunts the site, the Demon searching, in a daze, for its "love."

"It's there, Ki," Dav shouted over the pounding rain. "It's buried in the mud."

"And the bodies? What about those?"

Davage closed his eyes and nodded. "Yes, your husband was right about those too. They're down there—hundreds of them."

"Can you see Syg down there anywhere?"

Davage looked around. Sure enough, moving with wet, boneless movements was a figure, semi-Cloaked, wandering around aimlessly in the mud, walking in a large, endless circle.

"There, Ki—there she is!"

Ki looked hard, and still couldn't see anything.

"Dav, if what my husband said is correct, then something's wrong with her. She might not be in her right mind."

"Would you be … after such an ordeal? You heard your husband. She was in a terrible battle, wounded, forced to kill over and over again."

"And then she flattens the place to try and cover it up?"

Davage didn't reply. He rolled the roaring ripcar and sat it down in the muck, engines thundering and struggling for compression in the rain. The skids dug in deep; soon the smooth bottom of the ripcar touched the mud.

Dav jumped out, boots sinking in the ooze.

He was standing over the *Triumph*—standing on its grave. Born in Provst not long ago, dead on Gelt.

Ahead, in the rainy, wet grayness, a black figure emerged—a figure wearing a drenched, hooded black robe.

He took a few tentative steps forward.

The figure stopped and stood there, rocking slightly, elbows out, hands held at mid-riff. Its face hidden under its large hood.

"Are you my love?" it said in an ephemeral voice.

A stake made of Shadow tech emerged behind it and stuck in the mud with a splat.

It was black, the silver gone. Back to Shadow tech. Davage felt his heart break.

"Yes, I am your love. Sygillis, Sygillis of Metatron, it's me—it's Davage."

"My love … my love?" it said.

"Syg, it's me … I've come to take you home. I've come to take care of you."

"Home?" it said.

It reached up and pulled its hood back.

Syg's face emerged into gray light: wet, wounded, thin, as though she had not eaten in some time. Her hair a long, red, wet smear. Her eyes were glassy, distant, her expression confused.

Her face crumpled into misery and anguish. "Home," she repeated with longing, "I want to go home … I want to see my love … I want to explain …"

He lit his Sight, hoping to pull her out of whatever state she was in. She looked at his eyes, and her expression brightened a bit, but still, she seemed lost.

"Syg, it's me. I'm right here. Wake up. Wake up, my love."

Weeping, rain-soaked, she wheeled around in a dazed panic.

"I … I did this … all of this, for my love. Look what I have become. Look what I did!" She pointed down at the mud.

He glanced down.

The *Triumph* was in its muddy grave far below. All around it, the hundreds of impaled bodies on Silver and Shadow tech stakes, buried forever under the earth that once made up the hills of the Seven Wives. Buried, covered up.

He shuddered.

"How will my love accept me? I did it for him … I did it all for him!"

She looked at him, eyes lost in darkness. "You! You'll tell him for me, won't you? Tell him how I love him ... tell him how lonely I am. Tell him how I want to come home."

Davage was lifted into the air and spun around. Ahead, the black stake loomed, its point gleaming and rain streaked.

"My love is in heaven ... among the stars. I have to send you there so that you can tell him for me. I have to send you to heaven ..."

"Dav, she's not in her mind!" Ki shouted from the ripcar. "Syg, wake up! Don't make me kill you!" She leveled her SK.

"No, no Ki—stand fast! I order you to stand fast!"

Davage drifted toward the stake. Syg rocked back and forth in a daze. He could see she was covered in terrible wounds.

He unsaddled his CARG, held it for a moment, and threw it into the mud. It sank deep. He then unclipped his gun belt where it fell, forgotten.

"Dav!" Kilos cried. "You are defenseless!"

"Syg!" he said. "If you want to kill me ..." He parted his coat. "*Then aim for my heart! It's yours. I gave it to you once. I freely give it again!*"

He stopped in mid-air.

"You? You gave your heart ... to me?"

"Remember, Syg, you are going to be my Countess. We are planning to be married, you and I! Remember my castle, in the mountains? Remember my ship and the quarters I gave you? Remember decorating your quarters with colorful fabrics and little trinkets? Remember the coffee we enjoyed drinking together there?"

"Coffee? Yes, yes, I like coffee very much. I used to make it for my love."

"You made it for me, Syg, as you waited for me to come off my watch, remember? Every evening, you always had it ready for me." He felt a pang of longing.

"And you ... you were always so happy to see me."

She blinked, trying to remember. "I ..."

She set him down into the mud. "I recall your face, your handsome face. I've seen it someplace before. What is your name? Please tell me."

"I am Davage, Lord of Blanchefort, and you are Sygillis of Metatron, soon to be the Countess of Blanchefort, my beloved wife. Your portrait will soon hang next to mine."

"Countess."

Countess ...

Married ...

House of Blanchefort ... the heirs she wanted to give him ...

Portraits.

A balcony in the clouds ... where she—

Her portrait ... SYGILLIS—COUNTESS OF BLANCHEFORT, hanging next to his.

Yes, yes ...

"You," she said. "You are my love ... Yes, yes, I remember. You came ... from the heavens just now ... for me? I saw you!"

"I did, Syg. I came here as quickly as I could. I searched all over for you."

She bit her finger and looked around at the bleak sea of mud.

"They wouldn't stop hurting me ... wouldn't stop. So, I—I hurt them back ... and then I couldn't stop."

She put her face into her hands and fell to her knees.

"Will you marry one who has done this—all of this? Could you love a demon?"

"You are no demon! You fought them fair and square. You did not ask for the fight, but the fight was there and you finished it. You were one against many. You're wounded, Syg."

Sygillis sat there in the rain.

"I ... I love you. All I wanted was for us to be left alone, so we could live our lives, and look what I became ..."

"They would not leave us alone, and you know that."

"What can you see ... when you look at me?"

"All I see, Syg, is the woman I love. The woman I've come to take home and keep safe."

The darkness left her eyes.

The stake changed from black to silver and vanished.

"Daaaaaaav!" she wailed.

Davage slogged to her and knelt down. They embraced. "Daaaaaav! I'm sorry, I'm sorry!"

"It's all right, Syg. It's all over. I'm taking you home."

"It almost had me ... the darkness. Not even your light could break it. It was you—your memory, your love—that brought me back."

"Truly ... you remember me, Syg?"

"I do, my love, my Captain Davage."

Davage bowed before her in the mud and the rain. "Then will you take this wretch, this wretch that lies before you, and be his Countess, now and forever? I have waited far too long to ask you this question."

She joined him in the mud and gently took him by the chin with her hands, her tears mingling with the rain.

"Yes, my love, gladly. And will you take me and be my Lord, now and forever ... and save me from the darkness that awaits?"

"I will never be apart from you again, Syg."

They held each other there in the mud.

"I want to go home, Dav. Take me home, my darling, and never let me go."

He took her in his arms and began escorting her back to the ripcar. As he did, he saw the deep, ugly wounds on her arms and chest up close. They were worse than he first thought.

"You're badly wounded, Syg. We must to the *Seeker* immediately!"

"The most terrible wound of all you have just healed," she said, looking up at him as he led her to the waiting ripcar. "How many times are you to save me? To save my soul?"

"As many times as is needed."

She reached up and kissed him, her lips wet and cold but warming.

"Lord Probert, Lady Branna, are they safe?"

"They are, Syg. You saved them."

She looked into the mud.

"Wait," she said. "Your CARG, your gun belt. You dropped them."

"Leave them. We must away."

"No, Dav, no. Your beautiful CARG."

She gently broke from his grasp and dug the CARG and gun belt out of the mud. She then took off the black robe she was wearing and threw it down. Naked, her body covered in wounds, she stood before him, holding his CARG and belt, the rain washing the dirt away from both them and her.

"This CARG belongs to our House, Dav, and I'll have nothing of either of us left behind in this terrible place."

Davage took off his wet Fleet coat and draped it over her shoulders. He put his hat on her head to keep the rain off. He then helped her into the back of the ripcar.

"Hi ... Ki," Syg said weakly from under Dav's hat, the lack of food and her wounds beginning to take their toll.

"It's good to see you, Syg. I'm glad you're back. I'd about had enough of the captain moping around."

"Raise containment and get us out of here, Ki," he said, and somewhat clumsily, she lifted it thundering out of the mud and into the air. He held the shivering Syg to him.

Soon, in his arms, she was asleep, dreaming.

The nightmare over.

And they climbed out of the rain and cold, the *Seeker* waiting high above as a star.

They rose into heaven.

15

COFFEE AND PASTRIES

Ennez had never seen so much blood poisoning. Syg's blood was foul, putrid, deeply poisoned, but not beyond saving. He cleansed her blood, cleaned and closed her wounds, and put her on a bland broth diet, as she was experiencing a mid-level stint of malnutrition.

Ennez had wanted her to get some sleep alone, but she would not see Dav leave her side. Ennez relented but insisted she honor the broth diet he'd put her on—her recovery, he said, depended on it.

No sooner did he leave the tiny dispensary than the hidden pot of coffee came out and a plate loaded full of those sweet pastries from the mess that she loved.

Syg drank the whole pot and had ten of those pastries. They giggled and wiped the crumbs from each other's lips as they ate.

Their first meal together as an engaged couple.

"Now that we're engaged," Syg said sleepily, "I suppose I'll need to start wearing Blanchefort gowns. Pardock will have my head if I don't."

"You only need wear them if you really want to."

"I do. Pardock said I could make them any color I want."

"We don't have a set color in our House."

"Then I want my first one to be blue … just like your coat."

She looked up at Dav with big eyes. "You look so tired, my love," she said, licking her fingers.

"I've not slept much, Syg."

"Worried about me, were you?"

"Somebody's got to be."

"Then you should get some rest."

Dav stood to leave, and Syg loudly cleared her throat. He looked at her, and she had moved over in the tiny dispensary bed to make room for him. She was patting the bed with her hand, inviting him to join her.

He slid in, and before long, their bodies and souls intertwined, they slept.

* * * * *

Davage never heard from Princess Marilith of Xandarr again.

Of course, he wondered what had happened there on board *Triumph* and on the rainy muddy plains of Gelt. The terrible battle that must have raged … one where all of the Fanatics of Nalls met their painful, impaled end before a darkening Syg, her pain and anger nearly consuming her soul.

But what of Marilith? She could not be dead. She will return—she always returned. He had heard rumors, there were rumors aplenty—there were always rumors and hushed tales floating around the parlors and ballrooms of League society. He heard whispers that there had been a terrible battle on wet Gelt—that two goddesses had fallen in love with the same man, and unable to resolve the matter, fought over him and tore at each other, each determined to not only kill the other but to also make her suffer terribly first.

As they fought, they fell from the sky and the land was torn apart, canyons were dug out, mountain ranges formed, and in the end, one goddess met her doom and was thrown down into the earth and was covered by it. The other stood, triumphant and terrible, and forgot herself in the process, roaming the land as a demon.

Dav never asked her what had happened—he really didn't want to know the details. On dark, windy evenings when the topic of conversation turned to Gelt and the *Triumph*, Syg would put down her coffee cup and look at him with pleading eyes, and he probed her no further. It was, perhaps, best left undiscussed.

But Marilith couldn't be gone, couldn't be defeated. In his mind Princess Marilith had become more that just a woman over the years, more than an adversary—she'd become a force, an irresistible, unpredictable presence, like the coming of a thunderstorm, that could be counted on only to never fully be defeated, to always be just out of reach, to always return and darken the skies again another day.

He had this ongoing dream—rather, an ongoing nightmare, that, one day Sygillis would come to him, throw off her Cloak and become Marilith, tall and blue-haired. That Marilith had killed Syg on Gelt and taken her identity, burying her tiny broken body in a shallow grave and spitting on it and had snuck into Dav's bed and been with him this whole time, undetected. He often Sighted her, concentrating, determined to see through any Cloak.

All he ever saw though was Syg, red-haired, green-eyed, and ever loving, her body flowing with Silver tech that he had built for a second time.

Marilith was gone, and that was sure enough. Perhaps she had moved on, pursuing her strange, fierce life elsewhere. Perhaps she had died of old age … she was past her Time of Goodbyes, after all.

Perhaps her broken heart had finally stopped beating.

That she could be entombed on that cursed ship *Triumph*, or impaled on a Shadow tech stake could never enter his mind. Princess Marilith of Xandarr would not be so defeated.

The Fanatics of Nalls met their end there on Gelt certain enough; their halls and places of meeting in the dark city of Nalls were left empty, all their knowledge and aspirations made extinct in one titanic battle. The scant few who survived on *Seeker, Caroline,* and *Blue Max* were hurried off to the Sisters' research centers and never seen again.

And despite himself, he found that he missed Marilith in some small way. He missed the game, missed the joust, missed that face on the screen, covered in frightening makeup, a sure sign that fresh adventure was in the offing. He supposed, in the end, Marilith owned a bit of his soul that no other woman would ever have … not even Syg.

He guessed that such a thing would have made her happy.

EPILOGUE

"So, what are we supposed to be doing, darling?" Lady Sygillis, Countess of Blanchefort, asked as she and Davage strolled arm in arm through the green passes and vine-covered lanes of the Telmus Grove. She carried a flattering pair of Blanchefort shoes—somehow, some way, Pardock had gotten her to wear them for the ceremony. Beyond, in the sun-washed distance, the tall central spires of Castle Blanchefort rose up into the cool, dark blue sky. It was fluttering with banners and flags. Lord Blanchefort had his countess at last. The ceremony was over; they were married. The baton had successfully made its way to the front of the chapel. The last guest to hold the baton, walk a few steps, and present it to the Elder cleric was a special honor, and many had hoped they would be selected to perform the task. Davage and Sygillis chose Countess Hortensia of Monama—a shocking choice as the strange, black-eyed Monamas were not at a high tier in League society. The countess, with her visions, had, in part, helped pave the way for their love, and Davage had never properly thanked her. He would not continue the error, the countess and her family were now honored friends.

"We are on our way to Dead Hill."

Davage looked down at his tiny new bride. She was wearing a colorful Blanchefort gown. She now had a whole wardrobe of them, and her red hair was set into an elaborate design. She had just had her portrait painted. Her picture would soon by hanging in the hall of the ancestors next to his. Davage had never seen her so beautiful, so happy. Her Shadowmark was decorated with red and blue dots, making her eyes stand out like emerald jewels.

She was flush with excitement. The thing she had long seen in her dreams, the portrait, the thing that had helped pull her from the waiting darkness on Gelt, had finally come to pass, and though she had to stand still for a long time, she savored every moment of it. This was her day, and she wanted it to last forever.

And tonight, she would allow herself to be seeded; tonight the next Lord of Blanchefort was to be conceived. Pardock wanted them to spend the night in the traditional wedding suite in Harn tower. Syg, though, insisted they wouldn't be there for long, as they planned on sneaking into Dav's old room—she wanted to put his balcony to the ultimate test.

"I see," she said. "And what are we going to be doing there?"

"Not we, darling—you. You have to go up to the tombs and commune with the spirits of the dead. I cannot follow."

"I have to do what?"

"You said you wanted to keep with tradition. Well, that's the tradition."

They arrived at the base of Dead Hill. There was the ancient stone gate, the winding gravel path going up the side of the hill about three hundred feet, and then the tombs at the top, the myriad of tombs, most covered in vegetation. Syg leaned up against Dav and looked up the path.

"I've got to go up there?"

"Yes. And you've also got to do it once a year from here on out."

"What!"

"It's tradition."

"How will I know that I've successfully communed?"

"I don't know, having never had to do this myself. I do know that nobody at the castle will get to eat until it's done. I recall my mother telling me that she had to wander around up there for two days. Maybe she'll come out right away to spare you such an ordeal."

Syg strained to see the tombs and looked dubious.

"If you don't want to, Syg, we can just hide out for a bit and then go back and begin the celebratory dinner."

Syg thought for a moment. "That's tempting, love, but no—I want to do this. You'll wait here for me, will you?"

"Yes."

They kissed, and Syg opened the gate. "I won't be long."

"I know you're not going to want to hear this, Syg, but you'll probably want to put your shoes on. Blanchefort ghosts will want to see you in Blanchefort shoes. Fashion, it seems, goes beyond the grave."

Syg sighed and put her shoes on. "You know, Lord Blanchefort, that I am going to have to punish you for this later on the balcony, yes?"

"One more thing, Syg. What you experience up there is for you and you alone."

She blew him a kiss and began walking the gravel path toward the top, her feet already killing her. She should have waited until she got to the top to put them on.

After a few minutes, Syg reached the top of the hill. The view from up there was lovely, the huge grove with its endless hidden nooks and courtyards. She even spotted a few that she'd have to remember to visit with Dav later—the great Vith castle in the distance, the fluttering banners and flags, the dozens of spires reaching up to the magical northern sky.

Her home.

Every so often, she caught a glimpse of silver here and there in the Grove—Poe with her little Silver tech animals and fanciful benign beasts she loved to create and turn loose. Poe's skill with her power was now quite impressive. She'd even created a silver seal with bright, solemn eyes that could talk and fly. She'd been inspired by Dav's stories of Carahil. Dav had to admit the seal, recalling his old friend, was his favorite.

She could vaguely smell the meats and dishes being readied in the great hall for their wedding feast—over a thousand people waiting to sit and eat and raise a toast to she and Dav. All their friends were there. Even Kilos was out of her beloved Marine uniform and was beautiful in a lovely dress, standing tall next to her handsome husband. The last they saw of Ki and her husband, they appeared to be heading off to some dark, quiet part of the castle for some alone time. She couldn't wait to sit there at the table with Dav together as lord and countess. She took a deep breath. The feast smelled good, and she was hungry.

Down below, she could see Dav waiting for her, his CARG glinting in the early evening light. She guessed she'd wander around up here for a bit and then go back down. She'd pretend to have had an encounter of some sort, collect her husband, and return to the castle. She waved at him, and he waved back.

Turning, she wandered into the hazy maze of tombs, hoping to see an old Blanchefort ghost.

*   *   *   *   *

She'd walked a bit, allowing herself to get lost in the boulevards, lanes, and alleys of tombs. She didn't worry; her Black Hat ability to sense her direction was available for her use should she need it. Her feet were pinching badly, and once or twice, she stopped to get those Blanchefort shoes off and throw them, but recalling what Dav had said, she kept them on. The things she did for her husband and his ghost ancestors.

Moving on, she reached the far end of the hill. The tombs here were ancient. They were weathered, shapeless with old age, and covered in vines and centuries of tangled growth. The name plates on the doors were written in Vith, which she didn't know. The doorways were open, and the stony interiors were dark. Syg went into one and sat for a moment, the smell of age and mildew heavy. Anyone else probably would have been pretty scared in such a place—the dark, languid interior, the possibility of an old Blanchefort shade lurking nearby high. Syg, though, felt nothing but a bit of boredom, an empty stomach, and a growing desire to return to her husband.

She heard something outside and went out.

In the distance she saw a figure reaching out for her. The figure, backlit with some ethereal light, retreated into the distance. Pulling her shoes off, Syg followed, running as fast as she could. If it was a ghost, she wasn't going to let it get away.

Soon, she reached the tomb of Sadric, Davage's father. The figure was there, sitting, misty, weeping.

"Never wanted me … he never wanted me," the figure moaned.

Syg stood there and watched the figure.

"Who are you? Tell me please," Syg said

The figure turned to her. There was a hollow space where the head should be.

"You," it said. "You only love him because I loved him. You feel what I felt."

"Lady Hathaline, is that you?"

The figure stood. "You were going to kill him in your dreams—as if you could. I stopped you. I stayed your hand! I helped you to see him for what he is. I stopped you so that he did not have to kill you in turn!"

"You've been among us? He's not seen you, though he's looked and looked."

"I hid from him. I hid from his Sight. I was ashamed. But I've never been too far away. Even in death, I cannot forget him."

Syg gazed at the figure. Her face, hazy, indistinct, appeared from nothing. It was her face—their shared face. Her wavy red hair floated on a phantom's breeze.

"Does he hate me still?" Hathaline asked. "Tell me he has forgiven me."

"Of course he has, and you know that. He never hated you. He regretted those words the moment he spoke them. He regrets them still."

"Does he love you?"

"Yes."

"Why?"

"I cannot answer that question—because he does. And I love him. Like you, I've been waiting for him my whole life."

"When he looks at you, he sees me."

"He sees us, Lady Hathaline. He loved you as his friend, and he loves me as his wife. I think there is room in his heart for the both of us, and in mine."

"Both of us?"

"I welcome you into my soul, Lady Hathaline. I've a place set aside there just for you. Come, let us together go to him as one and be his Countess."

"Together? I can be with him still?"

"You can, as part of me. Come, join me, and let us be a complete person at last."

Hathaline glowed with happiness. Her figure tentatively moved toward Syg, passed through her, and was gone.

Syg took a deep breath and smiled.

A bit of herself had come home to her. The joy she felt—such joy.

*   *   *   *   *

Syg bounced down from the hilltop. Down below, Dav waited. He saw her coming and opened the gate.

She threw herself into his arms.

"Well," he said, "that didn't take too terribly long."

She squeezed him tightly.

"Did you encounter anything?"

"Yes, I did, in fact." She kissed him.

"I hope whatever it was wasn't too disturbing."

"Not at all. I'm glad I went up there. And now, Lord Blanchefort, I believe that your countess is going to attack you right here and now!"

"Syg," Dav said as she began undressing him. "Our friends are waiting for us. Our dinner ... aren't you hungry?"

"I'm starving, but that can wait. Our friends can wait a moment too. I intend to have my husband. I intend to conceive the next Lord of Blanchefort."

"I thought you wanted to go to the balcony for that."

"The balcony can also wait for all that follow. I've a son to conceive, and I wish to do it right here surrounded by all these old Blanchefort ghosts. I want them to see that their line is safe with us, that their House will continue."

And in the vast interior of the Grove, they came together as husband and wife. Overhead, in the darkening early evening sky, the first emerging stars came out and twirled.